THE
FINAL
CHAPTER

Also by C. B. Everett

The Other People

THE FINAL CHAPTER

C. B. EVERETT

SIMON & SCHUSTER

London · New York · Amsterdam/Antwerp · Sydney/Melbourne · Toronto · New Delhi

First published in Great Britain by Simon & Schuster UK Ltd, 2026

Copyright © C. B. Everett, 2026

The right of C. B. Everett to be identified as author of this work
has been asserted in accordance with the Copyright, Designs and Patents Act, 1988.

1 3 5 7 9 10 8 6 4 2

Simon & Schuster UK Ltd, 1st Floor
222 Gray's Inn Road, London WC1X 8HB

For more than 100 years, Simon & Schuster has championed authors and the stories they create. By respecting the copyright of an author's intellectual property, you enable Simon & Schuster and the author to continue publishing exceptional books for years to come. We thank you for supporting the author's copyright by purchasing an authorised edition of this book.

No amount of this book may be reproduced or stored in any format, nor may it be uploaded to any website, database, language-learning model, or other repository, retrieval, or artificial intelligence system without express permission. All rights reserved. Enquiries may be directed to Simon & Schuster, 222 Gray's Inn Road, London WC1X 8HB or RightsMailbox@simonandschuster.co.uk

Simon & Schuster Australia, Sydney
Simon & Schuster India, New Delhi

www.simonandschuster.co.uk
www.simonandschuster.com.au
www.simonandschuster.co.in

The authorised representative in the EEA is Simon & Schuster Netherlands BV, Herculesplein 96, 3584 AA Utrecht, Netherlands. info@simonandschuster.nl

Simon & Schuster strongly believes in freedom of expression and stands against censorship in all its forms. For more information, visit BooksBelong.com

A CIP catalogue record for this book
is available from the British Library

Hardback ISBN: 978-1-3985-3456-8
Trade Paperback ISBN: 978-1-3985-3457-5
eBook ISBN: 978-1-3985-3458-2

This book is a work of fiction. Names, characters, places and incidents are either a product of the author's imagination or are used fictitiously. Any resemblance to actual people living or dead, events or locales is entirely coincidental.

Typeset in Sabon by M Rules

Printed and Bound in the UK using 100% Renewable Electricity at CPI Group (UK) Ltd

RUSSIAN DOLL

A novel of death and identity by
JONATHAN DURWARD

Introduced, annotated and edited by
C. B. Everett

Publisher's Note

Following the events surrounding the re-emergence of *Russian Doll*, purported to be Jonathan Durward's missing – perhaps final – novel, events which you will no doubt be aware of due to the extensive media coverage, we wish to state that going forward we will no longer be working with C. B. Everett. The decision to publish this book as it stands has not been one we have taken lightly but ultimately we felt it was the right decision for Jonathan. In no way do we condone Everett's activities but we do believe this contentious book should be presented as written in order for the reading public to make up their own minds and draw what conclusions they can from it.

Introduction

Neil Young (in his 1979 song 'My My, Hey Hey (Out of the Blue)') said 'It's better to burn out than to fade away'. This phrase was violently rebuked by John Lennon in a 1980 interview who was angered at the thought, arguing it was better to keep going and eventually just fade away, 'like an old soldier'. Lennon wasn't one for idolising early death. When asked about Lennon's comments Young doubled down on the song's sentiment saying it was the spirit of rock 'n' roll. Ironically, and tragically in Lennon's case, the reverse happened to both men. Neil Young at time of writing is still with us and still making rock 'n' roll – albeit in a rather more appropriately faded capacity – while Lennon, sadly, barely made it to the end of that interview.

The line migrated from the song, sliding into popular culture where it gained an unwanted notoriety, popping up in the scrawled suicide note of Nirvana singer Kurt Cobain, who killed himself with a shotgun in April 1994. Overwhelmed by despair, he had reached out for help to his friend, singer Mark Lanegan, who at the time was dealing with his own demons, and didn't answer his phone. This haunted Lanegan for the rest of his life. Again, like Young and Lennon, Cobain was taken early while Lanegan enjoyed – or endured – nearly thirty more years of life and creativity until he died following a debilitating bout of Covid in 2022.

So is it better to burn out than fade away? And what has that to do with the introduction to the novel you hold in your hands? Chances are, if you've picked up this book and are ready to read it, you're familiar with the work of Jonathan Durward. You may even be familiar with my work too, under at least one of my pseudonyms. But let's be honest, you're probably more familiar with Jon's books, since he sold so many more of them. This was during the 1990s and 2000s, when the newspapers (remember them?) were eager to proclaim any artistic or cultural enterprise as 'the new rock 'n' roll'. They had already declared the YBAs, the Young British Artists, the new rock 'n' roll and made them arguably more famous than perhaps the majority of their work warranted. Stand-up comedy was also declared the new rock 'n' roll for a while, a decision which in hindsight, considering the amount of laddish toxic masculinity it enabled, seems more egregious than the YBAs. And so, inevitably, through laziness rather than anything else, the media alighted on literature. Young British Authors, for want of another moniker, were declared the new rock 'n' roll.

Jon in particular was tailor-made for this. Tall, good-looking, sharp of both cheekbone and mind, he could rock a leather jacket as well as James Dean and artfully sweep his hair back as well as any Romantic poet. And he had swagger. Rock 'n' roll swagger. Yes, it sounds pathetic saying it now, but at the time we all went along with this – obviously, every writer is a frustrated rock star – happily complicit in what the media was doing, happy to believe the hype, but most of us were the also rans. Jon was the one the camera loved.

THE FINAL CHAPTER

'Live fast, die young and leave a good-looking corpse.' James Dean there. Compare him with his contemporary, Marlon Brando (the Young/Lennon, Cobain/Lanegan analogy still applies here). Jonathan had the talent, the looks and the (supposed) appetite for fast living. The bright burning followed by the disappearing. No fading away for him. But where did he disappear to? To even attempt to find that out, we need to go way, way back into his background.

Born to a working-class family in the terminally unfashionable town of Dudley in the West Midlands in 1963, he was an only child who lived in the battlefield of his constantly warring parents until they broke up when he was sixteen. His mother left home, never to be seen or heard from again, leaving Jon in the care of his angry, alcoholic father.

He attended a local sixth form college, his father by this time not caring what he did or where he went, then following that moving to Bristol where he attended university. Contemporaneous accounts of his behaviour at the time talk of an angry boy sublimating his unresolved adolescent rage over his parents' split and the disappearance of his mother, by turning it outwards into an obnoxious confidence, sometimes bordering on arrogance (his first mask, note). This description is at odds with the lonely, bullied misfit who existed in Dudley before that, and it seems Bristol had something of a galvanising effect on him. That, coupled with a precocious natural intelligence, led to a First in English, Drama and Art.

This wasn't the first persona he tried on. During this time he constantly, and consciously, reinvented himself as young people wanting to both find and prove themselves are wont to do. Nothing suspicious in that, we all do it to some degree. It's how we find our way, our identity, our voice. And voice, obviously, is the most important thing a writer can possess. Over the course of his schooling and then university, Jon played at being several different kinds of people before settling on the persona he took with him to London.

He arrived in London at the fag end of Thatcher's Eighties. The era of conspicuous consumption, money, money, money, the City as God, survival of the meanest was just about to tip into the Major years and a looming recession, the Nineties hangover after the asset-squandering party before it. Jon claimed afterwards to have hated being in this milieu, and allied himself wherever possible with the voices of dissent, the counterculture of the time. He also claimed to have been in the poll tax riots of 1990 although there is only his testimony to prove that. The experience at first hand of seeing mounted police, batons drawn, leading a charge against defenceless, unarmed civilians, he said, made him a proud socialist. How well those socialist views survived once success came his way, we shall see later. For now, he was playing the lead character in his own story, and he was doing so exceptionally well. Perhaps this is why his first career as an actor didn't work out.

Clearly, he had the looks, not to mention the presence and charisma. But, crucially, not the ability to let go of the character he had created and inhabit others. Still, he tried. Got an agent, managed a few parts in some profit share fringe productions (off West End, as they'd be called now), and a couple of glorified bit parts in TV shows and commercials. However, by all accounts he was wooden and unconvincing. Look up some of his commercials on YouTube for proof. Still, he gave it his best shot. Took dead end, cash in hand jobs to leave himself free for auditions which hardly ever came and which never led to acting jobs. Perhaps he was just enjoying the feeling of considering himself creative without actually doing any creating. If so, he wouldn't be the first or the last to live that self-conscious, semi-bohemian lifestyle. During this period he took bar work to keep him going.

And it was while doing this he began writing in his spare time. This was more like it, he thought. Acting, he began to realise, wasn't for him. Or rather he wasn't for it. Unable to let the character he had worked so hard to create go, he chose to let acting go instead. But that desire to create still burned within him. So he wrote. He read writers not covered by his degree course, Bukowski and Kerouac, Harry Crews and Nelson Algren. Classic angst-ridden outsider literature from the alternative canon. Perfect for an educated white boy like him. Yes, this was more like it. As if the character he had created for himself had graduated towards the literature he was meant to read. He leaned into it fully. Recited Tom Waits lyrics in the pub to the customers, even read aloud during down times from whatever book he had in his back pocket. This was *him*, who he was, who he could be. Who he was supposed to be. And he didn't just have to read it, he could write it too. And so he wrote. And wrote and wrote. His new obsession. He was desperate to become a published writer. The next Kerouac.

He became a familiar sight around the bars and cafés of Clapham where he was living in a house share. With his quiffed hair and black overcoat, Levis and DM shoes, he was every inch the stereotypical young wannabe writer. Or at least a certain kind of writer, the romanticised image of one. He looked the part, totally and completely. Scribbling away in his notebook, a dog-eared copy of one of his previously mentioned heroes, or Camus or Hunter S Thompson or whoever he was mimicking that week beside him. There was just one thing missing. Having decided to become a writer he quickly realised he had nothing to write about.

He had the hair; he had the look. The attitude and literary outsider library. He just had nothing to say. That didn't stop him from trying, of course. And trying and trying. Each time getting worse and worse and more derivative. And he might have stayed that way, growing into the kind of parochial, bitter middle-aged failure literature is littered with. Had he not met the person who was to change his life.

Gwen McCulloch.

An assistant to a literary agent, based in the West End but living, and more importantly for our story, socialising, in Clapham. They met while he was doing his usual Friday night shift behind the bar at the Prince of Wales in Clapham Old Town. This would have been the early Nineties. Immediately the two were smitten and from then on inseparable. Their language of love was the most popular method at the time, exchanging mixtapes. Jon was listening almost exclusively to jangly indie guitar bands with angst-ridden lead singers. Gwen broadened his musical horizon considerably. She introduced him to soul and jazz, Stax and country. Blues. Women singers, not just the men he was exclusively listening to. In return he would read to her from his latest work in progress, walking round his bedroom, declaiming from his tattered, over-written notebook. She listened and, while not exactly liking what she heard, recognised that there was something there. It just needed, in her professional opinion, work. Lots of work.

There was talent there, Gwen realised. She had made a discovery. But before they could go any further, he needed to hear some harsh truths. His reading was stuck in 'sixth form boys masturbatory fantasy land' and needed broadening. It would improve his writing. So out went the Bukowski, in came ... everything else. She brought him new books from authors her agency represented. Asked him what he thought, explained why they were being published and his stuff wasn't. Read the classics by all means, she said, even the ones he was reading, but more importantly read what's currently being published. If you want to write about now, read about now. She became his private mentor and muse. And he responded, working and working under her guidance to become as good as he could be. They moved in together, renting a house in Streatham. Gwen then presented Jon's work to her boss and he had an agent. That's when his career began to take off.

You might be thinking that the obvious thing for a woman so driven as Gwen would be to represent Jon herself. And I'm not saying she didn't give the matter much thought and was severely tempted. However, she concluded that working with him at home was one thing. Putting that aside and turning the relationship totally professional was another. She didn't want to stress test their relationship if it was put on that kind of footing.

The Nineties became Jon's decade. His first novel, *Perfect Circle*, was published in '92 to instant acclaim. It also managed to do something few novels do, especially first ones: fly up the bestseller charts to become a commercial success as well as a critical success and have the rights bought by Hollywood. The holy trinity of book publishing. Usually that would be it for a film version, as most projects end up floundering in development hell before being quietly dropped. But a copy came across Martin Scorsese's desk and he quickly attached himself to the project. This was when he was hot off the back of *Cape Fear*, so consequently the film was instantly greenlit. It cleaned up at the box office and made quite a showing at both the BAFTAs and Oscars. Now, if you're reading this and think this is the normal trajectory for a novelist, especially a first time one, let me explain. It most definitely isn't. Usually, a book is either commercially successful or critically well-received. One or the other. Rarely both. And, for most writers, usually neither. Jon's book was both. Films that actually get made from books usually go the same way too. Either box office success or awards-season fodder. Very little crossover. Again, Jon did both. And again, most films made from novels end up in that so-so limbo. Now we would write them off as just streaming content.

But was he just a one hit wonder, asked the critics? Was it just beginner's luck? Hype? Right place, right time? Would he succumb, as so many did, to the curse of difficult second album syndrome? In a word, no. In '94 his follow up, *Black Snow*, was, if anything, an even bigger hit. Rave reviews, top of the bestseller lists for months in both hardback and paperback. It became not just the novel to read but the novel to be seen reading. Like schoolkids in the Seventies carrying round LPs to show their allegiance to their tribes, people would ostentatiously carry Jon's novel around with them. And the obligatory movie came next, this time David Fincher, his warm-up act for *Seven*. Obviously, you've read it or seen the film (or carried it round to impress people). So you don't need me to tell you how it did.

Jon was now untouchable. The British publishing industry's golden boy. Could he do it again? Of course he could. In '96 came the Booker Prize-winning *These Dark Tomorrows*. And the subsequent movie, Fincher again. Jon bestrode the publishing industry like a colossus. He was the cultural zeitgeist. The new rock 'n' roll writ large, the Britpop novelist.

Publishers, with their customary speed of a supertanker turning in an ocean, always at least eighteen months behind trends, scrambled to find writers like Jon that they could market like Jon, make as big as Jon. Ride the same wave as Jon. Make them as much money as Jon had for his publisher. And I guess this is where I enter the picture in a big way. Jon and I were already friends. We hung out at parties together, went for dinner together, became, in publishing terms, best friends. My career at the time was plodding along, not reaching the stellar heights of Jon, but now my association with him meant I was a possible contender to be another Jon. I didn't complain, in fact I was happy to go along with it. In Britpop terms he was Blur and Oasis combined. I used to kid myself that I was Suede. I guess in reality I was more like Supergrass.

If you want to check all this up, bear in mind I had a different name back then.

Novels followed. From both of us. These were the good years. We were on the big wheel of success. But the thing with big wheels is, they never keep you at the top for ever.

The millennium came and went and we were still being published. Jon was still a publishing powerhouse and I was ticking along beside him. Actually no, if I'm honest my sales were starting to slip. And I know you're only one poor or poorly received novel away from being dropped by your publisher or even worse, being banished back to the midlist. So I knew I had to do something. The party was coming to an end.

Jon, however successful he might have seemed from the outside, was beginning to be plagued by the vicissitudes of a media who thought his time in the sun was due to end. They had papers to sell, column inches to fill. New, younger faces to photograph. His reviews for the later novels became more respectful. Instead of being greeted as they had been previously, each new novel was now declared to be a great return to form. He still sold well, top ten bestseller, big draw at literary festivals. But as the Nineties gave way to the Noughties, I sensed that Jon was tiring of it all. 'I think I've only got one more in me,' he once said as we were drinking one night in the Groucho. 2007, I think it was. 'What'll you do then?' I asked. He didn't answer. Just smiled.

I've thought about that smile and what it meant a lot in the years since.

There were, as I'm sure you're aware, plenty of stories swirling around about Jon. His behaviour, both professionally and personally. What happened between him and his publisher. Between him and Gwen. I hate to use the word controversies because that gives those stories from the time more weight – or at least a one-sided weight – than they perhaps deserve. Jon was, like all of us, a complicated person. And out of complications arise misunderstandings. He became the subject of lurid, prurient pieces in the same newspapers that had praised him several years previously. He was even the subject of a particularly tawdry, hack-written biography. But none of them have come close to the real Jon. The one I knew. The one I was with when all this happened.

I – and everyone else – never got to see Jon's final book, as you know. Because he disappeared. Not just ran away on holiday or had a breakdown. I mean, he may have done those things, but we have no way of knowing. It felt like one day he was there, the next he wasn't. As if his life had ceased.

At first, no one took his disappearance seriously. Critics, as critics are wont to do, sensed a publicity trick. The media sensing a big story about diva literary star behaviour swooped down. But it genuinely wasn't a stunt. His publishers expected him to appear once again, in the manner of Agatha Christie in a Harrogate hotel, but he never did.

Sensing something untoward, they hired private detectives to search as far as their budget extended, and couldn't find him. Gwen had no idea where he was, she was distraught. Newspapers, realising this was serious, offered big money for any sighting of him. Nothing. He had, to all intents and purposes, disappeared. As if he had never existed.

Eventually it was accepted that he had gone. Just burned out instead of fading away. James Dean to my Marlon Brando. Kurt Cobain to my Mark Lanegan. And so on. (I'm still writing now. Fading away slowly, as all writers do. Or rather most.) The comparisons are numerous. So what happened? He had conquered the cultural mainstream. Did he just get bored and want to disappear? Was he a man who contained too much emotional damage to fully control his artistry? Did he die? Either an accident or murder? The general consensus at the time was of a talent that had burned incandescently bright but burned itself out too soon.

And his final book never appeared. Until now.

The book you hold in your hands, *Russian Doll*, was delivered in hard copy to his old publishers by motorbike courier. A hand-typed note was attached saying this book was written in 2009 and is definitely by Jonathan Durward. His signature was at the bottom.

Which begs the question: is the book real? Or is it a fake, a hoax? You, the reader, will have to do the same as his publisher, his agent and I did. Make up your own mind. Jon is (was?) too important a writer not to be given the benefit of the doubt as to the veracity of this book. It should be published, should be read, should be discussed. And it has been.

Because of my longtime history with Jon, his publishers asked me to prepare the manuscript for publication. I've made small edits for the sake of clarity, got rid of typos, that sort of thing. But I've left the text as untouched as I possibly could. It was my intention just to provide a notes section after each chapter in which I explain some of his more obscure references, or private in-jokes, or give more detailed explanations to the background of certain words and phrases. Sometimes the origins of whole scenes. However, as you will see once you come to read it, those notes became more extensive. It soon became apparent to me that small edits and notes weren't going to be enough for this project. The story in the novel, I began to believe, presented possible indications as to Jon's whereabouts or ultimate fate. He had left us clues throughout the text if we know how to interpret them. I felt strongly that I took it upon myself to follow these clues, turn literary detective if you like, and to try to reach an explanation for Jon's absence and whereabouts for the past two decades. I make no apologies for my actions in doing this and hope that rather than distract from the story itself, it enhances it. In fact, more than anything else, the publication of this novel and my actions in editing it should, I hope, give a sense of closure over what Jon's ultimate fate was. Or is. And that, I think, is the most important thing about it.

So please, sit back, get comfortable, pour yourself a beverage of your choice and enjoy this story of an international assassin who decides he doesn't want to be an assassin any more and instead decides to disappear by assuming his latest target's identity.

I give you *Russian Doll*.
By Jonathan Durward.

C. B. Everett
March 2026

1

The European Parliament Debating Chamber is vast, built to resemble an old Roman amphitheatre, the difference being the spectacle now is for consent and cooperation, not gladiatorial contests, tearing and ripping an opponent limb from limb. Apart from one MEP, currently standing up, currently attacking the head of the European Council. And currently being most boring about it.

The `far right grifter's` voice drones on, his face smug at the sound of it. He loves his own voice. He loves everything about himself. His ridiculous choice of [REDACTED], usually paired with a [REDACTED] and [REDACTED] shoes. The comedy patriot. Wrapping himself in the flag, inviting the gullible idiots back home to fall for his act, embrace it and him, the man of the people, bravely going into battle against the enemy, the establishment, on their behalf. Of course, that's all bullshit. The man's establishment through and through. His populist schtick just there to hide his extremist far-right views. He's the worst thing that can happen to any country.

How do I know all this? Because I've been by his side for months. I've watched him in action, close up. I've been a faceless, nameless functionary in the employ of `Toad of Toad Heil` himself. One of his party's activists, hired with next to no vetting and allowed a seat on their Euro gravy train in his entourage, comprising all the different factions of his party: the wife-beaters, the child abusers, the tax-dodgers and the racist thugs. Embarrassingly easy to get next to him. Just laugh at his racist jokes, mainly. I also have to wheel him away from potential flashpoints, avoid meetings, both planned and accidental, with non-partisan journalists, protestors, other MEPs and anyone else with a working bullshit detector. As per my job, I threaten to hurt those people if they don't desist. He likes that. He likes wielding that kind of power. He's different with those on his side, though, which isn't surprising for a man who chose to spend Remembrance Day with the German far right instead of in Britain. Unguarded with tame journalists, the mask slipping totally, then at the sign of a photo op with a supporter he's up, getting rid of his preferred large glass of expensive red and grabbing his props – a [REDACTED] in one hand and a [REDACTED] in the other – fixing his grin in place and he's off. Disingenuously greeting them, mentally counting the money he's making off them while laughing along with them, then once again in private grimacing and wiping his hands after any accidental contact with the great unwashed as he calls them, slagging them off and bad-mouthing them for the gullible, lumpen marks they are. Then off to spend more quality time with his paymasters, helping to facilitate their next incursion into Western democracy.

I should say I don't normally become partisan during an assignment. I don't get paid to do that. It's seen, quite rightly, as unprofessional. Breaking the first rule. Allowing emotions to become involved always gets in the way of work, of executing a clean job. No pun intended. But occasionally I make an exception. As long as I don't allow irrationality to cloud my judgement, to give in to emotionalism, to make any mistakes that could sew the slightest seeds of doubt in what I'm about to do, then I'm golden. And when it's someone as hideous in every respect as this one is, it's actually a pleasure knowing what's going to happen to them. (1)

He takes a sip of water, pauses. Looks round the chamber, hoping he's upset as many people as possible. Up close he's smaller than you think he is, in every aspect, with the voice of a golf club bore. However, he thinks he's the finest orator Europe has witnessed since Adolf Hitler.

And off he goes again. '[Blah blah blah drone drone drone personal attack attack attack to get his optics up up up . . .]' Pause for laughter – which isn't forthcoming because the whole chamber's ignoring him – and off he goes again. '[Smug attack smug attack smug attack . . .]' (2)

There's movement behind him. I lean forward in my seat, ready to get down there on the floor. Suddenly interested in what's going on, the rest of the suited party thugs with me do the same. We're watching on a monitor in a private room just off the main chamber itself. It's where entourages are parked, ready to walk into the chamber and escort our prize buffoon out when he's finished. Ensure he's not stopped en route to wherever. They've made their way through the free beer they asked for, I've played along, feeding the rubber plant next to me most of mine, knowing I'm going to need my wits about me when events move up a gear. Which they will do soon. But this guy standing up behind him in the chamber? Looking directly at him? This isn't part of the plan.

In a way it doesn't matter. If this guy's got bad intentions towards the right-wing shithead, then that doesn't bother me in any way. As long as he acts on those intentions and ensures the Poundshop Enoch Powell's not walking away afterwards. I still get paid, whatever happens. But if, as so often happens with amateurs, he fucks it up and leaves him alive, then we've got trouble. And so has he. Because he's just been added to my list.

One of my compatriots has noticed this guy as well. 'What the fuck …'

The guy behind's taking something out of his jacket, still staring at our boy.

They're all on their feet now, ready to rush the chamber. So am I, but not for the reasons they think.

The guy gets what he wants from his jacket pocket.

They're by the door, ready.

He unfolds a piece of paper, holds it up.

THIS MAN IS A LIAR, it says, with an arrow pointing to the right-wing populist. (3)

The thugs make their feelings known about the man. As loudly and angrily as possible. They're disappointed they didn't have to rush into the chamber as well. Even more disappointed there wasn't any violence. They may wear expensive suits and ties but they're still football terrace hooligans at heart. And always will be, bless them.

The delegate, acknowledging the laughter in the chamber, puts that piece of paper away, gets out another one.

AND BORING AS WELL.

More laughter. He sits down, pleased with himself and the reaction.

'Reckon we stand down,' I say, trying to sound disappointed. Also, knowing they'll be back on their feet soon.

I watch the feed on the screen. The rest of the delegates are really laughing now. He thinks it's for him, unaware of what the man behind him has done. Never mind. He'll see it on the news later. Oh no. Sorry. He won't. He'll go to his grave thinking he was hilarious. Maybe not the best orator in Europe since his hero. But at least the funniest.

And he's still banging on. The target of his ire no longer looks angry or indignant, just bored. As do the rest of the chamber. The President is asking him to sit down, to retract those remarks. This is playing into his hands. This is what he wants. He's now loudly proclaiming about free speech, something that only runs one way with him, of how they're trying to take it away from him. He pauses, takes another sip. Good lad.

Yes, it's in the water. It's undetectable. Completely untraceable. As I said earlier, I'm a professional. I don't do an amateur job. It won't look like he's been poisoned. It won't show up at all. Heart attack, that'll be the official verdict. He smokes way too much, drinks way too much. No one will be the slightest bit surprised. In fact, I'm sure people have money on him going sooner than later. I wish I could too. But that wouldn't be professional.

Another sip, bigger this time, more of a gulp. He's frowning, loosening his collar, looking like he's getting even more thirsty. Another mouthful, draining the glass. He's stopped talking now. Visibly sweating. Panting. He puts one hand on his desk to steady himself, looks around like the room's spinning, like he doesn't know where he is any more.

One of his legs gives way. He grabs at the desk, trying desperately to hold on.

People around him are beginning to notice. So are the thugs with me. They're on their feet again, but this time they don't seem to know what to do. This is out of their sphere of experience. If a situation doesn't demand violence or intimidation, they're useless.

He collapses completely to the floor.

And the house is in uproar.

The thugs have no choice, they leave the room. I stay where I am, keep watching the monitor. Someone rushes over to him, administers CPR. After what seems like minutes, hours, but is probably only seconds, they look up, gesture for someone else to come over. I see the look on their face, the slight shake of the head. The universal sign for: He's gone.

I smile to myself. But the smile isn't as big as I'd like it to be. I'm not feeling the satisfaction I thought I would. Perhaps it'll come later. Perhaps it never will. This is why I have to detach myself from my work. Good or bad, they're just a target. If I take any joy from this at all it should be the joy of a job well done, and only that, and not this emptiness I've been increasingly experiencing after my target has been eliminated.

But I don't have time to concern myself with that. I have an escape to make.

I leave the room. The thugs are all milling about outside, not knowing what to do. I know it's a cliché to describe them as headless chickens, but that really is what they look like. Headless chickens, their bloated bodies flapping about. It would be funny to watch, satisfying even, if I had time. But I have to be off.

Out of this building and as far away as possible. Shedding the skin of the person I've been as I go, the identity I've used dropping away. Disappearing with every step I take.

Job done.

1 – Notes

1. I'm sure you've spotted who this is supposed to be. Surely you have.

    Now, I should state at the outset, and you've probably noticed, that some of the text of Chapter 1 is in a different font. This is deliberate. In Jon's original text, he had written the name of the person and given him identifiable markers. Now, the publisher's legal department have had a look at this and told me we can't have that. Because the person in question is still alive and could potentially sue. So I've had to go through and change every reference to his name to something else. I didn't want it to look like Jon had written those things, so a different font for me seemed to be the best way forward. I hope you, dear reader, are fine with that. And that the legal department is too. Right. Onwards.

    Obviously the actions in this chapter raise questions. I mentioned in the introduction that doubt has been cast on this novel's authenticity. And no sooner have I said that, as if to prove my point, here's the first scene. If, as is claimed later in the text, the novel is set in 2009, where does that leave this section? It shows remarkable foresight to predict the rise of the far right in Europe, Russian disinformation and destabilisation of the West and its interference in the 2016 Brexit referendum. Was Jon that good an author? Is anyone? This also leads to the next question: Was the novel written in the year it's set, 2009? Jon disappeared that year. If he did indeed write it, it must have been 2008 or earlier, in preparation for publication in 2009. Again, this shows a degree of prescience that one has to, but can hardly, suspend disbelief at. At the time, this man was an MEP, not turning up for the committee work he was supposed to do, milking his expense account. An irritant to the militant wing of the British Conservative Party, but not taken seriously by anyone else. So, could Jon have spotted this grifter's potential and run with it? If that is the case, who was giving him this information? If that isn't the case, then it leaves us with a third, and possibly more obvious, option. The novel was not written before 2009 and is in fact contemporaneous or at least more recent. Or is there more to it than that?

2. Case in point. This is interesting. I've researched this, and there's no record of this person (if it is the one we think it is) haranguing anyone in a speech during 2009. In fact, he could barely be bothered to turn up most days. There is a record of him making a personal attack on someone in the chamber but that isn't until 2010. It seems impossible that Jon, however good his powers of clairvoyance might have been regards the rise of this man, there's no way he could have foreseen this attack. Not to this level of detail. Which, again, casts doubt on when it was written. But if it's more contemporary, then where does that leave us? What are the implications? The first, and probably easiest claim to make is that it's a straightforward forgery and leave it at that. Write it off as the work of a clever prankster (remember the Hitler Diaries?) and dismiss it. But this also ignores the larger questions the text presents. Mainly, why do something so glaringly obvious in the first chapter to demonstrate that it couldn't possibly be a novel by Jon

Durward from 2009? Wouldn't that, conversely, prove that it isn't a forgery? And if that is the case, then it must mean Jon is still alive somewhere and working. Or was when he wrote this, which we have to presume, given the subject matter, fairly recently. So if we take that at face value it leaves us with other, more pertinent questions. Where is he now? What's he been doing in the intervening years? And why has he chosen this particular story to make a return with? I believe, as I said in the introduction, the clues are all in here. Read on.

3. Again, there's a record of something similar to this happening, but not on the date stated. It's as if this chapter is playing his greatest hits.

Addendum: I first met Jon at the launch party for some anthology or other that he was in and I wasn't. I was just at the party, ligging, *networking*, as I justified it to my accountant, drinking weak bottled lager and chatting, one eye on the door in case someone more important that my present conversational colleague came in, someone who could help my career stagger up to the next level. Ingratiating myself on my agent's orders. I think it was in Black's Club. Or the Union. One of those very expensive faux-dilapidated private members clubs in Soho that I never had membership for but somehow always managed to get into.

Publishing in the Nineties in the heart of London's glittering West End. Taking the night off from the shift work of my second job in a pub to come here. To try and feel like I had arrived. Like I was living the dream. My dream.

I had written one novel. I thought the world, or rather my world, was going to change overnight and the papers the next day would be full of stories about how the future of British literature had been discovered. And it would be me. This never happened, of course. For the next few weeks I scoured the papers for a hint of a review. Finally I found one, a tiny one, in what seemed like an abandoned corner of the Literary Review. I measured it. Two and half centimetres high. It printed a rough precis of the story then said: 'Well-written and thought-provoking'. And that was it. There was the strapline for the paperback. The only strapline. Well-written and thought-provoking. It managed to be both simultaneously exultant and crushing.

It had been a tiny advance, but still established authors I met at parties told me what a good deal I had. When I say established, I mean ancient alcoholics whose best work was years behind them. Decades, even. At first I was delighted to be in their company, writers who I'd actually heard of, whose books I had read, talking to me. But gradually I realised that they were only there because they had nowhere else to go. And they couldn't face going home to be reminded of their failure. I wouldn't allow myself to become like that. I told myself frequently. Every time I talked with them. Whatever happened, I wouldn't allow myself to become like that.

So that's how I ended up at this party. I was trying to move away from the living dead and join the living. Writers my own age. Writers who I had something in common with. The next generation. The new generation. *My* generation. But I seemed to be struggling to get anyone interested in me. A new author with a tiny advance published by a small publisher to barely any acclaim. What was there to get excited about?

Anyway. The next person to walk in was Jon. Obviously I knew who he was. We all knew who he was. I'd read *Perfect Circle* along with everyone else and fallen into line with my praise of the novel. It's easy to say, looking back with hindsight, that there was something special about him, an aura of success or nascent success, something like that. But there wasn't. He was handsome, undoubtedly, with a confident smile which endears one to people. But there was something else I noticed about him. A certain amusement in his eyes. As if he couldn't quite believe he was here, that they were taking him seriously, and he was going to make the most of it. As I say, hindsight is wonderful, so maybe there was none of this and I'm pre-loading all the things I later discovered about him in one, possibly inaccurate, info dump. Memory cheats, and all that.

Anyway, we got talking over the weak lager. He'd heard of me, he said, but hadn't gone quite so far as to have read my first, and at that time, only novel. He made a mental note of it, though, and said he would. Yeah, right. Writers always say that. If they actually read all the books they claim to read they would never have any actual time to write their own. Still, I was impressed that said he had heard of me. Most of them didn't even bother to do that.

He told me where he lived: Tufnell Park. 'Just moved there not so long ago. With my wife. Used to live in Streatham. Thought we should move north of the river.' He laughed. 'Show I'm serious about being a writer.'

I laughed along with him, thinking of my home with my wife in a terminally unfashionable part of East London bordering on Essex. 'Absolutely. Don't blame you.'

I asked him how his book was doing. He tried that self-deprecating thing of shrugging and claiming not to know. I didn't believe it for a second. I knew how well he was doing. Everyone in the room did. People were looking at him while pretending not to. He was making those kinds of sales. People wanted to talk to him but he seemed to be sticking with me. I was quite pleased about that. Hoped some of his success would rub off on me. Hoped I'd become interesting to the people looking.

'What d'you think of this anthology?' he asked.

I said I hadn't read it.

'Don't waste your time. Bunch of preening fucking posers who spend more time getting their publicity photo to look moody than they do sitting at their desks actually doing the work. Fucking awful.'

I laughed aloud at that and looked round, seeing, for the first time that evening, the rest of the guests through Jon's eyes. It was a sad pathetic spectacle. Gurning idiots vying to be taken seriously, to be adored. I'm not saying I wasn't like that, but here was a successful author who seemed to have got where he was by not being like them. I could learn something from him.

'Fancy going somewhere else for a drink? Gerry's is just down the road.'

I had just started frequenting the venerable old Soho drinking club and was quite amazed at the regulars, half-remembered old sitcom actors, clustering round the bar wondering what had happened to their careers. I loved it.

'Yeah, why not?'

So off we ambled into the Soho night. And a friendship was born.

2

I step out of the lift on the top floor and through the concrete walkway. The windows either side of me show London down below and far away. I stop to look down and sigh. I used to sigh at the sight of the city from this vantage point. Now all I feel is tiredness. An absolute total bone weariness.

It hasn't changed. I have. Where I used to find the view exciting it now gives me a melancholic weariness. Every time I returned from an assignment I would stop here, look down and check the world below was still functioning as I left it. I used to believe that I did what I did for those people down there. To make their lives safe, unaware they were ever in any potential danger. Knowing I'd made a difference, given something back. Isn't that what we're all supposed to say when we're asked about work? It seems a long time ago, that I thought that. Or actually believed it. Like I was someone else. Because the more I became involved with my job, the less I had in common with the people I was protecting. Maybe it was always just a lie I told myself. Maybe I only ever said it to justify to myself what I did for a living. What I *do* for a living. And the thrill it gave me. In reality I have as much in common with the people down there as they do with the movie, TV and music stars they idolise. And yet I still stand here after every job, every return home. Not because it gives me the giddy, illicit secret thrill it used to, to know I'm protecting them and they don't realise, their guardian angel on high, no, it's something I do out of habit, ritual. And because I'm so far up here and above them all, I can.

I'm good at what I do. I'm a professional and I'm well rewarded for it. That's how it's always been.

Until recently.

Until now.

Getting out after the job was relatively easy. There was no chase, no cat and mouse trying to escape from the police, nothing like that. I don't work that way. There was a mass of people running around switching to damage limitation mode while simultaneously trying not to panic. It was chaos inside the parliament building. As I say, relatively easy to sneak away while all that was going on. No one even noticed me leave.

I never come straight back home either. For many reasons. One, it's not a very clever idea. If (and it's a big if) someone does connect me with what's happened or even suspect and try to follow me, I have to make it difficult for them. I keep my wits about me, look for anything out of the ordinary. Any tails. I always plan a circuitous route away, one without a seeming pattern. That way no one will know where I'm going. I take modes of transport that afford me some degree of control if I have to change my plans quickly, and that keep me under the radar as much as possible. I have many passports in many aliases. I favour the train over the plane as an initial escape. I've even tried buses, but there are too many variables and they often don't get me away quick enough. So I get the train, pull into the nearest large city or urban conurbation with an airport, get off, change of clothes, change of identity, take a plane from there. Always wary, always on the look out. I never relax until I'm sure I'm not being followed. Once I'm certain of that I go to the place I always head to after a job. Somewhere only I know about. And when I'm ready, I come home.

I turn away from my view of the city and cross the walkway into the body of the building. More concrete, the shimmering promise of coloured glass at the far end brightening and lightening the corridor, promising hope in the brutalist gloom. Giving my walk an almost spiritual dimension.

I live in Trellick Tower, West London. (1) My main residence. You'll know it. Everyone has an opinion on it, even if they've never been inside it or only glimpsed it from the train window coming into Paddington. It's an icon of Brutalist architecture. A huge slab of concrete, brick and glass dominating the skyline. Cairo has the pyramids, West London has Trellick. Ian Fleming hated it so much he stole the name of the architect, Erno Goldfinger, making him the nemesis of his hero, the archly unprogressive conservative James Bond, and in the process creating one of the most famous villains in the history of spy literature and cinema. You would think just from a description and the virulence it's attracted down the decades that the building should be ugly, but it's beautiful. Or beautiful in its ugliness. Ugly-beautiful. And of course, I take a certain delight in living in a building most think of in relation to a supervillain's lair. How could I not?

I live on the top floor. Apartments here are like gold dust. Rarely coming on the market and when they do the private ones go for increasingly extortionate amounts. But the majority of the apartments are council owned so you get the flashy architectural fanboys and girls looking for lifestyle bragging rights living alongside people who just call it home. I was lucky. The previous tenant of my top floor flat died unexpectedly and left the place to me. I've always been lucky that way.

I open the door and enter, putting my bag down with another sigh. Home again. I don't bother with elaborate motion sensors or hidden CCTV cameras. Or even anything old school, like a single hair licked and plastered across the door and frame.

There's no need. Only a handful of people know I'm here. And they keep that information quiet.

The interior matches the exterior: minimal and modernist. You don't move to Trellick for Georgian opulence. The walls are stripped back to the bare concrete, the only accidental decoration the runnels from the original embedded lighting cables which adds to the authenticity, I think. The furniture is all mid-century Scandinavian, which, when I started to furnish the place was easy to come by and cheap, but now the Sunday supplements and TV design shows have fetishised it into the mainstream it's becoming a lot more expensive. Again, I see it as being true to the surroundings.

A minimalist environment forces you to confront yourself. Question who you really are. Most of us, our lives, our identities, are an accumulation of our years. We amass and surround ourselves with stuff that reminds and reinforces us of who we are, where we came from, where we are now and how we got here. Records, books, CDs, furniture, DVDs, cars, watches, clothes. Our possessions become our diaries, and anyone can read them. We build life-libraries around ourselves and lock ourselves inside. This is who I am, we cry out silently, because this is what I've got. Look and you will know me.

I have next to nothing. (2)

It was a conscious choice. Possessions hold memories, memories hold ownership over you. Memories hold regrets. A life without possessions is a life without ownership, without regrets. A life lived in the moment. Like anyone else I want entertainment. I still read books, watch films or listen to music. It just has no claim on me. If something is memorable it'll be stored somewhere inside me, if it's not, it's forgotten. Obviously I wasn't always like this. If it makes me sound like an alcoholic who can no longer drink or a drug addict who's now clean, then so be it. The choice to live this way wasn't made in a vacuum.

I pocket my house keys, enter the kitchen. Bare walls, as I said, with a work unit fitted at one end containing a sink and an induction hob, oven underneath, cupboards next to that. Two long wall-to-wall shelves above hold kitchen items. I put the kettle on, make myself a cup of tea. Listen to the silence. I'm alone.

That tiredness persists. That melancholic weariness. I feel it even more keenly in the quiet of my home. That sense of motions being gone through. Of a joy snuffed out. It's not a homecoming, in the sense of relaxation, of being pleased to be back. It's been a long time since I felt like that. If I ever did. All I feel now is the emptiness of the apartment. It mirrors the emptiness I feel in me.

I cross to the kitchen table, sit down. Take a small ornately wrapped package from my overcoat pocket, place it on the table. I don't open it. It's not mine to open.

I do this every time I complete a job. It began as a gesture. It evolved into a ritual. Others may call rituals superstitions but they're wrong. Rituals are commonly believed to be small occult practices invoked in order for an embarked upon endeavour to reach the desired outcome. Success is, therefore, offered up to a higher power. My rituals are the opposite of that. They allow me to compartmentalise my life, differentiate my working self from my waiting self. To give a sense of structure. There's no higher power involved.

You'll have gathered by now I kill people for a living. But I'm not a common hitman. My job is more specialised than that. The very term, the words, 'Hit Man', smacks of pulp sensationalism, low-rent drama. It speaks of guns and incompetence, of poorly targeted anger and inherent psychosis. Hitmen are always portrayed in shabby spy stories, popularly illiterate crime novels and tabloid journalism as conflicted, angry souls, whose inner turmoil ultimately leads to them either subconsciously making a mistake or consciously messing up their assignment while seeking some form of redemption or deliberate damnation. Either that or they're stone-cold psychopaths, whose barely contained and poorly channelled maniacal blood lust spirals out of control, leading to ever greater atrocities. Both narratives lead to the same conclusion: they're either caught or killed. A third option is that they're somehow near-supernatural beings, appearing and vanishing at will, killing and leaving no trace, fading back into the shadows like they were never there in the first place. The stuff of urban legend. Three popular misconceptions. None of them describes my actual job.

Question: how did my target die? Was he shot? A sniper bullet? No. His water was poisoned with a tablet that brought on a swift heart attack.

Question: how did I know he would take it? Because I did my research. I studied him for months. His habits, his foibles, his life. I got so close to him I understood him better than he did himself. *Became* him. And with that knowledge planned his death. Everything went as planned.

Question: what if it hadn't have done? There was no question of that happening. I studied. I prepped. I planned.

That's why I prefer the term assassin to hitman. It's fairer and more accurate. History lesson coming up. Assassin is one of the oldest recorded tools of power politics. The name derives from the Arabic *asasiyyin* meaning 'people who are faithful to the foundation of the faith' – the inference being they would kill anyone diverging from that faith. The modern assassin differs, though. I'm not loyal to the foundations of any particular faith. However, I am most definitely an agent of power politics. And for me, that means the work is of paramount importance. The money too, obviously, as it enables me to live as I want to with no economic worries. As is professional pride. I've never failed in a job yet. When I say I'm the best at what I do I'm being neither falsely modest nor arrogant. I'm merely stating a fact. Although, sitting here and studying the small parcel on the kitchen table, I do wonder if that's enough. If it's ever been enough.

Many people think they can do what I do but my business is highly specialised. Armchair killers think it's easy. How hard can it be? Pull a trigger, walk away. That's that. And on that basis, plenty of people think they've got at least one kill in them. And that's where it should stay because most of them are wrong. It's much harder than it looks. There's a professional standard which most of them will never aspire to. It takes its toll, physically, mentally, psychically, emotionally. Every way. And you have to find ways to cope with that. Most people who try it quickly realise it isn't the idealised lifestyle they expected it to be. Some stick at it, scraping a kind of living at the bottom of the list, but the attrition rate is high. Very few last in the long run. Even fewer prosper. Which is why those who do, like me, are well rewarded for it. (3)

My reverie is cut short. I hear a key in the lock.

2 – Notes

1. It's interesting that Jon should choose this location for his assassin to live. Firstly, he's making an obvious joke here. An espionage novel? The lead character lives in a building designed by Goldfinger? As jokes go, it's not subtle. Also, and I think this is more interesting, this is the very opposite of the kind of place Jon himself would and indeed did live in. Actually, I'm more likely to live somewhere like this than Jon ever would. He favoured an older style, Edwardian, Victorian. Even Georgian, although that was more his wife's taste than his. He preferred high ceilings, old wooden doors, space. A sense of history. 'A proper house', he used to say. I'll talk more about that later. This may be (or have been) not only something that fits his lead character but a deliberate attempt to counter one of the most frequently asked questions that writers get: Is your lead character just an idealised version of you? Someone braver, or stronger, or thinner, or cleverer than the writer? Someone who could get away on the page with things you could only dream of doing in real life? And the answer is yes. But that's not the whole answer. The writer is the good guy. Or wants the reader to identify with them as the good guy. But the writer is also the bad guy and all the other characters in between. They've all stepped out of the writer's imagination. That hero? The writer. That comedy office worker? The writer. The murderer? That domestic abuser or paedophile? The writer too. Does that mean

the writer actually wants to do those things? Of course not. But it means that since the writer can imagine those things then the writer is capable of doing those things. Possibly. Or at least thinking about it. Working things through to such a degree that they can write a whole novel about it. This is not a great revelation. All it demonstrates is that everyone, writers, readers and non-readers alike, all have within us the capacity for great good and great evil. Depending upon the circumstances, of course.

2. Again, the opposite of Jon himself. His personal decorative style, if such a phrase could be used, ran towards maximalism. Some less charitable folk would say clutter. Framed pictures on the walls, often originals since he could afford them, shelves lined with knick-knacks such as toy robots, a pair of spurs, a Batman ukelele, plus, of course, awards. Many, many awards. And books. Shelves and piles of books. Plus, if there was any wall space left, the occasional film poster from one of his books. This clutter used to drive his wife Gwen mad, so he ended up keeping it all in his study. The clutter looked, to the untrained eye, like a mess. But Jon knew where everything was and everything was in its place for a reason. It all meant something to him, some memory or emotion, a remembrance or perhaps even a warning, a caution. It was like standing in the centre of his mind. By making his lead character the exact opposite of himself as far as home habitat goes, was Jon showing a different kind of lead character to himself? Or was he trying to indicate that he was running as far away from himself as he could?

3. This is the first clue that he's talking about something else rather than what the character is experiencing in the narrative. Is he still talking about assassination here? Or is he now, in a thinly veiled manner, talking about writing, and specifically his own place in the literary landscape? Is he, in fact, telling us that he's tired of writing, of being the best at what he does (or did) and wants to retire or just disappear? Here's a thing. Most writers when they are writing put themselves into a story. Obviously they do. It's all they've got, all *we've* got. Ourselves, the sum of our experiences, and our voice. Ally that with our imagination and, as I said earlier, an array of characters both good and bad (and in between) and you've got the beginnings of a novel. But another layer to the construction of a narrative that we can't resist doing is putting our own thoughts and even pieces of our own lives into a story, sometimes in such a way that only ourselves, or some notional, hopelessly devoted scholar of ours when we are long dead, will notice. This is an instance of Jon doing just that. Proving that this novel is not just a story. It's both an allegory and a puzzle he's given us to solve. Although even that idea isn't so simple: is he saying he wants to disappear? Or is he just saying the identity he invented for himself – Jonathan Durward, Internationally Famous Bestselling Author™ – should disappear?

Once we had become friends, the next logical step was to involve our partners and families. Dinner parties and the like. Proper friends. My then wife wasn't happy about this. She wasn't happy about many things, to be honest. She didn't like me writing, or wanting to be a writer. And she certainly didn't want to meet other writers. She thought somehow it would change me. I, for my part, hoped it would. That was a large reason for writing in the first place. I was working two jobs at the time, both dead end ones, bar work in the evenings and in a call centre during the day. I'd tried to make a living as an actor for a few years like Jon, and still had that freelance mentality of not wanting to be tied down, so the only work I could get was undemanding to the point of boredom and paid by the hour. I had to do that in case something good came along in my proper job that I couldn't resist. It also left me free for any castings or auditions that came up. But these were getting few and far between. I don't know whether acting was giving up on me, or I was giving up on acting. At least I had the writing to still be passionate about. Even if my wife didn't.

We were invited round to Jon and Gwen's house in Tufnell Park a few weeks after we'd met at the book launch and I was immediately struck by how much the house was an extension of them. Their shared confidence that they would be successful. Furnishings were tasteful and expensive. Bare wooden floors with authentic Persian rugs covering old, recycled wooden chests and overstuffed furniture. Bought because they were top quality and they knew they would last. Gwen and my wife (with customary reluctance on her part) were left to chat while Jon showed me his study. It was as I've described above. Considering I was currently writing at a makeshift desk in our bedroom it was something that I don't mind admitting I coveted. I'm not prone to jealousy but I really, really, wanted that room.

'Love this room,' I told him.

He smiled, self-deprecatingly, but also accepting the compliment at the same time.

'Love the whole house, really.'

He looked around as if not wanting to be overheard then

leaned in close to me. 'I've always wanted something like this,' he said. 'Ever since I stayed over at someone's house after a party. A drama student, but a posh one, you know?'

I laughed. 'Weren't they all? Apart from me, of course.'

'Yeah. Going to university when you're working class, you're the diversity hire, the exotic.'

I nodded. 'You too?'

'God, yes. The working-class autodidact. If you've got an accent, they're amazed you can write.'

I noticed, for the first time that there was no trace of Jon's Midlands accent. Like something he'd left behind that he no longer needed.

'I went to a party and stayed over with this girl. Yeah, we slept together, but that's not the main thing. The next day when we got up, I actually took notice of the flat we were in. Stripped floors, a big Chesterfield and Indian rugs on the floor. And an old steamer trunk used as a coffee table. And then coffee, you know? Coffee in the morning. From a cafetière. First time I'd ever seen one in action. And I ... wanted it, you know? All of it. Not just the coffee and the flat, but the whole thing. The life. The confidence that came with it. Of being able to put all that together and be comfortable in it. All of it. You know what I mean?'

'I know exactly what you mean. The whole thing's a badge of, I don't know, middle-classness.'

His eyes lit up. 'Or the creative classes. The bohemian classes. That was the thing I was aiming for. And writing, you know, it's the most middle class of all professions, isn't it? And bohemian. Sitting around all day making up stories then complaining how hard you've got it?'

I smiled along with him and nodded, but thought of my days, working dead end jobs, trying to find time to write in between them, my hours patrolled by a wife who hated to see me do that and would complain every time I did. 'Yeah,' I said. 'Isn't it?'

He laughed. 'But you've got to do it, haven't you?'

I agreed that you did.

I looked round the shelves. I've always been interested in the books people have on their shelves. Is that a writer thing? I suppose Formula One drivers are interested in what kinds of cars other drivers drive. Probably. I wouldn't know. There were the usual suspects there. The kind of books you should not only read but be seen to be reading. Jon and I had come up the same route at the same time. But still, he had good books on the shelves. The kind we shared a common interest in. And the expected titles were all present and correct.

'Steinbeck, Faulkner ... Philip Larkin, Vonnegut ... the gang's all here,' I said, still looking. And I began to notice something. An absence of books more than a presence. 'Where's all the Kerouac, then? Bukowski? Aren't you supposed to be the natural heir to all that?' I was smiling as I said it.

Jon looked embarrassed in return. 'Yeah, that was fine for a while.' He laughed. 'My sixth form male masturbatory books, as Gwen called them. The Klan of Kerouac and the rest.'

'You've gone off him, then?'

'They've ... served their purpose. You've got to move on, haven't you? Can't keep reading that same stuff over and over. Need new things to inspire you.'

I looked at the 'new things'. Yes, there were the latest books the broadsheets had reviewed, the latest literary works, all present and correct. But something else.

'What's all this?' I asked. 'Michael Crichton? Seriously? Where's the Jeffrey Archers? You hiding them?'

He turned, about to answer when the door opened.

'Don't diss Michael Crichton,' said Gwen from the door, wine glass in hand. 'The most successful writer going. Possibly ever.'

She came into the room, my wife following, looking like she was hating every second she was inside the house with these people.

'Yeah, Michael Crichton,' said Jon. 'Don't knock him.'

'He's a genius,' said Gwen. 'Literally. Could have been a doctor, a surgeon, instead decided to become a writer. Wrote some crime novels while he was studying at Harvard to earn money and they ended up winning awards.'

'Crime writing awards,' said Jon. 'But still.'

'He could have been a professional tennis player, he was that good. Could have done anything. Decided to be a writer. Sold his books to Hollywood, even directed some. Never directed in his life, but that's what confidence allied with genius can do. You know he plots all his novels on a graph?'

'Graphs? Isn't that, I don't know, anti-creative? The whole point of writing is to create something, go on a journey, come out changed on the other side. The writer as well as the reader. If you're plotting by graph it's just ... formulaic rubbish.'

'Formulaic, maybe,' she said, 'But rubbish? Perhaps it is. If you don't have the talent to make the prose shine as well as his does.'

'Yeah,' I said, 'but his books are, you know, trash.'

Gwen's expression became serious. 'Really? Trash? Go stand at an airport or railway station and watch how many people buy them. And keep coming back. You don't do that for trash.'

'You don't buy into this, Jon?' I asked. 'You don't work on a graph. You're much better than that.'

Jon hadn't spoken during any of this, letting Gwen carry the conversation. He didn't answer now.

'Anyway,' he said eventually, bashful smile, 'something to think about.'

Then my wife announced it was time for us to be going.

I thought about that all the way home. Jon didn't seem the kind of writer – the kind of person – to live like that. To plot his books on a graph or use any of the Michael Crichton approaches. But seeing how Gwen took over the conversation there, talked more about writing than he did, made me wonder. Publishing power couple? Publishing power imbalance? And the other thing: what if she was right?

'Well, that was a waste of time,' said my wife.

I didn't reply.

3

'Hello, Julia.'

I turn. She stops dead, hand still on the door handle. Stares at me. I'm sure I've startled her but she long since learned never to let anything show on her face. I can read just about anyone. And fast. It's a huge factor in why I'm so successful in my job. But not her. Not any more.

'You're home.' Understated, simple, giving nothing away. Is she pleased to see me? Upset? Irritated? I don't know. And that should infuriate me. But it doesn't. Not with her.

She removes her key from the lock, closes the door, enters the kitchen, places her bags on the table. Looks at me again. 'Hello.'

Wide eyes, blank face. Nothing. Do I kiss her? Hug her? Ignore her? I don't know. I decide to kiss her. That's what couples do after they've been apart for a length of time. I move in towards her, take her in my arms. She doesn't resist. I kiss her on the lips. Again, she doesn't resist. Kiss dispensed with, I step backwards. I don't know whether her eyes closed during it or not. They're open when I look at her.

She's a very attractive woman. Hair characterfully tousled. No hints of grey, still as dark as when we met. Perhaps she dyes it. I don't know. Like me she's mid-thirties. (1) Her body has the same curves as when we first met. She may work out to keep it that way.

Her face is a beautiful, blank mask, eyes lit from behind by an unknowable intelligence, like she's always keeping secrets from me. Or wants me to think she is. Her mouth opens slightly as if toying with the idea of telling me something I'd either love to hear or hate to know but ultimately deciding to keep whatever it is to herself.

'I'm home,' I say. And fall silent.

Her turn to speak. 'How was your ... job?'

There it is again. That pause, that slightly open mouth. That faint smile.

I become a different person when I'm with her. Although it might be fairer to say we've both become different people over the years. I read people for a living. I need to understand them, work out their flaws and strengths. My work depends on it. With Julia I can't read her at all. Not any more. Which makes me wonder whether I ever did, or just convinced myself that I could. I should probably hate that feeling, that I can read everyone but my own wife. But I don't know. Part of me actually feels thrilled by it. Challenged.

'Good,' I say.

'Job done?'

I nod. 'I've got you something.'

I pick up the small wrapped parcel from the kitchen table. Hand it to her. She accepts it without any change of expression. She unwraps it. Examines it.

'It's very lovely. Thank you.'

It's a piece of netsuke, those small intricately carved Japanese miniatures. She once told me she liked them, so when I'd completed my first assignment, I bought her one. I thought it would be a symbol of my love for her. Our love together. I saw her admiring them in a gallery once and the thought stayed with me. Now it's something I do every time I complete an assignment. Another ritual. She seems to like them. Or at least always thanks me for them. (2)

This one is particularly beautiful. It's no more than four centimetres in diameter and has been carved from a single piece of ivory. It is a webbed sphere containing fully rotating, free-fitting, but progressively smaller, webbed spheres. Like worlds within worlds. It should be impossible to accomplish but the carver evidently managed it. I can't imagine how many hours they spent working to turn that one ivory marble into something so sublime. Creating like that is, to me, unknowable. I literally couldn't imagine how to do it. Any of it. Do you select a piece of ivory that you know has this inside it, freeing it through the act of creation? Or do you take a piece and turn it into something else, impose new ideas, new structures onto whatever is already there, transforming something already attractive into something astounding? And then what tools would you use to do it? How would you even start? And would what you see in your mind's eye translate to the finished piece? Would you be happy with it? Disappointed? Thrilled and elated? I don't know. How would you judge? To me, on the outside looking in, it's unknowable. To me it's immaculate. My definition of a masterpiece.

'I'll put it with the others,' she says, and walks away, taking it with her.

She goes into her room, the third bedroom, unlocking it to enter, locking it behind her. I don't know what's in there. I've never been invited in. Like the creation of the netsuke, I can only stand on the outside and guess.

Eventually she returns. Busies herself at the kitchen sink making herself a coffee with the expensive machine we have. 'So how long are you back for this time?'

'Depends where they send me next. And when.'

Her back is to me so I can't see any reaction.

'How have you been while I've been away?'

'Fine.'

'Good.' Again, I feel I need to add something. 'I'll try not to get in your way.'

No reply this time.

'It must be difficult having me back when you've had the place to yourself so long.'

Again, no reply.

She makes her coffee and enters the living room, sitting on the sofa. I join her, sitting on the armchair. No TV, no music. What the journalists would call companionable silence.

She finishes her coffee, places the cup on an end table, turns to me and gives me *that* look. It's about the only time I can read her. She wants sex. Here and now. I almost allow myself a smile. At least that's one thing that hasn't changed in our relationship.

'Come on then,' I say.

We stand and make our way into the bedroom where we'll undress, get into bed and we'll commence lovemaking. I know exactly what she wants, what she needs. And she understands and caters to my needs as well. After so long we should know at least that much about each other. But with that knowledge has not come boredom or repetition. We still genuinely take delight in each other's bodies. We're still able to, dare I say it, surprise each other in that sense.

Later, with Julia in the shower, I'll lie on the bed, staring out of the window at the sky, lost in my own thoughts. I'll think of Julia, how I know her and yet don't seem to know her at all any more. Then I'll think of the carver who made that exquisite piece of netsuke. I can't imagine their life, their urges, their drive, their skill. Their genius. They're unknowable to me.

But here's the thing. If I was given that carver for my next assignment I *would* know them. I'd get to understand them so much I could become them. And then dispatch them. Because that's what I do. I could do it with anyone.

Apart from Julia. (3)

3 – Notes

1. It's always said by writers (I can't remember who said it first, probably plenty of people will lay claim to it) that your lead character is always an idealised version of the writer themselves minus five years. This would be about right for Jon/Garrick. The lead character, it's usually said, is stronger, cleverer, wittier and more empathetic than the writer. Supposedly. One does always make oneself more heroic in the writing. And of course, we're all our lead characters. That's the way we want the world to see us. As for Julia . . . I can't really see many similarities between her and Gwen. Or at least none at this early juncture of the novel. Julia seems much more reserved so that Garrick hardly ever knows what she's thinking or feeling. And while it is possible to enter into a relationship with someone like that (I did, after all), Gwen has never struck me as that sort of person. Quite the opposite, actually. She's fiery, committed, opinionated, straightforward, forthright. And funny, lest you think all of the above just makes her sound like a tedious old harpy. Can I still say that? I mean, I've just said it, but you know what I mean. I'm old enough and out of touch with this week's latest list of dos and don'ts that lead to cancellation. Unless we don't even do that any more? I don't know. And I'm too old to care. Anyway. You know where you are with Gwen. Because she'll tell you.

2. The netsuke. Have you ever seen these things? Beautiful. Miniature sculptures originating from

seventeenth-century Japan. There is, of course, a story behind Jon putting them in his book. You might have even heard it, probably more than once. It became one of his well-honed anecdotes that he prepared for media interviewers and festival audiences. I'm not saying it isn't true, I'm sure it is. Or the majority of it. Based on a true story. A kernel of truth nestling amongst the juicy flesh of fabrication. Netsuke took on a symbolic meaning for Jon. When he was a boy – a teenager – living in Dudley in the West Midlands in the most unstimulating, not to mention exhausting, of environments due to the constant warring of his parents, he used to take the bus into Birmingham on a Saturday. As there weren't a great deal of activities happening in Dudley, most of his peer group did the same. Where Jon differed from them was in his destination. Jon would go to the library, take books out, read them there. If there was a book he was suitably impressed with he would nip over to Hudson's, the main bookshop at the time, and buy it. From there just over the plains of post-war concrete, was the Museum and Art Gallery. That was also a draw for a neurotic boy outsider like him. The gallery is justly lauded for its extensive collection of pre-Raphaelite paintings but it also has – or had, not sure about now – quite a collection of netsuke. Jon told me he would spend ages staring at them, admiring the craftsmanship, trying to work out how someone could create something so small and intricate and beautiful. How much time it must have taken, the concentration, the patience. And the one piece that fascinated him the most is the one that turns up in this chapter. The sphere within a sphere within a sphere, all carved out of one single piece of ivory. To this working-class kid from

Dudley it was a glimpse into another world. Even more so than the paintings or anything else in there. Painting could be taught. Understood. Brushes on canvas. He'd dabbled himself, even. But this was something else. And this particular piece spoke of worlds within worlds. All of them seemingly out of reach. Or was it? Jon already knew he wasn't like his contemporaries – the fact he was haunting the library, bookshop and art gallery on his own at weekends told him that. He knew he didn't fit in at home or in his school life. He knew – or at least sensed – that his future would be away from Dudley, and hopefully at the first opportunity. You'll have gathered from this that Jon was quite a loner as a child, not many friends. Unhappy, he often said, later. Obviously, he reinvented himself once he left the West Midlands, but it was during this time, these Saturday day trips, that the initial impetus, that spur, happened. He might never be able to create anything as beautiful as netsuke but he could appreciate the artform it was. And that appreciation was something in itself. He began to wonder about the life of a netsuke carver, what it must have been like, where they came from, where they trained, how they went about their art and craft. Did someone pay them to train? Was there a school they went to? Or did they have to practice in their spare time until they were good enough to sell what they made? Then there were the questions of how they got paid, how they could afford to live. Perhaps they had been like him, looking at art, any art, and wanting to contribute in some way. Perhaps they even came from a background like his, where he was mocked and derided for liking things others didn't. The sensitive oddball kid, bullied. Abused. Perhaps they didn't become artists until they left that abusive background behind and found their own kind. It was, he said, what he told himself every Saturday. Seeing those netsuke and thinking about those creators gave him the confidence to leave, to find himself, to be himself. The fact that someone had created something like that all those years ago that stood the test of time demonstrated to him that an artistic life could be lived. Even by someone like him. All he had to do was want it enough. And work for it enough.

I'm sure you've heard him telling that story loads of times. I have. I don't doubt it happened, or a version of it did, but I do question whether that single act gave him the confidence to leave his family and become a creative artist. I'm sure the act of standing there looking at them most weeks gave him a kind of solace away from the family home. But the impetus to leave it? We just have to take his well-worn word for it. Once he left he never went back (well, only once, which we'll come to in a while), never spoke of his parents in interviews, dropped contact with them. We know his childhood was hellish, but we don't know just how bad. Unlike a lot of writers who, when they reinvent themselves for a paying public, tend to big up their impoverished, struggling childhoods and the part played in the creation of their art, especially if that backstory is entirely fictional, Jon was the opposite. Yes, he reinvented himself, but that was a character he lived in during the present. He wouldn't talk about his childhood, except in the broadest of strokes. How abusive was it? Worse than he let on? We don't know. And how important was the netsuke? Was there more to it than what he said? Remember, this may be a childhood tale of young Jon. But it was told by a reinvented adult Jon. So who's to say the story itself isn't part of that reinvention too? In fact, the use of it in here makes me suspect, not for the first time and definitely not the last during this narrative, that Jon's written this book with me in mind. There are things I know about, confidences that only he and I shared, stories that would be meaningless to anyone else, peppering this book. As I said earlier, clues. But the more I read, the more I feel the clues are specifically meant for me. I'm meant to recognise and interpret them. He's expecting me to use them to unlock memories, follow the trail, find him. Not anyone else. Specifically me.

3. I should say straight away that as shown here, Garrick and Julia have an entirely different kind of relationship to the one Jon and Gwen enjoyed in real life. I should say that although Jon and I shared many confidences, I knew, and still know, nothing of their sex life. And I'm happy to remain in ignorance.

4

It wasn't always like this between us.

We met through work. (1) Or rather, given the nature of our employment and employer, through 'not-work'. Julia was a diplomat's daughter, with both her parents working various jobs in the diplomatic corps. Posted all over the world by the Foreign Office but mainly to the Middle East, she grew up the classic unsettled brat, indulged by her parents with everything apart from their time and attention. Given various nannies and servants by various embassies, she acted out and played up as much as possible, thinking she was the first ever rebel, not yet realising she was only following a long-established pattern. Defying her nannies and breaking out of whichever compound she was supposed to stay within, indulging in underage drinking, clubbing and drug-taking, having look-at-me-aren't-I-shocking relationships with unsuitable suitors.

One of which was me.

Her parents were always vague about the capacity in which they worked for the Foreign Office, usually citing something to do with trade or diplomatic missions. All of which, we know, is nudge-nudge wink-wink code for MI6 field agents.

So how did I come to be involved with MI6? Firstly, you should know that I wasn't one of those posh braying hoorays who fast track from public school to Oxbridge to spy recruitment. My background is far less rarefied than that. I entered MI6 during one of its occasional recruitment drives among the lower classes and minorities, making a token bid to be more inclusive. What that actually means, deciphering MI6's coded message, is a hope to get more brown faces through the door in order to infiltrate Muslim communities. And by lower classes they didn't mean the real lower classes of course, the inner-city, bog-standard comprehensive kids. They meant the lower middle classes, whose offspring had passed the eleven plus and could afford to get a scholarship to attend a fee-paying grammar school. Which was me.

I come from somewhere past England but not quite Scotland. A no man's land for accents and cultural identity. (2) My parents recognised I was, in the parlance of the time, gifted and talented. Hence a scholarship to the local grammar. This set me adrift from all my previous friends who trudged off to the local comp and set me apart from all my new classmates who regarded my lack of a moneyed background with mostly suspicion and sometimes outright hostility.

In time I came to hate them. I was a quiet kid, brainy, with no aptitude for team sports, especially those involving coordination and balls. But I was surprisingly good at those in which I was only ever in competition with myself. Cycling. Swimming. Long distance running. Even though there were others involved, I was never in competition with them. I competed alone, the only person to beat being myself. A previous time. A personal best. I worked at it and in time I represented the school then the county. There was talk of aiming for the Olympics. (3) However, that required dedication to something I didn't want to dedicate myself to. I demonstrated to the rich kids that the scholarship boy could beat them. That was enough.

I'm sure they hated me too. I didn't care. I never sought, nor had, many friends as a child. But I learned how to be friendly from watching the others. I learned how, on the surface at least, to fit in with people and environments my upbringing would have considered alien. I could have gone to Cambridge or Oxford; my teachers ushered me in that direction. But I had been enough of an outsider at school, and either of those two places would have been the same thing in extremis.

I took all my learned skills with me through university. By this time I'd reinvented myself. I was now playing the part of a confident, strapping, handsome young man. Yes, handsome. Here's the thing about being attractive: if you believe you are, you make others believe that too. This works for just about everything. Exude an air of belief, that you are the person you say you are, you can do the thing you say you can, and people will believe you. It's a confidence trick. It's how the elite, no matter how incompetent they actually are, get away with running our society. It's how I'm able to be successful at my job.

On leaving university with a First in International Politics, I thought of a career in spying. It seemed the obvious thing. After all, hadn't I done that all my life so far? Pretend to be someone I wasn't?

Turns out I didn't need an Oxbridge education to become a spy. You only need two things. Firstly, you can't be a good person so by default you have to be a bad person. Or at least a duplicitous one. And you have to choose something to be loyal to. Reconcile those two things and you're in.

There is another aspect to this tale that I haven't mentioned. And since it's pertinent to my relationship with Julia I feel I should mention it here. At university I developed a, shall we say, penchant for posh girls. Couldn't get enough of them. Befriend them, flatter them, flirt with them, fuck them then ... forget them. Usually. Some intrigued me enough to keep them around for a while, most didn't. Why was this? Well, maybe I was just enjoying swimming in this exotic sea with these exotic sea creatures, the kind I would never have met had I stayed in my hometown. Or if I had met them, they wouldn't have given me the time of day. The alternative explanation, and I'm sure Freud or Jung or whoever would agree, would be to say I was taking my revenge on all those posh kids at school who hated me for what I was by fucking their beautiful sisters. If that was the case, then it was the most enjoyable form of revenge I could possibly think of.

And this, to cut a long story short, is how I came to meet Julia.

The commoner and the diplomat's daughter. Star-crossed fuck buddies in some god-forsaken [REDACTED] Middle East hellhole. By this time I had been accepted by MI6 and was working out there as a field agent, my cover being a hapless trade envoy who enjoyed the illicit local nightlife a bit too much, a perma-wasted loudmouth who ended up in all manner of seedy places meeting all stripes of unsavoury local characters. My clandestine drinking buddies believed I was an idiot, ripe for squeezing dry of information when in reality I was doing the squeezing.

I still had my thing for posh girls and this coincided with Julia still going through her rebellious phase. Or perhaps I was just something to do to ally the boredom. Whatever it was, it worked. *We* worked. And when we ended up staying together despite other placings and eventually married, no one was more surprised than we were.

I never tell Julia I love her. But she never tells me either. Love is something we have just taken for granted that we have. Or don't. Either way it doesn't impede on our life together.

I don't think we reached a stage where we stopped being romantic with one another. It was never that kind of relationship.

Sexually charged, yes. Undoubtedly. And still is. And I guess you could say we're fond of each other, as far as that goes, living well together without one unduly angering or irritating the other. Beyond that we both have our separate lives which we're tolerant of. It may not be the kind of relationship that works for everyone, but it does for us.

I just wrote 'dies' instead of 'does'. A Freudian slip or a clumsy-fingered keyboard slip?

Because until recently I would have said we were happy together. Or at least sharing whatever passes for happiness between a couple who have been together as long as we have. I can't read her. Which makes me wonder whether I've ever been able to read her or if I was just lying to myself by believing we had something of depth and mutual understanding together. Maybe we didn't. Or don't. Or never have.

Would Julia miss me if I wasn't there? Would she notice, would she even care?

And am I going to put that thought to the test?

4 – Notes

1. There was nothing like that when Jon and Gwen met for the first time. I think their real meeting bears repeating, however. Again, this might be a story you've heard before, so if you have please bear with. As I said in the introduction, Jon was working behind the bar in the Prince of Wales pub in Clapham old town, waiting for his glittering career to start but not knowing how to make it happen. He worked Friday nights, back when Friday night was a big night out. The place was always rammed. And if the punters didn't crowd the place enough, there was always the décor. It was what you might call maximalist. It looked like an accumulation of tat hanging on the walls, off the ceilings and draped over every surface. It was like a junk shop. Old mismatching chairs and tables, school desks, antique lighting, theatre programmes, pictures, anything and everything, including a mannequin dressed as a sailor stuck on the roof outside. Eclectic, an estate agent would describe it if forced.

    This was at the time when Clapham was going through its next phase of gentrification, going from student/hipster to properly monied trustafarians. The last gasp, really. And Jon loved it there. A few night shifts and time to sit in his attic studio and write during the day. An artist starving in his garret, he would later say. This was when he was going to be the next Kerouac, the next Bukowski. Sitting in cafés with his black notebook, incessantly obsessively scribbling away. Black quiff, black overcoat, black boots, distressed Levis. The uniform at the time for the soulful artistic outsider. He told me he sometimes wore thick, black rimmed glasses with plain glass, just to make him look more like a European intellectual. This was his first London attempt at reinvention and he was living it large like a method actor.

The main thing, of course, is that behind his carefully constructed façade, he was getting nowhere. Oh, in his head he was a literary giant, the next undiscovered outsider genius. But not in reality. No one wanted anything he wrote. No agent, no publisher. He would phone up agents, (landline, pre-mobile days, remember, how we did things back then, kids) all naivety and excitement, big plans and big dreams, and he was often so convincing that they would be swept along on the other end of the line, eagerly asking to see what he was working on and he would be more than happy to send it. Unfortunately, his telephone charm offensive was never backed up by anything approaching decent work and the answer was always a form letter rejection. He then tried calling publishers directly but never got past the secretaries who informed him that no publisher would look at unsolicited work unless it had come through an agent. After months and months of this, Jon was getting pretty downhearted. It seemed like the world didn't want a one-man Beat revival. Or at least it didn't want him doing it. And so, finally realising that this might not actually work out for him, he dragged himself off for his usual Friday night shift at the Prince.

On the walk there he dared to confront the thing that he had avoided so long: reality. He might have to get a proper job, the kind you have to wear a suit for and get excited about lunchtime meal deals. Where with every commute you watch your dreams recede further and further away until one day you can't remember having any. That was the kind of life that was stretching out ahead of him. And it was in this less than cheerful mood that he met Gwen.

Amazingly, considering it felt like he had personally called every literary agent in London in an attempt to get representation, he hadn't spoken to Gwen before. She was an agent's assistant at a big central London agency. Not saying which one, do your own research, but it was one of the ones named after its founder who had died years ago. That should narrow it down a bit. She was young and eager. Breathing in ambition like air. She had plans of her own. She wasn't going to be an assistant for ever. She would be running the company within a decade, if not before. And if not this company, then another one. She was going to bend the British publishing industry to her will, remake it in her image, populate it with her choice of books. But at this point she was still at the smiling graciously and doing the legwork stage. Paying her dues. But there was no doubt that one day soon, those dues would be paid in full. However, none of that mattered this Friday night. She was out with friends, unattached, wanting to enjoy herself and what do you know? That barman looks quite handsome. In an obvious sort of way, of course. But he has presence. The fact that Jon was looking miserable, sullen, just made him seem even more unattainable. He looked like a challenge. And she liked a challenge.

She made sure he served her. And she smiled at him. What she thought was a smile with unmistakable undertones, letting him know what she thought of him.

He didn't seem to respond. She went back to her friends, who could all see she clearly fancied the barman and the fact that he wasn't responding just made her want to get his attention even more. So she did. She spent all night working at it until he noticed her. Her friends knew what she was like. She wouldn't rest until she got what she wanted. The barman was just the latest thing. She talked to him all night, every chance she got. And, despite the pub being hugely overcrowded, he always made a beeline to serve her. They were both smiling now. This attractive, confident young woman was just what he needed to get out of his post-writing funk. A bit of fun, just to prove he'd still got it, a fun night, maybe even a weekend, and then back to work again. Exactly what he needed to take his mind off things.

'You going on anywhere after this?' she asked him.

'Hadn't planned to. What did you have in mind?'

She turned back to her friends who were all staring at them, expectant smiles, then back to him. 'Well, they're going to that pub on the common with the club upstairs.'

'And you?'

A smile he had no trouble interpreting. 'Depends what you're doing.'

He didn't know what to say. Despite his good looks and his reinvention, inside he was still that same bullied kid from Dudley, the one who spent his Saturdays in the libraries. The one who didn't know how to talk to girls. Especially attractive ones. But something told him that he shouldn't let this one go.

'I'll . . . come and join you there, then. Yeah?'

She smiled again, and again there was no mistaking the intention. 'Make sure you do.'

And with that she turned and was off.

Jon couldn't believe his luck. He finished up as fast as he could, turned down the usual afterhours drink and offer of food at the late-night Italian opposite where the staff often ended up and followed her. He found her straight away. She was with her friends, surrounded by a bunch of young men. Or boys, really. But they all looked like new Clapham. Monied, trust fund kids with public school backgrounds, who thought they could have anything – and anyone – they wanted. And right now they wanted Gwen and her friends. Jon felt jealous just watching. And wounded. There was no way he could compete with them. They were everything he was not. Rich, confident, successful. And Gwen was talking to them, making them laugh. It sounded like the howl of hungry wolves.

He was about to turn round and walk out when she spotted him, waved. And came straight over.

'Sorry,' he said, 'you're with someone.'

She glanced back at them, back to him, made a pained, patronising face. 'Seriously? One of them? I'd rather vote BNP. That's a lie, obviously. But you know what I mean. I had enough of those kind of entitled wankers growing up. No thanks.' Then she looked at him. Really looked at him. And smiled. And that was it. He was lost. 'I'm glad you came.'

'So am I.'

And that was that for their first night. Their meet cute, I suppose you'd say now.

It didn't go the way either of them expected it to, though. And no doubt the way you, dear reader, would expect it to. In that, they didn't go back to Jon's (or Gwen's) and have sex. When the club closed, they went for a walk. They had spent the whole time talking. Gwen had detached herself from her friends and the two of them sat together. She told him what she did for a living and he told her what he was trying to do and immediately she was interested, and there was a connection. A huge one, Jon always said. 'I'm not a religious man but there was something of the divine about that night', he said on several occasions. Anyway, the walk. They left the club and meandered, talking all the time. Like they couldn't stop, like they had known each other for years or if not known each other then were waiting for each other and all the things they wanted to say to that person just poured out. They ended up walking all the way to the side of the Thames at Vauxhall. It was a still, warm night so they found a bench by the river, sat down and kept talking. And talking. And talking. Until it was light. Then they made their way back to Jon's studio flat in Clapham North, ordered bacon and egg sarnies from the hole in the wall café on the corner of his street and went upstairs.

He said about that night that he felt he had known her for years, and she him. And simultaneously that they had only just met and had so much to tell each other. A true meeting of soulmates.

His words, I hasten to add, not mine.

2. Not Dudley, interestingly enough. And even more interesting, to me at least, is the fact that I'm from where he claims Garrick hails from, the North East of England. And because of that, the distance from London, I've never felt truly English. I have to assume that giving Garrick my roots is intentional, making him feel like a man without a cultural identity either.

3. Olympics? I ask you. Talk about self-aggrandising wish fulfilment. Jon told me he was always the last to be picked for football at school. Or any games for that matter.

5

I've been back in London about a month now and I have my debrief coming up. Business as usual, nothing to worry about. My work was exemplary, also as usual. I'm not bragging, just stating a fact. But I am worrying. Because even though there are no problems, I may be about to create one. I've been thinking a lot about this since I returned to London. And now I've come to a decision. I want to retire.

Do assassins retire? *Can* assassins retire? In theory, yes. Anyone can, obviously. There just has to be an evaluation done by the pointy heads and a decision taken at the end of that. Hopefully there should be no problem with me quitting. I've been an exemplary employee, I won't sell my secrets, I can't be compromised in any way. They know that. So why am I still worrying?

Because it's impossible to predict what they will say, that's why. Any of them, handler up to pointy heads up to the bosses. This isn't just spying, this is calculatedly taking another person's life through assimilation of their identity, exploitation of weaknesses and consequently unimpeachable results. There isn't much demand for those transferable skills in the job market. The only options open to me in the service are an in-house desk job or teaching. Neither of which I feel I'd be able to carry through to the best of my abilities. So if they turn down my retirement, I think disappearing is probably the best option for me. A new identity, new home, somewhere where I won't be found. I've devoted my whole life to pretending to be other people. Now I should put those skills into practice for myself. Do it for real. And permanently.

I have provisions in place for just such an occurrence. Have done for years. I like to think the company doesn't know about them but I have to assume they at least suspect. After all, they are spies. To that end, I have two different escape plans that they may know about. Or that I hope they know about. Because therein lies the deception. There's one I have that they couldn't possibly know about because the detail of it only exists in my head.

Worst case scenario: If they say no, I have a problem. A permanent, terminal one. In-house work aside, it's rare for an assassin to receive a pension and a golden handshake. And even though it's one of the rules of espionage and I'm supposed to accept that, I know I won't.

Espionage. That word. Try it yourself. Say it. Roll it around the tongue, extract everything you can out of it. Espionage. Coming up, we had a lecturer who couldn't say that word without sounding like an arch Kenneth Williams impersonator, extending the fourth syllable well beyond its natural length. (1) Try it. Espion-*arrrrjjjjuuuhhh*. Once you've heard it that way you can't say it any other way, and every time I hear the word, or even think it, I still hear him say it like that.

He would say it that way to make a point. The word, he would say, sounds exactly like what it's supposed to sound like. Sophisticated. Complex. All shadowed alleyways, long trench coats and forward-tilted fedoras. Cigarette cupped in hand to avoid the red tip acting as a sniper's mark.

Historically, he would continue, it speaks of mysterious, exoticised destinations that when spoken hold their own cachet of mystique, like Prague and Marrakesh, places once far beyond the reach of the average package holidaymaker. Too unknowable, too foreign, in every sense of the word. Such destinations, mysterious and exotic, fuelled the imaginations of a credulous post-war public fed by hack-written spy paperbacks, big-budget film cycles and low-budget TV action shows featuring character actors – usually from Wales and the North – blacked and browned up as untrustworthy foreigners in Elstree Studios' facsimiles of souks and medinas. These places must, by their very definition, be exciting if James Bond goes there. Or their old cut-price TV equivalents Simon Templar and Jason King. (2) We'll have a bit of that, said Sixties Britain. Yes, espionage.

I soon realised it's nothing of the sort. Just a posh word for spying. Used by the kind of people that think themselves cultured and well-travelled, the kind that say las-*arrrnneeeah* instead of lasagne. Or, of course, Kenneth Williams impersonators.

But what he said struck a chord within me. Perhaps he was right and there's some excitable, impressionable childhood hangover left within me since I still experience that slight exotic Marrakesh and fedora frisson at the sound of the word. That's why I like to use it. Maybe a part of me never grew up. Maybe it's an impressionable boy's attempt to sound sophisticated. Maybe retaining that sense of excitement's why I ended up doing the job I do. Or at least partly.

In the four weeks since my return I've tried to cultivate a sense of normality, of grounding. I keep fit, go to the gym, run, practice the Israeli martial art Krav Maga. Keep my body ready to return to the field. But when it comes to giving my head downtime, when you do what I do for a living, that's when it proves difficult. Especially if you've cleared out anything else from your life that could prove a barrier to that. To continue to do what I do at the level I do it I need no distraction. To continue to work successfully I need complete focus. Complete control.

I can't just round up my (non-existent) mates and go for benders at the pub. Not any more, anyway.

And there's Julia, of course.

She anchors me. Keeps me grounded. Moored. I appreciate it must be difficult for her having me come back into her life after such long spells of absence. I can't, for obvious reasons, contact her while I'm away, which does nothing for the kind of ongoing building and maintenance a relationship needs to flourish. When I'm back I try to be normal, take her out for dinner, to the theatre – not that I know what's on – and try to go to the supermarket but I don't even know what she wants to eat. She might have become vegetarian in my absence. The days when you can put your order in online and supermarkets deliver to your door can't come soon enough. That would do away with at least one big hassle. (3)

I ask her what she's been up to, who she's seen, where she's been and she replies in generalities, mainly. Prefacing always by saying things like, I wouldn't know this person, or that wouldn't mean anything to me. She only asks me the bare minimum concerning my work. Partly because that's the way she's been brought up but now, I think, because she doesn't want to know. I'm less of a corporeal presence to her and more of a ghost that occasionally haunts the flat she lives in. And who she fucks from time to time.

I should, of course, ask her what she thinks of my notional plan to retire. We should discuss it, as husband would with wife, me telling her exactly how I feel, how the decision would impact the both of us, her listening, adding to the conversation. But we won't. We should discuss the financial implications if nothing else, even though we both have enough money to be comfortably well off for the rest of our lives. Hers comes from her parents, mine from my work. We could, if we wanted, have several houses around the world. For all I know she may have.

And could take off there and live her life – her real life – when I'm away. And for all she knows I could be doing the same. But I don't discuss it with her. Obviously I'll let her know what's happening once the wheels are in motion, but for now it's something I have to sort out on my own. And deal with the immediate consequences of that decision on my own.

I've tried to run every possible scenario through my head in advance of meeting my handler. To be prepared for whatever she says. I can't rely on any of them to have my back; allegiances in this game being written in water. (4) I've even, and this sounds desperate, come up with a scenario where they ask me to assassinate Julia. My final job, then I'm out. The rational part of my brain tells me that's a ridiculous notion but something still niggles about it. It seems like the kind of thing they would do. One final, painful test then I'm out. If I manage to complete the job successfully, of course. And if I don't? Then that gives them every justification for letting me loose with extreme prejudice. They'll make it look like an accident, of course. An unknown colleague of mine will see to that.

Doubtless I'm not the first person in my profession to think and feel this way. It's something you immediately contemplate when you start in the job – the day you won't be able to do it any more. But you put that to the back of your mind, box it away. Try to forget it. You'll be different, you tell yourself, you'll be the one such a future will never happen to. You'll keep working right up to the end. And that end is so far in the future it doesn't matter. Well, the future is now. And that moment, kicked into ever lengthening grass for the whole of your career, is finally here. And it has to be dealt with.

And yet.

And yet ...

Part of me says I'm worrying over nothing. That I don't actually want to retire and this is just the feeling I get after the thrill of a successful job has worn off. Normally I would agree but this is something that's been building over time, so I'm more inclined to listen this time.

The part of myself that tells me that everything is normal is always there. More than normal, fine. Tip top. Good to go, never been better. It counteracts the darker thoughts. Tells me that all I have is the between assignment jitters that, given time, I'll soon be ready to go back to work when I'm needed. That I've got away with it again, dodged a proverbial or even literal bullet, and there are years of usefulness in me yet.

Normally, I recognise this in myself, and need both of these moods in order to function, to do my job. It's a seesaw that has to be kept in constant balance. On the one side is doubt and despair – constantly thinking I'm not good enough for this, I've only got this far through luck not skill and the next job will find me out, expose me. On the other side of the seesaw is the arrogant, brilliant killer. The one who has succeeded this time and will do so again. And every time to come. Nothing's going to stop him. And these two diametrically opposed feelings need to be balanced. Because I can't work without them being in alignment. The doubt, the yearning to do better, must be balanced with arrogant self-belief. It's only in that sweet spot that I can operate. (5)

When I visit my secret location and decompress after a job I undergo a kind of personal primal scream therapy to shed the persona I've had to adapt in order to get the job done and allow some semblance of myself to resume control once again. And then, coming home, once I am myself again and have nothing else to do, I begin to worry. And that's what all this is. Just illogical, unnecessary worry. Birthed from boredom and restlessness. That's all.

But not this time. This time it's something different. This time it's real.

I walk to the meeting with my handler.

And the difficult conversation to come, the one that will decide my future.

Permanently.

5 – Notes

1. Kenneth Williams (22 February 1926 – 15 April 1988). Actor mainly remembered for his appearances in the *Carry On* films during the 1960s and '70s. Small and camp, he always felt he was better than the low-brow, crude shows and films in which he appeared and dismissed with disdain, but not good enough to be taken seriously in more high-brow material which he loved.

2. Simon Templar and Jason King. While the cinemas of the 1960s had Sean Connery's James Bond representing Britain on the world stage, the TV shows of their counterparts were more cut-price affairs. Simon Templar, aka The Saint, was played by Roger Moore who himself went on to play Bond in the 1970s and '80s. Based on a character appearing in a series of pulp novels, short stories and novellas between 1928–1971 written by Leslie Charteris. Likewise, Jason King, played by the flamboyant Peter Wyngarde. He first appeared in the TV series Department S (1969), in which King was a crime novelist as well as a secret agent and used one profession as cover for the other. In real life, Wyngarde (real name Cyril Goldbert) was a master of self-reinvention and hiding in plain sight. His dandified dress sense made him a style icon of the time and he was always surrounded by adoring female admirers. However, he was in reality homosexual and his career ground to a halt when he was found guilty of gross indecency with a crane driver in the public toilets of Gloucester bus station.

3. Supermarket home delivery. Again, this might be an attempt to make the novel appear to be genuinely of the time it was written – late Noughties – as supermarket delivery wasn't as widespread then as it is now. However, supermarkets were delivering then. This is nothing new. I can only assume he's talking about online delivery which, again, was available at that time. Is this just lazy research on his behalf? Or yet another attempt to muddy the waters and throw us off balance?

4. 'Written in water'. The quote comes from the poet John Keats (31 October 1795 – 23 February 1821) and appeared on his tombstone. 'Here lies one/Whose name was writ in water' is the full quote, with the date underneath. Keats didn't even want his name on it. I've always found this quite fascinating. All we can do as writers is produce work. Sometimes, if we're lucky, that work lives on after us (if we're really lucky the work makes money for us during our lifetime). Did Keats think he would be remembered? Did he *want* to be remembered? And that begs another question: is it more important to have recognition while one is alive or posthumously? Some writers who were huge in their own lifetimes have been completely forgotten in death as times and styles change. Almost overnight, in many cases. Some are always with us, some rediscovered. But the worst thing of all as a writer is to be forgotten before you've died. To still be standing in that water you have written your name, and indeed your work, on. Ignored. Unwanted. That could lead someone to take drastic action in order to be remembered. Or even noticed.

5. Which gives me cause to wonder: why was I, in particular, chosen for this editorial job? It's true I knew Jon well. Possibly better than any of his contemporaries. And he opened up to me about things more perhaps than he did with others. So I'd say that gives me an unparalleled up-close view of him. And of course, the events contained in the novel, I was there to witness and expound upon if needs be. But is there another reason?

    The publishers were pretty insistent that I be the one to do it. In fact, they claimed it was one of the terms involved in publishing this novel. I felt I was left with no alternative but to accept. And it has been interesting to take a walk down (cliché alert!) memory lane. I'm not usually one for looking back. Glance at the past, I always say, but don't stare. Live in the moment. But this has really unearthed things, both about Jon and myself, that I've long since buried. How I felt about certain things, how I behaved in certain situations. All of that. And I'm also able now to see those times more clearly in hindsight, which has allowed me to put some kind of perspective on what happened. This, I'm sure, will hold me in good stead for what's coming up.

6

'Coffee's as grim as always but I think they've switched to a new supplier for their pastries. I can recommend the pain au raisin. If you're hungry.'

I go to the counter, order myself an Americano with oat milk and a pain au raisin, return to the seat and join her.

'Oh you did. Good.' She appraises me. 'Suits you. But then I suppose it would, wouldn't it?'

It would. We're meeting in the café at the front of the British Library, (1) a cordoned off section before the cavernous business of the building gets started properly.

Most people in meetings such as this would meet in the office, or possibly a restaurant if going for an informal look. Sit over a table, eating, drinking and discussing work. But unlike most people in whatever profession, I don't like going into the office. I could be spotted (bad) and identified (even worse). Restaurants are good, though. The noise and ambience ensures eavesdropping is kept to a minimum especially if you sit beneath a speaker, lip readers can be kept guessing by judicious use of menu and napkin. Some restaurants and clubs are even well-known safe spaces where those in our profession are actively welcomed, usually because we own them. The British Library, as far as I know, is not one of ours. My handler prefers cafés to restaurants. More unexpected and it gives me a chance to practice my disguises.

I'm dressed for drinking coffee and eating pastry in the British Library coffee shop. Well-worn selvedge jeans, chunky desert boots, a Breton top under a plaid flannel shirt with a canvas chore jacket on top. Brown tortoiseshell glasses, stubble, hair swept back. Even my socks, glimpsed when I cross my legs, are colourfully hooped in a way that screams Creative Person. A writer, specifically. (2) It's the kind of person this place attracts, obviously. I've altered my posture too, round shoulders, hunched forward, as if I spend all day crouched over a laptop. It's camouflage. If we were meeting somewhere like Rules, I'd be wearing a conservative stockbroker suit and tie, clean shaven, hair neat and short, Grensons polished to within an inch of their lives. My posture would be different too, straight backed. Like I'm used to being listened to. I'd also have entered carrying the newest, most ostentatious iPhone, laid it on the desk next to my cutlery and kept glancing at it, just to let anyone watching know my time is important and I'd rather be somewhere else.

We used to meet, at my handler's insistence, in the Conservatory at the Barbican and walk round pretending to look at the massive palm trees. Standing, walking, making a moving target of ourselves, ensuring any interested parties had to keep up with us and in the process give themselves away. But now it's the British Library café. Keep any observer on their toes.

I tear a bit off my pain au raisin. Put it in my mouth.

'You're right,' I say. 'Good.'

She smiles, nods, as if she baked it herself.

My handler isn't what you'd expect. Assuming, that is, you're expecting some severe grey office functionary, which given the circumstances most would. She's anything but grey. With her wild red hair, her clothing all layered scarves, chunky jewellery and designer bohemianism, and large framed glasses, you could be forgiven for thinking she works in the arts or is some kind of visiting lecturer at a private but very expensive girls' school. She's not doing it for the same reason I am, not to attract suspicion, she looks like this all the time. Maybe that's a cover she's carefully cultivated. But as someone once said, we have to choose our masks carefully because they can end up wearing us. Or something like that. (3)

'So how are you adjusting to home life once again? Bored yet?'

'Pretty much,' I say. 'I'm keeping fit, keeping up the training, putting in a few shifts in at the gym. That sort of thing.'

'And Julia?'

'She's ... fine.'

'You hesitated.'

The defences come up. My expression flattens. 'Not much more to say. She's fine. We're getting along. That's it, really. No monumental change in our life together. Back to business as usual.'

'Must be difficult for her, you being away half the time. Well, most of the time, really.'

I shrug. 'We manage.'

She nods. Pastoral care over, she gets down to business. Although I don't believe for one second she's let that pass without filing it away. 'So. Debrief.'

I've already filed a full account of the job from my perspective. But this is where she gets to talk face to face, see if I'm lying about anything. Rate my reactions. I wait. Her turn.

'How do you think it went? From your point of view.'

'Fine. The job was executed exactly as asked. Doesn't seem to have been any repercussions from my actions.'

'Apart from the obvious.'

'Apart from that, yes.'

'Any witnesses?'

'Apart from the whole of the European Parliament, none.' I notice the change of expression. 'Why? What's happened?'

She smiles. That's when I always see how dangerous she can be. 'Someone noticed.'

My character almost slips. I lean forward, slouch. 'Who?'

'One of the interns who worked for that gurning idiot. No one important. But they spotted you had disappeared. Started asking around about you.'

'Oh.' I could see my next job shaping up right in front of me. 'So you want me to—'

'No need.'

'Why not?'

'Terrible situation. Terrible.'

I frown. She continues.

'This poor person was shopping in central Brussels, minding their own business when they must have stepped out into the road. Distracted, I suppose. And you know how terrible those drivers are in Brussels. Belgium is famous for it. Awful. Lawless. Hit and run. Driver never stopped, no one got the registration number. Never caught. Tragic.' She shakes her head, looks appalled. If you didn't know her, you would believe it was genuine.

'It is,' I say.

Her expression changes. Like concrete hardening. 'Getting sloppy, Garrick. Not good.'

I bristle. 'I carried out everything perfectly. If some overstimulated intern who's read too many crime novels starts snooping around, I can't be held responsible.'

'Slightly unprofessional, at least.'

I sit back, fold my arms. 'Not at all. This job was no different to any other. I made no personal connections, fitted in, did as I was supposed to do. I played my part perfectly.'

She takes a sip of coffee, winces, sits back, scrutinising me. 'Tell me, have you been contemplating retirement?' (4)

Her question takes me by surprise, my heart skips and I chastise myself for it. I should be better than that. 'What makes you say that?'

'I've been your handler for years, Garrick, and for others too. I'm adept at spotting moments.'

'What kind of moments?'

'Tipping moments. A career, especially one like yours, is like a big wheel. You start at the bottom, work your way up to the top. And when you reach the top, the view's wonderful. You can see for miles. And the people down below are inconsequential. So far away from where you are up there with their lives and their cares, they may as well not exist. But wheels turn. That's what wheels do. You can't stay on the top for ever, it's not possible. So slowly, ever so slowly, you start to descend.' She drains her coffee. 'This time it was an inquisitive intern. Easily dealt with. But next time it could be someone higher up the food chain who notices something amiss. You see what I'm saying?'

'I've gone over the whole operation. Several times. I always do. And I could find no fault in it. Not one. I was as conscientious as always. That intern thing could have happened to anyone at any time.'

She says nothing initially, presumably letting what I've said sink in. But I know her better than that. What she says next will define the rest of the conversation. Perhaps more than that.

'I suppose you think you'll take a desk job, be office-bound. Was that the kind of thing you had in mind?'

'You seem to have made my retirement decision for me.'

She smiles. 'Perhaps not a desk job. D'you think you're temperamentally suited for a desk job? I'm not sure I do. Your skills in the field are highly commended. No doubt. But they're not the kind of transferrable skills that would make you happy in a desk job, are they?' She laughs. 'You'd be planning to kill someone by the end of the first week, wouldn't you?'

I smile. 'Don't most people who work in offices do that?'

She looks at me closer than ever. Really sees me. She knows I've been thinking about giving this all up. Somehow. This meeting wasn't to go over the previous job as such, it was to sound me out about my future. To see what I thought my alternatives were.

'If we're speaking hypothetically …' The look on her face tells me we're not, she's only humouring me. '… then, no, you're right, I wouldn't want a desk job. Too boring.'

'So what would you suggest?'

'I could do your job. Handle other agents.' I go for a wry smile. 'How hard can it be?'

She says nothing, just raises an eyebrow.

'Or I could teach. Go to the academy. Impart my knowledge to the next generation.'

'Is every footballer cut out to be a manager?'

I'm becoming angry now. I tamp it down. 'You tell me.'

She scrutinises me once more before answering. 'You know, you've been doing this job a lot of years. I don't want to count how many because then I'll age myself and we don't want that, do we?' She sits back once more, a quizzical expression on her face. 'You know one of the things I've never understood about you? Why you stay in that Godawful flat. I mean, why? The money you've made from this, you could have houses all over the world. Passports in lots of different names. Perhaps you may have, for all I know.' She sits forward again, looking me straight in the eye. 'I mean, if you really wanted to retire, that would be the best thing to do, wouldn't it? Just disappear, become someone else, somewhere else in the world?'

She holds eye contact. She may as well tell me it straight. It doesn't take a genius to work it what she's saying. Once I've finished in the field, there's no future role for me in the organisation. So just disappear and no one will ask any questions. End of story.

I keep my expression as even as possible. Smile. I break the moment, move away. 'As you say, though, this is all just hypothetical. I'm not thinking of retiring. I'm just waiting for the next assignment. Which I hope will arrive soon. There are only so many lengths of the swimming pool I can swim.'

'And then you'll go out in a blaze of glory. Hypothetically, of course.'

'Of course.' I don't believe her for one minute but I continue as if I do. 'But I'm still at the top of the big wheel and I have plenty of time, intern or no intern, before that wheel hits the bottom again. And you know that. You know how good I am.'

'Indeed I do.' She nods as if confirming something to herself. Then looks at her watch. 'Look at the time,' she says. 'Have to go.'

'I'm glad we've had this chat,' I say. 'Good to know where we both stand.'

'Absolutely.' She busies herself by wrapping her pashmina/scarf thing round her neck, picking up her bag, bracelets jangling all the time. When she's finished, she stops, looks at me over the top of her oversized glasses. 'We'll be in touch. Soon.'

'With another job?'

'Of course. As you say,' And here she smiles. 'You're still at the top of the big wheel.'

And with that she's gone.

I hang around a while longer, not wanting to leave at the same time. For camouflage I take out a paperback, open it and pretend to read. No one around me moves or notices me.

When I'm sure it's safe to do so, I leave too.

6 – Notes

1. It's interesting that Jon should choose to set a scene in the British Library. This is where I used to meet my clients when I was working a side hustle as a freelance editor and mentor for unpublished authors. This happened after I became more established and stopped working evenings in the pub and tried to get more suitable jobs. Working as a mentor and editor to unpublished writers is always a good one. Writing books is a transferable skill and I was able to help others become published writers. For a fee, of course. There are rip off courses, obviously, but I like to think I offered value for money and great insight. Of course, when the writer you're working with becomes better known than you and more successful – and it happens, more than you might think – it hurts. You say you're pleased for them, you have to, but it hurts.

   Once we'd got to know each other, and knowing I did this as a sideline, Jon asked me to look over his new novel. I was honoured, I suppose. 'You're a mate,' he said. 'I trust your opinion.' This would have been his third novel, *These Dark Tomorrows*. 'I feel like I've stepped up a gear with this one,' he said. 'Like I've really found my own voice. Yeah. Good.'

   And he had. This was a serious step up. The language was denser, the characterisation more subtle, the narrative more engrossing. I loved it. Part of me hated him for writing it, for being this good. I also noticed something else. Things I remembered saying to him popped up throughout the book. Phrases or exclamations. He'd remembered them, jotted them down and appropriated them as his own. Just a small thing, I suppose, but it rankled. I read it again and realised it wasn't so small. These weren't just a few odd phrases, these were situations I'd described to him from my own life that he'd inserted wholesale. I recognised the marriage of one of the main characters in the novel as mine. Yes, I know, all writers have that little chip of ice at their heart, according to Graham Greene, and everyone and everything is material, but wasn't this going too far? I thought I was his friend. Not a subject for one of his novels.

I confronted him about it. Gently. Or as gently as I could. We were seeing a band one night at the Borderline just off Charing Cross Road. I can't remember who, but I remember everything else.

'Oh,' he said, looking quite startled, taken aback, even. 'Had I? Written about you? I wanted to write about a marriage, but I didn't know ... Is that where I got it from? You? Wow, I'm sorry. It must have just ...' And then his face changed as he said something that I know he didn't mean. 'I'll change it. Take it all out. Start again. I'll ... make sure it's not you. That you're not recognisable.'

This was the bit where I was supposed to say that it didn't matter, that he could keep things as they were. No problem. And I should have said that. Spared him the embarrassment. But I couldn't. And I told him why.

'Well, yeah,' I said, 'there's only one problem. That's what *my* new book's about.'

'What, your marriage?'

'It's falling apart, Jon. I mean, you know that. I

started writing about it to try and understand how and why, you know? To find out who we were then and who I am now. I was just ... using the novel to, to explore all that. Hopefully come up with some answers. And get a book out of it.'

'Oh, sorry, mate,' he said, eyes brimming with empathy and sincerity. 'I didn't know things were as bad as that. I mean, I knew it was bad and all, but that's it? You're separating?'

'Well, I don't know. I mean, it looks that way, but that's why I'm writing the book. To try and work everything through.'

He became thoughtful. 'Listen,' he said eventually, 'this is what I'll do. I'll change it so that no one will recognise you. Yeah?'

'But no one recognises me now in it. It's only because I know who it is.'

'Yeah, yeah. I'll sort it, don't worry.'

The band chose that moment to make their entrance and we didn't discuss it any further. But I knew there and then. That Jon had written a great book. And he had no intention of changing anything.

And I was right. His book came out before mine and, of course, took all the column inches in review space, got him on radio and TV to talk about it and sold the film rights straight away. Reviewers praised it as 'a bravura performance, a nuanced, heart-rending but also anger-making portrait of a failing marriage.' 'Exceptional insight into a crumbling relationship.' 'Stunning.' And all the rest. And I suppose the supreme accolade for him was when it was shortlisted for the Booker and won. And when mine appeared a few months afterwards from a smaller publisher and with less than a tenth of the marketing budget of Jon's, what reviews I managed to scrape talked of how it was 'derivative of other, better novels on the same subject.'

The publishers did spring for a launch party. Probably where all the marketing budget went. And Jon came along to it, such as it was. When he entered the room, all the attention turned to him. No one wanted to talk to me any more. My book and me, forgotten. He looked apologetic about it, shrugging, and deflected all the conversation back to me. Which was kind. But which he could afford to do. As someone at the party said to me in the pub afterwards, when the publisher's money had run out and we were drinking out of our own pocket, 'Like he was doing you a favour, coming here. Bet he wouldn't be so fucking cheerful if it was the other way round.' I said nothing. Too drunk to reply, for one thing. But I filed that away.

My marriage ended. No surprise to anyone who read my novel. Or Jon's for that matter. However, if you believe the reviews, I couldn't work out what went wrong and just wasn't good enough to put it right.

2. This is, of course, a description of Jon. Or me, for that matter. A generic description of an early-middle aged writer. His lead character in disguise, playing a part. It's like he's not even bothering to hide it any more. He's putting things like this in just for the reviewers to realise, so they can pride themselves on understanding the subtext. Bring in on the joke. Because a great writer would never bother with anything as tedious as a genre novel. A book about spies and assassins. No. It would have to be about something else. Something *better*.

3. Jon, with Gwen's help, had been taken on by one of the best agents in the business. And this is a portrait of her. A disguise of onion skin thinness. He's basically describing a meeting with his agent. As far as I'm aware they never met in the British Library. That was reserved for my students and I (another detail he took from me?). He always met in her office or out for dinner. He was often wined and dined. It happens to the ones who bring in most of the money. Her offices reflected that. All minimalist Scandinavian wood panelling in Soho. Discrete potted palms, comfortable sofas. By contrast, I was with an agent who operated out of the upstairs of a pub in King's Cross (pre-gentrification). He wasn't one of the biggest and best in the business. He believed it was his job, as he said, to manage my expectations. If I could have, I would have left him. But my options weren't upwards, only sideways or downwards. So I stayed with him and tried to do what I could for myself. Hence networking every night. Making myself one of the most familiar faces at publishing parties, sticking my foot in as many doors as I could. Being as entertaining as possible. Selling myself as a commodity. And it would work until some editor went in to work the next day, remembered me from the night before, thought I might be a good fit for their list and checked my sales rankings. And that was the end of that. So I had to stick with my agent. And just say nothing, grinding my teeth when he said things like, 'Got to call one of the big editors this afternoon. Hate doing that. Get really nervous.' Then find out which parties were happening that night, get myself invited, fix my false grin and start the whole tedious networking thing all over again.

4. Wow. He's definitely not hiding it now. Retirement? He's not even subtly hinting at it, just coming out and saying it. Or his lead character, five years younger and better looking, is. Is he dropping more clues? Has he got houses secreted away around the globe? Is that where he disappeared to?

Obviously there have been sightings of him. At one point he even outdid the ghost of Princess Diana for tabloid spottings. One true crime blogger put together an intricate murder board, like the one in that online meme of the guy raving in front of a wall of newsprint joined together by red string. This blogger was sure he had gone to Kerala in Southern India and wanted Jon's old publisher to finance a trip for them to prove it. It turned out to be a dead end but a lucrative one for the true crime blogger, who got a very nice holiday out of it.

The *Daily Mail* ran a piece about a year or so ago saying they had a positive sighting of him in Portugal, running a surfboard hire shop on the beach at Maceda. Again, it wasn't him. Even psychics were enlisted in the search for him, with predictably useless results.

So, is he letting us know? Teasing us? Giving his editor (i.e. me) more desk-based detective work to do? Yes. This whole section was put in for a reason. If he's hiding, he's hiding in plain sight. I just have to find out where.

7

I browse the British Library bookshop before I leave, outwardly looking intently at what's on the shelves, in reality scanning the room for any watchers and followers.

When you've spent a lifetime dealing in code you end up speaking it. Like the conversation I've just had. They're planning to get rid of me and she thinks my wisest option would be to disappear. The inference being they wouldn't look too hard for me if I just quietly slipped away. Obviously, she didn't say that in so many words, but then she didn't need to. As I said, we've both had a lifetime dealing in code.

No teaching job for me, no handler job either. And no desk job. Not entirely unexpected. People who do what I do tend not to be the kind of people you'd like in an office next to you. My job is mainly for psychopaths and sociopaths. I now regard myself as a sociopath. What's the difference? Sociopaths can hold a conversation at a party. We may not be interested in other people, but we can give a convincing impression that we are. Psychopaths can't. This shouldn't mean that psychopaths and sociopaths are natural killers. But it is true we are drawn more to that kind of profession. It's that little chip of ice in our hearts that make us good at what we do. (1)

Have I always been a sociopath? Or did I become one?

Nature/nurture, I don't know. The pointy heads with their tests would be best suited to tell you that one. And I've had tests. Plenty of them. They wouldn't let me loose in the organisation without testing me first. And not to tell if I'm a psychopath or a sociopath. Just to let them know that I'm an *employable* psychopath or sociopath. A company asset, even if I am a deniable one.

How did I get into this line of work? How did I go from lower ranked spy to assassin? Well, it happened when I killed a man. (2)

Accidentally, I should say. Or that's what I thought at the time. But looking back, I'm sure there must have been an element of pre-meditation involved. It's impossible to grow up harbouring that level of hatred and anger I had and not wanting to vent it on someone.

Working for MI6, I felt like an actor playing a part. A character, and the fun lay in getting people to believe in that character, trust that character and tell that character things they weren't supposed to. I wasn't a le Carré spy, a posh outsider, nor was I a James Bond type, who isn't a spy anyway, just an enforcer with a veneer of snobbery. A thug in a tux. I was just enjoying being someone else and seeing how far that could get me.

It happened in Prague. (3) I mean, where else? There was a time when Prague was shorthand for Euro-noir sophistication in popular spy language. With its brooding neo-Gothic architecture and cobbled streets, its shadowed alleyways and palpable air of menace, it was just far enough away from London to be thought of as exotic, just enough behind enemy lines to be considered dangerous.

When I was posted there it was a city at a crossroads. The ex-Soviet satellite Czechoslovakia was rebranding itself the Czech Republic, with ex-playwright Vaclav Havel as president and avant-garde rock guitarist Frank Zappa as Special Ambassador to the West on Trade Culture and Tourism. Prague, the capital, was trying to reinvent itself as a centre for art and culture, hoping to attract West Europeans on that basis. It eventually became known as a cut-price stag and hen party destination.

But I'm getting ahead of myself. (4)

Once again I was there as a UK Foreign Office trade envoy, ostensibly welcoming our new neighbours to democracy and displaying the myriad opportunities now available to them as new business partners, but in reality keeping an eye out for any lingering hangers-on from the old regime sporting new clothes and new haircuts but unable to disguise old habits. Spies, basically. Inserted into trade delegations. Like me.

Back in those days, I still had a youthful belief that I was one of the good guys. Naive enough to believe there was a gulf between what us and the other side – the bad guys – did and that our aims were more noble than theirs. I was also a cocky, arrogant arsehole, who I'm sure everyone hated, but I thought I was wonderful, because I was one of the good guys. It was the persona I'd chosen to play, and it was easy because it wasn't a million miles away from who I was at the time. Invincible, but more than that, *right*.

And it was in this mindset that I came to kill someone.

I'd been out drinking and dining – but mostly drinking – as part of the UK delegation entertaining our Russian counterparts. We were playing the game, each sizing the other up, each trying to work out who, if anyone, was genuine, who was the spy. There were two of us who weren't who we said we were in our party. Myself and an older, more experienced operative I'll call Charles. Charles was perfect; a gracious host, an informative and witty conversationalist and the kind of person who you'd never in a million years suspect of being a spy. Which is why he was so good at it. And there was me. Eager, young, straining at the leash to throw off these dreary old guys and hook up with the younger ones, head off to see what the new, unregulated nightlife of Prague had to offer. In hindsight I was clearly too enthusiastic in my portrayal as an obnoxious, coked-up entitled prick. And that arrogance allowed me to become involved in a situation with no back up or extraction plan. But being invincible made me bulletproof.

There was a younger guy on the opposite side, let's call him Granit. He and I struck up a conversation over dinner and I suspected that he was as bored as I was. As I said, Prague was still wriggling out from under the Soviet jackboot and although they were trying hard, they hadn't quite got the hang of things yet. As I remarked to Granit.

'First time I've ever seen chewing gum on the menu as a dessert.' I laughed when I said it.

He tried to return that laughter but it didn't quite take. 'We're trying. We may not be as prosperous as the West – yet – but we're trying.'

I sensed his embarrassment and said nothing more on the subject.

We talked of other things, of how different things already were since the tanks rolled out.

'It's good, free. We speak freely to each other. Not terrified of saying the wrong thing and disappearing, you know? We can be confident.'

'Does that mean people have stopped complaining?'

A shadow I couldn't quite read passed over his features. 'People always complain. No matter what you do for them.' And then it lifted. He glanced round the table. Charles was getting polite but knowing smiles from some bureaucratic anecdote. 'But anyway, why don't we shake off these ancient ones and I'll show you the new Prague? The real Prague.'

I didn't have to be asked twice.

We waited until a suitable break in proceedings then stood up.

'Granit's taking me on a tour of the nightspots,' I told Charles.

His response I thought, at the time, was heavy-handed and prohibitively, patronisingly paternal. Thinking back, I realise he was trying to warn me to be careful. Or not to go at all. Charles had either decided that, or been given information on, Granit, and he couldn't be trusted. And I wouldn't be safe with him. Or our mission, for that matter. However I was too young and arrogant then to read codes so I missed all of this. Told him not to worry, I wouldn't do anything he wouldn't do and left with Granit.

We hit the bars first. One, the Whisky Bar, very popular with the burgeoning hipster scene, sold mainly bottled East European beer and local vodka. Whatever whisky it had was imported and expensive and went largely untouched and anyway was beyond my Foreign Office budget. However, I did discover that vodka, which I've never been a fan of back home, was surprisingly drinkable, especially neat. Although this was the local and the best stuff which, like the Irish and their Guinness, they kept for themselves.

We went bar hopping, picking up a kind of rag tag entourage of Granit's friends and colleagues, or that's how he introduced them to me. All young, wearing designer gear that I doubted was knock off although I couldn't be entirely sure, all with a level of testosterone-fuelled arrogance that threatened to become violence at the slightest provocation. Yes, they were lively and lairy, but I still didn't feel Charlie's coded warning had been warranted. And it wasn't. Yet.

Another bar, then another and another. More vodka coupled with increased laughter from Granit's friends which took on a dangerously manic edge, more back slapping, more pulling me into their circle. I was very drunk by this time. That, and the cocaine I had snorted in the toilets at the restaurant with

Granit – bonding, I had told myself, all in the line of duty – was hitting me hard. Pills were passed round. No idea what, but I was expected to partake. That manic, dangerous energy the group gave off made it impossible to say no.

By the time we hit the club I was on one level wiped out but on another ready to keep going for another few days and nights. The music was hard and heavy house, pushed up to ear bleed levels. The barely dressed clientele were all going for it, sweat flying off them in all directions. The walls and ceiling of this former warehouse dripped with moisture. It was a vision of psychedelic hell. I loved it.

I hardly registered that we didn't have to pay or that we were led straight to the roped off VIP area where magnums of champagne were hurriedly placed before us. And I definitely didn't notice the fear with which Granit's entourage was greeted by the employees.

'This is all right, isn't it?' I said above the din, glass of champagne in hand.

Granit laughed. 'You did this. All of you. The West. Showed us a better way of living. A better way to be free.'

'Well, here's to us!'

We chinked glasses.

At that moment a waitress appeared to replenish the bottles. I didn't notice how badly her hands were shaking but I did notice her spill some champagne on the leg of my trousers. She looked at me, terror in her eyes. I smiled, shrugged. It happens. Don't worry. I picked up a napkin, began dabbing at it.

Granit grabbed her wrist, twisted it hard. She gasped, screamed. 'This man is a guest in your country. Is this how you treat a guest?'

'Hey Granit,' I said, placing my hand on his arm, 'It's OK. No harm done.'

He ignored me, kept twisting her arm. His eyes were off

somewhere else. The faces of his entourage became suddenly hungry, waiting for something to happen. Something unpleasant they could get off on. Equally suddenly, I wasn't drunk.

'Let her go, Granit.' My voice had steel in it, was louder than I'd expected. The cocaine had made me brave. Or something else.

Granit stared at me. Challenging me. He kept twisting her arm.

'Stop.' I increased my grip on him.

Granit wouldn't let go. It became like a surrogate arm wrestle with this poor girl in the middle.

'Granit. Let her go. She's apologised.'

More staring. More twisting. He'd reached the point where if he didn't let go, he'd snap her bones.

He let go.

The girl flew away from him, out of the VIP area, crying. He stared at me. Eyes lit by raging fires.

'Do not do that to me again. Do not challenge me. You are guest in my country. Remember that.' He sat back, staring ahead. His anger unabated, just waiting for another target.

I stood up, not wanting to be there any longer. 'I'm going to the gents.' I made my way out of the roped off area, looking for the toilets. The full noise of the club hit me as I did.

I was guided by a bouncer to the VIP lavatories. I stepped inside, relishing the relative coolness inside. It was spacious but empty. I crossed to a mirror, turned on the tap, threw water on my face, stared at my reflection. I looked dreadful.

'Get a grip. Come on . . .'

I was aware of the door opening behind me. I turned. There stood Granit.

He was enveloped in stillness. A brutal, ugly, dangerous stillness. He stared at me.

'We know what you are.'

'I'm sorry?'

He didn't move. 'I said, we know what you are.'

I swallowed. The mood he was in, it didn't matter what or who I was. I was who he decided I was. I'd stopped him having his fun with the girl, made him back down in front of his friends. And now I was going to pay for that.

I played the dumb Englishman, giving it my best Hugh Grant. 'I'm sorry, I really have no idea what you're talking about.'

He took a step towards me. 'Foreign trade envoy? No. MI6 spy. Here to watch us.'

'I can assure you I'm nothing of the sort. I'm—'

'Do not bullshit me.' His voice now matched the glare in his eyes. 'You're a spy. You only play the wanker.'

'I ... I don't know quite how to take that ...'

Another step. 'But that's OK. Because I too am spy. FSB. Here to make sure the right people come out on top. To make sure you don't fuck with what we've spent years building.'

'I ... I can assure you I'm ...'

I saw his fist coming towards me. Pills and coke had heightened my senses. I ducked. He caught me on my right ear. Jesus, it stung. I backed away as he came forward, ready to go again.

All pretence now gone, I fell back on my training. Exploit your opponent's weaknesses. Use them against him. Easy to say in training. But when your opponent is some coked up rage and 'roid machine, much harder to carry out.

He telegraphed his next intentions. I managed to dart around him, get clear out of his grasp.

He was more compact, more muscular than me. Was that a weakness? It didn't seem so.

Yes it was. It made him slower. And the pills had made me sharper. Right now I'd take any advantage I could.

He was still in the same position, his punch having failed to land. Before he could turn towards me, regain his fighting stance and go again I reached behind him, took what hair he had in my hands and slammed his head down on the rim of the sink as hard as I could.

He screamed. Blood from his broken mouth sprayed over the white porcelain.

No time to think, to let him back into the fight. I did the same thing again. Something cracked. Bone or porcelain, I didn't know and I didn't care. I readied my hand to do it again but his meaty fist swung up, clamped onto my arm, spun me round.

Suddenly I was the waitress from earlier. Unlike her I turned into the movement, let my body go with it until I was facing him. He was a sight. Broken nose, broken teeth, possibly, from the jutting angle of his face, broken jaw. The pain had enraged him even further.

He came towards me, screaming, his free hand going for my face. He grabbed me by my neck and squeezed. His hands were huge, enough to encompass all of my neck in one, and immediately I felt my blood supply constrict.

I put both my hands on his forearms, trying to break his grip. I may as well have tickled him.

Training. Weakness.

I grabbed instead either side of his head with my fingers, extended my thumbs.

Plunged them into his eyes.

He screamed even more.

I kept pushing. He took his hands from my neck and arm, placed them on my arms and tried to push me away.

I ignored him, kept pushing. In … in … as hard as I could.

He screamed even louder. Trying to walk my body back all the time.

I didn't let up. No matter how hard he squeezed my arms. I pushed further. Felt my thumbs in the middle corners of his eye sockets. Felt his eyeballs start to dislodge, like squeezing two huge cysts.

He realised what was happening and stopped pushing at me. Instead he tried to pull away from my grip, get away far away from me as possible. He succeeded. Stood there in the middle of the bathroom, hands to his bloodied eyes, pained, blinded.

I didn't wait for him to recover.

Lifting my leg I brought my foot down on the outside of his knee, hearing a crack as the bone split from cartilage. He screamed once more, went down on one knee. I stamped on the same knee again. His leg now went in a different direction from the other one.

I stood back, stared at him. He was beaten but still dangerous. The man was FSB after all. I couldn't leave him like this.

I glanced to one side, saw the sink I'd earlier smashed him head into. There was a massive crack running down it. One good pull and it would separate into two parts.

I pulled.

A whole section came away easily.

I turned to Granit. He was trying to get to his feet, using another of the sinks to aid him.

I swung the lump of porcelain at his head. Put everything I could behind it. It connected, hard.

Granit slumped to the floor.

Breathing heavily I knelt over him, and, arms raised as high as I could, brought the sink section down as hard as I could on what remained of his face.

Once I realised he wasn't moving I slumped back against the pipes of a neighbouring sink, trying to get my breath back.

No one had entered while we fought. Presumably Granit had put a guard on the door.

So I couldn't just walk out. His entourage would be waiting for me in the club. I doubt I was the one they expected to emerge.

I looked around for another exit. Even VIP club bathrooms in former warehouses have windows. I stood up, found the window. Old, metal-framed, consisting of small panels of wire-reinforced glass. I pushed it open. Not big enough for me to leave by. Plus I didn't know if there was a drop at the other side or not.

However, I didn't have a choice. I ran my fingers round the frame, found the plaster to be old and crumbling. I climbed onto a toilet cistern, eventually standing. Balanced myself on the cubicle frame and kicked my foot out at the window.

It didn't take long before it was hanging off and I could pass through.

Before I did I looked back at the prone figure of Granit. He wasn't moving. Had stopped breathing.

And in that instant I knew that something had changed in me. I had crossed a line that I could never cross back. I had become someone else.

I climbed through the window to find out who.

7 – Notes

1. Ah, that Graham Greene quote again. Is he saying all writers are sociopaths? Possibly not all. But definitely some, I should imagine. Depends how big that chip of ice is, I suppose. And how well you do in keeping it from melting. But all writing, all fictional writing is supposed to be about empathy, I hear you say. Aren't writers supposed to be natural empaths? Isn't that how they're able to work? Well, yes, I suppose so. But they (we) will suck you dry of experiences to use for our work. Just look at Jon appropriating my crumbling marriage for his novel. But if a writer can then turn it into something relatable, that's where the empathy comes in. Or at least the faking of empathy. Sociopaths do that too, remember. Writers especially so. As they always say, fake it till you make it. And if you can fake sincerity, you've got it made.

   It hurt, what he did to me. Using my story for himself. I mean, I tried to play it down but it was hard. Especially after he won the Booker. Not just for using my story, but for using my life. The thing was, he couldn't see anything wrong with doing that. Everything was material to him. And part of me agrees. I mean, I'd used it myself. Only difference being, it was mine to use. Which I suppose leads to a question of authorship. Whose story can you tell? Since Jon's heyday, a lot has been written about cultural appropriation. Taking the story of someone else from a different culture and telling it yourself. I can see both sides of this argument. Yes, the life of a mixed-race teenage girl on a social housing estate in Tottenham is miles away from my day-to-day experience. But does that mean I shouldn't be allowed to tell her story, made up though it may be? Or should she do it herself? Does she even *want* to do it herself? Should I not tell it, even if it's crucial to my book, just in case she might one day want to tell it herself? I don't know. I may be old, but I thought the whole point of writing was to become someone else. To get away from yourself and try on a different personality. I just know that no one would be interested in my daily life, or what goes on in my head. If I wanted to write about any of that I would disguise it. I would have to. And obviously, that's what Jon's doing here. If he wants to hide certain aspects of his life by dressing them up in a fictional framework then so be it. All novelists do that. That's fiction. But there's still a difference between making up a fantastical story, even if it is in order to tell truths about the human condition, and borrowing someone else's life.

Because it still hurt that he stole my life to write about. I mean, we kind of forgot it – or at least he did – and we remained friends. Good friends. Jon was such a dazzling personality that it was hard to stay angry at him for long. So we were soon back in harness together, drinking our way round the literary parties of Soho, deluding ourselves into thinking we were like those great hellraising cultural boozers of yore, Dylan Thomas and Oliver Reed, people like that. Jon would even say on occasion that we were a modern-day Byron and Shelley. Loudly declaim it, even. Then laugh. And I would laugh along with him. But it was only afterwards, when that whole era was gone, that I thought about that phrase. And he was right, as far as it went, we were a contemporary Byron and Shelley. Byron, in his own lifetime, was massively successful. Shelley barely known and certainly not read. Was Jon being cleverer than I thought he was in saying that? Did he actually know that, and used it as a dig against me? Or did he not have a clue and said it because it sounded self-aggrandising? I don't know. But there's a margin of doubt there that there never used to be.

And here's the other thing about that time. Yes, looking back it seems to have been one long Britpop type party. But the thing I didn't notice about Jon at the time was that he wasn't keeping up. Oh, he pretended to, went along with whatever drink or drug was going, but it was all an act. Quite a sly act, all things considered. I need to be honest here. And this is a difficult thing to write about oneself honestly. No character to hide behind, no fancy words to deflect away from me. Just *sincere* writing. No matter how bad it makes me look. You see, like I said, it was only afterwards, years afterwards, that I noticed Jon never kept up with me, drinking-wise, carousing-wise. He would be the one to get us into places, unlock those magic members' club doors, and once inside he'd kind of stand back and push me forward. Leave me to do the majority of the entertaining. He was the suave one, I was the comedy sidekick.

You can make a case that he did this to humour me, patronise me even, for not being as successful as him. Or am I being too paranoid? I don't think so. Maybe he thought me being entertaining was the admittance price I had to pay to be allowed into this rarified cultural atmosphere along with actors, film directors, rock stars, the lot. His court jester, only along because he, and those around us, found me entertaining. Yes, I could imagine them saying, he's not much of a writer, quite a failure, but he's good value at parties. And because Jon had instructed them all to laugh at whatever I came out with. And poor deluded me would wake up the next day thinking I'd been dazzling, charming company. Little realising people weren't laughing with me but at me. Or at least behind me. Yes, you can certainly make a case for thinking that.

But. On the other hand...

Jon didn't need to do that. Didn't need to spend so much time hanging out with me when he could have been with more important writers, more successful ones. With film directors and rock stars. He certainly wasn't doing his career any good by hanging around with me. My agent at the time, the one who was frightened of editors at big publishing houses, told me I shouldn't be spending so much time with him, and other writers of his level because it was giving me unrealistic career expectations. I would start wanting to be successful next and I should get that kind of thinking out of my head. But, no. Whatever else Jon was, he was my friend. And he was a good friend, all things considered. When my marriage ended, he helped me find a flat in his old stamping ground south of the river, in Clapham. A one-bedroom, rented, that I was paying well over the odds for (or I thought I was – it was actually the going rate). But it did me. It was what I needed. My bachelor pad. My writer's garret, even if it was only on the first floor. And from that room, buoyed by the successes of my successful friends, what masterpieces would I create!

Yeah, right. But considering what happened next, I probably should have had more faith.

2. Oh, here we go. Supervillain origin story alert.

3. Well, this is interesting. More of me in his book. Not as contentious this time. We used to read thrillers during this period, Jon and me, which might well be where the idea for this novel came from. And one of the things we used to say was the word Prague. Just the word. It was always used for a setting at that time and we both found it utterly hilarious. Like doing a Kenneth Williams on the word espionage, Prague could have its vowels sounded out. And we would. Every time we read the blub on the back of a book, or saw a film trailer set there, we would look to one another and say: PRRRRaaaagggueee ... However, unlike espionage, Prague was said in a deep enough voice to sound menacing. One could imagine some twisted, facially scarred, emaciated, long leather-coated and fedora-wearing, gravel-voiced Euro spymaster rolling it out. Probably curling his fingers into a fist while saying it. PRRRRaaaagggueee ... We would then burst out laughing. I'm smiling now thinking about it.

4. There are two ways to look at the rest of this chapter. And since we're currently looking at how Jon appropriated things to put in his novels, this one bears repeating. Not long after his first novel came out and was a success, Jon went back to Dudley.

   He took Gwen with him. It was the first time she had been away from London with him to meet his family. He had tried to put it off indefinitely, because he didn't want her to see where he came from. But she insisted so he relented. *Perfect Circle* was riding high in the bestseller lists and the film rights had been sold. If ever there was a time the prodigal son of Dudley could return it would be now.

It wasn't a successful visit. His father and he had never had a good relationship and now he was particularly dismissive. He was unimpressed by Jon's achievements. He didn't like Gwen and told her so. What was Jon thinking, he said, bringing a posh bint like that here? Got too full of himself. So Jon, burning internally with rage, took Gwen out on the town.

And something from that depressing experience made its way into this chapter. At least with a changed, cathartic, fictional ending. Jon took Gwen to one of the pubs he had occasionally frequented as a teenager. It was busy, the clientele local. Jon ordered while Gwen found a table. It was clear they didn't belong. Equally clear they were unwelcome.

Jon was proposing drinking up and heading into Birmingham for a curry when Gwen noticed someone staring at them. Not just casually looking over, but actually leaning forward, not bothering to disguise the fact. Unblinking. Unfriendly. 'Friend of yours?' she asked.

'Never seen him before in my ...' Then Jon recognised him. 'Yeah. I went to school with him. And no, not a friend. Let's just drink up and—'

Too late. The starer was coming over. He sat down on a spare stool next to them. 'I know you.'

'Hello, Grant.'

Grant looked at Gwen with a mixture of positive appraisal and anger.

'Who's this?'

'My … fiancée. Gwen.'

'You from round here?' he said before Gwen could introduce herself.

'No, I, live in, we both live in London.'

Grant nodded as if that explained everything. 'What you do, then?'

Jon and Gwen glanced at each other, nervously. Jon looked back at Grant. Decided not to lie. 'I'm a writer. Write books.'

Grant frowned. 'What d'you mean, books?'

'I write them. Books. Novels. I—'

'What you doing back here?' The subtext clear: *You don't belong here.*

'Just, erm, back to see my dad. You know. Then a quick one in here. Just for, you know. Anyway, we've got to be off.' Jon was painfully aware that he was regressing, back to that frightened little misfit he'd been as a teenager. Coming here had been a bad idea, a *very* bad idea.

'Right,' he said, draining his pint in one go, 'nice seeing you, Grant. We've got to be off now.' He stood up, hoping Gwen would do the same. She hadn't yet moved.

Grant still stared at him. 'You always thought you were better, didn't you? Better than the rest of us.'

'Come on, Gwen, let's go.'

'Always thought you were better than us. Laughing at us, sniggering because we didn't like the things you liked. Because we didn't like *books*. You thought we were thick. You thought you were better. And now you live in London with some posh bint … you're not. Not better than us, not better than me.' His voice raising now, attracting attention.

'Yeah well,' Jon said, 'We're going now, so—'

Gwen stood up. Squared up to Grant. 'You dare to stand there and say that? To my fiancé? And about me? When you don't even know me? Yeah. Jon was right about you. Clearly.'

Jon grabbed Gwen, tried to steer her to the door.

'Posh bitch,' shouted Grant.

'Fuck you, saddo,' Gwen said in reply and they left.

'Jesus Christ,' Gwen said, once they were putting their coats on and walking away. 'I'm sorry. I'll never ask to come back here with you again. I'll—'

She didn't finish her sentence because Jon was on the ground. Grant had followed them out and attacked him from behind, punching him in the back of the head. Jon rolled round in agony. Gwen who stood there in shock, Grant staring at her.

'Yeah,' he said, 'Fuck off back to London. We don't want your sort here.' Then turned and walked back inside.

Gwen helped Jon to his feet, checked that the damage to him was fairly minimal. She was angry, wanted to go to the police. Jon just shook his head.

'No, I don't ... no.' He managed a small smile. 'Bad publicity. Let's just go home.'

'And never come back.'

And he never did.

Now. You may be wondering what this has to do with the chapter you've just read. Well, the physical description of Granit is the same as the one he gave me for Grant. He's also used an embarrassingly small amount of disguise over the names too. Remember what I said about a writer's lead character being an idealised version of themselves but five years younger? There you go. The Grant story ended up in a novel after all. And, just like the real-life experience had been a cathartic moment for Jon, realising that he could never go home again and had to keep moving forward, so it becomes a pivotal moment in the progression of Garrick, his fiction character in the narrative. That's writers for you. Never let anything go to waste.

Now, having said all that, there's the question of the other way of looking at this chapter. And that is to regard it as some of the most clichéd spy writing you'll ever read. It sounds like he wrote it in an armchair during the advert breaks of a Mission Impossible film, cribbing what was going on onscreen. Appropriating again, but to a much less original degree. If I were to play devil's advocate, then I suppose we need these kinds of scenes. It is that kind of book. And yes, you're saying, maybe I'm just bitter, having dredged up what he did to me and my marriage for his own gain. How he's put our private jokes in this chapter too. You might think that colours my impression of this section now. And fine, you're entitled to think that. Just as I'm entitled to think what I want to about Jon. I knew him, after all. He was my friend. Until he wasn't. But that comes later.

Great last line of the chapter, though.

8

Charles's face froze when I explained what had happened. He listened, unspeaking, as if I was talking to a rock. Then he took to action. And all the derogatory things I'd previously thought about him went out the window. (1)

I made it back to the embassy through the back entrance, reserved for tradesmen and disgraced spooks. It was swept daily for surveillance, but you never knew. You couldn't trust anyone in this game. Charles was up waiting for my return, ready to debrief. One look at the state of me – torn, bloody clothing, bruises and cuts – and he knew things had gone badly wrong. He didn't need to be a spy to work that one out.

My training deserted me as I jabbered disjointedly about what had happened. Charles listened patiently until I recomposed myself, then questioned me. Hard, sharp, focused questions. At first I batted them away, but he forced me to think, reply with clarity. Replay events as coherently and dispassionately as I could. To remember my training.

'Right,' he said, after thinking for some time. The expression on his face had changed, his whole demeanour had altered. Hardened. There was no trace of the upper-class twit I'd been with previously. I didn't actually realise until that point that he had been playing a character too and he was a damned sight more convincing than I had been. Afterwards, playing all this back in my head, I felt ashamed to have misjudged him. But that was just one more thing to feel ashamed about that night.

I was shipped out back to the UK straight away, barely having enough time to grab my belongings before I left. I couldn't take an obvious route such as an airport, where I'd be recognised, so it was to be under the radar. They cleaned me up, dressed me as gap year student and put me on a coach with all the other backpackers. A different identity, of course, since the last one was blown. I was dropped off at Prague bus station sometime in the early hours where I joined all the other backpackers making the most of the recently opened borders, cheap travel, cheap accommodation, cheap beer. Everyone sat around waiting for the bus which, given the fact the new regime hadn't yet managed to make the trains run on time, had taken on the frequency of a sighting of the Loch Ness monster. I struck up a conversation with two lads from Halifax who saw themselves as intrepid explorers, bless them, and got on the bus with them when it finally arrived. (2)

I got off at Dresden and dropped out of sight, surfacing again in Hamburg, still with the backpacker identity. By this time the enormity of what I'd done was starting to penetrate. I'd taken another life. *Another life.* How did I feel about that? I sat alone in a bar, drinking German beer, eating German food and reflected. Indulged in self-examination, tried to discover who the last few days had made me. I wasn't yet ready to go back in, but I didn't want to run any more. I had to get my head straight before I made my next move.

I had expected to feel guilt, remorse, a crushing black weight inside me resting forever on my soul and stopping me from being a fully functioning human being for the rest of my life. The horror, the horror. But I didn't feel any of that. I just felt . . . nothing. Granit – or whatever his real name was – was a piece of shit. He was no loss to the gene pool. Had I done the world a favour by taking him out of it? I didn't know. From my perspective, I hadn't *not*. I tried the 'he was someone's son/brother/father(?)' argument to see if I felt any guilt but it didn't seem to. If someone had brought him up to behave like that then he was either a chip off the old block, in which case no loss, or a massive disappointment, in which case a relief to be rid of. The lack of a feeling of shock at how I was thinking should have shocked me. But I didn't even feel that. (3)

Did my actions excite me? Exhilarate me in any way? I couldn't say. I suppose in a way, yes. I had killed a man and escaped from a foreign country after doing so. Made my way overground across Europe without attracting attention, and evaded capture. I had got away with it. I felt some excitement at that. I think the nearest emotion I felt was pride in keeping myself together and not going to pieces. Any exhilaration came from the fact I could drink beer and eat bratwurst and calmly reflect on my actions. The fact that I'd killed someone didn't bother me. What did that say about me? I wondered then for the first time whether I was a psychopath or a sociopath. Looking back now, after years of company mandated therapy, I'm not sure it really matters.

There was something else that happened, though, something which I later realised was quite important and had happened as a direct result of my actions. I felt incredibly horny. When I returned to the embassy, told my story to Charles and was dispatched on my way, I really, really wanted sex. Not just fancied it, as if some attractive young woman in the club had pushed my buttons, but actually *craved* it like my life depended on it.

I feel awkward even admitting that. I can explain in detail how I killed a man and tell you of my subsequent escape. But mention how horny the experience made me feel and I want to clam up, pretend it didn't happen. Why are we more comfortable discussing violence rather than sex? By 'we' I mean we as a species here. Sociopaths or not. We feel more comfortable with death rather than creation (especially even the practice of it), the negative rather than the positive. And presumably happier reading about it too.

Anyway. I got talking to a young female backpacker on the coach and I knew she was going to be the receptacle for whatever was coursing through me even if she wasn't aware at the time. I charmed her, flirted with her, flattered her, excited her and as soon as we got to Dresden we holed up in a cheap hotel and fucked each other raw for days. It was one of, if not *the*, best fucks of my life. I came like never before. Having been responsible for death, did I now want to feel as alive as I could? I don't know. But it worked.

I stayed in a safe house in Hamburg for a few days, where I was debriefed, analysed, monitored, interrogated, questioned, requestioned, requestioned again, the whole works. They were thorough. It was one of the most intense periods of my life. While they were making me talk, no one would tell me what was going to happen to me next. Would I face arrest and trial? In return for my actions was I going to be bumped off? Or could I be the makeweight in a trade deal, swapped with a British spy coming out of Russia? In their silence my anxiety grew. Which, combined with the interrogation was the point. They were assessing me. Testing me. And I passed.

Their work done, my inquisitors departed, leaving me confined to barracks alone in the safe house. I was then visited by a woman who I took to be a visiting lecturer in Humanities at the local university. She informed me that I had failed as a spy. No future in that department after what I had done. I was gutted, truly gutted. My whole future had ended. I had no idea what I would do now.

I asked if my actions had caused a diplomatic incident, and

was that why she was telling me this, but she said no. The whole affair had been swept under the carpet. Granit wasn't much of an asset to his own side, and she gave me the impression his spymasters were secretly pleased that someone had got rid of that irritant for them. No. She wanted to talk to me about another job in another department. Her department. A job I had demonstrated myself to be eminently more suited to. I needed training but the basic aptitude was there. The tests of the last few days had shown that. What was the job? Assassin. What did I think?

I thought that would do nicely. (4)

8 – Notes

1. Charles is based on Jon's first editor. I won't use his name (Google if you want to) as it's not really necessary for the enjoyment of the novel; I'm only saying this as a means of clarification. 'Charles' was an editor of the old school, or that was how Jon (and me) thought at the time. As I've got older, I've realised he wasn't old school, he had just been around a lot and was very good at his job. He'd seen writers like Jon (and me) come and go and was still there to talk about it. He'd also made writers like Jon (not so much me), given them their careers. Jon knew he was the real deal so listened to him and took his advice to heart. As he always said, 'If someone else comes up with a good idea that makes my novel look better, I'll use it. After all, it's not their name on the cover, is it?' This, experience has taught me, is the best way to treat editors. Good ones, of course. I can't say I was having the same experience as Jon at the time. We used to laugh about 'Charles', but in an affectionate way. Same as Garrick's reaction to the Charles character in this chapter. And yet another deliberate mining of his life and career for this novel. In fact, I've started noticing there's so much of Jon's life in it – veiled, of course – that at this point in the narrative it's beginning to look like a farewell tour.

2. Jon told me about a holiday he'd taken during his time at university. He and his uni girlfriend had gone backpacking round Europe one summer. Young, carefree,

bohemian, etc. All the usual clichés. Probably took his notebook and his plain glass glasses and pretended to be Kerouac off on some great literary journey of discovery. And that's what he's drawn on for this section of the narrative here. It reads pretty much like an early-twenties backpacking experience. I think the only difference is that Jon headed through the old Yugoslavia and down into Greece. Where, and this is an interesting point, his girlfriend finished with him. Now, you may think if she was going to do something like that, she'd have done it before they left Britain, wouldn't you? I would. And I know Jon certainly did. But when he asked her why she had done it, lying on the beach of some Greek island one day, she replied, 'Because if I'd done it then you wouldn't have come away with me and I'd have had no one to go away with.' Which does have its own logic to it, I suppose. Well, she found out what it was like to have no one to go away with, as Jon left her there and travelled back overland on his own. He told me he'd had a much better time without her, and it's from those experiences that this section is really drawn, clearly. Incidentally, he received a letter from her (pre-email days, remember) when he got back to university, saying what she had done to him was unconscionable and she hoped he could find it in his heart to forgive her. He was about to, but read on. Where the letter said that after he left, she teamed up with some Irish boys and had a great time. He tore the letter up. Vowed never to be taken in like that again. Another step on the road to his reinvention.

3. This reads like he's still thinking about the guy in Dudley. It feels like he's working through his feelings

about him, and any imaginary retaliation he might have wanted to make. He's clearly unforgiving about it. I wonder whether writing this also triggered the memory of the actions of his college girlfriend too? If so, he's equally unforgiving to her. And I'm not sure I could blame him for either one. I would have been the same, in his situation. In fact, I'd have probably behaved worse. I was always the angry one of the pair of us. Usually with good reason.

4. A parallel for Gwen pushing his career as a bestselling author? And if so, what does that say about Jon? In fact, what does that say about any of us?

9

And so ends my super villain origin story. (1) Or at least the first part of it.

After Granit's death, the company sent me for training. Spook School. Which meant I was training with wannabe spies, the only difference being I was also taking the Killing for Country module. Once I'd finished the training, I'd either be given a job – MI6 most probably – or let go. Obviously, given what I had just done, I realised just how important this opportunity was, perhaps the most important opportunity I would ever get in my life. Not only did I have to prove myself equal to the challenge, but I had to demonstrate how much better I was than all the others on the course.

They had the usual advantages over me. Privileged backgrounds, Oxbridge educations. Ex-special forces. Clever, well-connected and clearly dangerous. I was at that point only one, perhaps two, of those things. I needed to be. I resolved to show them I could be all three.

The physical training was brutal. Ex-SAS commanders put us through our paces. Even the ex-special forces guys found it hard going. I was determined not to let my inexperience show. I worked on my body, hardened it, toughened it, tested it to a level of endurance it had never been near before. I can't describe the pain I went through. I realised that the over-privileged prick I'd been playing hadn't just weakened me, softened me in both mind and body, but had become me. Like Granit, he too had to die in order for me to move on.

Alongside the physical training there was classroom-based work. Equally as rigorous in its own way, perhaps more so, and a lot of the SAS guys struggled with it. Not their skill set. They were used to a more hands-on approach to problem solving. This is the part I excelled at.

Mental puzzles. Conundrums. Lateral thinking. And not just hypothetical stuff. For instance, in one exercise we were given an assortment of random items and told to construct something that could kill someone, or severely maim them, then be disassembled once again to its basic, harmless, components. Like a particularly malevolent edition of Blue Peter. This played right into my way of thinking, and I came alive. Top marks in the class. My teachers were clearly impressed with how many different ways I managed to combine those harmless objects into killing machines. Impressed, and perhaps a little unnerved?

This all ran alongside the therapy sessions. And that was where I ran into trouble. I knew I was there to train as an assassin but in work of this nature they still need to carefully select who they employ. They can't just let any psycho loose to kill people. Can they? I soon found out.

One day I was taken out of my class and asked to accompany one of my tutors somewhere. She wouldn't tell me where we were going, face as blank and unreadable as a Sanskrit tablet. I was led through the building to a section I'd never been in before. I was ushered into a room, my tutor not bothering to knock. There was a woman behind the desk, a burst of colour totally at odds with the grey drabness of the room. She was sitting behind a desk and asked me to sit before it. My tutor hovered somewhere behind us.

'I hear you're doing very well,' she said. There was nothing on the desk in front of her. It was as bare as the rest of the room.

I didn't know what to say. I had thought I was in trouble initially and the look on her face, completely blank, wasn't helping. Immediately I felt myself going on the defensive.

'I think so. Ma'am.'

I didn't know who she was but she had power. I could sense that.

A small smile broke across her features. 'Oh you do, do you? Well, I must say, you don't lack confidence. That's a good thing in this profession. But it is to which aspect of this profession I wish to speak to you today.'

I said nothing. I was starting to get very bad vibes from this meeting. Really bad vibes. I was going to be kicked out. Worse – I was going to be assigned something totally unsuited to the work I wanted to do. I waited for her to speak again.

'You're ahead of a lot of your peers. Well done.'

'Thank you, ma'am.' Still waiting.

'The classroom-based disciplines, even the physical ones. All good. Mental aptitude . . . all of it good. Sometimes exemplary, even.'

'Thank you.' Here it comes, I thought. I'm being buttered up for something.

'But not everything.'

And there it was. My heart sank as soon as she said those words. And I felt anger towards her. Real anger. All the training I'd done, the work I'd put in, was going to be for nothing. Clearly, I didn't have the right background or something. Clearly, I wasn't one of *them*. And she was about to tell me I never would be. I felt my body stiffening, my hands flex into fists.

She smiled. 'Your therapy results have been brought to my

attention.' A sharp intake of breath. 'Not good, I'm afraid. Not good at all.'

I didn't dare move. If I did, I had no idea what I would say. Or even worse, do. But I knew it would be bad.

'I'll be blunt with you. You're better than ninety per cent of the other students here. However, the results of your psychiatric evaluation ... well. You're a sociopath at best. A psychopath at worst.'

A shiver of dread passed through me. 'Does that mean I'm out, then?'

She looked taken aback. 'No, not at all. You'll make an excellent assassin.'

I relaxed. 'Well, that's what I'm here for.'

'Absolutely. But your other results show something else. You have, as they say these days, the skill set to also make an excellent spy.'

'Oh. I didn't think—'

'Neither did we. But you've also mastered spycraft excellently.'

'So what does that mean?'

She sat back, smiling at me. 'You've passed the first test and you'll be fast-tracked. Congratulations. Welcome to your future.'

A soldier is made by breaking down a person's personality and reassembling them as a killing machine. Perfect in a war zone, useless back in civilian life as has been demonstrated time and again. To create an assassin, a much more rigorous, finely tuned approach is needed. Any soldier can pull a trigger. For an assassin it's the most basic of entry requirements.

The place I was transferred to was, in a lot of respects, the opposite of where I'd been. And the people the opposite of who I'd been with. And far fewer. I suppose that'll happen when you put a group of sociopaths together. We were living and training in some old Second World War barracks at the back of an air force base somewhere in Norfolk. Conditions were cold, harsh and seemingly designed to make it as tough and unpleasant as possible for us. It had been done deliberately, certainly, but whether that was to prepare us for life in the field or to act as a kind of punishment for being the kind of people we were, I couldn't say. Probably a little of both.

Friendships weren't actively encouraged or discouraged. We bonded as well as a group of our sort could bond, which is to say superficially at best, unsociably at worst. And the training was even more rigorous than it had been at the previous place.

We were constantly assessed to ensure that we understood the risks of what we were about to embark on, the potential damage it could do, long term, to our psyches. We were given coping strategies to use on a daily basis. Exercises to help distance ourselves from what we were doing, protect our core selves from the extremes of the job. They were thorough, covering everything. From the euphoric thrill of being allowed to kill without consequence to the attendant guilt that such an act could bring. It was truly fascinating. I dived in as deeply as I could and really discovered who I actually am. Who I was meant to be all along.

Obviously I passed the course. Slightly higher grades for the mental side than the physical side, and no significant red flags from the therapy. You know, considering what and who we all were. Not everyone made it and some who dropped by the wayside were the most surprising ones, the ones you'd have expected to be a shoo-in for the role. I guess coming from a privileged background doesn't help you in everything. (2)

There are three tiers in our organisation. Depending on the results of the course you're assigned to, the tier the bosses believe you'll be most suitable for. The lowest level is Mechanic. Hitman, in pulp parlance. Someone who can do a messy job as cleanly as possible. For when it doesn't matter that everyone knows the target has been murdered. One shot and it's all over.

The next level up is the Accident Men. That's not a sexist description, just what the department has always been called. There are female Accident Men working there, just as there are female X-Men. It's their job, obviously, to make a death look like an accident. Think Princess Diana or, for more clumsy examples, any number of Putin opponents taking a long fall from a conveniently open window.

The top tier is where I work. We're the Shapeshifters. Called so because we become our target. Think like them, feel like them, live like them. Inhabit them. All the better to find the most plausible way of killing them. It never looks like an accident. Always natural causes. It's never a quick kill; it can take months of preparation and the execution – in every sense – has to be airtight. The targets are always top tier. So we have to be. To establish yourself as a Shapeshifter is, to put it mildly, very difficult indeed. To continue as one, successfully over the years, without getting clumsy or burning out or going insane, is a rarefied skill. There aren't many of us able to operate at this level for any great length of time. That's why our skills are so highly sought after. (3)

And why the conversation with my handler set off so many alarm bells.

I don't have to wait long before my next assignment arrives. (4)

The package arrives while I'm out walking following a swimming session. Julia was out doing whatever it is she occupies her days with, and the package was waiting on my return. It's been placed on the kitchen table so I can't miss it when I come in. This is the usual way – I assume the courier has a key. It's too important to be left to the vicissitudes of the postal system or an independent carrier and a paid external courier might be tempted to look at what's inside. So a trusted internal courier is always used. They, I assume, have never seen me. I've never seen them. Or at least I'm not aware of their identity.

It's a large bulky padded envelope. The kind you'd expect if you ordered an oversized art book. I open it. A document folder. With one word printed on the front:

Prizrak.

I sit down. This, as they say, is the big one.

Prizrak is Russian for ghost. Or spectre. Or spook. Whatever. And there's a very obvious reason for that. No one has ever seen a ghost. And no one's ever seen him. Or, if they have, they haven't been aware of it. Or lived to tell the tale. He (we assume they're a he, as that's about as much intelligence as any agency has managed to gather) has been behind some of the greatest terrorist atrocities of the last thirty years.

The file in front of me is extensive as I knew it would be. It details everything we know about the Ghost and every atrocity the Ghost is supposed to have been behind. It'll take me quite a while to read it. There's a lot. It's in three sections: Known, Suspected and Supposed. A truly international terrorist. If he's my next target there must have been some breakthrough chatter, some new intel received on him that I can utilise. Terminally. They wouldn't send me after him unless they had something concrete.

I make myself a pot of coffee – a large pot of coffee – and sit down to read.

No one's ever seen Prizrak. Not that they know of. Most terrorists and terrorist organisations clamour to claim responsibility for acts they have done and even those they haven't. They're very media-savvy in that way; they know that spreading terror isn't just about the act itself, it's the perception, the fear, that they might strike at any time. That they walk among us, unknown, and could be anyone. Their leaders pride themselves on becoming the West's latest feared bogeyman. Prizrak doesn't go in for any of that. He's much quieter, more subtle. The general, news-watching public are, a few, poorly researched investigative think pieces aside, unaware of him. But he exists.

He's the power behind whichever loudmouthed, self-proclaimed throne he's working for at the time. Most terrorist organisations are crudely run affairs. They exploit the passion of willing idiots prepared to die for a cause. And, once indoctrinated, there is no shortage of them. What they don't have is expertise and resources to see them through long term. That's where Prizrak comes in. You go to him when you've found the money and you've got a plan. He works for the highest bidder whether that be a rogue state, an organisation, a cartel, a corporation or an individual. Which side doesn't matter as he's always on the same side – his own. He has no ideology, no religion. No moral or political persuasions. That's for lesser people. He would just as happily work for ISIS as for, say, Greenpeace, if they decided to embark on a more radical approach. As a Shapeshifter I know I'm good at what I do. But Prizrak is on another level. He can provide any organisation – or individual – with anything they need for a plot to succeed. For a price. A very large price.

Some of his greatest hits from the last few years that fall under the 'Known' section of the dossier: the ricin attack on the Tokyo underground. Obviously he didn't claim responsibility, but we know it couldn't have been achieved without him. Bombed trains in Spain and Italy. Again, Prizrak. A consultancy role to the IRA in the Nineties leading to the mortar attack on Downing Street and the insurance company bomb blast in the City in 1992. And the biggie, of course: 9/11. Indirectly, of course. He helped establish and run the Al-Qaeda training camps in Pakistan and Afghanistan that played such a major role. And again, far too modest to take the applause.

He's the most major of major players. And he's my next target.

The kind of assignment that can provide the capstone to a successful career.

Or the tombstone.

9 – Notes

1. There's that phrase again. I like to think I used it first.

2. This section deals with Garrick pitting himself against the others (and as they think, betters) on his training course and coming out top. Again, it could well be an allegory for Jon's rise as a novelist against the Oxbridge-educated, entitled masses that thought all they had to do was sit down at a keyboard and whatever came out would be a critically acclaimed, award-winning bestseller. Public school teaches them to expect that. Experience, once they've left education, shows them that's how the world (their world) works. But Jon/Garrick was determined. He turned his underdog status into a virtue, working twice as hard – if not more – to prove himself better than them. He didn't just play their game, he reinvented it. I guess a remembrance of mine demonstrates that point. I was round at his house one day. We were sitting out in the back garden so it must have been summer and no doubt we were on our way to some launch event that night. He was smoking (Gwen wouldn't allow him to do that in the house) and we were both nursing coffees. I happened to glance over at his shed, saw something slumped against the glass window. I did a double take.

    'Fuck's that?'

    He turned to look, saw what I was seeing. A look of embarrassment crossed his face. 'Erm ... golf clubs?'

his voice went up at the end of the sentence, as if he was as surprised as me to find them there.

'Yours?'

'Er ... yeah. Mine. Yeah.'

'But you don't play golf. You hate golf. The last refuge of the wanker, a good walk spoiled, and all that. You used to point and laugh at golfers. We both did. Rightly so. What you got golf clubs for?'

'Well ...' He shrugged, uneasy. Scratched the back of his neck, another sign of nerves. I got asked to play by [REDACTED]. You know [REDACTED]?'

'Know of him, obviously. Never met him. The head of [REDACTED]?' I named one of the biggest publishing groups in the UK, if not Europe.

'Yeah, that's him. Well, I met him one night at some do and he lives nearby. Asked me out to play a round, get together.'

Even though I hated golf I could feel the jealousy rising inside me. 'And you went?'

'Yeah. Been a couple of times now. Good fun. Good guy. I mean golf's shit, obviously,' he said, not very convincingly, 'But [REDACTED] is good company and you never know. I might need to move publishers one day. Nice to have a foot in the door.'

I said nothing, just nodded. But in that moment, I realised that no matter how close Jon and I were, there was part of him he wouldn't share with me. The ambitious part. Up until that point I think I'd been kidding myself that because I was friends with more successful writers that it was only a matter of time before I stepped up and joined them. But when he behaved so sheepishly about [REDACTED], I knew it was never going to happen. At least not unless I made it happen myself.

Like Jon was doing. He was quietly ruthless. And he hid that ruthlessness from me. But that moment made me realise how ambitious he was, ready to do anything, betray everyone to get where he wanted to be. And it wasn't just from seeing a set of golf clubs. It was Jon's reaction to them.

We went out that night, to the party. But I didn't play the fool. I was quite serious, standoffish. And I left early, sober. I knew what I had to do now. In order to be successful. To get somewhere. To actually be one of *those* writers, not just hang around with them. Oh yes.

And it didn't involve playing fucking golf.

3. The three tiers of the industry. Again, he isn't just talking about assassins here, he's talking about writers. In the film *American Fiction*, the analogy of whisky is used. Cheap whisky, middle grade whisky, top tier 'mucho expensivo' whisky. All made by the same manufacturer but aimed at different audiences. That's publishing. You've got your commercial fiction. The bestsellers. The literary equivalent of cheap whisky. Undiscerningly made and appealing to the widest market. Picked up in airports, flicked through on a sun lounger and, if they actually make it back home, destined for the charity shop. And like cheap whisky, they sell very well. Then there's the middle tier. Middle brow. A cut above in terms of quality, but not necessarily sales. The decent, well-crafted novels. This is where I've spent most of my career, if I'm honest. No shame in it, but it doesn't have the literary cache, the glamour. A good, decent range whisky. Which leaves the top tier. Where Jon was (is?). That rarified level where the writing is considered so good it illuminates the human

condition just by existing. Think Hemingway, or James Baldwin. Or before that, Shakespeare. Massively expensive whisky. Just taste it, sip it, don't gulp it. Savour it. Feel it go down smoothly. That's the good stuff, all right.

Publishers have their prestige authors, the top tier, that get column inches and fawning reviews. Publishing houses scramble to get these because of the cache, the reflected star quality it gives them. And the media play along because they've got papers to sell (if there are any left by the time you read this), clicks to be clicked, legends to be created. And booksellers play along too, dividing everything up into literary and genre.

But here's the thing: it's all bollocks. There are only really two kinds of writing. Good and bad. And those two types range across all three tiers. And you don't need to be told by a publisher or the media or a bookseller when you've got a good one, you'll know when you read it. And – whisper it – that's all readers really care about. And *they* know, the industry people, but admitting it would bring their whole cosy house of cards down.

But Jon, of course, in this narrative, just as in his real life, has to consider himself to be in the top tier. He wouldn't bother to play golf otherwise.

4. Couple of things here. Firstly, Prizrak. The Ghost. Who is this character meant to be? An actual person? The publishing head Jon was attempting to cosy up to? Or someone – or something – a little more insubstantial, metaphysical, even? A career pinnacle impossible to reach because it doesn't actually exist? I'll keep reading. And secondly, the assignment. Here we go. This

is where the novel starts to pick up. The hero has his assignment. To shadow a man who's never been seen. To ghost a ghost.

And, as I said earlier, at this time in our relationship, I had given myself an assignment. Jon wasn't going to like it, but I didn't care. It was *my* turn to drink the expensive whisky now.

10

I couldn't leave without letting Julia know.

I waited until she returned, packed and ready to go. As she walked in, she noticed the bags beside the front door. If she was startled by this, she didn't let it show.

'You off?' she said.

'The call came though,' I reply, getting up off the sofa. 'They want me back in the field.'

She nods. 'How long will you be gone?'

'You know I can't answer that.'

Another nod from her, slight this time, confirming something to herself. She glances towards the bedroom. 'Have we time for ...?'

'Afraid not. They want me gone straight away.'

She almost smiles. Whether from relief or disappointment, I can't tell.

I feel like I should say something, bridge the gap that's larger than the physical space between us. 'Will you be ... all right when I'm gone?'

She can't hide the surprise at my words. Have I not asked her this before? She's behaving as if I haven't.

'I'll be fine. I'm always fine.'

'Good. Good.'

We stand there, both looking at each other across the space of the living room, neither moving one way or the other. I cross to the front door.

'I'll be off, then.'

Before I can pick up my bags, I feel her hand on my arm. I turn, stop, surprised. I look at her. Her expression has changed, as if she's too tired to keep her guard up. Her eyes soften and she opens her mouth, starts to speak.

Then stops herself.

Her guard is back up, her eyes have deadened once more. She removes her hand, pats me as she does so.

'Be safe,' she says, then turns away, off into the kitchen.

Feeling as if I've been dismissed and knowing better than to engage her further, I pick up my bags and let myself out.

'Bonjour Monsieur Nolan. Very pleased to see you again. Back so soon?'

'Believe me, no one's more surprised than I am.'

Unusually for me I was in quite a state of inner turmoil on the plane. Whatever Julia had left unspoken was playing on my mind. That, and the sudden change in her expression, no matter how quickly, that spark, that connection, unlocked something in me that I thought had been lost long ago. I was going away without my head fully focused on what was to come. I never do that. I had to get myself reorientated quickly.

I opened the travel documents waiting for me at the airport and when I saw the name of where I was staying on the travel manifest my heart skipped a beat. *They know*, I thought. *They know.* I checked the name on the passport too: Nolan. This was too much. Warning signs were clanging inside my head. Turn back now.

But the professional in me took precedence. There must be a reason for this. I just, on top of everything else, had to find out what it was.

My destination hotel in Marrakesh that the company was sending me to is the place I always return to whenever I've completed an assignment. Where I go to decompress, shed the skin of the previous few months, reorientate myself, regain my identity. Its location isn't secret, it's a hotel complex. I've always prided myself on keeping my presence there secret, though. But just because no one at the company has ever mentioned it doesn't mean they're not aware of it. I should have expected that. But this is the worst way to discover that fact. (1)

And the name on my travel manifest: Nolan. That's the name I use when I always check in here, the name the hotel knows me by. They've gone with that too. A passport, cards and documents in that name. Even the photo, aged, looks like the one I use in my own Nolan passport. Usually my identity is just a formality, a name assigned at random, I've always been told, without any particular care or forethought. But not this time it seems.

I doubt it's a coincidence because coincidences don't exist in my trade. So why have they chosen to send me here? And why for this job? My first thought: if I saw the destination and the name I would refuse to go, thus giving them an excuse to fire me for whatever reason they think credible. Did they expect me to see those details, panic and disappear off into the sunset using one of my other identities? Again, that could be something the pointy heads suggested to try and get rid of me.

After giving it more thought I came upon another option. One they must have been sure I'd consider. If it's not the company's way of letting me know I can't keep secrets from them then it must involve Prizrak. If he's staying at the same hotel then that's where I should also be. It's a possibility. And if that's the case, then obviously I should use the Nolan identity since that's the name I'm known under at the hotel. Whatever the truth of the situation is, I know to proceed warily. Hopefully the contact I have to meet in Marrakesh this evening can shed more light on it.

I admit, the hotel does fit the profile of the kind of place Prizrak would stay at. It's expensive and exclusive. It's situated just outside Marrakesh, in an area known as The Palm Grove where cinderblock shanty homes rub up against official government residencies, where exhausted and aggressive camels wait at the side of the road to reluctantly give tourists rides through nearby palm trees and rubbly desert. The Atlas Mountains can be glimpsed in the distance, their snow-covered peaks at odds with the stifling dry heat all around.

As for the hotel itself, well, if The Village from the TV series *The Prisoner* had been in Northern Africa not Portmeirion in Wales, it would look something like this. (2) It's some kind of literal oasis on the fringes of the desert with a vast expanse of Andalusian style gardens, including fully grown, overhanging trees and lush green grass plus its own organic kitchen garden. The daily irrigation bill alone must be stratospheric. Not that you would know because the place has an ambience of discreetly monied luxury; a calm, swan-like surface of nothing is too much trouble, we're-here-for-your-every-need smiling staff.

The architecture is authentic Moorish, going back centuries and clearly once having been something else, now sympathetically repositioned as a complex of landscaped gardens, outdoor restaurants and drinking verandas, a swimming pool and lounging area, an open-air barbershop, indoor restaurants, not to mention the four-poster beds dotted around for people to lie in all day and get the sun, and the hammam with every kind of local spa treatment. Accommodation consists of rooms, luxury suites, apartments and riads, some with their own pools. All discreetly private, all safely within a walled enclosure. It's one of the attractions of the place and presumably so for Prizrak too.

The main building houses the bars and restaurants, along

with terraces and verandas where many an evening could be whiled away taking in the hotel complex's old-world charm, looking out over the gardens, watching the peacocks strut while drinking a perfectly prepared Manhattan. You could imagine you're about to join Howard Carter's expedition to the pyramids the next morning.

I wait in the small courtyard, watching the turtles sunbathe by the fountains, drinking sweet mint tea under overhanging palms and eating complimentary fancies while my luggage is taken to my suite. My expression doesn't show it but, like the swan-like service at this hotel, underneath I'm racing.

If I had been presented with my travel documents earlier than the airport, I would have questioned my handler. The trouble with that approach, though, is that it's difficult not to come across as petulant. I would be tipping my hand about my secret identity and knowledge of the hotel. She would either have to admit she knew and had known all the time about it, or meet me with amused obfuscation or just plain stonewalling, so I shall be patient instead. Wait to see how events unfold and adapt my approach accordingly. That's what I usually do on assignment.

In my room I change clothes. I always travel Economy and dress like a typical tourist. I never say or do anything that could attract attention to myself. I make myself as inconspicuous as possible. Now I change into something a little more expensive, something that a guest at this hotel would wear. I change watches, check the time. Take a deep breath. Another.

Go.

10 – Notes

1. This makes me smile. The hotel he describes here is one that Jon and Gwen went to and Jon, impressed with it, described to me in great detail on his return. In fact, they loved it so much they went back repeatedly. Got on to first name terms with the staff and owners by the end. Big deal, you might say. Well of course. It's not in the slightest bit unusual for a writer to use somewhere they've been. Everyone does it. If we didn't, we'd have nothing to write about it. The only difference with this place is that Jon once said to me: 'I love that place so much. I've got to find a book to put it in. Not just because it's so great, but because we go there a lot, as you know. So much so that I've got to find a way to make it tax deductible. That'll do it.' Well, it took him long enough, but he finally managed it.

    Also, the section at reception may serve a dual purpose. As it stands, it plants a seed of doubt as to whether his handlers know about his secret identity and, by extension, want him to know that they know. Fine. Good narrative writing for this kind of book. But is he also letting us know that this is the place he's known at? Is he, in fact staying there, or near there, since his disappearance? Under an assumed name, perhaps? I can answer that. No. Or if he did, he hid it very well. I wasn't the only person who knew about his love for this particular hotel. When he disappeared, this was one of the first places the publishers and tabloids sent their private detectives and reporters. And, despite extensive questioning and the running up of huge expense accounts, there was no trace of him there. So why is this particular place in the narrative? Is it because it's been so conscientiously searched? Another wry joke at the reader's expense? Or is it just the right location for this section of the story? And, if he's still paying tax wherever he is, is he getting a deduction for doing so.

2. The TV series, *The Prisoner* (1967–8). One for the kiddies, there. *The Prisoner* concerned a secret agent who wants to resign but his bosses decide what's in his head is too precious and cart him off to an apparently idyllic place called The Village. He soon realises that, despite being surrounded by luxury and wanting for nothing, he can't leave and the Village is a prison where they perform psychological experiments on him to find out the real reason he wanted to resign.

Again, in making a comparison to The Village, right after hinting his handlers know more about him that they've previously let on, is he making a bigger statement? One that might lead us to him in some way?

11

My driver takes me into Marrakesh old town, the drive being an education in itself. Car lanes are at best a vague indication, at worst a hindrance. Taxis the colour of sand mixed with baby diarrhoea and made of seemingly perma-crumpled metal weave through the near gridlock, making their own paths. Mopeds buzz about like blood stealing insects, their drivers rarely solo, often carrying a passenger, sometimes a relative and children, all balanced on the back like a family of circus acrobats. Occasionally, the family is replaced by goods. One moped we pass has what appears to be the whole contents of a soft furnishing warehouse piled high. I admire that kind of enterprise. Making the best use of what you've got. My whole career's been based around that.

As my driver makes a fourth lane for himself to turn left at a notional junction, I wonder what a car chase would look like in Marrakesh. I decide it wouldn't make much difference. They drive here with a casual aggression and abandon that makes drivers in Rome seem polite and stately, a courtly gavotte from a Jane Austen novel.

I'm heading towards the market square, where I'm to meet my contact at a nearby tourist restaurant. The driver drops me off at the opposite side and I walk the rest of the way. I've been here before several times, and it doesn't seem to have changed much. Tourists mill around the place at most times of the day or night. And spread out on the ground before I reach the souk itself are traders with cheap metal lamps, attempting to pass them off as authentic but bought in bulk from Taiwan. Juice and food stalls proliferate, everything from orange and strawberry drinks alongside food stalls that amount to a serial killer's guide to not wasting any part of a dead animal. Unidentifiable innards sit in greasy, bubbling pots alongside more recognisable meat and whole sheep heads, their dead eyes staring out, waiting to be eaten. Merchants laden down with cheap tat follow tourists, repeating their siren cackle, clinging to them like an unshiftable bout of flu.

It's hot and dry and uncomfortable, the air filled with grit from the city, dust from the desert and fumes from the revving cars forcing their way through and the proliferation of wasp-like scooters weaving in and out of strollers and workers, tottering with goods or people. As I near the warren-like souk itself I notice the casual animal cruelty this part of the world is so famous for. Robed and gap-toothed old men sit cross-legged before old straw baskets, attempting to charm ancient, defanged and drugged cobras out with carved wind instruments. Elsewhere captive monkeys, chained and held, are thrust onto startled passing tourists for photo opportunities. The monkeys look depressed beyond breaking point. Nearby stalls display massive multi-coloured pyramids of local spices, their owners waiting for tourists to photograph them before jumping out and forcing a sale. Beyond all this activity the Medina starts in earnest.

Some of the architecture in this maze is old, ancient, in fact. And beautiful. Exquisite brick and plaster work, minarets and gorgeously carved old wooden doors. Exactly as you would expect from Marrakesh. However, some of it isn't. After my first trip round the market, on my return to the hotel the receptionist asked if I'd got lost. I told her I hadn't, but that wasn't true. Even though I pride myself with an excellent sense of direction, I was hopelessly lost within a few lanes. The lanes themselves are about the width of a single bed, with pedestrian traffic going both ways plus mopeds and hand carts coming and going. It's easy to lose one's bearings, especially since the shops seem to proliferate, cave-like, covered and filled with their wares. Carpets, kelims and rugs take up every available space, pottery bowls and plates, lighting, leather goods, jewellery. Outside of each stall a merchant sizes up the travellers, decides immediately which nationality they are and greets them accordingly, enticing them into the shop. They may be plied with tea, conversation and offers of eternal friendship as inducements to buy. It's a calculated show, theatre in itself. And it has a high hit rate; they wouldn't do it if it didn't work. That's the front of house guy. There's usually an older guy at the back, lacking any of the forced bonhomie, clearly hating the tourists and having as little to do with them as possible but balancing that with the fact he has to make a living. He's the one who brings items out from the storeroom at the back letting the showman display them properly.

I'm not intending to go deep into the lanes on this trip, but I think I know a short cut to the restaurant I'm heading to, so I make my way into the medina. (1)

The further I walk into the medina the fewer tourists I see, which is unusual and makes me think I've taken a wrong turn. The stalls give way to restaurants and bars. Hotels and riads spring up, alongside hammams offering traditional spa treatments. And apartments and houses where people live. Yes, I've definitely taken a wrong turn. (2)

I cut through the alleyways, following the map in my mind yet feeling increasingly lost as I do so, heading towards the restaurant where I'm to meet my contact. If I've memorised the route correctly then it should be on the other side of this labyrinth of alleys which should open out on to a square. All the while I'm walking, I can't shake the feeling I'm being followed. Or at least watched.

My paranoia is always high in new surroundings, usually with good reason. And my fears are usually more substantial than just paranoia. I've learned to trust my instincts. I shall do so now.

The claustrophobic lanes feel like they're closing in on me. Tiny windows above and to the sides of where I'm walking could harbour anyone, even snipers. This would be the perfect place to get rid of me if someone wanted to.

I move quickly, glancing about as I do so.

There are no tourists here. The silence in this lane is so dense it seems hard to imagine that all of that noise is taking place only a few streets away. I pass a coffee bar, strictly for locals. It has nothing of the flamboyance of the earlier places I saw. Strictly functional. The few men inside look up as I pass, clearly unhappy at my presence. I hurry along.

I hear something behind me. A noise, distant, but getting louder. I turn.

A scooter like the kind I saw earlier is coming towards me, the rider's face obscured by a keffiyeh tied around their head. They've seen me but they're not slowing down. If anything, they're speeding up.

I look round. There's very little space for me to manoeuvre. I could run but the scooter is faster than me. It'll easily catch me.

It's getting nearer.

I look up. Nothing I can reach for, to jump away from it. I look to the sides. A huge old doorway on my left with an enormous wooden carved door in it. Slightly recessed from the main lane. That'll have to do.

I flatten myself against the door, hoping I'm not protruding too much, making myself too much of a target.

The wasp-like whine of the scooter gets louder.

I stare at it as it approaches. It's on me.

And it's gone, right past me, the rider giving a jeering laugh as the drone subsides into dusty silence.

The men in the coffee bar have witnessed all this, the foreign tourist scared of a scooter. Hiding from it. It's given them something to laugh about for the rest of the day.

I ignore them, walk off to meet my contact.

Once my heart rate has returned to normal, I realise I still feel like I'm being watched.

11 – Notes

1. These pages here read like the Jon of old. Evocative, muscular, colourful, immersive writing. *Proper* writing, we used to say, only half-jokingly. I think it's the first time his old style of writing, the kind that makes me think without a doubt that this novel is written by him, has appeared in the narrative. Remember what I said previously about the three tiers of writing? Well so far, I'd say this novel has been in the middle band. Not trash but not art. But this section here reads like high prose. Top tier. Perhaps self-consciously so, deliberately so. To show that, yep, the old guy still has it when he needs it. And that's the other thing about this kind of writing. Some novels are composed entirely of sections like this. Top tier novels. But this is a spy novel (or whatever) and consequently needs to be more propulsive. Middle tier are always better plotted. High, rich prose like this and propulsive writing aren't mutually exclusive, but they need to be used accordingly. As the situation in the narrative demands it. And that's what he's doing here. Remembering what kind of book this is. But also remembering what kind of writer he once was.

2. The rest of the chapter reverts to a middle-tier type of narrative. But evocative: being watched, feeling excluded. Paranoia. It is, as I said previously, knowing when to use the right kind of writing for the right effect.

THE FINAL CHAPTER

It's at about this time in our relationship that a wedge began to lodge between us. Not a particularly wide or deep one, but a wedge, nonetheless. Possibly of my own doing, it may be said, but I prefer to think of it as Jon's response to me getting a bit of success. Maybe, in hindsight, it was a one-sided relationship and I'd just been deluding myself otherwise. Maybe.

Here's what happened: I approached Jon's agent. Asked for representation. After all, she'd done wonderful things for him. Why not for me? Admittedly, some of my sales figures read like sub-Arctic temperatures, but it had nothing to do with the *quality* of the writing, only the *perception* of it. Jon was seen as a great novelist, I wasn't. Although taken on a blind test, my writing was just as good as his. If not better. It's just that when you're programmed to think something, when you're told something enough times to believe in it, especially by the media tastemakers, you do. Because you want to be part of that crowd. You don't want to be outside it, uncool, unhip. Even if you don't like it, you wouldn't dare to speak up and say so. That way lies ostracism.

Me, I had no particular cache like Jon, so it didn't matter. But I was looking at my work objectively now I wasn't married any more and had no one to consider except myself. And I found it ... pretty good, actually. Deserving of a wider audience, certainly. Hence the approach to Jon's agent.

We met for lunch. Rather like the earlier scene in the British Library. I may even have been dressed somewhat similarly to how Garrick is described there, funnily enough. Which, again, makes me think he's doing this deliberately. Toying with my memories. We chatted. I told her, quite openly and frankly, that I was sick of lesser talents coming up around me, getting further than me because they were better connected or had the right kind of profile. Especially sick when they were nowhere near as good as me. She listened. Nodded. All this was off the record, of course, but stored away for when she needed it. Literary agents are like spies themselves. They trade in information. It's their currency. Deploy it strategically when needed. Never give it away for free. Only when they get some kind of quid pro quo for it. So I knew this would go no further, even if she didn't take me on. I knew that it wouldn't get back to Jon, no matter how much money she made from him.

After I'd finished saying my piece she sat back, appraising me. And spoke.

'I think I might have a place for you on my list,' she said.

I felt my heart literally skip a beat. Just like they do in books. This was it. I was in. Next level. My career was about to take off.

'But,' she said.

And that brought me crashing back down.

'But what?' I said, trying hard to keep my voice under control.

'I'll be honest with you. I think you're a great writer. Really, I do. And yes, I agree with you, you haven't had the success that someone like Jon has had. I mean, let's be honest, hardly anyone has. But still. I do think your books and his are very similar. Possibly too similar.'

My heart, previously skipping, was sinking.

'But here's the thing. There's one thing that you're better at than Jon. Much better, in fact.'

'Go on.'

'You can plot. You know how to tell a story. How to rattle through a story, in fact, bringing the reader along with you.'

'Erm, thank you.'

'So that's why I want to make you a proposition.'

I listened. Said nothing.

'I've been talking to [REDACTED] from [REDACTED] just this morning and he's looking for a new thriller writer. Fast paced, but involving characters. Well-written. As you know, I already handle some crime writers but they're at the high end of the market. The literary end. [REDACTED] wants someone who can tell a story. Would you be interested?'

I thought before answering. So this was it. Even my attempt to emulate Jon's success – without playing fucking golf – came with strings attached. It seemed that I couldn't get anywhere on my own merit, that I just wasn't good enough to ... Well, that was it. I just wasn't good enough. A second rater. A perpetual second rater.

'Of course, because of your track record,' she said, '[REDACTED] would want you to write under a pseudonym.'

And there it was. Would you like to be a successful writer, but write crap? And not even under your own name? I thought again of Kenneth Williams, who I mentioned in earlier notes. Too good for the rubbish he appeared in, not good enough for the stuff he wanted to do. That's me. The literary Kenneth Williams.

'So what d'you think? Are you up for it?'

'Yeah,' I said. 'Course I am.'

And that's how I became a famous writer. Even if it wasn't my name on the cover.

12

'You are from England?' The enthusiastic young waiter smiled as if he had made a lifelong friend. 'I love your country. My cousin lives in Birmingham. King's Heath. Great place. Loverly jubberly!' (1)

I smile in return, nodded, expecting the next question to be whether I knew his cousin.

I'm sitting on the open-air terrace at the top of a restaurant looking out on the square by the Medina. Opposite are apartments and hotels, another similar restaurant doing local cuisine and a Chinese restaurant which I couldn't imagine did much business. All original old Moroccan architecture.

'Where do you live in England?'

'London,' I replied, not thinking it could do any harm.

His eyes widened, as if I'd said some mythical realm. 'I would love to visit there one day. It's a spectacular city. So welcoming.'

I just smiled, not wanting to disabuse him of that notion.

The terrace was doing brisk business. Far enough up from the people below but open enough to still catch the excitement that so many industrious bodies in such a contained space brought. The chairs and tables were all authentically Moroccan, carved wood and colourful tiles, but then I would have expected nothing less in a restaurant catering primarily to tourists.

'Is this seat taken? I don't mind sharing.'

I looked up. That was the correct greeting. I now had to give the correct response.

'Not at all. Glad of the company.'

'Thank you.'

The waiter looked slightly put out as the newcomer sat down opposite me. His new lifelong friend already had a friend. And he was a local.

The newcomer addressed the waiter. 'Gin and tonic. And you?' The question was to me.

'Same.'

The waiter went off, somewhat deflated, to get our drinks. I looked at the newcomer.

'Mister Nolan,' he said. 'I'm Kharis.' (2)

He was middle aged, trim and muscled, wearing what looked like a simple but expensive designer T-shirt, jeans and trainers. He hooked his sunglasses on the neck of his T-shirt. He took me in as I did him.

'The company sent you.'

'Indeed.' He smiled. 'I guess I'm here as the local colour.' He spoke with a slight American inflection. Local, but well-travelled. Educated abroad.

We said nothing until the waiter returned with our drinks, asked us if we were ready to order. We told him another few minutes. Once he had gone, we began talking in earnest.

'So, what can you tell me?' I ask.

Kharis looks round, checking no one was in earshot. I had already checked the other diners for anyone or anything suspicious. Found nothing. He leans in close, elbows on the table, making it look to an observer as if he's about to share a confidence. When he speaks he casually covers his mouth with his hand to foil any lipreaders. A professional.

'So. Your target. Prizrak, right?'

I nod, leaning forward myself, surreptitiously covering my own mouth with my hand. 'What can you tell me?'

'You're staying in the right place. Prizrak and his entourage are due there tomorrow.'

'How do you know?'

He smiles. 'It's my job, Mister Nolan. Intel. I'm surprised you asked. Why did you ask? D'you doubt me?'

'No,' I say, 'it's just there's been a few things about this job that have felt off, that's all.'

He looks concerned. 'How so?'

I pause. Is this person I've just met asking me to confide in him? Should I? Of course not. And I'm sure he wouldn't do the same to me. 'Just a few things. Probably just me being overly sensitive.' I attempt a smile. 'Our line of business will do that to you.'

He returns my smile. 'Indeed it will.'

'So how will I spot Prizrak? Any idea what he looks like? What should I look out for?'

'No idea. The chatter says he will definitely be there, though. As soon as I heard I contacted the company and here you are. Already a guest. Good.'

I say nothing. So far, it all sounds like a coincidence. Which I don't believe in, of course, but which, if this is the truth, I might have to. However, I know the truth is a rare commodity in my line of work.

'Do you know what to do when you meet him?' asks Kharis.

'My job,' I say.

Another smile from him. 'Good. I'll be your contact on the outside. Your liaison with the company. You're to report to me when you can. I have devised a method of doing so. There is a shop in the Medina. Once we have finished here, I will walk you to it. We shall communicate there. The owner is a friend of mine. He often does me favours.'

THE FINAL CHAPTER

'Can he be trusted?'

Kharis shrugs. 'For a price.' The jovial exterior drops. Something much harder, steelier appears behind Kharis's eyes. 'Plus he knows what will happen to him if he betrays me.'

'Fair enough.'

The twinkling smile returns. 'We will work out a relay system of messages through the shop.'

The waiter returns and we give our food orders. With business talk temporarily concluded, a silence falls between us that. If this was any normal encounter between two new workmates, we would now be filling the silence with small talk, getting to know each other better. Especially if we were to be working together. That's not something I do. I don't care about their family or their background. All I need to know is that I can rely on them for when I need them. But Kharis seems to want to talk. So I let him.

'Have you worked in Marrakesh before?'

'I'm familiar with it,' I reply. 'I've not worked here before, though.'

Another smile from him. 'I'm sure I would have heard about it if you had.'

'Not if I did my job properly.'

He laughed at that.

'Is that an American accent?' I ask. Not because I want his life story, just to know if there's any conflict with whom I'm working for.

'More or less,' he says. 'You know what this life can be like. We get around. I've spent a lot of time there. You pick up all their habits. I guess that's cultural imperialism for you.'

I actually smile at that.

The food arrives and we eat. Two tagines, of course. Once we're finished Kharis drains his glass, summons the waiter and pays. 'My expense account for this one.'

I don't argue. We stand up.

'And now I'll take you shopping,' he says.

We walk the same alleyways I'd walked earlier, but this time with a sense of purpose and direction. I mentally marked my route so I would know how to find it quickly and easily when the time came. We stopped in front of a shop filled with lighting. It was dazzling; every spare centimetre of space was filled with standing lights, hanging lights, wall lights. All blazing. The proprietor nods to Kharis as we enter.

'We'll be easily spotted in here,' I said.

'Shows what you know,' he says. 'Come on.'

He walks me through to the back of the shop and immediately it's much darker. I can't see the front, the Medina, for the lights. And for the same reason no one can see us back here. The light reflects outwards towards the front of the shop leaving the back in darkness like we're in some deep cave.

'Perfect,' Kharis says.

I have to agree he's right.

'We'll arrange a time to meet, say ... Tuesday afternoon? Two?'

'Fine,' I say.

'And you can give me updates. And, of course, if there is anything I can help you with just let me know.'

'I usually work alone. No back up.'

He shrugs. 'This time you've got me. I'm a resource. Use me.'

I nod. Check my watch.

'I'd better be getting back. I've got a target to acquire.'

He smiles. 'We're all set.'

I say nothing. Just try and keep those niggling thoughts at the back of my mind tamped down.

12 – Notes

1. Loverly jubberly. This might need some explaining for non-UK readers of a certain age. It was one of the many catchphrases of a much beloved TV sitcom character called Del Boy Trotter, played by David Jason. Del Boy, along with his younger brother Rodney, were market traders in South London and the series revolved around them trying to strike it rich. Del Boy had big dreams and small pockets but this working-class chancer, half wide boy, half naive dreamer, his mangled malapropisms and failed get-rich-quick schemes captured the public's imagination and the series, called *Only Fools and Horses*, ran between 1981 and 2003.

   It has an added resonance between Jon and me because of something that happened to us in San Francisco. We were over there attending a literary festival and, on our day off, decided to play tourists and visit Alcatraz. We got the boat over there and queued up for admittance. As we were being given our audio guides for the walking tour, the guy giving them to us asked where we were from. Now I should say, this guy didn't look like a typical tourist worker. He looked more like one of the inmates. Stocky, muscled, scowling. Slicked back black hair, a few scars on his face, bursting out of his uniform. Samoan American, we'd heard him tell someone else.

   'So where you from?' he asked us.
   'London,' said Jon, his voice strangely quiet.
   'England,' I added.

Hearing our words, his face split open. It was someone taking a machete to a melon. 'Loverly jubberly!' he said, laughing. His voice sounded like he had been gargling nails. 'Del Boy, yes?' he said, following with 'Rodney, you plonker!', another of the show's catchphrases. Still, it broke the ice and we both laughed at the incongruity of it. Here in Alcatraz was a gangster-looking guy quoting an old British sitcom in what he thought was a good Cockney accent. We never forgot the encounter with that Samoan American and the way he pronounced that phrase. We would use it to each other like a private joke. It never failed to make us smile, even if Gwen would just roll her eyes whenever she heard us using it.

The use of it in here makes me suspect, not for the first time during this narrative, that Jon's written this book with me in mind. There are things I know about, confidences that only he and I shared, stories that would be meaningless to anyone else, peppering this book. As I said earlier, clues. But the more I read, the more I feel those clues are specifically meant for me. I'm meant to recognise them and interpret them. He's expecting me to use them to unlock memories, follow the trail, find him. Not anyone else, me. Specifically me.

2. And this is proof, if it were needed by this point, of what I've just being saying.

His contact is called Kharis. The name might mean nothing to you, but both Jon and I were fans of old horror films. And the name Kharis has real meaning. Kharis was the name of the titular Mummy in three Universal black and white films of the 1940s.

The Mummy's Hand, *The Mummy's Tomb* and *The Mummy's Ghost*. Not, as popularly thought, played by Boris Karloff but by Tom Tyler and Lon Chaney Jnr. Karloff played Imhotep in 1933's *The Mummy*, but not in bandages. When Hammer remade the Universal horrors in the 1950s Christopher Lee played the titular role in *The Mummy*, this time bandaged and called Kharis.

So what has this to do with a character in this novel? A Moroccan? As I said above, it looks very much to me that Jon is dropping clues and hints just for me. He would know by calling a character Kharis that I, and probably only I, would pick up on it. I would get the joke. Such as it is. For the purposes of this novel (middle-tier thriller, remember), a character with a notional Egyptian name in Morocco would work fine. After all, Egypt is just next to Morocco, isn't it? Yeah, near as makes no matter. Whatever. No one'll notice, couple of bus journeys and this novel's finished with. Spine bent, pages turned down and creased, on its way to the charity shop. Egyptian? Moroccan? Meh. Whatever. That'll do.

I hate that phrase, *That'll do*. Especially when writers use it. It implies that no real effort should be involved in creating a novel. The path of least resistance should always be taken. Don't put yourself out, don't put anything of yourself into it. If there's an easy way, use it. If it works, and *they* won't notice, stick it in. *That'll do*. Hate it. It implies that writers are lazy, that they don't respect their readers, that they can feed them any old shit and they'll lap it up uncritically. And maybe I was guilty of thinking that way about thrillers like this one and crime novels in general before I started writing one (under my non de plume). But writing one soon disabused me of that notion. It was just as hard as writing a *proper* novel, harder in fact because everything that I'd put into my previous work was needed for a crime novel. It wasn't a lesser thing, it was demanding more of me. Because I needed a compelling narrative and a good plot on top of that.

So that's why I think that this is another of Jon's little in-jokes. Calling this character Kharis when he could have done his research and chosen any name at all, is deliberate. It shows that yes, if I want to, I can think of this novel as a lesser work because it's a thriller. That's the joke. But the fact that he chose a name that means something to both him and me – and only him and me – lets me know he's telling me something.

It started off sitting at his house watching old films with a few beers. That's how we stumbled across the Mummy films. They weren't very good, to be honest, and we gave them the respect we thought they deserved. As in we tried to outdo each other making witty/nasty comments all the way through. Amusing ourselves at the film's expense. When they first called the mummy Kharis, Jon piped up, 'Cerys? That's Welsh, isn't it? A Welsh girl's name? Are they saying this mummy is from Wales, then?'

And on we went, riffing on that all through the next beer.

Which is how I know that Kharis is deliberate. He's drawing me into this, making me work, making me follow him. And I am doing. I am doing, Jon, mate. And I'll find you. It'll soon be time to put the pieces together, and I'll find you.

Thinking of the name Kharis reminds that this would be around the time Jon had a protégé. Her name was Kari and she was his ... what? Assistant? Nanny for their non-existent kids? Intern? I don't know. He just brought her along to dinner one night, introduced her to me.

'This is Kari,' he said.

She just smiled like she had every right to be there. I smiled back, gave her my name.

'Oh, I know who you are. Jon's told me all about you.'

'Oh, right. Well, he hasn't mentioned you.' I glanced between them. Was Jon about to tell me that he had ditched Gwen and this was his new girlfriend? His much younger girlfriend?

'Kari is my assistant. Or rather protégé. She's hugely talented. Going to replace both of us eventually.'

She laughed self-effacingly, but I could tell there was self-determination behind that laugh. She believed it even as she laughed about it.

I studied her. Small, good looking, dark-haired. Elfin-like, I suppose you'd say. Gamine. Not my type at all. And then another thought hit me: had he brought her along as a potential date for me?

'I gave a seminar at—' He named a prestigious university. 'And Kari was one of the students. One of the brightest and best,' he said, looking at her and smiling. She returned that smile. 'And when she asked if I needed an assistant and if I'd read her work, I knew we could do something together.'

Oh my god, I thought, are they fucking?

'That's ... great. And, er, what are you working on?'

'Well, it's not finished yet, but I've got Jon helping me, so I'm sure it'll be great.' She beamed up at him like he was a benevolent god and I wished I'd stayed at home.

We ordered, chatted, ate and drank. At one point Kari excused herself to visit the bathroom. I leaned across the table.

'What the fuck's going on, Jon? Who is she?'

'Exactly what she says she is. My protégé.'

'And are you fucking her?'

He widened his eyes in mock shock. 'However can you suggest such a thing?'

'Well, are you?'

He shrugged. And I knew that he was keeping something from me. It was probably the first time he had done that. Usually if he didn't want to tell me something he would anyway, eventually, after much wheedling. But not this time.

'What does Gwen say?'

He looked at his glass. 'She's fine about it. It was her idea, actually.'

'Really?'

'Yeah. Pass the benefit of my wisdom on to the next generation. Giving something back.' He laughed. And for the first time between us, it was like hearing a joke that I wasn't in on.

She returned to the table and the meal continued. Afterwards, I declined their offer of going for a drink, thinking that the pair of them wanted to spend some time alone.

I went back to my flat. Disappointed. I had been going to tell Jon about signing with his agent, about writing thrillers under a pseudonym, all of that. And then we'd have laughed and got drunk and spent the evening riffing on all that. But that wasn't the way it had turned out. I thought of the way Jon had been looking at Kari. At first I thought it was pride in his protégé. But it wasn't. It was something altogether more creepy. Predatory. Like an old Seventies rock star salivating over a (too) young groupie. You can be in your forties and still be considered a young novelist in this country. But he was getting older, Jon. We both were. And seeing him with that much younger woman emphasised that.

And something else he said to her during the course of the evening, something that I didn't really think about at the time and had forgotten about really, until I just read it in the previous chapter. Kharis says, 'I'm a resource. Use me.' Jon used the same phrase to Kari during dinner.

And the way she looked at him. Adoringly ...

Someone was going to get hurt. Really hurt.

13

Back at the hotel I check out my suite in more detail. A large double bed. An ornate, functional fireplace on one wall and a set of old double doors of shuttered glass opening out to a private courtyard with two recliners and small swimming pool – for days when I'm feeling unsociable. A huge bathroom with a bath inset in what looks like a large Moorish redbrick cavern with small stained-glass windows. Like bathing on an altar. A toilet and wardrobe space beyond that.

None of the locks are strong; the old carved glass double doors looking particularly vulnerable. But this is the kind of place, heavily fortified from the outside and near impregnable, where the only criminals lurking would be the wealthy guests. So individual security isn't a real priority. There's a safe in the room, bolted to the concrete floor in the back of the wardrobe. That would have to do.

I don't have anything with me that could be incriminating apart from a spare passport in a different identity and enough travel money to get me out of the country, one way or another. I never travel without these things. My insurance should an operation fall apart and I need to leave in a hurry. They're already in the safe. Everything else in the room just demonstrates I am who I say I am. My usual cover when I'm here, Mike Nolan is a businessman who copes with burnout from his high-powered stressful job by taking himself away on solo expensive holidays to relax. That's how they think of me at this place. And I'm leaning into that now. All I have to do before Prizrak arrives is play the part. Lie by the pool, swim an occasional few lengths, dinner in the restaurant, drinks on the veranda. A dog-eared airport paperback at my side which I always start to read but never seem to get into. That high-flying exec struggling to re-ground himself and get his mojo back. The book also makes the perfect cover for watching the other guests.

Once I find a seat in the restaurant that doesn't have one of the many hotel cats curled up on it, I take a light dinner. The other diners don't look in any way suspicious, in the same way I hope I don't. I always try to work out their life stories when I watch them. Their relationships with the others in their party. Even if it's just a couple, I try to work out the dynamics between them. I don't get the feeling that any of them are Prizrak or connected with him. If he's there, then he's better at blending in than I am. Which in all modesty, I strongly doubt. The surface in the restaurant, in the hotel, is as calm as it should be. It's not until I'm sitting alone on the veranda afterwards nursing a Manhattan, listening to the cicadas, ignoring the begging cats and watching the peacocks strut the lawns in the floodlit darkness, that I become aware of a disturbance in that calm.

It feels like a change in the air. Like it's become electrically charged. The atmosphere in the hotel has shifted and a different kind of energy now surrounds me. I look up from my Manhattan to find two large men staring at me. Polo shirts and chinos painted over muscled torsos. Hair cropped to military shortness. Blank expressions that wouldn't change whether they were having sex or torturing a victim. I know hired muscle when I see it.

One of them makes a slight movement with his head. 'Move.'

I look up. 'Excuse me?'

'I said move.' Heavily accented. East European. Russian?

I hide a smile. Was this him?

If this is who I'm thinking of then it's time to play up my character. 'I don't think so, old chap.' I turn away from him, pick up my drink, take a sip. He's dismissed.

The other one moves in front of me. 'We are being polite. Move.'

I replace my drink on the table before me. Look up. Letting them know they're not the only ones with hard boiled stares. 'I'm being polite as well. I'm sitting here, all alone, enjoying my drink. I don't move for anyone.'

I stay where I am. I think of taking another sip but moving my attention from them would lead them to believe they've won this encounter, so I return stone with stone.

Impasse.

They're so still and monolithic, they look as if they've been planted.

'I can do this all night,' I say. 'And if you want to make something of it, trust me, you'll have a fight on your hands.' I clench my fists. I'm ready to rise at the slightest movement.

'Stefan, Georgio, what are you doing?'

A smaller man appears through the double doors behind me, steps onto the veranda. I say smaller. I mean in contrast to them. He's about my height and build, white, casually, but expensively, dressed. Cashmere sweater loosely tied over his shoulders, linen shirt and tapered chinos. Slip on loafers, no socks. Hair quite long and swept back, small beard. He looks like Matt Berry playing a Russian oligarch. And sounds like it too. (1)

They stare at me, talk to him. 'He won't move,' says the first one.

The man looks at me, at the two of them. Back to me. 'I must apologise for the behaviour of my associates, they do tend to get overzealous in the application of their duties. Please, feel free to stay where you are. There are plenty of other tables for my party to take. I hope you haven't had your evening ruined.'

'Not at all,' I say.

The man smiles. 'Again, my apologies.'

He nods at the bodyguards who, well-trained and without changing expression, leave me alone. They escort him over to another table with a similar view of the grounds, on the other side of the veranda out of earshot of me. The man sits down. The other two remain standing, trying, and failing, to look inconspicuous.

Out of the bar comes another man. Small, wiry. Frowning. Chewing his lip constantly, mouth moving. On someone else it could be a sign of coke addiction. On this guy it looks like he's working out advanced calculus or giving a constant commentary on himself to himself.

But it's not him I'm looking at. There's a woman in their party too. And she is stunning. Statuesque, blonde, she looks like, and probably is or has been, a model. She moves with a languid, bored grace, in her short cocktail dress and heels. She knows everyone else in the place, and me, are looking at her. And wants her. She's totally aware of her power.

These two join the other three at their table. Soon their drinks are brought. As the waiter is returning to the bar he stops off at my table. Places a fresh Manhattan on the table.

'From the gentleman in the party over there. With an apology for any inconvenience.'

I look over. Russian Matt Berry is holding his glass up, toasting me. I raise my own in response. He turns back to his party. Becomes engrossed in conversation with the small, wiry nervous man. The woman looks around, sees only me. Is disappointed, bored with the fact that on this terrace I'm the only worshipper of this goddess. The bodyguards stand there as if they've been powered down.

I pretend to sip my drink. Smile inwardly.

Contact, I think I can safely say, has been made.

13 – Notes

1. Matt Berry. Known to all – even Americans – for his portrayal of Laszlo Cravensworth the vampire in the comedy series *What We Do in the Shadows*. The BAFTA award winner is famously a large-voiced, long-haired British comedy actor. But that's *now*, while I'm writing this. What was he doing in 2009, the year this was supposedly written? Would he have been so recognisable? In a word, no. His TV comedy work was getting him noticed in the UK in a cult kind of way, but even so that was interspersed with typical jobbing actor gigs on TV, and small film roles. So why does Jon mention him here? Not just mention him, but make a deliberate point of reference for the reader to imagine as Prizrak?

    I think, as I've said before, this is another clue for me to pick up on. We were both fans of Matt Berry back in the day (*hate* that phrase), especially his work with cult comic double act The Mighty Boosh and *Garth Marengi's Darkplace*, a spoof of Eighties horror films. He was beginning to get noticed for his work and we had spotted him on numerous occasions drinking in Soho House. In fact, I think we may even have joined him one night. But again, this wouldn't be information anyone else would be privy to. A memory no one else would have. So why does Jon keep doing this?

    All part of the trail of breadcrumbs he's leaving for me to show he's still alive. Everyone he's used so far, from `that far right grifter` to Matt Berry, is someone we'd discussed (or in Berry's case, met) at length and had strong opinions on. We knew what a threat `that idiot who stood for Parliament and was beaten by a man dressed as a dolphin` posed to the UK years ago and saw with dismay how he was being courted by both the BBC and the right-wing billionaire newsrag owners. We'd seen through him straight away and couldn't believe anyone fell for his fake man-of-the-people act. This was Jon's way of letting me know that he agrees with me, that the world would be a better place without `that twat` in it.

And there was no way we could have known that Matt Berry would become so famous. I think from now on we can assume that Jon is still alive. And then it's just a question of searching for more clues as to his current whereabouts then tracking him down. I must admit, when I agreed to do this, I didn't think it would lead to such literary detective work. I'm finding it enjoyable, rewarding even. I hope you are too. It's also bringing those years Jon and I were inseparable back to vivid life. I have a feeling that as we go further, these memories will be providing more than just context.

After that disastrous dinner with Kari, Jon and I didn't see each other for a while. Nothing in particular was said, we just drifted slightly. He went over to LA to spend some time with film people, trying to establish himself as a scriptwriter. With his assistant, muse, intern, protégé, whatever in tow, of course. Ultimately little came of that, so he returned to the UK and began work on his next novel.

It was during this time that I bumped into Gwen at a party for the launch of a novel by a writer with the same agent as Jon and I. The first thing she asked was what I was doing there.

'Oh, erm, I've just signed with her.'

She stared at me like she hadn't heard me correctly. 'Sorry? You've signed with her? With Jon's agent?'

'Yeah. She asked me if I'd do a series of crime novels. Pseudonymously.'

'And you said yes?'

'Obviously, yeah.' I looked round, smiling, but feeling like I had to explain myself to her. 'Here I am.'

'Does Jon know?'

'I haven't told him . . .' I said. '. . . yet. I was going to when we went out for dinner but he brought his protégé along so I didn't mention it.'

I thought I saw her facial muscles tighten at that but her expression never changed.

'A protégé,' I said, continuing. 'Bit of a shock, that?'

'Why?' Said almost as a threat.

'Well, just seems a bit surprising, that's all. That Jon would do that. He's never shown any signs of wanting to do anything like that before. Just shook me a bit.'

'Jon is very altruistic.'

I'd never noticed. But I didn't contradict her. I just nodded.

'I mean,' she continued. 'Look at all the time he spent with you.'

I stared at her. I'm sure my mouth fell open. What the fuck? What the actual fuck? Had she really just said that? Aloud? To my face?

'What?'

She smiled, like she had just scored a point. And in that moment, I realised something: I had never liked that woman. She was poison. I tried to change the subject.

'So where's Jon tonight? Thought he'd be here.'

'LA,' she said, as if it was a goal I could never attain. That's when she told me about him trying to make it as a scriptwriter over there. 'He's very suited for it.'

'Yeah. Maybe I should give it a shot.'

She didn't reply. I wasn't finished. I wanted to get her back for her remark. 'So, is he there on his own? Or is his protégé with him?' I tried to put mental speech marks round the word when I spoke.

She drew back from me, like I'd tried to strike her. Yes. A hit. Good.

'She is,' Gwen said, as neutrally as possible.

'Pretty girl,' I said. 'Very pretty. And young too.' I gave a sharp intake of breath.

'Bet he's really enjoying himself over there.'

She turned and, without saying another word, walked away from me.

I watched her go, smiling to myself.

Later, as I was about to leave, she came over to me again. The way she was walking, eyes like fire, arms and legs like pistons, I thought she was going to physically attack me. But she didn't. she stopped right in front of me, just as I was putting my coat on. Jabbed a finger right in my face.

'Don't presume that you know anything about Jon and me. Anything.'

I just stared at her.

'You know nothing about our life. Nothing.' And with that, walked away again.

I went home.

Meanwhile, I was working on my own novel. And quite enjoying myself. I had taken the work seriously. Approached it professionally. First thing I had done, bought a whole load of thrillers that mine was going to be sitting on the bookstore shelves alongside. Then I read them critically, pencil in hand, working out what the genre demands for this kind of book and how I could not make mine derivative, while at the same time fitting in. Harder than it sounds. Something different, but not that different, was what I'd been asked for. In fact, there was a whole shopping list of things I had to do. And I gladly did them; not just because I was being paid for them but because I was, as I said, taking the work seriously. It may not have been what I would have chosen to write given the option, but it was what I'd been asked to write so I would do it as best I could. And I did. And, while I can't say I saved any of my top tier prose for the narrative, or even invested myself soul deep, I wrote a thoroughly entertaining thriller. Resolutely middle tier, but at the same time not stinting on anything I would put in one of my own novels.

After handing it in I started work on the next one. Things were going well for me. OK, not as well as they were going for Jon, but everything is relative. One shouldn't compare oneself to others in the same profession. That leads to rage and disappointment. For once, out of Jon's shadow, I was making my own way, ploughing my own, quite lucrative, furrow. Obviously, that meant something was about to change. In fact, a whole lot of things were about to happen, with repercussions that would carry on down the years, for both Jon and myself. But before that: a surprisingly happy and unexpected rapprochement.

14

After that I watched them. Constantly. Without letting them know I was observing them. I sat on a lounger by the pool like the other tourists, reading my same paperback, occasionally going for a swim to loosen up. My straw hat was pitched forward, my sunglasses on. Sometimes I wore a Hawaiian shirt and shorts, other times just shorts. Mixing it up a little. Letting them know I was in good shape should the bodyguards want to tussle again.

The party sat round the hotel pool as well, more often than not. Like the other residents they would drift to the Pergola restaurant for lunch then resume their spaces on the loungers. Out of all of them, the woman spent the most time lounging. There was usually no shortage of attractive women around the pool, most of the female residents being young and privately educated at places that included lessons in eating disorders, judging your self-worth only by your appearance and ability to snare a dull stockbroker. This woman was a league apart. She was aware of the power her body exuded and proud to show it off. She was the kind of woman who ended up on the arms of millionaires, billionaires and international arms dealers. She wasn't a prostitute or an escort. Those words should never be used to describe her. Her body was her life's work, her currency, her career, and she worked hard maintaining it. She wanted her audience – wherever and whoever they were – to appreciate the effort she'd gone to, to take satisfaction in a job well done. Constantly performing for the camera in her mind's eye, recording her fabulous life. She had to work hard at it – there would always be someone younger, prettier, more willing to do whatever was needed to take her place. She had a limited shelf life in her chosen career, but she was going to get everything she could from it while it lasted. Lying, lounging, walking or swimming, she was at pains to show herself off. It must have been exhausting. (1)

Stefan and Georgio lurked constantly in the background. They too sunned themselves and swam and even eventually approached some semblance of relaxation, but only after thoroughly checking the surrounding areas for threats. They were like a malign off-screen presence, lurking at the periphery of everyone's vision, disquieting. The man who'd toasted me, the Russian with the beard and the catalogue model hair I assumed was Prizrak, was, more often than not, lying next to the woman. He carried an air of unhurried relaxation, the kind that extreme wealth or power imbues. He also seemed expectant, waiting for something or someone but not agitated about it, clearly used to biding his time. The ratty little accountant constantly accompanying him less so. He buzzed around the Russian like an irritating insect. Worry defined him. He adapted poorly to a sun lounger and had to be told to dress like he was on holiday, as he would attract attention. I knew this because the man I assumed was Prizrak told him so. I heard because I was listening. If any others heard they said nothing. This place is discreet like that.

They were very definitely types (2) and, therefore, easy to work out. If your career is built around such skills, of course. Although apparently *my* skills weren't as good as I thought, as one day I looked up from my paperback to find a face staring down at me.

'Enjoying your book?'

The Russian. Standing right in front of me. I hadn't heard him approach. And it wasn't because I was enrapt in my reading material.

'Yeah,' I say, caught off guard. 'It's OK. Not taxing. Just something to relax with.'

He sits down on the lounger next to me. He's wearing pastels and beige, those expensive, delicate brown loafers again, looking as much in disguise as I am. He's tanned and his body's taut with muscle, but not the kind you get from a gym. His perfectly swept back hair is showing grey close up but his beard is expertly trimmed. His eyes hidden behind sunglasses. But I know they're scrutinising me.

'I've been watching you,' he says, leaning in, confirming it for me.

'Stop you right there,' I reply. 'You're not my type.'

He smiles. His face creases as if it's used to smiling. But not at anything funny. 'You misunderstand me. Perhaps deliberately so.'

I say nothing.

'You've been watching me, haven't you?' he says. 'Why?'

'Sorry to disappoint you,' I say, keeping my heart rate even, as I'm not used to a target being so bold as this. If that is indeed what's happening. 'But you're wrong. I haven't been looking at you.'

'I think you have.' Something hard creeps along the edge of those words.

'Not you,' I say, letting my eyes drift to where the woman is sunning herself on the opposite side of the pool.

He follows my eyeline, then back to me. Smiles. 'Understandable. Want to try your luck with her?'

'I don't think so.'

'No?' He sounds surprised, as if he's never heard this answer before. 'You never know, she might be amenable to you. She's gone for more surprising people in the past.'

'That's as maybe, but I'm just content to watch, thank you.' (3)

He studies me from behind those sunglasses again. I'm also wearing sunglasses but his gaze is so intense it feels like I'm hiding behind mine.

'You say you are not gay and you don't strike me as the kind to feel irrational guilt at betraying the little woman back home, in fact, I doubt you have a little woman back home. So why aren't you interested?'

I turn my head to him now, giving him my full attention. 'I'm sorry, are you that woman's pimp, or something? Is this some poolside service you provide for everyone or are you just singling me out for this special treat?'

I've deliberately raised my voice and it's attracted the attention of Stefan and Georgio who are suddenly on point like attack dogs scenting meat.

The Russian just smiles. 'If I've offended you, then I apologise. Let me make it up to you. My associates and myself will be dining tonight. I would like you to join us. As my guest.'

'Why me?'

'You are here alone. And of all the people around this pool,' he says, gesturing with what looks like disdain at the other residents, 'I find you interesting, Mister ... Nolan.'

Nicely done. So he knows my name. He could have got it from the hotel register. Not that impressive.

'I'm afraid you have me at a disadvantage, Mister ...'

'Ivanov. Alexander Ivanov.'

Of course. Like saying John Smith in English.

'Mister Ivanov.'

He stands up. 'Good. I shall meet you in the restaurant at seven thirty.'

Not a question, a statement. He smiles, nods, and with that goes back to the sunbathing woman and twitchy accountant. Imminent threat averted, the two bodyguards stand down.

I pretend to go back to my book. But there was no way I was reading. I had way too much to think about.

14 – Notes

1. My hackles rose when I read this description of 'the woman'. More on that later.

2. *Types.* Or stereotypes? These are characters usually found in thrillers. The meat-brained bodyguards, twitchy 'accountant', beautiful woman/gangster's arm candy and suave but dangerous Russian. Has Jon deliberately used stock characters, or is it a case of something becoming a cliché because it's true? Surely there must be something more to it than that. A good writer shouldn't be content with writing stereotypical characters. They must at least want to subvert that stereotype, make it interesting. Is that what he's doing here? Is that the game he's playing? And, given some of the other choices we've seen him make in this narrative, are these characters to be taken at face value? Or is there something more to them than that? Just to reiterate what I said earlier, the characters in this novel aren't who they are by accident. Even Prizrak – the Ghost – looks like Matt Berry. A private joke between Jon and me. And there's Kari. And the woman who he's just introduced, if my suspicions are correct. So. These others. Surely he hasn't just got lazy and decided to pop in a few stereotypes because he can't be bothered to come up with something better? Or has he written them this way to *disguise* their real-life analogues? Are they that important? Perhaps they are who they're meant to be and he's just writing the kind of characters he thinks

should be in a spy story? Or is there something more to it than that? We shall see. Or perhaps not.

3. This is another cheap shot, making this woman out to be a whore, and his lead character just 'content to watch'. It reads perfectly in character for the scene, but, as I've said, there's more to it than that. Writers often have little in the way of recourse when it comes to righting wrongs. They only way they can get revenge for real life slights – or perceived slights – is to explore that in the pages of their novels. Remember the pub bully Jon encountered in Dudley. That's how to take revenge. For instance, an old editor of mine appeared in one of my novels. I'm sure he didn't recognise himself, even though I gave a detailed physical description of him. He wouldn't have recognised himself because his ego is too big to even think he could be the pathetic, snivelling coward begging for his life at the hands of a knife-wielding psychopath. And then finding himself disembowelled in the most graphic and painful way possible. But I recognised him. And I enjoyed every single second of writing that scene.

But I digress. I think this woman is going to become an important character in the story. And she's based on someone who became a very important character in my story. Even though her real life counterpart is nothing like this description, I know who this is supposed to be. This is Bette. And knowing what I know about what happened later, and how heartbreakingly horrible the fallout was, makes me really want to hate Jon for doing this.

15

Contacting Kharis was going to be tricky at such short notice and under such apparent scrutiny, so I decide it's best not to attempt it. Also, I work alone and don't feel the need to give someone else a running commentary on my actions. I would call him as and when I needed him. And he would have to understand that. If he was the professional he said he was, he would.

In the meantime, I prepare for dinner. Work my legend deep into my mind until it becomes second nature. Each assignment, each new personality, is like becoming fluent in a new language and wanting to pass for a native speaker in as short a space of time as possible. Time, no matter who you work for or what you do, is money. And deadlines have to be met in any business. Mine is no different. Especially when my deadlines are literal ones. Shapeshifters, out of all the levels of assassin in the organisation, play the long game, but that's only comparatively speaking. We still have to work quickly, earn trust, get on with it and produce an end result. Yes, be a perfectionist but do it on time.

I look at my clothes on the bed, decide what will make the best impression. I choose the chinos with the near-military crease down the middle, sturdy loafers with no socks and a blue short sleeved shirt to show off my worked-out arms. The outfit screams ex-military, which is the impression I want to give. All part of my legend. As Alexander Ivanov will find out.

I do a small work out, meditate. Focus myself for the evening. Get my head where it should be. Banish doubt, increase confidence. I'm sure this is what actors must feel like before going on stage. Preparing in their dressing room, reciting their lines until they come naturally, then waiting in the wings for the lights to change, hopping foot to foot, nervous before the call to action when a silent kind of stillness falls over them. Then: on. And the character has taken over.

I check my watch. Time to go.

We all arrive at the restaurant at the same time.

'Mister Nolan!' Alexander, all smiles. 'What a happy coincidence!'

I'm sure he believes in coincidences as much as I do.

'It certainly is, Mister Ivanov.'

'Please, Alexander. Alex, if we're to be friends. And I sincerely hope we are.'

'Very well, then, Alex.' I'm all smiles now, too. The bodyguards and other two, not so much.

'Come. They have our table waiting for us.'

We walked into the restaurant. Traditional Moroccan décor with contemporary flourishes. A huge, vaulted ceiling. Waiting staff giving the impression of effortless attentiveness. Muted lighting and an atmosphere that doesn't scream luxury but whispers it, quietly and seductively.

The six of us take our seats round the prepared table. I sit between Alexander and the woman, flanked on either side by the bodyguards. The nervous man sits opposite. Although not obvious, it feels like I've been deliberately ushered to my chosen seat.

I turn to the woman. Give a small, confident smile, a Mike

Nolan kind of smile. 'We haven't been introduced,' I said. 'Mike Nolan.'

She turns to me, looks me up and down, her eyes calculating, as she works out my potential worth to her. She smiles. Evidently I'm good for something. 'Elizabeth,' she says. (1)

I try to place her accent but can't. Flat, neutral. Could have been from anywhere, any number of countries, the original one having been presumably deliberately erased.

I smile, showing her my even, white teeth. 'Pleasure to meet you.'

She returns the smile. 'And you.'

A glance from her over my shoulder and I become aware of Alexander watching us. His face still smiling but that smile not quite meeting his eyes. He gestures over to the other side of the table. 'And this is Julien, my accountant and constant companion.'

I stretch my hand across the table to shake. Julien takes it reluctantly, his grip weak, his skin clammy. 'Pleasure,' I say.

He doesn't reply, merely sighs. The heat seems to be melting him.

'And this is Stefan and Georgio.'

No hands are offered so I tailor my response appropriately. A nod from each, a nod to each in return.

'Right,' says Alexander, pleasantries concluded, 'let's drink, eat and toast our new friendships.'

We did so.

I order a gin and tonic to start with, then settle back, apparently open to conversation.

'So, what brings you to Morocco, Mister Nolan?'

'Mike, please. This hotel, really,' I say looking round. 'I'm quite a frequent visitor. I feel at home here. Whenever I need a break, work getting too much, that kind of thing, I take myself off here. Get looked after for a couple of weeks. Pop into

Marrakesh for the day – or night – if I need anything the hotel can't provide but mostly just sit around the pool, relaxing and recharging. What about you? What brings you to this part of the world?'

A smile plays on Alexander's lips. A smile is never far from Alexander's lips, I've noticed, but it seems to be there primarily to camouflage whatever's going on behind his eyes at any given moment. 'I move around a lot. Work keeps me busy. I tend not to stay in one spot for too long but find I am much happier staying in places like this than ... what would you say in your country? A Travelodge?'

He laughs. I join in.

'Couldn't agree more,' I say. 'And what is your work?'

His smile becomes an inscrutable mask, his gestures and voice vague and he sighs while answering. 'Consultancy. Advising various international organisations on, you know, strategy, growth, brand awareness and perception in the marketplace, that kind of thing. Boring. But boring can be lucrative.'

'Nice work if you can get it,' I say. Mike Nolan is, you might have guessed, the kind of person who speaks in those kinds of clichés. 'You got some work coming up in Marrakesh, then?'

'No. But North Africa is a growth area for my kind of expertise.'

'Developing countries.'

'Exactly. As long as they develop in the right direction. For me.'

'You've got your work cut out for you, I'd say.'

'How so?'

'Very unstable, some of them. Not very welcoming, either. Libya? Gaddafi? (2) Bit of a handful.'

Alexander gives an elaborate shrug, takes a drink before answering, as if weighing his words carefully. All for my benefit, I think. 'A handful? Perhaps. To those in the West. But to his own people? Something else entirely.' He looks at me from over the top of his glass, scrutinising me once more. 'But I sense you might know something of this already. Would I be right in thinking, Mike, that you have a military background?'

'You would.'

'And that perhaps you are not unfamiliar with the political situation in North Africa? Or even this general part of the world?'

I put my head down before answering, as if my cover had been blown, or I'm unsure how to proceed next. It sounded like he'd been checking up on me. And the legend is holding.

'Yes, you would be right in thinking that too. But how did you …'

Alexander shrugs. A guess? 'An Englishman who keeps coming to Morocco, or rather returning to Morocco because it relaxes him … I would guess a military background. And the way you dress gives you away. You just can't give it up, can you, those military creases. What were you, Army? Which regiment?'

I nod. 'Doesn't matter. All in the past now.'

Alexander thoughtfully reaches for his drink. 'Is it, though? Is it ever?'

I'm about to reply when the food arrives.

We busy ourselves with that for a while. Tagine for Alexander and me, salad for Elizabeth, a massive amount of protein for the bodyguards and something bland for Julien. When we've started eating, Alexander speaks again.

'What was I saying?'

'You were wondering whether you were the only consultant here in North Africa.' Julien, talking with his mouth full, making consultant sound like a terrible insult.

Alexander snaps his fingers, making a show of remembering. 'That's right.' He turns to me. 'And am I? The only consultant here in North Africa?'

I stutter, hold my arms up uselessly and laugh. 'What, what d'you want me to say?' Perfect Hugh Grant.

'The truth, Mister Nolan?' Alexander's gaze is sharp enough to cut glass.

I drop the Hugh Grant. Business now. 'Why are you asking?'

'Because I would hate us to be in competition with each other. Especially since we've just become friends, Mike.' The *Mike* as pointed as Julien's *consultant*.

I return his gaze, just as sharply. Masks off, as far as he's concerned. Mask on, for me.

'That depends, doesn't it? On who you're working for and in what capacity.'

The atmosphere at the table drops a few degrees. Even Julien can feel it. Stefan and Georgio slowly put their cutlery down. Wait for a command.

'Well, that's killed the party,' says Elizabeth. 'How fucking boring.'

Her outburst manages to defuse the atmosphere. I'm not sure Alexander's entirely happy with that, judging from the look of irritation he gives her. He turns to me.

'Let's not ruin our dining with work talk, Mike, shall we?' He smiles. It seems to require something of an effort. 'Let's finish this conversation on the veranda once we've finished.' He dredges up a laugh. 'I promise you won't be asked to move this time.'

I manage a smile in return.

My tagine has suddenly lost all taste.

15 – Notes

1. Elizabeth. He couldn't be less obvious with the name if he tried. Elizabeth/Bette. There's no mistaking it – Jon is not just writing this book to get my attention – because that's working – he's also trying to get a response from me. And if he keeps on like this it won't be a very complimentary one.

2. Muammar Muhammad Abu Minyar al-Gaddafi. Known mainly in the West as Colonel Gaddafi (1942–2011), he was a Libyan revolutionary and politician who ruled Libya from 1969, he came to power in a coup, until his death at the hands of rebel forces in 2011. Considered a terrorist in the West, he was deposed during the so-called Arab Spring uprising involving Western-friendly revolutions in Tunisia, Egypt and Libya. He was found hiding in a drainage pipe and murdered by rebel forces. Jon wouldn't just bring him up as a throw away. Like Chekov's revolver on the mantelpiece. If it's placed there in act one, it's going to be used by act three. So, Gaddafi, we can assume, is Chekov's revolver.

    What's interesting about the mention of him here is that this novel, supposedly written in 2009 remember, is prior to the uprisings in Tunisia and Egypt and certainly hadn't spread to Libya yet. Is it just well-researched prescience for what was happening or about to happen in that part of the world? It could be. A writer such as John le Carré would do that. Given his background, he did have extensive knowledge of the world of realpolitik and plenty of contacts in it. He would be able to come up with something like this, mentioning Gaddafi and his increasingly tenuous position as ruler of Libya at a time when most people in the world wouldn't be aware that was happening. The other alternative, as with `cunt face` in the first chapter, is that this novel *wasn't* written in 2009 but far later, even contemporaneously, and is only being claimed to have been written then. Again, that would be something that would change everything else in the novel, throw a different light on everything. My mind is still open at this point. However, the time is rapidly nearing when I'm going to have to make a decision. This may involve (what am I saying – *will* involve) some extra-curricular detective work. I will, of course, let you know when I'm about to do that. And I'll report my findings in full in these notes.

My writing was coming along now, just as Jon's time in LA was limping towards an ignominious end. That sounds harsh and spiteful and perhaps I don't intend it to be that bad, but I have to admit there was some bad blood between us by that point. Gwen had made me believe that. Made me think that that was what Jon really thought of me. That I was the comedy sidekick and nothing more. I guess that was the spur I needed to make these crime novels successful in their own right. I worked tirelessly on them and was actually proud of the results. They were good. Very good. Not award winners, of course, at least not the legitimate writing awards. Perhaps the crime fiction ones.

The first one was released. Prior to that, the publisher sat me down and explained what would happen.

'You'll chart at about fourteen,' she said. 'First week. Then rise up to seven, we think. Then from there it's down to word of mouth, really. That's the marketing budget gone.'

'So you can make a bestseller?'

'If we want to, yes. We've put money behind you and behind this book. We want to see a return on our investment. It's good business, that's all.'

I was silenced. Commercial fiction was a whole different dimension from literary fiction. I thanked her and nodded. And left.

And she was right. Reviews – what there were of them, as it wasn't the type of book that usually gets reviewed – were good. I was also told its rewards are supermarket sales and those sales were also good. It was part of a promotion in WHSmiths with a tabloid newspaper. Buy the paper, get my book half price. I stood in a branch one afternoon watching people come in, see the stand, pick up a paper and buy the book. And, because my name wasn't on the cover I couldn't say anything. Success at last and there was no way I could get recognition for it.

But, as I was told, the sales were the reward. And with them, the money. Quite a decent amount of it. I wasn't complaining. I moved out of my tiny flat in Clapham to a small house in Clapham and set about decorating it. And that's when I heard from Jon.

He phoned, said he'd heard about my success and did I fancy a drink to celebrate? I was taken aback. I honestly didn't think I'd hear from him again. Especially after my encounter with Gwen. I said yes, sure. We arranged a time and place at a pub in Soho.

He greeted me like a long-lost friend. All hugs and smiles. And for my part I was genuinely pleased to see him. We settled in for the night.

'So how was the States?' I asked him.

I wasn't sure because of the pub lighting, but I think he blushed. Looked self-effacing. 'Not what it's cracked up to be,' he said, smiling ruefully. 'I'm glad to be back. Cheers.'

We clinked pint glasses. I didn't say any more, but he continued.

'It's a factory out there and not a good one. Like an industrialised farm that treats cattle as commodity. I mean, I didn't think I had any illusions about the place having been on set when films of my books have been made, but Jesus Christ. Being there on a day-to-day basis ... it's shit. Really shit. You know they always say if you knew how sausages were made, you'd never eat a sausage? Yeah. Hooray for fucking Hollywood. And you know what? I sucked at it. Fucking sucked. I'm genuinely glad to be back. Cheers again.'

Another clink. This wasn't the Jon I'd been expecting. I mean, I assumed he hadn't had a good time out there, but I thought he'd put more of a brave face on it. Even making claims that the decision to come back was entirely his own. I'd even anticipated a prepared speech about how he didn't want that place to corrupt and sully his art, or something. But no. Honesty. Wow.

'So hey,' he said. 'I hear congratulations are in order.'

'You mean the ...'

'Yeah. Your new novel.' He smiled. *Really* smiled. Like he meant it. 'I'm proud of you, man. Really proud of you. Cheers!'

We clinked.

'Yeah, it's ... different. A whole different world, really. I'm getting to see the other side of publishing.'

'About time. It's a great book.'

'You've read it?'

'Course I've read it. Loved it.'

'Can I put that on the cover?'

He laughed. 'I'm sure they can get better names than me for it. I'm good in my lane but I'm sure they can get somebody like Dan Brown to say something nice.'

'Yeah, but he's shit.'

'Yeah, but he shifts units. And that's the name of the game.'

This was a different Jon. Relaxed, open, non-competitive. A genuine equal. It was like having my old friend back again. I couldn't reconcile the person in front of me to the one his wife had talked about. Maybe there was something between them, some row or something that she'd decided to take out on me that night? Speaking of which . . .

'How's Kari?'

Something passed over Jon's features then. A kind of brief darkness, then it was gone and he was himself again. 'Oh, she's fine. Yeah, fine.'

And he said no more about her. So I didn't push it.

'You know, I thought you'd be pissed off with me.'

He frowned, looking genuinely puzzled. 'What for?'

'Approaching your agent.'

His eyebrows rose in surprise. 'Really? Why? No. Honestly, no. I just feel a bit bad about it. If I'd known you wanted her to represent you, I'd have mentioned it to her. Ages ago. Sorry.'

'No, no . . .'

'Yeah, I should have done that. You should have said. I mean, I knew you weren't happy with your agent – I mean Jesus, who could be? – but I didn't know you were interested in mine. Seriously, you should have said. Right. Another drink. We're still toasting your success . . .'

And that was it for the rest of the night. We kept

drinking, went for an Indian, popped into the Groucho where we saw two famously heterosexual TV actors underneath a table snorting cocaine off each other's dicks, laughed about it, went and sat somewhere else.

'There's one for the autobiography,' I said to Jon.

He laughed. 'No way you'd get that past Legal.'

I laughed too. He was right, of course.

I felt like I was shining. For the first time in that place, I felt like I belonged. Not that I wanted to snort cocaine of anyone's dick, no. Not like that. But that I was there on merit. Not because I was Jon's friend but because I was a bestselling author in my own right. I was nobody's comedy sidekick any more. I was the main guy. And I would keep on being the main guy for as long as I could manage.

16

The artfully placed lights show the lawns at their best as peacocks roam, cats meander and cicadas chirred. My Manhattan tastes as good as it looks. Across from me Alexander sips his drink. We replace them on the low table between us, sit back. Appearing, to anyone watching, like two old friends relaxing after dinner. He plays the game as well as I do.

Stefan and Georgio are on a different table, not looking like old friends relaxing. Elizabeth has gone to bed, taking a bottle of champagne with her, and Julien, much against his wishes, has been banished somewhere.

'It's like sitting in your colonial British past, is it not? This place, this veranda? We could be in colonial Egypt. Howard Carter and Lord Carnarvon sipping drinks and planning another day of tomb robbing. Instead, we're in the here and now, just two guys shooting the breeze,' Alexander says, attempting an American accent. 'How pleasant.'

'Yes,' I say. 'We should both be wearing white linen suits.'

Alexander laughs. Once it tails away his face changes. 'To business.'

I make a gesture: you first.

'Cards, as you English say, on the table. I work as a consultant for many different parties. Countries, organisations, corporations. Individuals even. Whoever can afford my services. There aren't many, I assure you. But the ones who can, pay well.'

'And what do they ask you to consult on?'

He stared out at the peacocks. 'Oh Mike, it's tiring, don't you think? This back and forth, back and forth. Let's just be honest with each other. Unless I am very much mistaken, you are in the same line of work as me. Why else would an ex-military man be staying alone at such a place as this on the edge of one of the most unstable but potentially lucrative parts of the world?'

'Why don't you just believe I am who I say I am?'

'Because you wouldn't have accepted my dinner invitation. You'd have found an excuse not to. You'd have felt somewhat out of your depth, I think.'

I try a self-effacing smile. 'Maybe I'm just bored and lonely?'

He fixes me with a stare. 'I don't think you're the kind of person who gets bored or lonely.'

I look away, take a sip of my drink. 'Assuming what you say is true and I am who you think I am, or do what you think I do,' I say, 'aren't you taking a risk by opening up to me? Even having this conversation?'

'Wouldn't I be taking a bigger risk by keeping quiet? If I found you to be in opposition to my plans then we would have a problem, Mike, wouldn't we?'

'And if my reason for being here aligns with your reason for being here? Would you have a problem with that too?'

Another smile. 'I doubt it. You see, I've been employed by certain parties to carry out a very specific set of actions leading to a very specific set of results. My skills, as I said, are highly prized. Highly sought after. I doubt very much whether the same people who have employed me have also employed you in the same capacity.'

'Perhaps in a different capacity?'

'Perhaps. But let me be honest, Mike. If our objectives coalesce, then good. You do your job, I do mine. Hey, there's space for both of us.' He leans forward, eyes shadowed. 'If, however, our objectives were to clash, then ...' He says, leaning back, picking up his drink on the way, pointedly looking away from me.

'I see.' I wait for him to speak again, playing the silence out by sipping my drink.

'I'm giving you a chance, here, Mike. I will complete the task for which I have been employed. And no one will get in my way. No one. So which side are you on, Mike?'

'That's hard to say, Alexander, since you haven't told me which side you're on yet.'

He sits back again, smiles. Almost laughs. 'Listen to us. Like too eager teenagers, dancing around each other, both not wanting to make the first move. Because once we've said the words, they can never be taken back, can they? And things will change for ever.'

'So, with that in mind, perhaps we shouldn't rush things? Perhaps we should leave the heart to heart until we know each other a bit better, yes?'

He nods, drains his drink. Stands up. Somewhere behind me, the bodyguards come to life also. 'I have enjoyed our little chat, Mike. Think on my words.'

He makes to go, turns, stops. 'Oh. I am heading into the old town tomorrow. All of us. Please. I'd like your company. If you're free of course.'

My first thought: if they're out I can go through their stuff. My second thought: if I say no, he'll know that's exactly what I plan to do. My third thought: I can do both.

'That would be very pleasant, thank you.'

'Good. We'll assemble after breakfast. Good night, Mike.'

I say my goodnights, wait until I'm sure he's gone, then head back to my room.

I have a phone call to make.

*

I think that's the end of the night, but it isn't.

I've been back in my room about half an hour and I'm about to get into bed when there's a tapping on the double glass doors. I throw on a robe, open the curtains and there's Elizabeth standing there, holding up the bottle of champagne she took from the restaurant earlier. It's the first time I've seen her smile since I met her.

'Can I come in?'

Believe it or not, this is quite the dilemma. I'm sure she's been sent here to get what she can out of me, so to speak, when my guard's down, but on the other hand Alexander might not even know she's here. Either option could be dangerous. I look at her, silhouetted in the moonlight and open the doors.

She steps inside. 'Getting chilly out there.'

I close them behind her. 'Is that an English accent?'

'Haven't you heard me speak before?'

'Not much. You've managed to communicate in other ways so far.'

She smiles, crosses to the small table and two chairs beside the empty fireplace. There are two glasses on the table. She sits in one of the chairs, begins opening the champagne. She's wearing a kind of silk kimono wrap. It keeps falling open. I'm sure it's meant to.

The champagne pops, she pours into the two glasses. I join her.

'Cheers.'

'To what are we drinking?' I ask.

'Who cares?'

We drink. She drains hers, pours herself another one. 'If we need more,' she says, 'we can always call room service.'

'You planning on being here long?'

Another of those rare smiles. No mistaking what this one meant. 'Depends.'

'On what?'

'On whether we can find anything in common.'

I take a sip, look at her. She's beautiful. Incredibly beautiful. Not just good looking, pretty, but the kind of beauty that makes others lose their breath and walk into walls. The kind of beauty that should belong to film stars or a race of superhumans. Now, I don't think I'm all that bad looking, but I'm not in her league. She should be with someone like Brad Pitt. Yet here she is, making eyes at me and 'accidentally' exposing herself. I'm too old to believe this is anything other than transactional. But still young enough to want a piece of what she's selling. It's just whether I can afford to pay the price.

'And what is it you think we may have in common?'

'I was watching you,' she says, after draining her second glass, 'at dinner and before that, round the pool. And I know you were watching me.'

'Along with everyone else.'

She smiles. Not in arrogance but in acknowledgement. 'And you liked what you saw.'

No sense in lying. 'Of course.'

'Well, I liked what I saw too.'

She leans forwards once more to get herself a drink, as her kimono falls open. Her breasts are as perfect as the rest of her.

'Oops,' she says unconvincingly. 'You still like what you see?'

'What d'you think?'

She stands up. Undoes the belt loosely holding the kimono together, lets it fall to the floor, the kimono along with it. She stands like a statue of some breathtaking Greek goddess.

'Won't Alexander be angry about this?'

'We have an understanding. It's a very open relationship.'

'Does he know that as well?'

She walks towards the bed, climbs slowly onto it, lies on it. Looks at me, her eyes locking mine. The embodiment of enticement.

I don't need to be told. On one level I'm aware that I'm playing a character, this is acting. It's not me doing this, it's Mike Nolan. But like all the best actors I know, it has to come from me. The passion in any performance has to be genuine for it to be convincing.

And right in that moment, I want to be as convincing as possible.

16 – Notes

First chapter with no numbered notes. That doesn't mean there won't be notes for this chapter, however. Especially after what you've just read.

Elizabeth. No doubt at all. This is meant for me. You see, the person I met, the one who I fell madly in love with, was called Elizabeth. Or Bette, as she preferred to be known. And while not bearing a one hundred per cent similarity to Elizabeth in this narrative – that may well be libellous – I'm definitely supposed to know that it's her.

Bette became very important to me. *Very* important. Unfortunately, as I said, things didn't end too well between us, as is so often the way. Is this Jon's way of telling me that Bette knows where he is? Or at least why he disappeared? Is he taunting me with her, telling me that if I want to know more I should go and talk to her? He knows I can't do that.

I first met Bette when my life was improving. I was writing my pseudonymous thrillers, making good money from them and getting decent reviews. My publisher and agent were taking me seriously, mainly because I was earning money for them too. Happy all round. And I wasn't short of ideas, either. Quite the opposite. I had more thriller ideas than I knew what to do with. It was trying to decide which ones I wanted to spend up to a year of my life with that was the tricky part. But good tricky, enjoyable tricky. I saw an interview with a TV writer about this time who said he'd actually been to a hypnotist to stop him having so many ideas, too many for him to develop within his lifetime. While I didn't quite have that problem I could kind of sympathise. But as far as I could see, working down the pile-them-high-and-sell-them-at-supermarket-discount mine as a commercial novelist, it was a happy problem to have.

Jon wasn't having the same happy problem as me, though. He told me so one night when I asked when his next book was coming out.

'Who knows, mate? Who knows?'

'What's happened?' I asked. 'You haven't been dropped. Not you.'

'Oh god, no.' He tried to smile but there was something haunting his features. I waited. He'd either tell me or he wouldn't. But the fact he'd asked to meet me tonight told me he wanted to tell me. He laughed. 'Well, not yet, anyway.'

'What's up? This isn't you.' And it wasn't. Whatever else he was, he was always positive about his work. He had that charmed aura about him that success brings. But it seemed to have deserted him this evening.

He sighed. 'Maybe I should do what you're doing. Can't be hard. Or not as hard as this.'

I bridled slightly. It sounded like a carelessly dropped insult. I decided not to pick him up on it. Maybe he hadn't meant it.

'What, you mean write crime novels?' I said.

'Yeah. I mean, you seem to be enjoying it. Doesn't look too taxing, book a year, sorted.'

Yeah, that was definitely an insult. Even if he hadn't intended it as such. 'Harder than it looks, you know. It's still writing, still making a novel. I have to do all the things you do, I just have to put a plot in as well.' I smiled when I said it, but it was definitely intended. If he could play at that, so could I. 'It's still work.'

He looked slightly taken aback, hurt, even. Took a drink. A big one.

'Next book not coming along?' I asked, voice low, consoling. Trying to get back on a friendlier track.

A sigh. 'Yeah. Really difficult. Just can't think of anything to write. I mean, what's there to write about? I've won awards, had my books made into films, been well paid, all of that. What is there for me to do next? I get up, have breakfast, drink coffee, sit at my desk, look out on to the garden, my big garden, knowing the house is paid for and all my money's invested well. So what have I got to say? What penetrating insights into the human condition can I throw before a reading public and make them applaud?'

He sat back and it was then that I noticed this beer wasn't his first drink of the day. His eyes didn't look right.

I wasn't sure what to say. I needn't have worried because he continued.

'I mean, you're all right. Someone gets murdered, someone solves it. Piece of piss, everyone's happy.'

I opened my mouth to argue but he talked over me.

'D'you ever feel like you're a fraud? Like you're not the person everyone thinks you are?'

'Well … yeah. I mean, imposter syndrome's a fucker. I'm always expecting to have someone putting their hand on my shoulder telling me it's time to leave, the real writers are here now.' I tried to laugh while I said it because, even though it was the truth, it sounded ridiculous when I said it aloud to someone else.

'I don't mean imposter syndrome. I mean a fraud. A real, fucking fraud. Not what or who you're supposed to be.'

I couldn't work out what he was getting at, but I tried to answer him. 'Well, I always think when I hand a new book in and it gets accepted that I've dodged another bullet. That I've got away with it again. I suppose we all think that, though, yeah?'

Another sigh and a shake of his head. 'You don't get it, you don't get it . . .'

He drained his glass. We were supposed to be going to a book launch after the pub, but it didn't seem like he would be much company there. He must have read my mind.

'I think I'll go home,' he said. 'Give this thing a miss. You go, though.'

'Very generous, thank you.' I laughed when I said it. He didn't.

'I'll see you soon.'

He stood up and, before I could say anything further, left the pub.

I watched him go, through the window, until he faded away into the crowd. Then drained my pint, checked my watch and headed over to the book launch.

It was in a West End bookstore, as most of them are, with the usual assortment of publishing types, poor quality alcohol and a smattering of bemused-looking civilian friends of the author. I went to the bar, helped myself to a bottle of beer, spotted another writer I knew, and began, like always, with the small talk, the gossip and the anecdotes.

It was always the same, but talking to Jon had got me thinking. This was the kind of event I often felt like an imposter at. I'd meant what I said when I told him I expected a hand on my shoulder guiding me towards the exit. I suppose that's why I always have a steady stream of anecdotes for these kinds of things, enough recall to get the facts about them straight, and enough practice to make them amusing. But then I'm sure a lot of other people do that at these kinds of events. And not just writers. Although it helps – or should do – that we're storytellers.

For some reason, probably that earlier conversation with Jon, I wasn't feeling the vibe, as the kids would say. I was going to buy a copy of the book, get the author to sign it – the price of admission at book launches and anyone who doesn't do that is a freeloading twat – drain my beer and leave, when I found myself in front of probably the most beautiful woman I'd ever seen.

She was tall, blonde and had a kind of vintage, 50s pin up style about her. I fell immediately in if not love, then certainly lust. I didn't even stop to think that she was way out of my league, which is what I would have thought if I'd had time to think about it and talk myself out of speaking to her. But she was right in front of me, we were blocking each other's path in the crowded bookshop so I had no reason not to talk to her.

'Oh hello,' I said, 'I don't think we've met.' I told her my name.

She smiled. 'Oh wow, you're the crime writer.' Her face lit up in a smile and she looked even more beautiful, if that was possible.

'Oh, you've heard of me.'

'Oh yeah. Mr Hot Shot Author,' she said, and laughed.

I had no idea if she was taking the piss or not, but I joined in with the laughter.

'Yep, that's me. So what are you doing here? Another writer?'

'PR. Freelance. Been called in for this book. In charge of the campaign.'

'And a great job you're doing of it, as well.'

'You think so?'

'Well I'm here, aren't I? I got the invite.'

She laughed again, even though the correct response to my words should have been vomiting.

And that was it. How we met. We talked and talked. She had to go off and talk to other people, as did I, but I always knew where she was in the room. She was looking at me too. At first I thought I was imagining it, but no. She was definitely looking over at me. And smiling. In a with me not at me way. And even, unless I was imagining it, in a 'where are we going after this' way.

Eventually the party broke up and, as is tradition, the ones who didn't have to rush for trains or other parties retired to the nearest pub. It was a well-worn route. As Bette was in charge of PR she led the party. I was more than happy to tag along, all thoughts of leaving early long since disappeared.

Once in the pub which was overcrowded and too hot, we tried talking again. Getting to know each other further. She had worked inhouse for several years before heading out on her own, setting up her own company. She got fed up of the office culture but not the book culture. I told her I knew what she meant. I was happy going into the office when I had something to drop off, but much preferred working from home. She was also single. As was I. Result.

Eventually it was time to leave and a curry house was sought. There were only about eight people left by this time, including the writer whose launch it had been, Bette and myself. I was sat away from her on the table, but we kept looking at each other still. There was no way I was imagining it. Not now.

Eventually it came time to leave.

'Whereabouts are you headed?' I asked her.

'West. I live in Hammersmith. You?'

'South. Clapham.'

We both stood there. The air seemed charged around us, between us. It was like standing on the edge of a precipice in the pitch dark, not knowing whether the next step would lead to solid ground or freefall and an unpleasant landing.

'Opposite directions,' I said.

'They are.'

'D'you ... fancy heading off to a club? The Arts, the Groucho?'

'I'd ... better be getting back.'

My heart began sinking. 'Right. OK.'

'But you could walk me to the tube, if you like?'

That sounded fine to me.

We walked to Leicester Square tube. 'Accidentally' brushing up against each other as we went. I loved her perfume. I'm sure I would have loved any perfume she was wearing.

We reached the station. Stopped. Looked at each other.

'Well,' she said. 'Here we are.'

'Yes,' I replied. 'Here we are.'

Silence. We stared at each other.

I spoke first. 'Look, erm ... I'm not used to doing this kind of thing, but ... d'you fancy coming back to mine? See where Mr Hot Shot Author lives and creates his Hot Shot Masterpieces?' I laughed when I said it. Obviously.

Thankfully she laughed too. Then said the words I didn't want to hear. 'Sorry, I can't I have to be up in the morning for a meeting.'

My heart sank again. I didn't want this night to end. I didn't want her to get home, think about what she'd done, who she'd been with, scream 'What was I thinking?' and block my number. I came close to telling her that but thankfully I didn't. 'OK,' I said. 'Fine.'

She gave me another smile and it was like the sun coming up. 'But you could always come to mine if you like?' She paused and, before I'd had time to answer, kept going. 'I mean, if you're not doing anything tomorrow, if you haven't got anywhere to go, if ...'

'I'd love to.'

Another look between us, the step after the precipice secured, the air changed and everyone else in the whole of London's glittering West End disappeared. There was only me and her.

'Let's go then,' she said, taking my arm.

The end of that chapter. Jon writing that Garrick/Mike was playing a character in this scene. What does he mean? Is he trying to tell me that he was sleeping with Kari? Is it as obvious as that? Or is it something worse? Is he telling me that he had an affair with Bette? Or that he wanted to? Or if he was somebody else, he could do that? Or maybe just to make me jealous, thinking that he could have done that if he had wanted to? Or is he with her now? I don't know.

I don't know.

17

It feels like a dysfunctional family outing. We meet up by the gatehouse of the hotel, waiting for the people carriers to take us into town. Alexander, Julien, Elizabeth and myself in one, Stefan and Georgio following on. Despite the heat, Stefan and Georgio are wearing linen jackets. They do very little to disguise their weapons. Julien is fussing, voicing his displeasure and unease to Alexander.

'I told you we shouldn't be relying on the hotel,' he says. 'We should have hired our own transport. We do everywhere else.'

Alexander barely looks at him. 'We're on holiday, Julien. Just tourists, here to take in the local atmosphere. Don't attract attention to yourself, you'll look like a pickpocket's easy mark.' He turns to him. 'Besides, Stefan and Georgio will be right behind us. And I'm sure that with Mister Nolan here with us, we won't come to any harm.' A quick glance at me, a quick glance at Elizabeth. A half smile. 'Or one of us won't at any rate.'

So he knows. She's reported back. I'm sure I'll find out what she said at some point.

Elizabeth only gave me a cursory greeting and hasn't yet made eye contact, hiding instead behind her massive shades. I've picked up her cues, responded accordingly. Hoping no one notices that the air's changed between us and if they do that they don't care. Alexander seems unperturbed. A couple of days ago he offered her to me like he was offering his car for a joyride. Since I said no, he must have thought the offer would be more tempting coming from her. Perhaps he thought her directness would weaken me. It did. Or that's what I want him to think.

The sex was good, No, great. Inventive, intense, athletic, hard. Enthusiastic but skilful. Sport sex with the goal of assured mutual satisfaction. I've had a lot worse. Especially in the line of duty. This was one of the better encounters and I would look forward to it happening again. Just because I'm working doesn't mean I can't enjoy myself.

And Julia? She understands. It's an assignment. It's work. I'm a professional.

Afterwards, we lay there side by side, spent. The fan wafted air over us but hardly cooled us down.

'Well, that was a surprise.'

'Really?' She turned on her side, looked at me. 'After the way you've been staring at me every day?'

'I didn't know that approach worked. I'll have to remember it in future.'

She gave a small smile. 'Arrogant shit.' Turned over on to her back.

'So you and Alexander have an understanding,' I said after we'd lain there a while.

'We do. We're not exclusive. He knew that when he first met me. He just had to accept it.'

'Did he have trouble doing so?'

'He wanted me,' she said offhand. 'Those were the terms.'

'He doesn't strike me as a man who likes being told he can't have what he wants. On his terms.'

'Then I'm an exception.'

'Unless those are the terms he actually wanted you on.'

She doesn't reply. I wait a while longer before speaking again.

'So how did you meet him?'

'How do you think?'

'I honestly don't know. You're English, clearly well-educated ...'

She gave a small laugh. 'You mean I'm not damaged goods? A project he set his mind on completing? Rebuild me in the image he wanted, like restoring a classic car?'

'I didn't say that.'

'I know what you meant. No. I was a hostess in a Tokyo night club when I met him. He was there for work. We became friends.'

Work. The sarin gas attack on the Tokyo subway? 'Right. And how did you end up in Japan?'

'My act of rebellion. Or one of them. I was a good, privately educated Home Counties girl. Mummy and Daddy had my whole life mapped out for me. The kind of man I'd marry, where we'd live, how many children I'd have ... all of it. The only thing was, they hadn't consulted me about it.'

'So you rebelled by going to Tokyo.'

'Not right away. I started stripping while I was doing my A-levels. Faked my age. It wasn't hard. Made good money too. If you can get over being objectified by some of the grossest specimens of humanity you'll ever see. Try it. It cures you of any empathy for the human race. Especially men.'

'I'll take your word for it.'

'From there it was a short step to modelling. Then glamour modelling. Then porn. By then I thought I'd made my point. Shamed my parents enough. So I put a pin in the map and took off there.'

'Which was Tokyo.'

'And that's where Alexander found me.'

'And saved you.'

She detects the unserious tone in my voice. Laughs. 'Exactly.'

'So, what do you do now? Exactly. Just travel the world with him wherever he goes for work?'

'Pretty much. He likes to travel with an entourage. Julien is his walking diary, his accountant, his lawyer, all of that. Stefan and Georgio are, well, Stefan and Georgio.'

'And you're the arm candy?'

'I'm more than that. But I know the role I have to play with him. We have a relationship, as you've seen, but I'm on the payroll. He deploys me when he's curious about someone or wants them to come onside.'

'So he wants me onside, is that right? That's why you've been deployed?'

She smiles.

'And what was this, a medical test to pass? Checking out my stamina? Have I passed? Am I onside?'

She makes a fake pout. 'Oh Mike,' she breathes heavily, 'did you really think I loved you? I'm so sorry ...'

I laugh. 'Don't worry, this isn't my first rodeo.'

'I'm sure it's not.' She looks down my body, smiles. 'And it looks like you're ready to ride again ...' (1)

The carriers arrive. Julien is making a fuss about something to Alexander, speaking *sotto voce* so I won't hear. Alexander is clearly becoming irritated. Eventually he turns to him.

'Then stay here. Please. Stay here.'

Alexander turns away from him, Julien is dismissed.

The carriers arrive. We get in.

'I'm sure you don't mind sitting next to Elizabeth, Mike?'

She's in between the pair of us. 'Not at all.'

'Good. Let's go.'

I say nothing. But Julien's just severely fucked my plans up.

17 – Notes

1. Right. I'm sure that this has been done to upset me. Anger me, even. Nothing more. The Elizabeth of this narrative is clearly meant to be some sort of escort-cum-gold-digger, weaponising her body to get what she wants, captivating Mike Nolan with athletic displays of sport sex, for which he's grateful. As I say, hurtful. Deliberately so. The real Elizabeth, *my* Elizabeth, my Bette, was nothing like that. And Jon knew it. Yes, she was younger than me. Yes, she was extremely attractive. But that's where the similarities end with this character. She wasn't with me because of what she could get, because I was a best-selling, successful author at the time. She was with me because of who I was, just as I was with her for the same reasons. We were in love. Pure and simple. And so what if people looked at us walking down the street and thought I was punching? I was. But she never made me feel like that. It was the greatest relationship I've ever had in my life. We were planning to spend our lives together. Grow old together. As you'll see, that didn't happen. But it was the opposite of what Jon presents here.

   So why has he done this? To upset me, first and foremost. I don't think he ever liked Bette. Some people are like that. It's fine for them to have partners but if their friend gets a partner then they see that as a competitor for their friend's affection. I didn't notice it at the time, but that was what was happening with Jon. I think he had problems of his own (more on which as we come to them) and couldn't bear to see me happy. Good career, good personal life. For once, everything was going right for me.

So what was wrong with him? I think him and Gwen were having a rocky time of it. On the rare occasions they ventured out together in public they barely spoke to each other and when they did, they would be short, sniping. There was no love in either of their eyes. Other people noticed, not just me. I mean, it didn't impact on his standing as a writer. At this stage he was still bringing in the money for the publisher. And there were no outright arguments in public. That would have been worse, not to mention embarrassing for all concerned. It felt like wherever they went in a room, the temperature dropped. The same as malevolent ghosts are supposed to do to haunted houses.

I tried to get Jon on his own, talk to him about it, offer some help or at least a sympathetic ear, but he seemed distant, depressed. Plus, I almost always had Bette with me, and I'm sure he didn't want to open up in front of her.

Away from Jon, Bette was opening up other vistas in publishing to me. Her work in freelance PR introduced me to plenty of different writers working in genres I'd never have normally bothered with. They saw literary fiction as just another genre, one they weren't particularly interested in. It made me feel better about myself and the genre I'd ended up working in.

So life was good. I was happy. I had everything I'd ever wanted.

Of course, it wouldn't last.

18

The old town was as I remember it from a few days earlier. I was wondering what we were actually doing here as Alexander might have said he was playing the tourist but didn't strike me as someone to go shopping for holiday mementoes. It didn't take me long to find out.

'OK,' he says when we reach the main square, surrounded by fruit sellers and snake charmers, 'I have some business to attend to. Elizabeth, why don't you and Mike amuse yourselves in the souk?'

He hands her a credit card. She pockets it, expression unchanging. She's used to this kind of thing.

'Where are you off to?' I ask.

'As I say, business,' he says lightly. 'I'll take Stefan and Georgio with me. I'm sure you're more than capable of handling yourself if anything were to arise.' A smile as he says this. Is that a double entendre? Is it aimed at me or Elizabeth?

'I'm sure I can,' I say.

His mouth smiles but his eyes run calculations. 'We'll meet you back here in, say, three hours?'

'Will that give you enough time?' I ask. 'To do whatever it is you've got to do?'

Another smile. He wears them like masks. 'Ample.' He sets

off walking away from the market, the two bodyguards falling in behind him.

I turn to Elizabeth. 'Does this happen often? Him leaving you to amuse yourself?'

'More than you'd think.'

I watch them walk away. 'Did he mention last night? Ask if you got anything out of me?'

Her smile wraps itself round secrets and in that gesture I feel a pang of jealousy about what she gets up to away from me. I know I've only spent a night with her and shouldn't feel so proprietary – for several reasons – but it's there none the less.

'He asked if I'd enjoyed myself.'

'And did you?'

Again that concealing smile. 'I told him I did.'

'And he doesn't get jealous?'

'Would you get jealous of someone who worked for you who did their job? Besides, people like him don't get jealous where things like that are concerned. We're all just pieces on his chessboard.'

'So if you're the queen, what piece am I?'

'I don't think he's decided yet.' She turns towards the market. 'Come on.'

As we walk I'm aware of all eyes on Elizabeth. Double takes, men walking into stationary objects, the lot. She affects not to notice but it's as if a goddess has chosen to walk among them. I just follow in her wake.

We pass the stall Kharis and I are supposed to meet at. The stallholder doesn't even spare me a glance. Elizabeth, I notice, has a real gift for finding the expensive shops in amongst the tourist tat.

'Surely the designer stuff's over in the new town? Don't you go for that?'

'There's designer stuff here. If you know where to look. And it's supposedly more authentic. Apparently.'

'Nice rugs here. Don't you fancy one of them for your home? Actually, where is home for you?'

'The hotel. When we leave it'll be to another hotel in another part of the world.'

'So you don't have a permanent base? Somewhere to call home?'

'Alexander believes the whole world's his home, as long as it's five-star treatment. But he's got a few houses and apartments dotted around the place. The main one's in Iceland, that's where he heads back to most often.'

'And you go with him?'

'Obviously. But I prefer the sun.'

'So what is it Alexander actually does?'

She smiles. 'Don't you know?'

'A contractor.'

'There you go, then.'

'You don't know more than that?'

'I don't care. We have our arrangement. That's enough for me. At the moment. When it stops working, or when either of us gets bored with it, it'll be time to move on. But we're not at that stage yet. So everything's fine.'

'And you're not curious about what he actually does for his money?'

'Not as curious as you, apparently. And I don't care how he gets his money. As long as I get my share. That's all I care about.'

We lapse into silence.

After walking around for a while, watching Elizabeth try on and buy jewellery, we decide to find a bar. Sitting down over afternoon cocktails she looks at her purchases.

'Aren't you supposed to haggle when you shop here?'

'What's the point? It's not my money.' She carelessly places the jewellery into her bag. 'He just wants me to look good and trusts that I will.'

I check my watch. 'We should be getting back. Don't want to keep him waiting.'

Sitting at the side of Elizabeth once more with Alexander on the other side, I reflect that it's been a curious trip. I've been brought along so Elizabeth can keep an eye on me. Alexander's meeting was important and he didn't want me following him. And that little spat with Julien before getting into the cars was just for my benefit. It was always Julien's intention to stay at the hotel. So he could go through my room. Elizabeth would have reported back the layout and what to look for. He would do the rest himself. He wouldn't find anything. Everything pertaining to the Nolan identity is in the safe, as expected. Everything else is strapped to me. Taking no chances.

The only thing I'm annoyed about is that I planned for Kharis to go through Alexander's private riad. With Julien there he wouldn't have been able to.

We arrive back at the hotel.

'Well, I'm heading to the pool for the rest of the afternoon,' announces Alexander. 'Anyone coming?'

He's looking at me when he talks. 'Be along in bit. See you there.'

I head off to my room. I expect Elizabeth to offer to accompany me, but she doesn't. Perhaps Julien has to debrief Alexander on what he's found – or not – first. (1)

I open the door to my room, step inside, close it behind me. The curtains are drawn and the room is in darkness.

'Buy anything nice?' says a voice.

Kharis. Dressed as a member of staff.

I remove the document belt from underneath my shirt around

my waist, place it on the table, sit down in one of the armchairs. 'How did you get on?'

'Well that ratty guy coming back was an unwelcome complication. But he wasn't around for very long.'

'I know. He was in here.'

'Yeah. Would he have found anything?'

I shake my head. 'No. What about you?'

'On the surface, nothing. There's a couple of laptops but I didn't have time to get into them. Besides, from what I know about Prizrak, he's not the kind of terrorist to entrust his innermost thoughts to anything electronic.'

'I assumed that's why Julien's on the payroll. A walking database. Or one of the reasons. Recognise him? Know anything about him?'

'Not familiar with him. I managed to snap a couple of photos, though. I'm sending them over, see if we can get a match. Same with the others. Getting a photo of Prizrak's quite a coup, though.'

'Did you get into the safe?'

'I did. Nothing there but passports. I took photos, though. What about you?'

'He had a meeting with someone in the old town. I was stuck with Elizabeth as a diversion. He's suspicious of me, but I don't think he knows why I'm here. He still thinks of me as another contractor.'

'The legend's holding.'

'For the moment. So you didn't find anything?'

'Well, just this.' He passes over his phone. There's a photo up on it. 'Tickets to Libya. Any idea?'

'We did mention Libya.' I think for a few seconds. 'Gaddafi? Regime change?' I hand the phone back.

'Could be. But who would be employing him? Whose interests would that be in?'

'Ours, probably. The West. Although it depends who he

wants to replace him with. But it doesn't change anything. I still have a job to do.'

'Found any weaknesses on him yet?'

'None. I'll have to step things up a gear.' I stand up. 'I'll be in touch. You all right getting out?'

'Yeah, no problem.' He smiles. 'Might have to deliver room service on the way, but hey. Might get a tip.'

Once Kharis has gone, I look round the room. Julien's done a good job. To anyone else's eyes it looks as if nothing has changed. But I can tell. Things a few millimetres different than where I left them. Something accidentally tidied up. I know housekeeping will have been in but I know the difference. I check the safe. Mike Nolan's life, tucked up safe and sound. I add the other documents in there, change the numerical code. I don't think they'll try the same thing again. Not right away.

I go back to the armchair, pour myself a glass of water.

Think how I can move the operation on to the next step. (2)

18 – Notes

1. He's very good at writing about the transactional nature of relationships, I think. How all these characters' lives are interlinked in a purely transactional way and they're under no illusions about it. I'm sure this is something he worked on observing how publishing works. And how friendships in publishing work. The truth is, when writers get together it's like any other bunch of people who share a common interest, usually a work-based one: they want the gossip. Simple as that. Who's shagging who, who's on the way down, who's made a huge mistake and embarrassed themselves in public, who's been dropped by their publisher, whose new book is terrible and shouldn't be up for awards, whose new book is cruelly overlooked, and on and on. There may also be a degree of jealousy if a writer is doing well or a sense of schadenfreude if a writer, especially an obnoxious one, is suddenly doing badly. But that's just natural human behaviour and writers are no different in that respect.

    But that's writers with writers. In the wider arena of publishing, namely the relationship between writers, their agents and their publishers, it's far more transactional. Totally transactional, in fact. And the better you were doing, the more of a chunk of change you got from the transaction.

    Take Elizabeth and Alexander. Travelling all over the world, never at a loss for money, but both aware of the parameters of the relationship. The same with publishing. If you were doing well, your editor or agent would invite you down to their weekend country residence. Put you up, lush you up and lay on entertainment. All on the pretext of discussing something or other. If you weren't doing well, they wouldn't even take you out for lunch. Jon is demonstrating a transactional relationship perfectly, with both sides knowing what they're getting out of it. Likewise, if you stop earning for your publisher or agent, the weekend invites disappear too. Incrementally – as the money drips away, so too do the social invites.

So what's Jon saying here? Is he talking about himself and his publishers/agents? Or is he talking about me and him? Or, given the nature of the relationship he's describing in the novel, is he even talking about himself and Gwen?

I will put a caveat in here. He's not talking about Bette and me. Definitely not. At this time, we were going from strength to strength. We moved in together, renting a house in Chiswick.

Bette and I had something different to what I'd had with my ex-wife. A mutual respect for each other and our work, and also a common knowledge of the industry we both worked in. I can't tell you the difference that made to our relationship, even just on a day-to-day basis. Since we both mainly worked from home in our respective studies, we knew what the demands of the job were on each other, also that it wasn't strictly nine to five. We understood each other. On every level. It was the thing I'd always wanted. A good career as a writer and a happy home life with a woman I loved. Yes, I had to write thrillers under a pseudonym but that was a small price to pay for everything they brought me.

And I was free to work on something else, something more literary, if I wanted to. Any time. I spent about six months at most writing a thriller, so I was free for the other six months. Why not write a novel under my own name? Why indeed. Because I didn't need to, that's why. This, here now, was giving me everything I wanted. Why push myself if I didn't have to?

And I suppose it's worth mentioning, the floor of the house was stripped floorboards on which, in the living room, was an expensive but comfortable sofa, a Persian rug and an old wooden trunk used as a coffee table. All the symbols of success.

2. The chapter ends with Nolan not knowing what to do next. I know what that means. I've done it enough times myself. It means the writer himself doesn't know what to do next. Raymond Chandler, the great private eye novelist, always said something like, if in doubt, have a man enter the room holding a gun. Obviously it's not to be taken literally – although it was in his case – but certainly, if one doesn't know what to write next, throw in an event to shake things up and write your way out of that. I wonder if that's what Jon's going to do?

19

Alexander, with good reason, doesn't trust me. But to move things along I need to make him trust me. And to do that I need to stage a scene. Not an obvious one because he'll suspect immediately and close me down. Perhaps permanently. So something subtle. Or even roundabout; planting a seed of trust but not obviously, so that even he doesn't know what I'm playing at.

It isn't the first time I've had to do this but there are no tried and tested methods to fall back on to guarantee the right outcome – every situation needs different handling even if the outcome is to be the same. Ideas that are out:

Saving his life. Too hackneyed, too clichéd, too incredible, in every sense of the word. (1) And he has bodyguards for that, why would I put myself in harm's way just for him? No. That's out.

Saving the life of one of his entourage. Please, no. See above.

Giving up something of myself for him. That's a possibility. If he thinks we're in conflict over our 'consultancy' work, then I could offer to give mine up and come over to his side. If there's a big enough incentive. Financial, obviously, but also some reassurances that it'll be worthwhile, that I'll be coming over to the winning side. This is risky because he may just decide to eliminate the competition, meaning me. To stop that happening he has to sense something in me that might be useful to him, some knowledge I have that he doesn't. Something in me he can bank now and use later? But I don't know what he wants. So I'm back to square one.

I'm getting nowhere and this isn't like me. I'm blocked. I've always trusted the process, capitalised on the opportunities that present themselves, but I can't think. Maybe they're right. Maybe I'm too old for this. Or maybe I just need a swim in the pool to help me think.

I change into my swimming shorts and drape a towel over my shoulder when there's a knock at the door. This, I realise later, is my big mistake. My guard is down, I'm in my own head, lost to the here and now, vulnerable when I should be aware of my surroundings. And I answer the door.

I have almost a second to realise there are two of them before they rush me. Instinctively, I'm ready to fight but I've lost time already and they're on me.

One has a sack which he throws over my head, blinding me, the other pins his arms round me from behind, stopping me from hitting out. Once the hood is on, the first one sends his fist flying into my stomach. Twice. Hard.

I try to kick out with my legs, but it's impossible to find a target when I can't see and just end up flailing wildly and losing my balance which gives them even more of an advantage.

I struggle, refusing to go down without a fight. Then there's a blow to the back of my head, stars, blackness, and I'm down. The fight is now irrelevant. (2)

I open my eyes but it's still dark. I blink. That's when I realise the sack is still over my head. I'm not sure what it previously contained but it's not pleasant.

I'm sitting down and I try to move. Can't. I'm restrained in a sitting position, tied to a chair. I try to pull my wrists apart. From the feel of the binding and the sound it makes, it's duct tape. Same with my ankles. I try to squint, see through the fabric of the sack. Can only make out light and shade. I inhale, but all I can smell is whatever the last gross thing was in this sack. I stay still, sensing. My legs, body are bare. I'm still in my bathing shorts. Still barefoot. I'm cold. I hear a voice.

'He's awake.'

I strain, try to recognise it. It's muffled. I'd need to hear more. I can't yet tell if there's an accent or if it's a man or a woman, young or old. Known to me or unknown.

Then movement. Someone getting up, crossing the floor. Coming closer. 'You with us?'

A male voice, I think, but still muffled. Disguised. Means I might perhaps know the person or at least be able to recognise them. Some kind of accent too, but I'm not sure whether that's been deliberately put on. So that, small though it may be, is something.

My heart races, pumping blood and adrenaline round my body like it feels fit to burst. My mind whirrs with possibilities and impossibilities, my brain making thousands, millions of calculations per second. Not reaching any conclusions, just increasing my confusion. I need to get a grip, remember my training. Fear reduces the intelligence by fifteen per cent, so I breathe slowly, deeply, controlling my thoughts and emotions, not giving in to the overwhelm. Control regained, I attempt to think rationally. Have an answer ready when my captors interrogate me. It's not the first time I've been in a situation like this, and I escaped. Make that experience count.

'Asked you a question.'

'I'm here.' Keeping it short, non-committal.

Silence once more. Maybe they're waiting for me to ask questions. Display fear. Again, I make the mental calculations, work out the alternatives. Are they expecting me to do that? Or stonewall? And which will work to my advantage?

And then another thought, the big one this time: is my cover blown? That hits like a stone to the chest. Or another thought: am I being tested? I breathe deeply, focus. I can only respond to the situation when I know more about it. I have to be patient. They'll tell me more. I just hold my nerve until then.

One thing is in my favour: the hood. They can't see my face, gauge my reactions to their words. So if they're willing to lose that huge aspect of interrogation that tells me something: I might recognise my captors.

'So, Mister... Nolan? What are you doing here?'

Do I know that voice? I do, I recognise it from somewhere. Or I think I do. Despite the attempt at disguising it. Get him to talk more, maybe it'll come to me.

'You tell me,' I say. 'I was heading out for a swim at my hotel when you grabbed me. Brought me here. Wherever here is. Is it worth asking?'

'You want to be clever, do you? Try to be funny.'

'I just want to know where I am, why I'm here and who you are.'

'And we want to know who you are.' Another voice, the first one that spoke. Is it a woman? And do I know her? Again, it's hard to make out anything.

'You already know who I am,' I say, allowing anger to rise in my voice, giving an approximation of fear as well. 'You've just said my name.'

'What's in a name?' The male voice again. 'Names can be fake. Identities... how do we know you are who you say you are?'

'Why would I not? And what fucking business is it of yours, anyway? Who the fuck are you? Kidnappers, is that it? Take a random Westerner hostage and hope someone'll stump up the money for his release? Well, I've got news for you, mate. You've picked the wrong person. I'm not worth a fucking thing.' Louder and throwing in a bit of swearing. I'm improvising, but this is the way an innocent man in my position would behave.

There's movement again. Someone approaching. Crouching down next to me. 'You're a liar, Mister Nolan.' The male voice, up close now. 'We know you're not who you say you are. So what are you really doing here and who sent you? Tell us.'

'I have told you. My name's Nolan and I'm here on holiday. I often come to Morocco on holiday. I like it here. I might not be back after this, though.'

'You think you'll be going anywhere after this?' The female voice this time. With a real edge to it. 'We're just going to believe you and let you go?'

'You have to believe me. I'm telling you the truth ...'

'Lower your voice, please.' The male voice.

'Why? Will someone hear me?' And then, much louder: 'Help! Help! I'm being held captive! Help! Hel—'

Another punch in the stomach. I'm still sore after the last one and this one huffs all the air out of my body, leaving me gasping for breath and in pain again. I breathe in ragged gasps.

'No one will hear your screams. No one is coming to help you. So answer the questions.

'My name is Nolan ...' struggling for air, breathing through gravel. 'Nolan ... I'm a British citizen ...'

'Stop this shit. We know who you really are, Mister Nolan. Admit it and this need not get uglier.'

'I've told you who I am, you fucking shit! Nolan! Mike Nolan!'

'Liar!'

Another punch. These really hurt. I'm in good shape but I'm not sure how much more my body can take and not have serious injuries.

'So who am I, then?' I just about manage to get out. 'If I'm not who I say I am, then who am I? Who do you think I am? Tell me ...'

Silence.

'Tell me ...'

Again, no reply. My mind whirring: is this a fishing expedition? Do they just suspect I'm somebody else and are trying to scare me into confessing? Maybe the hood is on so they don't give away the fact they know nothing.

'My turn now,' the woman says.

The male voice gives a harsh, sharp laugh. 'You think I'm bad? Wait till she starts on you. If you do get to leave here, it won't be in one piece. And no one would recognise you.'

'And what's she going to make me say that you can't? I've told you everything. Whoever it is you think I am, you've got the wrong person.'

No response to my words. I listen hard, trying to make out sounds. I hear something. Metal scraping against metal. A blade being sharpened. Footsteps coming towards me.

I involuntarily breathe in as the blade is placed on my bruised abdomen.

'You feel that? Cold? Sharp?'

'You tell me. You're the one who can see it.' I wish I was as brave as I hope I sound.

I've never liked knives. Never used them, don't like being around them. They're messy, unprofessional. The tool of the amateur, the kind of person who kills for the enjoyment of it. The psycho sex killer's weapon of choice. Something in the woman's voice tells me she wouldn't need payment or a reason, she would do this for fun.

Things have escalated.

'Tell us what we want to know,' she says, pushing the blade in slightly, 'and then I'll stop.'

I try to sit up straighter, pull my stomach back, away from the knife. It doesn't work.

'Tell us. Save yourself the pain ...'

I feel the cold of the blade being dragged along my stomach. It's like being scraped with a razor. I gasp. I know I'm bleeding.

'Tell us who you are. And who is Prizrak ...'

I tense, expecting another cut but instead I hear the sound of a scuffle. The male has raised his voice, shouting at her. Ignoring the pain, I try to focus on what they're saying.

'Don't, you don't ... not yet ... you ...'

There's more to it but their voices are reduced to hushed spitting. I can't make anything out. But it sounds like cutting me wasn't part of the plan.

'No,' the male voice says, 'we do it my way now. No argument.'

She makes to reply, he cuts her off. Loudly. 'I said no argument.'

Someone moves quickly towards me and I hear the unmistakeable sound of a gun being cocked. Before I can properly process this information there's a loud, close explosion, a shattering pain in my left ear, followed by a stunning, swift deafness. I scream, jerk my head away from the noise. I unbalance the chair and fall over, landing painfully on my side on the floor.

I'm still screaming, but I can't hear it.

The deafness is sudden and all encompassing. But gun deafness isn't the absence of sound it's the replacement of it. A wasp's nest has been planted in my head while I'm in front of the speakers at a Motorhead concert. This silence is deafening. Gradually it fades until it's one long high-pitched scream, a freight train coming towards me that I can't get out of the path of.

I close my eyes and the train passes. I hear it go, receding into the distance and as it does, the pain subsides. I'm back in the room and still alive. Hands grab me, roughly right me again. The gun is cocked once more.

'What you going to do now? Shoot me? First one was just a warning, that it?' I'm aware I'm shouting too loudly. 'You can't, can you? Because you want me talk, you need me alive. So you can't kill me, can you?'

The male voice sighs. My logic has worked.

'Now you can use your knife,' he says.

'What?' I try to move. Can't.

Then someone is behind me and the knife is against my skin. Against my hands. I instinctively try to pull away from it.

'Get off me ... get off me ...'

But the knife doesn't break my skin, let alone touch it. Instead, the duct tape binding my wrists is cut. I don't have time to even think about getting away as the person behind me grips me round the neck with one arm while outstretching my left arm with the other, holding my hand out.

'Kill you?' asks the male voice. 'Not yet. But we will make you talk.'

I feel the still warm barrel of the gun being placed against my left palm.

'Ready to tell the truth yet?'

I close my eyes. (3)

19 – Notes

1. You're telling me, mate. One of the oldest, most overused tricks in the book. A really, really clichéd and hackneyed book. This reads like a blocked writer thinking aloud and writing it down. Hoping to find inspiration where to take the story next by having the lead character think the same thing. Is this too close for the lead character/writer to be? A lazy way of working through your problems? Or a legitimate way of working, getting involved in the narrative structure in a meta kind of way?

2. Well, it wasn't exactly a man with a gun, but it was near enough. For all his literary pretensions, Jon isn't too proud to take advice from Raymond Chandler.

3. This whole chapter is starting to resemble some kind of spy/espionage novel tick list. The wondering what to do next/action hero rendered inert at first. Then events are taken out of his control by external influences coming to bear. The attack, knocking out and subsequent dragging off somewhere. I mean, does that ploy still work in this day and age? Or are we wise to that now? It can't create much in the way of tension, surely, can it? We don't think the hero is in too much jeopardy, do we? I mean, it's a first-person narrative and you can see how many pages are still to go. So unless he starts to narrate it from the perspective of a ghost then he's going to be, ultimately, OK. Or, again, is it an expected trope?

The kidnapping and interrogation scene? As I said, we know they're not going to kill him. He's got the rest of the book to live out yet. I choose to think that a scene like this demonstrates character under duress. What would Character A do in a situation like that? When they don't have B, C and X to fall back on? That kind of thing. It shows a different aspect to the lead character. He's been in control all the time up to this point, now we see him in a reactive situation. How does he cope? That's what I, as a writer, look for in scenes like this. It's the same with sex scenes. Now bear with me here – I know what I'm talking about. Sex scenes, which a lot of writers hate (usually the ones who aren't very good at writing sex scenes), aren't there for titillation in my opinion. They're there to show power dynamics in relationships. A shorthand way of seeing how characters behave when the trappings of politeness are removed from them. You can get more about a character from a well-written three-page sex scene than some writers can do with a ten-page chapter.

But I digress. Back to tropes and clichés in this chapter. I mean, there are so many I'm surprised that someone hasn't offered Nolan a drink and he then gets dizzy and collapses. If you're keeping score for that kind of thing, that should be in here somewhere.

You may be wondering why I haven't gone into detail about myself in these notes. My backstory, as it were. Well, the main reason is you don't need to know. It's not that interesting. And not that dissimilar to every other writer's backstory. But, you might say, you've inserted yourself in the narrative, even in a reactive, passive way, and we know very little about you. And again I say, it doesn't matter.

You know Jon's background? Pretend that's mine, too. It's not, but the themes are similar. As they are for all writers. There's a phrase of Tolstoy's in *Anna Karenina* and I'm paraphrasing here, that says something like all happy families are the same in their happiness but all unhappy families are different. Reverse that and you've got a writer's backstory. All writers have the same things (the same unhappiness?) to some degree that led them to a life of standing on the margins observing and making notes rather than being in the middle of the action and living. And when writers get together, they can always recognise that in each other. No matter our class, race, gender, whatever, it's the one thing we all have in common. You can't see it, but when you carry it yourself, you can sense it on others. This is why you don't need to know anything specific about me. All you need to know is here already.

Jon and I were still friends at this point. Good friends. I'd tried not to think too hard about the whole 'if I was successful, he wouldn't want to know me' thing. It wouldn't get me anywhere. Just let things happen organically.

'You look really happy, man.'

'Thank you.'

Jon had just got a round in. We were in our usual pub in Soho. It was where we went at the start of the evening before heading out to whatever the night had in store for us. Bette was at her own party this particular night. By this time we would go to events together. I loved walking in with her. She looked beautiful and I knew plenty of people were staring at her. And she did too, which didn't hurt.

But anyway.

'No, you do. Really happy. You look ... content.'

'Well, I guess I am, really.' I smiled, laughed even. 'First time ever.'

THE FINAL CHAPTER

I noticed Jon had his head down, distracted. 'Good for you, mate, good for you. You deserve it.'

'You OK?'

He looked up. 'Yeah, I'm ...' He sighed. 'I dunno. I mean ...' Another sigh, another large mouthful of beer. 'It's ...' He shook his head. Took another mouthful.

I waited. Eventually he looked up.

'How d'you do it?'

'Do what?'

'Be happy in this ...' He looked round. 'In this ... all this. Amongst all this shit.'

'Well, aren't you happy? Awards. Huge sales, films? Doesn't that make you happy? Isn't that what you've always wanted? It's what all of us want. You're successful on a level most of us can't imagine.'

I could say things like that now since I'd found my own level of success and was content within it. Sure I'd like what Jon had and maybe that was the next step. But I was enjoying where I was at present.

'I just ... I can't see a way forward. Just ...' He trailed off.

'Is everything okay with you and Gwen?'

'What?' He looked startled, like he couldn't place the name for a few seconds. 'Oh yeah, fine. Yeah. Yeah.' Nodding to himself again. 'Yeah. It's just ...' Another mouthful. He'd just about drained his glass. He looked up, stared straight at me. His eyes held a kind of desperation in them. 'How do you do it?' he said again.

'How do I do what?'

'Be happy. How?'

I leaned forward, like we were exchanging confidences. 'Jon, you've got it all. Everything. *Everything*. I'm just ... yeah, I'm making money. Not under my own name. And not writing the books I'd write given the chance. And I'm nowhere near in your league. I don't know how much you earn, but it's a shitload more than me, I bet. Jon, you've got the life I've always wanted.'

He looked up them stared straight at me. 'No I haven't. I really fucking haven't . . .'

'OK. OK. Fine.' Something about that look, that outburst . . . it was as if he was becoming unhinged, unmoored. As if he didn't know which way he wanted the story he was telling to go.

I think he sensed this too, composed himself. Settled down again. Drained his glass.

'I just, I just can't do it. I can't seem to do it.'

'Do what?'

'Find a way forward. From here to . . .' Another sigh. 'Oh, I don't know. I don't know.'

'Is there something you want to tell me, Jon?'

He looks at me again and his eyes this time seem imploring, as if he wants to confide something but knows he shouldn't. The walls are thin, I can tell. He's about to say something. Then thinks better of it, looks at his empty glass. 'Another one? That'll cheer me up.'

'Yeah, go on then.'

He got up, went to the bar, got a couple more drinks. We drank them and skirted round what he'd just said, or just tried to say. It was a massive elephant in the room, but Jon's mood improved as we talked and by the time we were ready to go to our party it was like the conversation had never happened.

We arrived at the book launch, worked the room, had fun, drank, told anecdotes, heard gossip and by the time Bette turned up to join me, Jon had disappeared.

I hadn't even noticed him leave.

20

The shot doesn't come. Instead, there's some kind of angry commotion, physical altercation. There is a gunshot, but it's directed away from me.

My arm is dropped, there's the sound of running and I realise I'm free. First thing I do is take the sack off my head, try to take in my surroundings. Stefan is pointing a gun and firing through a doorway. Georgio is walking towards me, knife in hand. I don't have time to react in any way as Georgio bends down and cuts the duct tape away from the chair leg for both my ankles. He then pulls me to my feet.

I look round. I've been held in a filthy, run down room. Dirt floor, painted breezeblock walls. Dust in the air. There's no evidence of my captors.

I try to ask Georgio what's going on. He doesn't even acknowledge me, just puts my arm round his shoulder and drag walks me out of the room. I want to walk under my own steam but the ordeal has affected me. I'm exhausted. I put my hand to my stomach, look down. Most of the bleeding has stopped. The wound is long, bisecting my torso, but thankfully shallow.

Georgio drags me outside. It's some dusty back alley in the middle of nowhere. A few more buildings, mostly derelict, resemble the one I've just been inside. Two storeys at most, flat-roofed. Either an area of lock-ups and storage or housing for incredibly poor families. There doesn't seem to be anyone else on the street. And it's dark now. I hear the disappearing buzz of motorbikes.

Alexander is leaning against the side of a black 4×4. He detaches himself from it, comes over to me.

'What have they done to you? Are you all right?' He looks and sounds genuinely concerned. 'You're cut . . .'

'I don't think it's anything important. It's not deep.'

'Nevertheless, you need to get it checked out. Come with me.'

He opens the back door of the black 4×4, ushers me inside. I climb in. He goes to the back, opens the boot, takes out a blanket which he then hands to me. 'Here. You must be freezing.'

I am. It could be shock setting in. I wrap the blanket tightly around me. Once I've started to warm up, questions come to me.

'What's happened? Why are you here? *How* are you here?'

'We saw them taking you. Or rather, Elizabeth saw them taking you. She was coming to see you when she saw a couple of people hurrying away from your room pushing a large wicker laundry basket. The speed they were going made her suspicious so she followed them to the gate. When she saw them dump what looked like a body, and was in fact yours, into a private car, she ran to tell me. And here we are.'

'Thank you.' I feel rather numb. I'm trying to take everything in.

'It took us longer to trace them than we thought it would. My apologies.'

'How did you do that?'

'Elizabeth remembered the number plate, told Julien. He excels at these kinds of things. We borrowed a hotel car and followed the GPS to here. Then Stefan and Georgio took over.'

'So who took me?'

'We don't know. Clearly they had some kind of warning

THE FINAL CHAPTER

procedure in place. As soon as we arrived, they cleared out. Stefan shot at them but they got away. We then had to decide what was more important. Chasing them or seeing you were OK.' Alexander gave what seemed like a genuine smile. 'You are my friend, Mike. It was no contest.'

'Thank you.' I think I honestly mean it.

Stefan and Georgio get in the front of the vehicle. Alexander gives them the name of a medical centre and off we go.

'So who were they? What did they want with me?'

'I don't know, Mike. Perhaps you could enlighten me. Did they say anything?'

Time to play the honest man, again. And, as they told us in training, the best way to lie is sound honest. 'They kept asking me who I really was. Who I was working for.'

'And what did you tell them?'

'Nothing. That I am who I say I am. It's all I could tell them.'

'And did they believe you?'

'No. Called me a liar. Started to cut me. They were going to blow my hand off. And they would have if you hadn't arrived.' I sound alarmed and vulnerable as I say that. Scared, even. And I might not be acting.

It looks like Alexander wants to ask me more but he sees I'm actually in a fragile state and could be going into shock. 'We'll have you sorted out soon enough.'

We ride the rest of the way to the medical centre in silence.

I'm soon patched up. The wound is quite superficial but its length makes it susceptible to possible infection, so I'm given a course of antibiotics and told to stay out of the swimming pool for the foreseeable future. The knock on my head isn't too bad, no lasting damage, no concussion. And the repeated punching hasn't ruptured anything. All in all, I've been quite lucky.

The treatment has been excellent and the medical centre itself isn't the usual kind you'd find in Morocco; Alexander has clearly paid handsomely for this. I feel like it's put me in his debt, although when I tell him this, he just waves my concerns aside.

'What are friends for, Mike?'

It feels like the ordeal has put us on a deeper level of understanding. Good.

We drive back to the hotel. The adrenaline's worn off now and I'm feeling done in.

'I've arranged for a late supper at the hotel,' says Alexander. 'Please join us.'

'I'd love to, but I honestly think I'm too tired. And I don't think I'd be good company.'

'As you wish. I don't want to force you, but the offer is there.'

'Thank you.'

Alexander smiles. 'Just be careful of room service. I don't want to go through all this again.'

I manage a weak smile in return, then close my eyes.

The next thing I know I'm back at the hotel. Even though I'm exhausted, I double check all the doors are locked before I get into bed. And double check my documents are where I left them. They are. Too tired to do anything else, I sleep.

But not for long.

Because I think I've worked out whose voice I heard.

Awake now, I spend the rest of the night deciding what to do about it.

20 – Notes

The power balance in our relationship had changed.

Jon was no longer his supremely confident self, self-deprecatingly shrugging away all praise – and he got a lot of praise, wherever he went – and smiling charmingly, eyes downcast like Princess Diana. Now, he always seemed nervous, anxious, on edge, looking over his shoulder, eyes widening at every new person who entered whatever room we were in at the time. Like he was genuinely waiting for someone to tap him on the shoulder and tell him his time was up, the real writers had arrived, and he had to leave now. The imposter syndrome fantasy made real.

I tried to get him to open up, with varying degrees of success. It was like he was clairvoyant, could see his own future. Like he was heading for a fall and he was convinced it was going to happen.

'Might not, mate,' I said one night over dinner in Kettners in Soho, 'I mean, we all think that, don't we? The next one's going to be the one they hate.'

He just laughed, as if he couldn't imagine what he was hearing. As if I was somehow naïve for even thinking that.

'No', he said, 'It's my turn, isn't it? I'm due a fall about now. I can't stay golden for ever.' He became thoughtful, eyes drifting away somewhere else. 'Golden.' A laugh. A very bitter one. 'What a fucking joke.' He looked back at me. 'It's luck, isn't it? Just luck. We try to dress it up, try to claim some, I don't know, divine intervention, some "things always happen for a reason" bullshit, some determinism, but it's a load of cock. And we both know it. It's luck. My first book landed on the right desk at the right time with the right person. And it happened to be the thing people wanted to read which made it a huge hit. All out of my hands after that. Then it was seen in Hollywood by the right person at the right time and a film was made. Miraculously, the film was good. And so they want another. And another. And another.' He sighed. 'You know what the odds are on us being here? Right now I mean, here?'

I frowned. 'You've lost me. You mean in Kettners?'

'No, I don't mean in fucking Kettners. I mean here, now on this planet. Life. Living, breathing intelligent apes. Us. The chances of life happening are tiny. Really tiny. The right rocks binding the right way at the right time to form a planet, the right kind of gravity, the right balance to support life... and then the choices and decisions along the way that lead us, after several billion years, to humans on the Earth. Living, breathing humans. Sitting here in fucking Kettners, aware of ourselves, our lives, our place in the universe and our mortality.' He leaned forward. 'What are the chances of that?' Before I could answer he answered himself. 'Fucking tiny. *Tiny.* You wouldn't put money on a horse with those odds. They wouldn't even give you those odds. That's how slim the chance of life on this planet is.' A slurp of his drink. 'And then, there's me. And you. Us here, born from the parents we had, the choices and decisions that led us in our lives to sitting here now talking to each other. Those chances. Equally fucking tiny. Equally.'

He sat back. Waited for me to speak. Challenging me to speak.

'Yeah, right. You're right. And when you think about it, it makes me realise how small we are in the universe.'

He smiled, patronisingly, as if I hadn't understood his point. 'Those chances. Tiny. Slim. One millimetre either side and none of this happens. *We* never happen. That's the same with publishing. That's the same with my books being a success. That's what I mean. Everything had to fall in the right place at the right time. I'm so fucking lucky. *So fucking lucky.*' And then he laughed again. Even more bitter than the first one.

Silence descended. I tried to formulate an answer, one he would want to hear.

'Yeah, you're right. It is just chance, it is just luck. But to keep going, to build a career out of it, that takes more than luck. That takes skill and talent. We're both here now. We've both done that.'

My answer didn't seem to convince him. It was beginning to feel like whatever answer I gave wasn't going to please him. Maybe I wasn't expected to answer. Maybe I was just supposed to sit here while he got this – whatever this was – out of his system. Sure. Yeah. That's what friends are for.

'You ever think about running away?' he said, suddenly, like it was both a change of subject and the thing he'd been building up to say.

'Running away? What, like just dropping your life and finding a new one? Or going on holiday with no plans to come back?'

'The first one. Just getting up in the morning, walking out the door and never coming back. That one. You ever think about that?'

'Not seriously. I mean, sometimes I think it would be interesting to move somewhere else, see what's out there. Get away from London.'

He shook his head slowly, features contorted. Clearly I still didn't understand.

'No. Not going away. Just walking out. Leaving

everything behind. Not telling anyone where you're going. And leading a whole new life, become a whole different person.'

'You've really thought about this.'

'I really have.'

'Where would you go?'

He smiled again, but this time it was almost wistful. 'Northumberland. Get an old fisherman's cottage in a village on the coast. Seahouses. Bamburgh. Somewhere like that. Just me and a dog. A rescue. And we'd walk along the beach, and go to the local pub, and sit and read and be ... I don't know. Happy?'

'Really? That would make you happy?'

He nodded, clearly seeing this existence for himself.

'What about Gwen? Wouldn't she come with you?'

It was like a cloud passed over his face, his expression changed that quickly.

'What about her?' Said really sharply, too quickly.

'Wouldn't she miss you?'

He shrugged. 'Doubt it. She'd have the books to keep her warm.'

I didn't even notice at the time just what an odd thing that was to say. It was coming on top of all the other odd things he was saying.

'And Kari? Doesn't she need your mentoring?'

He laughed out loud this time. 'Kari doesn't need anything from me. Never did. Never will.'

I didn't know what to say to him after that. We continued the meal as though he hadn't come out with all that, talking about music and gigs and industry gossip. Keeping it light. Not stepping on any conversational or emotional landmines.

It was only, a few months later when his next novel came

out and was universally hated and failed to make the impact that his previous ones had, that I began to understand the despair he must have been feeling and had tried to explain to me. Knowing that what he had written was bad and just waiting to have that opinion confirmed. Feeling, for the first time in his career, anything but golden. Realising he was just as mortal as the rest of us.

That realisation had clearly hit him hard. Very, very hard.

A fisherman's cottage in Northumberland. Something to go on. At last. There must only be, what? A few thousand? Is that where he's gone?

21

'Had to rearrange things pretty quickly to make this meeting. Sure they won't suspect anything?'

Kharis is sitting in the darkened back of the lighting store in the medina. I'm even further in the shadows.

'I doubt it,' I reply. 'After what just happened, I think I might have proved myself to them. They're not watching me as I leave any more.'

'Least you hope not.'

'At least I hope not.'

The meeting had been arranged quickly, Kharis is right. As soon as it was light, I left the hotel and came straight to the old city, contacted him. He came as quick as he could and I filled him in on the ordeal I'd just been through. His eyes widened, shocked as I told him everything.

'Jesus, man, that's incredible. You sure you're OK?'

'Yeah, I'm fine now. Don't know how I'd be if Alexander hadn't got there when he did, though.'

'Yeah, yeah.' He becomes thoughtful. 'Funny he turned up when he did, though. You think he might have been behind it?'

'I thought that at first, yes. It seemed the most obvious thing. A set up to get me to talk, find out who I really am, scare me into revealing secrets, but do it all at arm's length. Leave a space for himself to enter at the last minute, make himself the hero by rescuing me. Just in time. Then, if I haven't opened up already, I'm so grateful to see him, I tell him everything.' I nod, looking serious. 'Yeah. That was my first thought.'

Kharis looked puzzled. 'You don't think that now?'

'I've been awake all night running through every possible scenario. And for a long time, yes, that seemed like the most promising one. Especially for the timing.'

'Timing?'

'When they arrived to rescue me. Just as I was about to have my hand shot off. Just as I was scared enough to reveal something. Or I might have been.'

'But you didn't.'

'I didn't, no. Which makes me suspect Alexander wasn't behind it.'

Kharis, perched on a cardboard box full of lighting, stirs uneasily. I'll admit, conditions aren't very comfortable in the back of the shop. 'How so?'

'Because, as I just said, I might have been about to reveal something. They could have scared me enough so I'd say who I really was, what I was really doing there. And if Alexander – Prizrak – was behind the abduction then he'd have waited to see what I had to say before coming in and rescuing me.'

'So you think that rules him out?'

'I do, yes.'

'Maybe it was just, I don't know, bad timing on his part?'

I almost smile. 'This is Prizrak we're talking about. He doesn't do bad timing. If he thought I was about to give something up, something he needed to know about me and how it impacted on him, he'd have let me get my hand shot off. Jesus, he'd have even shot it off himself. So no. It wasn't him.'

Kharis becomes thoughtful then, features lost in shadow.

I watch him. 'Maybe ... maybe he thought he had all he was going to get? Time to call a halt to the whole thing?'

'Why?' My voice is dead when I ask the question, eyes unblinking.

This makes Kharis nervous, for some reason. 'I don't know, he could have ... heard everything he wanted to. Decided he could trust you now.'

I give a half smile. 'Decided he could trust me. Right. You see, that's the thing. The sticking point I keep coming back to.'

Kharis's voice is quiet now, question more like a statement. 'How so.'

'What if – hear me out now – what if the kidnapping was staged. Just not by Alexander.'

Kharis swallows. Hard. 'By who, then?'

'By you, Kharis.'

I see his eyes dart around the room, like the answer he's looking for is somewhere else. A mouse looking for the tiniest crack of an excuse to escape through before the cat pounces on him. I wait, completely still, totally patient, for him to speak. Eyes never leaving him. I excel at being patient.

Eventually his gaze drops. He sighs, knows there's no point in pretending any longer. He nods. 'Yeah. It was me.'

'I know it was you, Kharis. I recognised your voice. You tried to disguise it, but when the shit hit the fan, you forgot and began speaking normally.'

He puts his head down, too ashamed to face me.

I'm still when I ask the next question, still and measured. My voice low. No histrionics, no anger. No emotion of any kind. I have long since learned to detach feelings from work situations. 'So what was the point? What did you hope to gain by putting me through that?'

Again, he looks round the room. Once he's found his answer, he looks at me. Still ashamed but wanting to be believed.

'They decided you needed something to happen. Something to make Alexander trust you. Get you both on the same side.'

'They.'

'Yes, they. You know who they are. Your bosses. *Our* bosses. They sent word that we were to stage a kidnapping, let Alexander's party see you being taken away, follow us, then come in and save you from being tortured or killed.' He's leaning forward, desperate to be believed. 'That's the truth. I swear it.'

'You staged it.'

'Yes ...'

'And you didn't tell me about it?' There's a hint of rising anger in my voice as I speak. I tamp it down. Control it.

'We couldn't! How could we? If I told you what was going to happen, you'd have been prepared. You wouldn't have been scared enough. Wouldn't have let us make it look like we'd roughed you up.'

'You did rough me up. You cut me.' Still in control.

'Not me. I didn't do that.'

'No, your amateur sidekick did that. Who was she, anyway? Where did you find her?'

'I ... I don't know. They sent her to me. I've never seen her before. She disappeared afterwards. Haven't heard from her again.'

He's lying. His voice and body language tells me. But I don't press him on it. Not just yet. I continue with my line of questioning.

'So this was all for my benefit. To help me get closer to Alexander.'

'It worked, didn't it? He trusts you now?'

'We'll see. Wasn't it a risk, though? Threatening to blow off my hand? What if he didn't come in at that time? What if he arrived later or earlier?'

'If he was early, no problem. If he was later then we'd have found another way to stage it. We'd have ... improvised.'

I just stare at him. Eyes like stone.

It works. He's flustered. He leans forward, pleading, desperate to be believed. 'The whole thing was smoke and mirrors. All of it. You were never in any danger. It was just a lot of shouting and banging to raise confusion, fear. That's all. Come on, man, I'm sure you've done these kinds of things yourself.'

I have, of course, but he doesn't need to know that. And that has no bearing on the situation here. 'And what if it had gone wrong? What if they'd burst in and started shooting straight away? What if you'd been killed?'

'There was a risk, but we had lookouts. Sentries. We knew when they were coming and we had an exit strategy in place. It was as safe as it possibly could be. Worst case scenario, we shot back, killed his bodyguards. Or wounded them.'

'The motorbikes I heard.'

'Was us getting away, yes. I know these streets better than they do. Knew which ways to go, to lose them if they decide to give chase. Which thankfully they didn't.'

'Thankfully for you, you mean.'

Kharis turns to me. His desperation has broken. I haven't treated his confession in the way he expected. So he moves on to the next emotion. For the first time I see real anger on his face. 'Hey, I just did you a huge fucking favour, man. You wanted to get in with your target? You're in with him. Use it.' He turns away. 'Thank you, Kharis, you really fucking helped me.'

I stare at him, unable to back down but knowing I should. He's right. About everything he said. He couldn't have let me know because I might have blown it. And I do have an advantage now.

'Sorry,' I mumble, 'you're right.' I'm not used to having

anyone else dictate my play, or the speed of it, but it's better to just swallow it this time. Get on with my job.

Kharis nods, not making eye contact.

I try a smile. 'Our first big argument. No relationship's complete without one.' (1)

21 – Notes

1. And here we are again. The interrogation set up, the reveal it's been perpetrated by his own side, the fallout. Cliché or trope? Is he running through every cliché in the book or is he demonstrating how the tropes of this genre are to be employed? In fact, there are so many clichés/tropes in this work – as we've seen already – that it almost doesn't read like a Jon Durward novel. And I must admit, going through this test time and again for just these sorts of editorial purposes, there were times when I – or part of me at least – thought it wasn't him. Couldn't be him. He wouldn't write something like this, it's against everything he ever claimed to love about literature. But then I think again. No. He's doing this for a reason. I made my name (or one of them) writing commercial genre fiction. And I like to think those books could still be recognised as being written by me and not just the pseudonym I was operating under at the time. Personal style is the one thing a writer can't fake. And this whole novel has Jon's personal style all over it. So we just have to believe that he deliberately set out to write a novel exploring identity wrapped up in the guise of an international espionage story. A story where no one is who they appear to be. Apparently. We also have to believe that this a novel he wrote to tell readers not only where he went, but, more importantly, why.

I bumped into Kari, quite by chance. This was after Jon's outburst over dinner. I hadn't seen him for some time after that. Not because we'd fallen out or anything as specific, just that we didn't seem to be appearing in each other's orbits for a while. So Kari. She was drinking coffee in the café at Foyles bookshop. Throw a stone in there and you're bound to hit at least six writers all working away behind their laptops. It's the ultimate central London writers' coffee shop.

But she wasn't working. She was sitting slumped, the remains of some half eaten baked good in front of her, staring into her half-drunk coffee. I was in two minds about approaching her. I mean we were friendly enough, but I felt uncomfortable because I still couldn't work out the relationship between her and Jon and he had never told me, which was a bone of contention of a sort between us. Friends shouldn't keep secrets from friends.

I decided to approach. I didn't want her saying to Jon that she'd seen me and I'd ignored her. Or saying that to Gwen. Her opinion of me, already frosty through no fault of my own, would plummet even further.

'Hey there, how you doing?' I said after being served, standing over her with my coffee in hand.

She looked up, startled, not realising for a few seconds I was talking to her, taking a few seconds more to realise who I was. 'Oh. Hi.'

I hadn't really spent much time with her until now. Certainly not one on one. And I'd never appreciated just how attractive she was. I mean, I know that's neither here nor there, but she really was quite stunning. In her own way, of course. Petite – although apparently I'm not supposed to use that word any more – and gamine. Can I use that one? Kind of like an elfin French film star from the Sixties. Not my type at all, but I could see what Jon saw in her.

But for all that, she looked rough. That was what I

noticed more than anything else. I would say her eyes were red rimmed as if she'd been crying but it was worse than that. She looked like whatever was troubling her – and she did look troubled, very troubled – was doing more than make her cry. It looked like it had been keeping her awake at night.

'Mind if I join you?'

I needn't have spoken to her, I knew that now. There was no way she would have noticed me, as wrapped up as she was in her own world and, clearly, her own problems.

'Yeah, sure.' She moved her stuff – bag book and coat – out of the way and I sat down opposite her. She tried to smile, just looked nervous.

'You OK?' I said.

She sighed. 'Yeah, you know. Yeah.'

She looked so sad, so pitiful, that I couldn't help but be concerned for her. 'What's up? You look a bit down.'

Another sigh. She took a sip of her coffee, seemed surprised to find it had gone cold.

'Can I get you another one?'

She shook her head. 'No, I'm good.' She went back to staring at her cup, as if whatever answers she was seeking would be found in there.

'You sure? You don't look good.'

'I've just had a meeting with my agent and publisher.'

'Oh, right.'

Another sigh. Bigger than the last ones. 'They're dropping me.'

'What, the publisher?'

'Both. Both. Yeah. Both.' She was nodding, eyes anywhere but on me.

'Shit, that's awful.' I wasn't sure I needed this from someone I barely knew, but she was in pain and needed help.

And, let's be honest, it was a situation I understood all too well. So I couldn't just walk off now. Or worse, get up and go and sit by myself. That would be particularly heartless.

'What happened?'

'Just that. My last two books haven't made the, as they said, splash they thought they would, especially since they came sprinkled with Jon Durward's fairy dust...' Her voice dripped with sarcasm. Some part of me, the gossipy part, wondered if she was speaking in euphemisms, alluding to their purported affair. Or not. She continued. 'Yeah, so that's it. That's it. Me done. Over and out.'

'That's fucking awful,' I said, 'but surely they can do something about it? I mean, that happened to me. I was in your situation, or kind of like it, but they offered me the crime novels. That worked out. Why don't you try something like that? Reinvent yourself, get a new name.'

She looked up at me then, straight at me. And the honesty in her direct gaze was almost too much. I had to blink, look away.

'Write under a different name?' She gave a bitter laugh. 'Are you serious?'

'It's not that bad,' I said. 'These things happen in our line of work. You've just got to be a ducker and diver.'

She said my name and it didn't sound pleasant. Neither were the words that followed it. 'I don't know if you mean well or not. But really, saying that to me, you have no fucking idea, do you? No fucking idea whatsoever.'

'Oh. OK. Right.'

Another sigh. 'Sorry. Didn't mean it like that.' She seemed to be in dialogue with herself more than me. I was just the sounding board who happened to be in front of her at the time.

'Couldn't Jon help?'

Another bitter laugh. 'I doubt it. No, I doubt Jon could help. Or would help.'

'Well, is there anything I can do?'

She looked at me with such angry pity that it was almost like being stared at by Gwen. 'No. There's nothing you can do.'

I said nothing. But I couldn't pretend it didn't hurt. And told myself that was why she was talking like this. Because she was in pain. So I tried to will my coffee to cool down, drink it and go. Clearly, there was nothing I could do to help her.

'I could go away. That's what I could do.' She was talking as if I wasn't there. Or as if my presence was her excuse to voice her thoughts aloud.

'You could,' I said, thinking of what Jon had said recently. Lot of it about. 'If you think that would help. Put a bit of distance between yourself and everything happening here. Get some perspective. Might be good for you.'

She nodded, absently, as if she was acknowledging my words only as part of her inner discourse. 'Yeah. Get away. Yeah. Just tell all these fuckers to ... to ... fuck off. Jon, Gwen, the lot of them. After all I've done for them, that's how ...' A huge, shuddering sigh. She looked up again, at me. Smiled. 'Yeah. I'm off. Yeah. I don't need this. I'm better than this. I'm going. Yeah.'

I'd finished my coffee. 'Listen,' I said, passing her my business card. 'Here's my number. If you need to talk any time, just a sympathetic ear, anything like that, give me a call.' I don't know why I did that. Probably because she was in such pain. That pretty, elfin face all twisted up in ways it should never be. And my friend seemed to be the root cause of it. And Gwen. I placed the card in her hand, held my own over it.

She looked up at me. And something in her gaze melted. She managed a weak smile. 'Thank you.'

I took my hand away, stood up. I hadn't even taken my coat off. 'I mean it. Any time.'

'Thank you.'

'Hope everything works out OK.'

'Yeah,' she said.

And that, I think, was the last I saw of her.

22

'Elizabeth decided not to call on you this evening. She thought you needed respite, shall we say, following your ordeal.'

Alexander smiles as he says this and I return the smile. His is broad and worldly while mine is slightly diffident. I'm wondering if he believes we're in some way bonded by sleeping with the same woman. Part of me, the professional part, thinks that might not be a bad idea. The rest of me thinks it is.

'That's very kind of her,' I say. 'Wouldn't want to rupture my injuries, would we?'

He laughs and there we are. Two old friends on the terrace, drinking small, expensive, potent drinks as the night moves in. Stefan and Giorgio are secreted so discreetly amongst the shadowed shrubbery they could have been planted in pots.

'Thank you for yesterday,' I say again, because I think I should.

He waves my apology away with a distinctly European hand flourish. 'No problem. At least now we should have less pretence between the two of us, don't you think?'

I take a sip of my Manhattan. 'I wasn't aware there was pretence between us.' (1)

Alexander laughs. It's as expressive as his hand flourish.

'Come on, Mike. We don't need to play games any more. Not after yesterday's ordeal. Let's be real with each other.'

'OK,' I say. 'What real things do you want me to tell you?'

'Let's start with why you're really here.'

My turn to laugh now. 'You sound like my interrogators from yesterday. Is this all part of it? They play bad cop to get me to talk? If that fails, you come in as good cop?'

Alexander looks genuinely hurt by my words. 'We're two friends talking, Mike. I thought we were beginning to trust each other.'

'I wasn't aware that we weren't.'

He takes a sip of his drink, something clear and potent and Russian in origin that could probably be used to sterilise wounds, and leans forward. Places his hand on my knee. 'I believe we are on the same side, Mike. Why we are both in this country, what we are here to do. It's not easy for people in our kind of profession to make friends so we really have to grasp every opportunity we can, don't you think?'

'What is our profession, exactly? Are we going to be honest with each other now? Because if we are, we might find we have some kind of conflict of interest. What would happen then?'

He sits back, smiling. 'Then I would berate myself for having made a miscalculation and you won't be heard of again.'

I laugh. I have no other choice. 'So this is what you mean by being real with each other.'

'Sometimes honesty is the best policy.' Something hardens in his gaze and in that moment. I can believe he is who he's supposed to be and has done what he's supposed to have done. 'Besides. After what I did for you yesterday, you owe me. Mike.' He sits back, waiting for me to speak.

'OK, then.' I take a sip of my drink. Another. Alexander is staring at me, his gaze laser like. 'I work for ... a western country. Intelligence.'

'Britain?'

'A western country, shall we say. And I'm here because we've picked up chatter about Libya.' I'm telling him what I think he needs to know, also what I've managed to piece together about what he's doing here so far. It's a calculated risk, but then so are all aspects of my job.

The bonhomie is gone. 'What kind of chatter?'

'Rumours, of instability, shall we say. Rumours of regime change.'

He nods to himself over this admission. 'So why are you in Morocco and not Libya?'

Some more improvising. 'Because I've heard that the regime change isn't being planned from inside the country . . . it's being planned from inside this one.'

He sits back, seemingly satisfied so far. 'You're very well informed. If all this is true.'

'As I say, just rumours. That's what I'm here to find out.'

'And what have you found out? About these rumours?'

'Not much, so far. But someone clearly thinks I must know something, given yesterday's turn of events.' My turn to question now. 'Is that something you can help me with?'

He smiles but it's like his whole face, his whole body has changed. He's no longer the laid back, rich but bored international traveller he's been projecting since he got here. There's something else there instead. Like his whole personality has changed. Revealed his true face. And it's much harder, colder. Ruthless.

Prizrak.

'Why would I want to help you?'

For the first time I feel a frisson of fear from him. I'm aware in my peripheral vision of Stefan and Giorgio, who've subtly altered themselves to a state of alertness, as if they've picked up some Pavlovian signal from Alexander only they can hear.

'Because as you said,' I say, taking a large sip of my drink, draining the glass, 'it's not easy for people in our profession to make friends. And we have to grasp every opportunity.'

'Assuming we have no conflict of interest.'

'Always assuming that, yes.' I keep my hands down by my side. I'm calculating odds now. Checking entrances and exits, mentally mapping out possible routes of escape. Glancing around for things I can use as a weapon against the two slabs, working out the odds of my speed against their bulk. Not to mention Alexander himself. He's never shown himself to be particularly physical but that was perhaps only in his previous persona. Now, I don't know what he's capable of.

He stares at me, eyes giving nothing away.

I try not to move, return the stare. I feel suddenly very warm.

A waiter chooses that moment to appear next to us, ask us if everything is all right. Alexander tells him it is. I attempt to break the mood.

'Could I have another Manhattan, please? And anything for you, Alexander?'

The look is broken, Alexander drops his gaze. Absently orders another drink.

The waiter retreats and we're left alone again. Thankfully the mood has changed. I wonder if he'll try to recreate it or move on, improvise around the change.

He smiles.

There's my answer.

'Regime change,' he says.

I don't reply.

'That's what you're here for. Libyan regime change.'

'Or the possibility thereof,' I say. 'Is that why you're here?'

Another stare, but after the moment was broken before he can't quite summon the same intensity again.

'Assuming I am, what then?'

'Then it seems we might have a common goal.'

'Really? You assume I would be working for Western interests as well? Perhaps I have another kind of regime change in mind. A kind the West would prefer not to happen. What then?'

I shrug, try for nonchalance. 'We can work together up to a point. Then, agree to differ and go our separate ways.'

He laughs. 'A gentleman's agreement. How quaint. How ... *Western*.'

I smile. He leans forward again, staring at me, about to say something that he doesn't want me to miss the point of. 'I thought I had a friend once. A good friend. Someone I thought I could rely on and in return he could rely on me.' He shakes his head, getting lost in his story. 'I'm going back several years now. To Chechnya. When I was, oh, barely more than a boy. We were both barely more than boys. But we had heart, spirit. And we loved our country. And hated the Russians. Or Soviets, as they were known in that incarnation. Same people. Anyway, we fought. This was nearly twenty years ago. We fought and, eventually, we won. The Soviet Union collapsed and we got our country back. Or so we thought. That drunken shit Yeltsin wouldn't give it back. So we fought again. Fucking hard. They even killed our democratically elected president. Took hostages in a hospital. But we showed those Russian bastards up for what they were. My friend and I together. Blood brothers.' (2)

He takes another sip, eyes clearly reliving all this.

'Eventually Yeltsin signs a peace treaty. Then turns round and leaves us. We ask for help to rebuild. It's his mess, he should clean it up. We get nothing. We are starving.' He hits the table for emphasis. 'Starving. We have to do something. We're no longer in the army, we have nothing. *Nothing*. As far as the world is concerned, we are nothing. So we take matters into our own hands. The world won't give us money so we'll get their attention. We start kidnapping. Westerners, like you. Ones with gentlemen's agreements. They don't count for shit. We take them, ask for money. We get it, they get released. If not...' He mimes putting a gun to my head, pulling the trigger. He laughs. 'We get it. And my blood brother and myself, we're rich men. You will have heard of this, no doubt?' (3)

'Oh, I certainly have.' I don't add that I was in Chechnya at the time. Working. He doesn't need to know that.

'It was a beautiful scheme. Until it wasn't.'

I think I know what's coming next.

'My blood brother betrayed me. He was caught by the authorities and he talked, told them about me.'

'Tortured, no doubt.'

'Oh, no doubt. But d'you think that is any kind of excuse? To betray me?'

I think the question's rhetorical but he's waiting for me to answer. 'I guess that deep down, no matter what, we'll always do what's best for ourselves.'

'Yes,' he says nodding, like I've given the right answer. 'Yes, you're right. Exactly. I know this now. But I thought differently then. Would I have given him up? If positions had been reversed? No. Of course not. No matter the torture. But that was just me being naïve. But nevertheless, he gave me up.'

He stops talking and I can see he's looking somewhere that I can't see. It's dark and it's lonely and it's painful and I don't want to go there with him. Eventually he looks back at me.

'They tortured me too. Wanted me to give them names of associates. Told me he had given me up. And that? That broke me. Really broke me. And in that moment I could have given up those names they so badly wanted. Told them everything. Confirmed what they wanted to hear. But I didn't. Because I wanted him to pay for what he had done. His betrayal of me. So I told them. It was all him. I knew nothing. Talk to him.'

He smiles.

'Apparently I was believable. They thought they had broken me and they bought my story. Went back in on him. He wasn't as strong as me. He died. Serves him right for betraying me. They came back to me then. But their attitude had changed. They still wanted names, but for a different purpose. I sensed this. So I bargained. Because that's what they really wanted, you see. Our network. Our methods. They had got who they thought was the top man out of the way so now, through me, they thought they had control of the gangs and a way to use them. Turn the black-market economy into their official economy. State-sanctioned kidnappers. That's what they wanted us to be.'

'And did you do it? Become a state-sanctioned kidnapper?'

'No.' he laughs. 'And do you know why?' He didn't wait for an answer. 'Because I had realised something. I had a skill. A talent. And people were ready to pay me for it. I didn't have to stay in Chechnya and work for these assholes. No. Especially after everything I've seen, everything I've been through, what I did for my country and what my country did for me. So I disappeared. And I vowed that I would never be so stupid to fall for their shit again. I came of age in a warzone. Why not use those skills I had developed for the highest bidder? The world is shit. I can't make it any better. But I can make myself richer. So that's what I did. I slipped away. And became a ... ghost.'

'And they've never caught up with you.'

'Never.' He settles back in his seat. Smiles again, but this time it's one of relief. As if he's put down something heavy that was a burden to him. 'Until you turn up. My *friend*.'

'I'm not in the business of selling people out,' I reply. 'I'm all about collaboration.'

'Go on.'

'I thought I knew who you were but thank you for confirming it.'

He says nothing, just stares once again.

'I was sent here to negotiate. To collaborate. We have a common goal. It's in our mutual best interests.'

'So your government would work with me?'

I smile. 'Our government has worked with worse. Reputationally speaking. To get what they wanted.'

He nods. 'So where's the money?'

'As I said, I'm here to negotiate. How do I know you are who you say you are and that you can get me to talk to the people I need to talk to?'

He stares at me once more, and this, I know, is the moment. Everything stands or falls on his reply. If it's a positive, I'm in. And my shapeshifting can begin in earnest. If not ... I'll have to resort to cruder methods.

He smiles. 'Let's a take a trip tomorrow. There's someone I want to introduce you to. Ah! Drinks!'

The waiter makes his way over, places our replenished drinks on the table, departs. Alexander picks his up.

'To friendship!'

'To friendship,' I reply.

We drink, replace our glasses.

'What a good night we're having,' he says. 'Just two friends together.'

I don't reply.

Loverly jubberly. (2)

22 – Notes

1. I should have probably picked this up earlier, but have you noticed the protagonist's drink of choice is a Manhattan? So what? you may say. It's my favourite drink. But here's the thing: Jon hates it. In fact, Jon's never tried it. Because Jon can't bear to drink whisky.

   Beer, yes definitely. Wine – if he's forced to. But spirits? Not for him. I asked him why and eventually he told me it was because of his family and growing up around them. They were heavy drinkers, especially spirits, and he came to associate the smell of whisky with his aggressive, abusive father. Consequently he never wanted to drink it, never wanted to be near it. Which begs the question: why would he give his protagonist a taste for whisky? And, in particular, a Manhattan?

   The answer's simple. Because, as I said earlier, it's my favourite drink. I think we've come to realise by now that all the hints, references and allusions he's put in this text are expressly for me to pick up on, and this is one of the most obvious. It's a message. Telling me he's still alive and waiting for me to find him. Just untangle the clues. He's also, I believe, making a less than flattering connection between his father, who, as we know, he hated, and me. As I said, when we last saw each other for what we didn't know then was the final time, we parted on unpleasant terms. This is him not only telling me to come and find him but also what he thinks of me.

   You may be thinking that I'm inferring a lot from

this one thing. And you'd be entitled to think that. But Jon, no matter how we ended up, was my friend. And I know this message was meant for me.

Jon, meanwhile, was getting progressively worse. He started getting into the papers for all the wrong reasons. Usually turning up at some party either drunk or high and taking it upon himself to insult, deride and embarrass everyone within his ambit. Of course, this behaviour backfired and he ended up making himself look ridiculous. And sad. Very sad. I was sad for him, and I daresay a few others were too, but he was so aggressively, unrelentingly nasty to everyone – even those who had once championed him – that he soon used up any goodwill remaining.

So what brought about this behaviour? Bad reviews. Bad sales. It was as if he'd been sitting at the top of the big wheel for so long that the guy operating it had forgotten it was supposed to move and let someone else come up towards the top. Of course, once the guy at the bottom does restart the motor, there's only one direction for the person at the top: down. And Jon knew it. So, in desperation, he acted out.

Conversely, I was doing really well. My crime novels were selling in huge amounts, I was getting money coming for doing nothing, royalties and residuals from all over the world. They hadn't been made into TV or films, but I was confident it was only a matter of time. And in the meantime, film and TV companies paid me handsomely every year to renew the rights to my books. Yes, things were going great. And the thought of writing under my own name again had receded entirely.

OK, there were a couple of things that were niggling me, but that's all they were – niggles. Blips. I seemed to have a new editor for each new novel and each new editor had their own ideas about what I should be writing. Yes, they were all younger than the last; yes, they all wanted to make a name for themselves; and yes, they were all fucking irritating. Telling me that my style of writing, the stories I was telling were quickly becoming old hat, obsolete. Boring, as one of them said. And that was the last time I spoke to her. I phoned my agent and demanded she be replaced. How fucking dare she. Boring? Me?

Anyway, I decided the notes they were giving me were no good. They didn't understand my writing or the culture of crime fiction that had grown up around it. My agent contacted me, asking me to reconsider, take the editorial notes but I refused.

'Your sales are slipping,' she told me on one phone call. 'If you want to halt that decline, listen to what your editors are telling you. Both here and abroad.'

'I don't need to,' I replied. 'I know what I'm doing better than them. They just turn up with their agendas, desperate to get ahead by pissing on established authors like me. They won't stick this business in the long run.'

She sighed. 'Please. Just listen to your editor. I've arranged a meeting—'

'No. I won't go.'

'No, stop this. You're being an idiot.'

'No I'm not. Sales are falling? Well, maybe. If they say so. But that's not my problem. It just means the publishers aren't doing their jobs properly. It's them you should be having a go at, not me. If they did what they were paid for, sales wouldn't be slipping. So get off the phone to me and get on their arses.'

I hung up. I'd given her something to think about.

*

And that was when I bumped into Jon. Another party, obviously. As I said, he wasn't well. And as soon as he saw me, his eyes lit up with stoned malevolence.

'Well look who it is,' he said, spilling his drink over his wrist as he spoke, 'the cunt's cunt.'

I just stared at him, open-mouthed. Too shocked to even reply.

'What's the matter?' he said, slurring the words together, 'can't think of anything to say? Not like you. At least, you can't think of anything to say to my face, is that it?'

'What?' I looked round, feeling very uncomfortable. Faces that I knew, had known for years, all turned away. Didn't want to be part of what was happening. Like he was diseased and contagious and they didn't want to catch it. So I, apparently, had to take one for the team. 'Jon, I don't ... why don't we go somewhere else and have a chat.'

There was spittle round his mouth. Like a rabid dog. 'Why?' Some of that spittle landed on me. 'What have you got to say to me that you can't say in front of all these people?' He made an expansive gesture with his drink, spilling plenty of it on those he gestured towards.

'It's not that I've got anything to say, Jon, it's just that you're—'

'Where's Kari?'

'What?'

'You heard, cunt. Where's Kari?'

'I ... I have no idea. Why?'

'Because she's not answering any of my calls, that's why. Where is she?'

'I don't know, Jon.' I felt shaky, now. Not just because of the spectacle he was making of himself and involving me in, but because if I told him I'd talked to her and told her to put some distance between herself and him, I didn't know what he'd do to me. At that moment, he looked like his father's son. His aggressive, abusive, violent father's son.

I continued. 'Why would I know where Kari is? I've barely spoken to her.'

He leaned in close. His breath was awful. Curdled chemicals as well as alcohol.

'You fucking her, that it?'

'What? No, course I'm not.'

He pulled back, appraised me. Looked like he wanted to spit on me. 'Yeah ... yeah, you must be fucking her.'

'I'm not, Jon.' I was starting to get angry now. I tried not to because I didn't want this scene to escalate but I couldn't help myself. 'Why would I do that? I don't know her, don't fancy her. And also, I'm with Bette. Why would I need to?'

He sneered. 'Bette. Oh yeah, Bette. How could I forget the sainted Bette?' He gave a bitter laugh.

I looked round. No one caught my eye.

'I'm going, Jon. Please sort yourself out. If not for yourself then for Gwen.'

It was like I'd physically struck him. He moved close up, right on top of me, almost. Face in mine again. Hand on my chest. 'You wanna fuck her, is that it? You wanna fuck Gwen? That's your game, is it?'

'No, Jon, I don't.'

I removed his hand, possibly more roughly than I intended to, and he staggered back, losing his footing. He stumbled into a couple of party guests, who moved out of the way, not wanting to have any physical contact with the contagious one, and he fell backwards onto the floor, drink spilling everywhere.

I know what I should have done. Knelt down, helped him to his feet. But I didn't. Couldn't bring myself to. I looked at his face. His expression had changed again; now he looked like a hurt and scared teenage boy, being bullied at school. He looked like the Jon he had told me he ran away from. I couldn't bear it. I turned and left the party.

'Yeah, that's right, walk away. You fucking coward ... coward ... supposed to be my friend? You're a betrayer, that's what you are. A fucking betrayer ...'

I hurried to get out of earshot.

Getting home later that night, I told Bette all about it.

'Oh god, that's terrible,' she said. 'Poor Jon.'

'And poor me,' I said. 'He dragged me into whatever psychodrama he's got going on in his head. And in front of all those people, too. I'd better phone my agent tomorrow, see if there's been any fallout.'

'You'd better phone her anyway.'

'What for?'

'To apologise for putting the phone down on her?'

'What? How d'you know *that*?'

'I bumped into her earlier.' She named another work event she'd been to that night. 'She told me what you did.'

'Well,' I said, feeling suddenly defensive, 'she was being fucking stupid.'

'What, telling you to listen to your editor? Read their notes? That's not fucking stupid, that's common sense. Something you seem to be lacking lately.'

'Oh, don't you fucking start as well.'

'Look, she's right. Your sales are slipping. People are getting bored with the same old, same old. You need to liven it up a bit.' She placed a hand gently on my arm. 'They're trying to help you. That's all.'

'I don't need their fucking help.'

She took her hand away. 'Well you might do. Because you're spending money like it's going out of fashion and you've got nothing to show for it. You can't keep that up. Babe, please, you've got to—'

'Shut up. Just shut the fuck up.'

I let her know how displeased I was with her.

Then I lay awake for hours, not being able to sleep.

2. Fuck off, Jon.

23

I had thought my hotel pretty bougee, but it wasn't even in the same league as the Royal Mansour. This is, as the cliché goes, the playground of the super-rich. We drive up to a gatehouse where the car is checked over for weapons or bombs. Then we head up to the main gates of the hotel. Huge, ancient wooden gates, part of what was once clearly a fortified castle of some sort. But where the walls once held off invaders, now they contain billionaires. It's almost impossible to believe that several meters away behind those imposing stones is the daily stick car rally that is Marrakesh's road system.

Once inside we are welcomed by traditionally liveried greeters and ushered into the building proper. It's exquisite. Walls of the most delicate traditional Moroccan filigree, floors of expensive stone tiles. Fountains, pots, interesting recesses and even a jewellery alcove with an armed guard stationed by the glass display cases. But this wasn't what we were there for. We walked on, ignoring all that. Or affecting to, in my case.

It was about as far from Alexander's origin as it's possible to be. But he wasn't letting it show. He walked through the gilded corridors as if he was doing the hotel a favour by being there. Staff seemed to sense this and averted their gaze accordingly.

I was dressed similar to Alexander, in a linen-and-loafers

ensemble. My hair was starting to resemble his and I hadn't shaved, cultivating a beard. If he noticed, he didn't let on. I, too, looked modern and monied. The kind of person who should feel at home in this hotel.

We walk through into the indoor dining area where huge circular banquettes and tables dominate, placed beneath enormous intricate crystal chandeliers. The whole place uses traditional methods but gives them the most high-end spin possible. This is several worlds away from the traditionally crafted stuff on sale in the old town market.

Following Alexander's lead, I sit down on one of the banquettes. A part time supermodel comes towards our table, smiling. Alexander tells her we're waiting for someone but that we'll have some tea in the meantime.

He had been near silent on the drive over, which had made me uneasy. I kept my face blank, hoping my cover hadn't blown, but after the way the conversation had gone the previous night, I thought it best not to say anything. Maybe he has a hangover, I thought. Maybe he said too much. Or maybe he just didn't feel like talking. I took my lead from him.

Now, seated and waiting for tea, he leaned across, his voice low. 'The people we are waiting to see have a villa here. They live here pretty much permanently.'

'Not short of a bob or two,' I reply.

He almost smiles. 'Rulers in exile seldom are. They may plead poverty but they do so from surroundings like this. Sometimes I think they don't actually want to take power again. It's much easier to live like this, don't you think?'

'They might get bored. What do they find to do all day?'

'In here? Anything they want.' His eyes took on a sheen of cruel amusement. 'Anything.'

The tea arrived shortly after that, then the people we were here to meet.

They don't look like rulers in exile. And certainly not rulers in waiting. More like the owners of a carpet warehouse or a pyramid scheme. Small, dapper, both wearing silk suits more off the peg than tailored and gold Rolexes so huge, shiny and fake-looking, that they must be real. One has on a tie, the other sports an open neck. Both have thinning, greasy suspiciously black hair combed back close to their heads. Relaxed and smiling, they don't appear to be grieving too badly for the loss of their country.

Alexander shakes their hands, introduces me to them. To protect their identities, I'll not repeat their names. Just go by appearance, not that there's much to tell them apart. I'll refer to one as Tie, the other as Open.

We resume our seats, they join us.

The supermodel appears at our side and, demonstrating their innate sense of class, the two exiles openly leer at her. She affects not to notice and hides her hatred of them very well. Needless to say, they don't notice.

They order something extravagant in as innuendo-laden a manner as possible and she responds as if it was the most hilarious thing she's ever heard. We just stick to our tea. She walks off, leaving them to believe they've given her one of the greatest experiences of her life. She really earns her tip if they're all like this in here.

'Perhaps I'll pay another visit to this restaurant later,' says Tie, watching her rear retreat. 'See if there's something more succulent on the menu.'

His companion laughs. Alexander and I give polite smiles.

'To business,' Alexander says.

The two of them look at me, as if noticing me for the first time. 'Who is your ... associate?' asks Tie.

'Mr Nolan,' says Alexander. 'He is another contractor. Here to hear what you have to say. He is an expert in his field and may be of assistance to you. I vouch for him.'

'We wanted to deal directly with you. That was our arrangement.'

'And you are doing so,' says Alexander. 'Nothing has changed.'

Mollified, they continue. 'Gaddafi is old. He is losing his grip. The people—'

'Our people,' Open chimes in.

'Yes, of course. *Our* people have had enough. They long for a new decade. A new Libya. They want their rightful rulers restored.'

'So,' says Open, 'what is your plan to achieve this? Tell us what we are paying you for.'

Alexander smiles. 'You know my reputation. You know my work. Obviously, otherwise you wouldn't have approached me. When you agree to my fee, then we can talk specifics.'

Tie gives a strained smile. 'We would prefer to discuss the specifics before discussing the fee.'

Alexander's features harden. No trace of lightness or mirth. Not a man to cross. Or question. He knows his worth and he demonstrates it to them. 'Then there's no further need for this meeting to progress. We've had this conversation before. I gave you my price, you said you would okay it. That's what the meeting is for today. How I go about earning my fee is up to me. You don't need to know what I intend to do. That's not our agreement. You're here to finance the operation. You're here to greenlight the money and transfer it into my account.' He leans forward. 'Is there a problem?'

The two men glance nervously at one another. Then back at Alexander. 'No,' says Tie, 'there's no problem. We have the amount of money you requested.'

'So what are we talking?'

'Not all of our assets are liquid,' says Open. 'It's a little difficult to come by all the money that you require up front.'

'Yes,' nods Tie. 'Perhaps if we can give you some up front, say perhaps—'

'No,' says Alexander with a finality that I doubt anyone would argue with. 'I've presented you my terms. I've told you how much it will cost. Overthrowing a country—'

'Returning it to its rightful rulers,' chimes Open.

This earns him a stare of contempt from Alexander. A stare he holds for long enough, ensuring they get the message. When he's sure its penetrated, he continues.

'Overthrowing a country is expensive. If it's to be done correctly. Apart from the military hardware needed, I also need propaganda services to destabilise. Neither come cheap. If you just want to talk about taking over your country once more then go right ahead. But we won't speak any more. I don't deal with fantasists. I deal with realists.'

Alexander sits back. The table falls into silence.

The waitress chooses that moment to arrive with the exiles' food. She lays it out on the table, smiling, but the two of them can barely muster the energy to sexually objectify her. She leaves looking relieved.

One of the men starts eating, the other looks like he's lost his appetite. Alexander is unmoving, staring at them, a malevolent Easter Island head.

This was him in business mode. I'd caught a glimpse of the real Alexander the previous night, but now I was seeing him in his natural element, at work. None of the learned social niceties that he used around the pool. This was him distilled to his essence.

Sitting next to him, I go to work. I don't just make mental notes. What I do is a kind of psychic osmosis: I absorb his thoughts, his feelings. His personality. I understand how and why he does the things he does. I've already built up a partial profile from being near him in the bar, at dinner, at the pool and drinking, but seeing him up close, working, this is where his true persona lies. My synapses are moving so fast I can barely keep up with myself. I score high on the cognitive empathy scale, as a lot of sociopaths do. So I'm an empath with a calculator: understanding my subject, every aspect of him, but simultaneously working out the flaws, the hooks that I can grab on to. Understand his life so I can organically engineer from that his death. This is when I love my job. When I feel myself soar. How could I ever think of doing anything else? Why would I want to?

Tie and Open are looking nervous. Alexander has said nothing. I'm fulfilling my role, watching.

Alexander's body language tells me he is about to get up and leave. 'Well?' he says eventually.

They both smile nervously.

'I researched you both fully,' says Alexander. 'Before meeting. I always do. I like to know who I'm dealing with. I don't like surprises. I also have to be careful. Just talking to me could sign your death warrant. Because as you know, there's a bounty on my head. Worth a lot of money. A *lot* of money. Enough to fund a revolution. More than enough to fund regime change in a North African country. Don't you think?'

Neither speak.

'Alternatively, enough to keep you both living in hotels such as this while you talk about returning to your country, but enjoy all the things that come from exile too much to actually do anything about it.'

Tie tries to speak. He doesn't get far.

'As I said, I've researched you both. Carefully. You aren't the first to try and capture me. I doubt you'll be the last. But this little game of yours goes no further. Even now my associates are in your apartment going through all your belongings. Destroying anything that links you to me.' He leans forward to emphasise his point. '*Anything*. The photographers you've installed in here to try and capture my image have been, shall we say, dealt with. Likewise the hotel's CCTV footage.' He smiles 'My associate here, Mr Nolan, has been seated exactly where I wanted him to be seated. If a camera points over here, his face is the one to be recorded. Not mine. I chose this seat for a reason. It's already been arranged for me. Like everything else.'

He sits back. I'm too shocked to speak. I should have known he brought me with him for a reason. And this is it.

If a mongoose could smile before it kills a cobra, this is the smile Alexander gives. He stands up. 'Enjoy your meal, gentlemen. Take your time. You won't be having another.'

And walks out, me following in his wake.

23 – Notes

You want to know how publishing works? When you've had a few books out, when you've built up a list of contacts that you're on first name terms with? You think you can just walk into a publisher's office, say you want to write a novel and leave with a pile of cash? Well, you'll be surprised to know, it doesn't work that way. Let me tell you by way of a digression.

Like Mike Nolan comparing the Royal Mansour to his hotel, this place I'm sitting in is far, far swankier than my own publishers. No question. Not even in the same ballpark. I mean, when I go to my publishers and I'm waiting to see my editor, the waiting area is what was once a corner piece of sectional seating, having seen its best days when John Major was being elected Prime Minister (1992 for the pedants out there), with a plastic coffee table holding a sad display of dying flowers, possibly as some kind of metaphor for the publishing industry, with torn posters of their vaguely latest books on the walls. Not here. It's all Eames chairs and blonde wood, hidden lighting illuminating their latest releases on the shelves behind me, hugely sofaed break-out areas around me. Well-tended house plants and space. Lots of space. Because nothing says success in central London like having offices with space.

I'm here following the conversations with my agent and Bette. Instead of listening to editors I don't respect and refuse to listen to, I decided to talk to other editors, ones I did respect, at other publishers. Bigger and better publishers, I might add. Ones who create – and more importantly retain – bestselling authors. This is the first one. It's someone I've known over the years. We became friends through networking, the way most people in this business do. And after the very public spectacle of Jon's behaviour, I decided to call in a few favours, have a few chats, sound out the lay of the land and other confused clichés and mixed metaphors. The grass being always greener, of course.

I looked up on hearing my name, my editor friend coming towards me, huge grin in place. I stand up, we do that manly hug thing so beloved of those in our profession, and head off to a meeting room, making small talk on the way.

Once inside, he puts in an order for two coffees from his assistant and we sit down at the large conference table. This publisher's office, like so many of them now, are all open plan, so there's no real sense of hierarchy or for that matter privacy. So private meetings have to book a room because sitting at a desk surrounded by all the other editors just isn't conducive for talking. This is progress.

'So,' he said, sitting back once the coffee's arrived, 'What can I do you for?'

Hilarious. 'Well, I'm just getting a little bit jaded where I am. Writing what I write, who I write it for. You know the kind of thing.'

He nodded. 'Yeah, yeah, sure.'

'I think we're just all too familiar, we're bored with each other.' I try to laugh as I say this and he gives a smile in response. 'I'm just seeing what it's like away from them.'

'Sure. Sure. So what did you have in mind?'

'What d'you mean?'

'Ideas. What ideas for books do you have?'

'Well, I thought I'd bring the series I'm writing over with me. Fresh start and all that. Give it a good kick, get it going again.'

He made a face, which I'm sure he didn't intend me to see. But nevertheless I did. It's not a pleasant face. 'Telling you now,' he said, 'Straight away, we wouldn't want that series.'

'OK. Why not?'

There's that face again. 'It's just ... well, I just think it's had its time. That idea, that approach, that pseudonym, the main characters ... all a bit old hat now. Sorry, I'm just being honest.'

I tried to keep my face straight. 'No, no. That's fine.'

'And the sales are declining as well. Not a lot we can do about that, I'm afraid.'

'Right. Yeah.' I was starting to see the inside, but I didn't say anything.

'So,' he leaned on the table, hands open, 'what else have you got for us?'

What indeed? How about nothing? I didn't have any other ideas because I was expecting him to take my existing series, up my advance and put it on the top of the charts. I had to think quickly. Come up with something.

'Okay. There's this soldier. Comes back from Afghanistan. Hates what the country's become so he becomes a vigilante, righting what he sees are wrongs, doing good. Like a British Lee Child. It's got legs. What d'you think?'

There's that face again. 'Yeah ... British Lee Child? You see, the whole point of that series is that it's set in America. The wide-open spaces. The vistas. Reacher gets off a bus and he's into a new story. You couldn't do that over here. Gets off a bus and he's in Redditch.' He laughed. 'Wouldn't work, would it? Anything else?'

'Yeah. It's kind of more of a horror novel than a crime novel.'

He winced. I caught it.

'About the laundries in Ireland. You know, where they sent the unmarried mothers to work? Run by sadistic nuns?'

'Yeah, I know. You want to set a novel there?'

'Yes, because it's a brilliant setting. You've got the rage and injustice right from the start. And you've got this, this girl, this unmarried woman, who's been made pregnant by this boy at church and no one believes her, and they all take this boy's side, so her family send her to the nuns. And she's treated horribly. In fact, she's beaten so badly they think she's dead. But she's not dead. They leave her outside and she's visited by this ghostly figure, this spirit of vengeance of all the other dead girls. And this spirit gives her the power to take on the nuns. So she—'

'I'll stop you there. That's not something we would be interested in.'

'Why not?' I've actually impressed myself with my ability to think on my feet. I genuinely don't think it's a bad idea.

'Well, for one thing, we don't do horror. There just isn't a big enough market. And for another, it's not your story to write, is it?'

'How d'you mean?'

'A young, unmarried Irish girl? Written by a middle-aged, middle-class white man? No, sorry. Too much appropriation, I'm afraid.'

That really makes me angry. 'You're saying I can't use my imagination to write something? Is that it?'

'I'm just saying there are other writers who'd be better suited to write a story like that, that's all. Anyway, what else have you got?'

I've got nothing more. I can't even make up another story, he's made me so angry. He sensed this, stood up.

'Well, thanks for coming in. Give my love to Bette.' A shadow falls across his face when he mentions her name. I don't know why. It made me uneasy, but I brushed the concern aside, gave him some platitudes, made my way outside.

Really angry now.

It wasn't the first publishers I'd called in to and that wasn't the first editor I'd talked to. In fact, it was the third. And I'd heard variations on the same story from the earlier two. They didn't want my series and they weren't interested in anything else I had to offer. If I didn't know better, I'd say it was me they didn't want to publish.

Anyway. Not to be too disheartened I tried new agents after that. If I couldn't find a new publisher, then I'd find a new agent who could find me a new publisher. Again, I'd made enough contacts through networking to be able to have frank and honest discussions. Easy. Except it wasn't. I got the same response from them too.

Something was up. I knew it. But I didn't know what. I wasn't imagining it, I was sure of that. I just had to find out what it was. Was Jon involved in some way? Was he trying to stop my career because we'd had a falling out? Was he that petulant and petty? I didn't know but I suspected it was something like that. There was nothing else for it. I would have to confront him. And be ready for whatever he said.

24

'So I was only there as a human shield, is that it?'

I kept my anger reined in until we got outside, through the massive, hangar-sized ancient wooden doorway, waiting for the car while liveried doormen fussed around us, and into the air-conditioned interior before I spoke.

'Only there to deflect attention away from you. Thanks.'

Alexander has dropped all pretence of bonhomie. The courting stage is over. Now that he has me where he wanted me all along, he doesn't need politeness. He turns to me, eyes dark coals.

'Why are you here, Mike? Really?' The way he pronounces my name, like it's the most unpleasant thing he's ever had in his mouth.

'To meet them,' I say. 'Fact finding, fishing.' I'm genuinely angry but I'm using it. Staying in character. Saying the kinds of things he would expect to hear after what he's just done to me. 'We heard the chatter about Libya. I was sent to find out whether there was any substance to it.'

'Well congratulations. I've done all your work for you. You can go home now.'

'And so can you.'

I sink back into the leather, as if sulking.

'Indeed.'

We continue along in silence. I look out of the window. The daily drama of Moroccan driving doesn't do it for me any more. I don't want to be here.

'Of course,' says Alexander eventually, as if we're still having a conversation. 'There may have been another reason for your presence here.'

'Like what.' I'm playing the grump, barely articulating my answer as a question.

He turns to me again, and again there are those dangerous, glittering coal eyes. 'To meet me.'

Shit.

Compose yourself.

'And what makes you think you're so special?'

'Don't fuck about, *Mike*. You know who I am.'

'And who's that then.' Again sulkily, but hopefully not over-playing it.

'Don't pretend you don't know.' His voice drops dangerously low, dangerously monotone. 'The time for pretence is long gone.'

I look at him. He's waiting for me to give him the answer he wants. I'm thinking fast. Do I give him what he wants? And what happens to me then? Or do I keep this charade going for longer, risking really pissing him off?

'You're some international fixer, I get that.' My voice retains its angry edge, the words seemingly reluctantly dragged out. 'You do this kind of thing for a living. I've met people like you before.'

'No. You've never met anyone like me before.'

He's still staring at me. Waiting for me to give him the answer he wants. This time I have to oblige. But I'll do it my own way.

My eyes widen as if in shocked realisation. Like I've just scrolled through my mental rolodex of international terrorists and come up with him. The top of the list. My face registers surprise, a touch of fear and then, thinking of the absurdity of the situation, I give a small smile, shake my head.

'No ...'

'Yes.' Still staring at me, deciding whether my response is truthful, hopefully falling for my act.

'Not the ... Ghost' I laugh. 'No ...'

'You think it's funny?'

'Not at all.'

'Here you are with the one person that someone in your line of business is desperate to capture. And yet, you can do nothing about it.'

I look to the front of the car. The driver is armed. I look behind us, out of the window, to see Stefan and Georgio are following in their own black 4×4.

'Please,' says Prizrak, 'don't take me for a fool.'

'Wouldn't dream of it. What d'you mean?'

Prizrak gives out an elaborate sigh. 'You almost had me fooled, you know. Almost.'

A shiver runs through me. 'What d'you mean?'

'The whole kidnapping thing, the shooting ... very good. Very good.'

'I didn't—'

He holds up a hand. 'Please don't patronise me.' His voice hard, cold. 'We've passed that time now.

I say nothing.

'You may not have been expecting it, I grant you. But it was all organised by your people. To get you nearer to me. A stupid trick, almost amateur. And it almost worked. Because you seemed so genuinely shocked by it. But it took only a small amount of digging before I found the truth, Mike.' He smiles. 'How are you going to shape shift your way out of this?'

Fuck. Fuck, fuck, fuck. My cover's blown. Spectacularly so. I don't reply this time because I can't actually speak.

'You're good. Very good. But I'm better.' Prizrak smiles. 'So, *Mike Nolan*, what happens next?'

I still can't speak.

Prizrak continues. 'I can't let you go. You understand that. I could take you with me, but I doubt you have any value as a hostage. Shapeshifters don't officially exist. So shall I just kill you?'

I find my voice. I need to. 'Why are you even thinking about it? If what you say is true about me, you have no choice.'

'If what I think is true?' He laughs, harsh and grating. 'It's what I know and it's true. Don't play for time, *Mike*. Begging doesn't suit you.'

'I'm not begging. Cards on the table? Truth?'

'Oh, this should be interesting. Please continue.'

'I wanted to resign. Leave all this behind. Disappear. But they gave me this one last job. I'm beginning to suspect they thought something like this would happen. That you would discover who I was and kill me. Maybe you even had help to uncover my identity, I don't know.'

Prizrak shrugs, noncommittally.

'And I was going to go through with my task.'

'I'm sure you were. Don't think I didn't notice how you started to dress like me. That's what your sort do, isn't it, you Shapeshifters? Mimic the target?'

'Usually. Helps us get into the right mindset.'

'Please continue.'

'I started to think, to question. Why am I doing this? What do I get out of it? I've got money put away in various locations to be comfortable for the rest of my life. Or comfortable enough until I can start a new one. But then I thought, we're getting on well. Why don't I tell you who I am? And ask to change sides?'

Prizrak falls silent for a moment, then nods. Smiles. 'Ah yes,' he says. 'I thought this would be it. Something like that.'

'What d'you mean?'

'Is this what they teach you? Is this what you've been trained to do?'

'What d'you mean?'

'When your cover's blown try and join the other side?'

'Why would they teach us to do that?'

'Because once you're on my side, once you get to know even more about me, you can carry out your mission perfectly. And make some money on the side. Very clever.'

'I'm not lying, Alexander. If that's your name. I've grown to like you. To regard you as a friend.' An image of Julia appears before me in my mind. I dismiss it. 'There's nothing for me back home. I was giving this up anyway. So what would I gain by still killing you? The job doesn't mean anything to me any more. And I'd be bored doing nothing. Plus, there's a lot in my head that people would pay good money to get at. So why not?' (1)

His mouth falls slightly open in surprise, genuinely considering my proposal.

'Very good, Mike. You almost had me.'

'What d'you mean?'

'Even if I were to take you with me. As an equal, not as a hostage, of course, I could never trust you. Not fully.'

'D'you trust the people you have now?'

'Implicitly.'

'Why?'

'I pay them better than anyone else would. And they know what will happen if they double cross me.'

'So what makes them any different to me? Pay me better than anyone else and I'll be as loyal as them.'

He goes quiet, thinking.

Sounds have fallen away. I can't hear the street or the air conditioning. All I can hear is my heart hammering, blood pounding in my ears. My life hinges on the next few minutes. Seconds, even.

Eventually Prizrak sighs. 'It's a tempting offer, Mike, but, as they say in your country, it's a no from me.'

I feel suddenly lightheaded. Tiny stars dance before my eyes. Despite the chilled air-con I'm sweating.

'I don't doubt that you have qualities I could use. And that you're better at what you do than most people. Not to mention, as you say, the information you hold in your head. But ... there will always be this sneaking suspicion of loyalty. To who you were, what you were. Even with what I could pay you. I'll gladly have the information you're carrying, no doubt. And I'll make sure I get it. But as for working together, as the phrase has it ... you're fired.'

I sit still, staring ahead. I have no time for self-pity, for reflection. It's time to be professional. Time to go to work. My mind spins, making calculation upon calculation as fast as I can go. Calibrating. Weighing up scenarios. Hopefully Prizrak thinks I'm fully in the moment and not calculating my odds of escaping this situation, which I am doing. He leaves me alone to think, doesn't break my silence.

I look out of the window once more. We're driving past what appears to be some kind of unofficial overflow market, outside the walls of the old town. It squats along an unmade track with a long, sloping, bank down behind it towards a dried riverbed. The bankside has been used as an equally unofficial rubbish dump with the consequence it looks like an unregulated tip with market stalls on top of it. The car is turning round a roundabout at the side of it, heading back towards the hotel. I realise I may never actually reach it.

Without overthinking, I reach forward and grab the gun holstered on the driver's waist. He's too shocked to react initially, making a noise of surprise, torn between keeping control of the car while completing its manoeuvre around the roundabout and getting his gun back. I take the guesswork out of the situation by shooting him in the back of the head.

The dead man's foot presses down on the accelerator, the car lurches forward, straight ahead, the market in its sights. I brace myself for impact.

The car ploughs right into one of the stalls, scattering plastic bowls, buckets and other household items as it hits. The stall-holder and passers-by jump to get clear, screaming.

The car doesn't stop, taking items from the stall with it, crashing over the edge, careering down the rubbish strewn bankside.

It comes to a sudden halt when the front end connects with the dried-out stone, rubbish and rubble at the base.

Even though I'm braced, I hit the seat in front of me hard. I look to my right. Prizrak wasn't braced. He's hit the seat with the full force of his face and he's out cold.

This isn't going to be elegant, but it is what I'm paid for. I grab his face, shove the gun into his mouth and I'm just about to pull the trigger when the car door is pulled violently open.

Stefan has arrived.

He reaches in and grabs me, pulling me off Prizrak. I have no option but to allow myself to be dragged from the car.

He draws back his free hand, making ready to land me a blow that'll probably break most of the bones in my face. He doesn't have time to do anything else, though, because I've still got the automatic in my hand. I bring it up and, point blank, shoot him in the face.

He takes a few seconds to stagger backwards and for his lifeless body, minus half his head, to fall.

I look up. Georgio is making his way quickly towards me. I fire off a volley of shots at him. All body shots. He too staggers as the bullets connect and falls to the ground. When I'm sure he's no longer a threat I turn back to the remaining inhabitant of the car.

But he's gone.

I look around, expecting to see him running away, but I can't make him out. The commotion has drawn a huge crowd and he's managed to disappear inside it.

Like a ghost.

Thinking that I should do the same, I fire off a couple of shots to clear a path through the shrieking onlookers.

Then I'm gone too.

24 – Notes

1. Even bearing in mind what follows this declaration, is 'Mike Nolan' being honest here? Would he change sides? Admittedly he says a few paragraphs later that he's only playing for time, trying to find a way to get out of the car and escape, but nevertheless, he's very convincing when he says this. What are we to infer from that? Is the protagonist, the 'hero' of this novel really that morally pliable? Are we still meant to root for him if he changes sides? Or is it only a ruse? I genuinely don't know, and I'm sure that's the effect Jon wanted here. It's a morally relative milieu he operates in, so this kind of thing is to be expected. So if that's the case, is Jon saying there's no such thing as loyalty? To friends, colleagues, a cause or a country? And if that applies to someone's professional life, would it also apply to their personal life?

I wanted to share all the things that were going on in my search for a new publisher and agent with Bette, but I couldn't. Because when I got home, admittedly the worse for wear after staying in the pub for too long, she was gone. And I don't mean just popped out to the shops or busy with work. I mean gone. The cupboards cleared of all her clothes and belongings and a note left for me. Handwritten. I'm not going to repeat what she'd written down. Suffice it say, it was pretty final.

I honestly didn't see it coming. I thought we were fine. Yeah, a few rows and sulks just like any other couple. But apart from that nothing major. We were good for each other. We worked well together. It was like a punch to the stomach.

I go round the house, looking for any trace of her. There is none. It seems that even her scent has vanished. How could she do that? Make her exit so complete that even that's gone?

I should be heartbroken and I am, but I'm not crying. I haven't broken down and sobbed. No. I suppose I'm still processing but at the moment the main emotion I'm experiencing is anger. Real, barely suppressed anger.

I think about all the reactions I've got from editors and agents I've spoken to, the shadowed, cautious way they behaved when they mentioned Bette's name. Did they know about this? That she was going to leave me? *All* of them? How?

Again, I can only suppose someone told them. And again, I bet I know who.

Later that evening I land on Jon's doorstep. It's dark, it's cold but the lights are on inside. I know he's home. I knock on the door. And Jon opens it immediately, as if he was waiting the other side, just for me to turn up.

'Well,' he says, and from the way he's swaying, I can tell he's drunk. That makes only one of us because my anger has sobered me up. 'Right on time. I knew you'd turn up here.'

'Where is she? Is she here?'

I make to step inside but he bars me.

'Whoa, fella, where d'you think you're going? You can't just come barging into someone else's house without being invited, now, can you?'

'Why, is she inside?'

'I assume we're talking about Bette?' He smirked while he spoke.

'Course we fucking are,' I said.

'Shh. Neighbours.'

'Then let me in and we'll talk inside.'

'I don't think so. You're not staying long, and everything we have to say to each other we can say here.'

'And what would that be?'

'Well, you want to know where Bette is. Or rather where she's gone. All I can tell you is that she's gone. Out of your life for good. You'll never see her again. She'll make sure of that.'

I stared at him. And realise my assumptions are correct. 'You told her to leave.'

He smiles.

'You *helped* her to leave.'

His smile widens.

I went for him. 'You—'

'Whoa there,' he said, pushing me away. The strength in his arms shows he's not as drunk as I first thought. 'I said, you're not going to find her. Now you know that, you can leave.'

Sorrow hits me then. The anger dissipates slightly. 'Why? Why did you help her?'

'She came to me, mate. She asked for my help. And I was only too happy to. Gwen and I. Both of us helped her. She told us how unhappy she was. How unhappy you were making her. So we told her to leave. She said she couldn't, that she didn't have anywhere to go to, no money, so we helped her. And that's all you need to know.' He started to close the front door. 'So, goodnight.'

'Wait,' I said. 'Wait.'

He stopped. Looked at me. Waited.

'Why? Why did you do it?'

'Because she came to me for help. So I helped.'

'But ...'

His smile widened again, became bitter. 'And because I knew it would really, really hurt you. It was worth it just for that.'

I just stared at him, not knowing what to say. I knew we'd had a recent falling out but we'd been friends so long, I couldn't believe he'd say that.

'Plus it's payback.' There's relish in those words.

'Kari. You told her to leave me. And she did. Well now we're even. Mate.'

And he slammed the door in my face.

25

Everything's blown. It's extraction time.

I lie low in a café, trying hard not to look like a wanted man. It's in the old town, where I can hide away for a while and think. A squalid little backstreet place, where the streets are alive with the noise of raised voices and moped engines, and the air choked with exhaust fumes, fried meat and rotting vegetables. A place where locals drink coffee and talk in Arabic about how much they hate Western tourists, especially how they have to rely on them to make a living. There's no alcohol, so I drink coffee too. It's bitter and black and surprisingly good. I ask for it in Arabic, so that endears me slightly to the burly old guy behind the counter.

I sit at my table, glancing round to be sure no one has followed me. I would spot them straight away. They would stick out somewhere like this, even worse than me. I think what to do next. I've still got the gun on me, tucked into the back of the waistband of my linen trousers, in time-honoured fashion. My loose shirt stops it being noticeable, my posture does the rest. I need to think.

I contemplated getting rid of the gun as they're not my style. However, my prints and DNA are on it. Not that my prints and DNA have been left on anything else over the years so they wouldn't be able to get a match with anyone on any system. But I don't like the idea of starting now. So I keep it with me for now. Given the way things are going, I may need it again.

I get my phone out, call Kharis. There's no need for secrecy now, just expediency. He'll have to arrange me safe passage out of the country and back to the UK. All my passports, documents, money and cards are back at the hotel and I'm sure Prizrak will be waiting there for me. Or worse, the local police. No immunity in my line of work, that's acknowledged going in. If you're caught, you're caught. And if they get me, I'm dead – one way or another.

Right now, my handler's idea of just disappearing into one of my fake identities, dissolving away where no one would ever come and look for me, seems damned attractive. But no. I had to do the one last job cliché. The one last job that goes wrong cliché. How fucking, tediously predictable.

Kharis answers. I tell him the meeting place, give him a time, end the call. No time for conversation, argument, anything. I order another coffee. There's an old TV on in the corner of the room, up high and the screen so covered in dust and grease it seems to be showing ghost transmissions. I've never found ghosts scary. Never. Always comforting. Someone coming back after death points to an afterlife, gives you hope. No matter how horrifically it may be presented. Hope is hope. But there's nothing ghostly about the images they're showing on the TV. And nothing remotely hopeful either. It's Prizrak's car face down in the dry ditch, bodies and debris strewn around. There's a reporter doing his piece to camera, making the most of it. He's gabbling with excitement, almost forgetting his training, but I can pick up a bit of what he's saying. Explaining how the car crashed, a shoot-out, then the lone gunman running away, getting lost in the maze of the old town markets. He gives a description of the wanted man. It sounds like me.

But to be fair, it sounds like any white western tourist. Only, not many western tourists would go drinking in a café for locals.

I feel eyes on me. Suspicious, wary eyes. Scared even. Possibly angry. I drink my coffee and, as casually and as unobtrusively as I can, leave.

'I need extraction. Now.'

We're in the lighting shop, standing in the shadows at the back, as per usual. I haven't let Kharis speak, no pleasantries even. This is the first time we've made contact since he admitted setting up his little kidnapping charade. I'm still smarting over that but don't have the time or mental energy to keep churning it over. This is more important.

'I take it that was you on the news?'

'Yes. And Prizrak gave me no choice. It's a mess, a fucking ugly mess, but I had to play the hand I was dealt.'

'And you got him? You killed him?'

'No. He got away. But my cover's blown, identity's gone, everything. I have to get out. Now.'

He rounds on me. Shows me a side to his personality that I've not yet seen. Playtime is over. 'So you try again. You go till you've got him. That's your job.'

'How can I go again? He'll be in the wind by now. And all my fake documents are back at the hotel. I need you to get me out. Now.'

I'm expecting him to jump to it, organise it, now. But to my surprise – and irritation – he sits back, looks thoughtful. Doesn't answer straight away.

'What? What are you waiting for?'

'I haven't been totally truthful with you, my friend,' he says.

'What d'you mean, what are you on about?' I'm irritable, struggling to keep composure. I have no time for this.

'That kidnapping stunt. I haven't told you the whole truth about it.'

'What d'you mean?'

'It was to get you on Prizrak's side, yes. And job done. It worked. But that wasn't all.'

He pauses, and it's like he's doing it for dramatic effect. I could throttle him.

'Tell me.'

'I received a message from London. An order. Telling me what I had to do, but giving me carte blanche to do it the way I saw fit. The most effective way. So I did. Killed the proverbial two birds.'

'What message? Why didn't I get a message?'

Something hardens behind Kharis's eyes. His laughing playboy mask has gone completely. There's now just the hard professional. The killer, if needs be. 'Because it was about you, not for you.'

I wait. Emotions are tumbling through me. I'm on edge, vacillating between anger and desperation. Wanting to do something physical but knowing I have to wait. I try not to let this cloud my understanding of what he's saying.

'The message?'

'Simple. Find out why you want to resign. Find out what you know. And more importantly, what you intend to do with all that knowledge in your head.'

'That's it? Find out why I'm resigning?'

He nods.

'You could have just asked me.'

Kharis looks directly at me, gives a pitying laugh. 'Oh really?'

The anger wells up inside me now. I turn, slam Kharis up against a shelf of dusty cardboard boxes. The whole shelving system rattles with the force. 'You could have just fucking asked me ...'

Kharis replies to my anger with his own.

'Yeah? Could I? And would you have told me the truth?'

'Course I fucking would.'

'Really?' His eyes, large and mocking, show he doesn't believe me. 'Then you're a rarity in our business. Just like the truth itself. Very rare. Haven't seen or heard much of it. Not sure I would recognise it if I was confronted by it. Certainly not if it was casually volunteered.'

I keep him pinned there.

'Why did you resign?' he says, eyes blazing. 'Just felt like it, got some fishing to do. Really? Really?'

Again, conflicting emotions are rushing through me. I want to take everything out on Kharis but I think back to what I said to Prizrak, how I would come in with him, share what I knew, sell it to the highest bidder, who I assumed was him. Had I meant that? Seriously? Or was I just saying that to get me out of that situation? Would I have honoured my word and told him or double crossed him the first opportunity I got, finished my assignment? I don't honestly know. I don't know what the true answer would be.

Kharis senses my anger has changed. 'Not so easy, is it? Giving a straight answer when our work, our lives are built on lying. If positions had been reversed, you'd have done exactly the same to me. Or anyone. Or perhaps even worse, I don't know.'

I let him go, step slowly back. Kharis remains where he is.

'A test,' I say. 'That's all it was.'

Kharis says nothing.

'Torture me to see if I'd break. Spill any operational stuff. Say who I was, what I was doing here. And more importantly, why I didn't want to do it any more. Tell you what information I was keeping in my head and what I was going to do with it. I assume you'd been given ultimate sanction?'

He nods.

'Right. And once I'd told you all that, once you'd broken me down, you could kill me. Plausible deniability all round. If in doubt, blame Prizrak.'

He nods again.

'But Prizrak got to me first. Spoiled your plan.'

'Not at all. As I said, either way works in our favour. You never told us anything, which makes both Prizrak and us believe in you. Job done.'

'Great.' I feel soiled from more than just heat, dust and dirt. 'Now get me out of here.'

Kharis shakes his head. 'Not so fast. There's still the little question of your resignation to answer.'

And the anger's back. 'Oh, for fuck's sake. I need to get out of here. We can do this another time.'

I'll never know what Kharis's response will be because at that moment there's a commotion at the front of the shop. We both glance towards it, thinking I've been discovered by the police, and how I'm going to get out of there. I reach for the gun behind me, check it's still there, rest my hand on it.

The commotion gets louder, voices raised, things being thrown around. Kharis pulls away from me, goes to see what it is. I take the gun out of my belt, ready.

I hear Kharis's voice from the front of the shop. 'No,' he says, 'no ...'

I move forward, follow his eyeline. Someone has entered the shop, causing the store owners to begin shouting. I see why. It's not the police. At first I'm reassured. But that doesn't last for long. This person, a woman, is dressed in black leather bike gear, including gloves and boots, wearing a full head, black helmet. But that isn't the reason for the shouting and confusion. It's the gun she's carrying. A gun she's currently pointing at Kharis as she strides towards him.

'No ... no ...'

He backs away, looking for a way out. Shelves of boxes line the walls behind him. He can't escape. She pins him up against the shelves. Fires repeatedly into his body, point blank. He drops immediately to the floor.

She turns towards me, gun ready. The stance she falls into tells me she's a professional.

I'm not about to let Kharis's fate befall me. I swing the gun up, aim it at her.

Stalemate.

She shoots. But not at me; she's aiming for one of the massive, elaborate light hangings above my head. I flinch as the glass and metal shatters from the bullet's impact. Cover my head with my hand, instinctively.

She uses that moment of deliberately created confusion to turn, make for the door.

I bring my gun up once more, take aim at her. Squeeze the trigger.

It's too risky. The store, the market is rammed with people. I'm a good shot but she's dodging about, weaving her way to the front of the store, trying to make herself a difficult target, deliberately scattering items from shelves in her wake, trying to stop me from following her.

I take a chance. I shoot. I only hit a metal lampshade, add a few more holes to it.

She ducks away again, looks round.

Her gun arm is down and I run after her, but by this time she's reached the front of the shop.

By the time I get there she's roared off down the lanes on her motorbike.

I look back at the shop, the anguished cries of the shop owners, the dead body of Kharis and get out of there as fast as I can.

25 – Notes

As you may have noticed, the notes seem to be less about the narrative than about the story behind it. Or rather the relationship between myself and Jon. Or, let's be honest, I'm just talking about myself now. And yes, it is a digression but one I think that's certainly germane to the main point. Being the background of Jon and my relationship, how I came to edit this novel and, the most important thing, where this novel came from and why at this time. Which we will come to.

However, at the moment, while the narrative itself is rattling along like a generic thriller and doesn't need me to provide any contextual notes, I'll continue with, as we call it in the trade, the backstory. Even though the next section is personally very unpleasant to deal with. There are memories I don't want to dig up again but, for the sake of full and frank transparency about my friendship with Jon, I'm going to have to. If I didn't think it was necessary to do so and enrich the reader's knowledge, believe me, I wouldn't do it. It would be too painful. But here goes.

After being turned down I returned, somewhat sheepishly, to my agent, ready to swallow my pride and resume my career again. But it wasn't to be.

'Listen,' I said, with as much contrition as I could muster in my voice, 'You were right. All along. I should have listened to you. I just wanted to say that. And now, I want you to apologise to my editors and tell them that I'm going to take their notes on board. I'm going to work with them to get my sales up again.' I managed a smile. 'I'm really sorry, and I want to start again.'

I waited, trying to gauge what her reaction would be.

'And what's brought about this sudden change of heart?'

'I just ... got a bit too full of myself. I gave myself a talking to. And now here I am. Ready to go. Again.' Another smile. But they didn't seem to be getting across.

She stared at me. 'So,' she said, 'putting all that to one side for a moment, I hear you've been having conversations with publishers. Behind my back.'

I felt myself reddening. I stumbled over my words. 'Well, I just wondered if they had anything to offer me. I was using my initiative. Using those contacts I've made over years of networking. I thought you'd be pleased I was being proactive.'

She nodded slowly, taking it in. 'Yes. Being proactive and using contacts is good. Very good. I suppose.'

She smiled and I thought I'd got away with it.

'But talking to other agents behind my back ... how is that using your initiative?'

I stared at her, open-mouthed. I didn't know what to say.

'Did you think I wouldn't find out?'

I look around the room, see the books of her other, more successful clients, their ten by eights hanging framed on the walls. Including Jon's. Obviously including Jon's. That's when I notice. I'm not there. My picture has gone.

I have nothing to lose now. I may as well speak honestly.

'I thought there was a code of conduct with agents? You can't poach each other's clients, and no one tells anyone else who's been talking to them?'

'Usually, yes. But in this case, it seems we've made an exception.'

'Why? Why in this case?'

'Because, and I can't sugarcoat this, I'm afraid, but no one wants to work with you.'

I sit back. It's like I've been physically hit. 'What? No one ... What? Why?'

'You're a liability, I'm afraid. Word's got round about how difficult you are to work with. And there's the other stuff as well.'

'What other stuff?'

'We all know you and Bette have separated. And she's very hurt.'

'But that's not anybody's business but ours. What's that got to do with anything?'

'Word gets round. This is a small business. People talk. And come to conclusions.'

I feel lightheaded, I'm shaking. This is the last thing I had expected to happen today. I thought I'd walk in here, beg, and everything would be all right again.

'Look,' I say, 'let's make a fresh start. I can change again. Become a different person, write under another name—'

'It's too late for that. Much too late.'

I sigh, not knowing what more I can say. And then I do. I've been on the backfoot too long in this conversation. There's one thing I've got that my agent hasn't, that the publisher hasn't. And I can just keep going. Somehow.

'Well, I'll just take my series and try somewhere else.' I didn't tell her no one else wanted it. That backlist was leverage. There was still money to be made out of that. And she knew it.

'You can try,' she said, 'but those books, that pseudonym, aren't owned by you. They're owned by the publisher.'

'What? You didn't tell me that.'

She almost laughed. 'Oh, yes I did. But you were in such a hurry to sign your contract and get paid that you didn't bother to read it. I tried to warn you, but you were having none of it.'

I just sit there, staring into space. Feeling like my life has come to an end.

'And this concludes, our business,' she said, standing up. I was being dismissed. 'I'm sure you can find your own way out.'

26

I don't know where to go, what to do. I put the gun back in my belt, walk aimlessly around the market. It's easy to get lost in its labyrinthine walkways when you're aware of your surroundings. When you're not paying attention, it's like being trapped in Dante's Inferno.

The job's compromised. I can't risk a return to the compound, I can't even go back to the café I was in previously. I just need to leave. But I can't do that without my documents at the hotel. There's no other way out. I have a debit and a credit card under my current name but neither will get me far without a passport. And I'm sure that by now the police will have a description circulating of me. It may be generic, but it only takes one person to spot a Westerner acting suspiciously. I'm unused to not being in control of a situation. It's a horrible feeling. I think back to the first time, when I killed that Russian in the club. I held it together then, got out, I can do it again. I'm a professional, I need to act like one.

I take several breaths, stop walking, steady myself. If anyone looks at me, they'll see a confused and lost tourist. I'm not the only one. I need to think.

Despite what Kharis said there has to be a way out. There must be. I'm sure I'm not the only agent we have working in this country. There will be safe houses, safe routes. Of course there will. It's just a question of finding them. I need to make contact with someone on my side, either here or at home. There must be some way to do that. Some kind of protocol that I should know about. I've never needed to fall back on support. Always been self-reliant in the field, prided myself on it. However, the thought of calling for help on what's supposed to be my final assignment feels like the worst kind of failure. Admitting defeat now will forever taint my memory of all my vast accomplishments.

I've just read that last sentence through again. And cringed. Jesus, just listen to me. Maybe what I always took for professional pride and belief in myself and my abilities was – *is* – nothing but arrogance. And looking at it now, through this lens of desperation, it seems to confirm that thought. (1)

I want to follow the protocol, phone home, even. But there's a part of me stopping that course of action. And I don't think it's arrogance, not altogether. It's remembering what Kharis said. About Home wanting to know why I was resigning and what I was going to do with the information in my head afterwards. And, if necessary, using ultimate sanction to discover that. Something tells me if I do that, I may not be received with open arms.

So, I need a plan. And the more I think about it, the more I realise I have to go back to the hotel. If I'm to get out of this country, get away, get anywhere, I need those documents.

It won't be easy. Alexander knows who I am now. What my objective is. So that's next on my list. Kill Alexander. Complete my mission. Go home. Avoid being trapped here.

Easy.

The gloves are off now. This is no time for finesse, to use my usual skills. Just rely on my basic training, take him out, grab my passports, get out under whichever identity I choose. Don't even need to arrange an accident. If he was a public figure, then definitely. But he's the opposite of that. I just need to dispose of him. As quickly and efficiently as possible.

And back to the hotel I go.

I check all around to make sure no one is watching me as I gently open the double doors into my bedroom.

It's dark by the time I reach the hotel compound. I took a taxi, still playing the part of the tourist, asking the driver to drop me off by the far wall at the opposite side of the gated entrance. I told him I didn't want to wake my wife up. He laughed. The wall is nearer to where my room is.

There's a small village by that side of the wall. I have to weave my way through the shacks and shanty dwellings to reach the wall. Luckily no one sees me and, more importantly, I don't alert any dogs to my presence.

It's a vast, old stone wall and takes some climbing. I pull myself over, keeping the grunts and huffing to a minimum, drop silently into one of the gardens. It takes a few seconds to orientate myself then I make my way round to where my private pool is, walking on the lawn while keeping within the shadows of the greenery and away from the artfully positioned night lights. I reach the veranda, my double doors ahead. I pause, look round, trying not to breathe. I've been careful. No one's seen me. Hopefully no one's heard me.

I turn the handle as slowly as I can, push the door open. The heat from inside the room hits me. And something else. Another smell. Perfume. With an undercurrent of something unpleasant.

I close the door quietly behind me and, using what little light there is from outside coming through the glass of the double doors, make my way lightly across the tiled floor to the bed. There's an unusual shape under the duvet. I throw it back, ready.

Elizabeth. She must have come to see me, let herself in, waited and fallen asleep.

I put my hand out, ready to rouse her, tell her to leave, but stop. Something's not right. She's not moving. Not breathing.

I drop the duvet, step back, fighting my quickening heart rate, not to mention the impulse to just get out of there. My first thought is to turn and run but I stop myself. This is so obviously a set up that I don't know who could be waiting for me once I leave this room. Perhaps that's why it was so easy to get in.

I look more closely at her. The indentations around her throat tell the story of her death. She's been strangled. From the look on her face, she didn't go gently.

I try to move backwards with composure but know I'm staggering slightly. My heart is racing, my mind trying to stop it, force myself to think rationally. Get the documents, get out the way you came in.

I turn, checking the room for possible assailants, not managing to see into the darkest of corners, when I notice something else. Crumpled in a heap by the far side of the bed, are a set of bike leathers, boots and a helmet. I've seen them before, fairly recently. So that's one question answered.

But more raised.

My mind spins, trying to work out what I should do with this new information, what I should do next, all the while a voice is screaming inside me to get the papers and get out of there. I'm so engrossed in my own scattergun thoughts, I don't notice there's someone else in the room with me.

'Well,' says Alexander, emerging from the shadows of the corner of the room, 'this is an interesting development, isn't it?'

26 – Notes

1. Oh. Breaking the fourth wall here, Jon Boy. Giving the readership a wave, letting them know you're there behind the story. Interesting tactic to take and the only time he does it. Is it a slip up or deliberate? Or is Jon here letting us know he's OK, that he (or Garrick or Nolan or whoever) lived to tell the tale? Or maybe it's this: another clue for me. I always used to bang on to him about not being able to write about places when I was there, that I had to be somewhere else to do it. 'Ah yes,' he replied, 'the Wordsworth approach.' I questioned it, and he told me the famous (to him at least) quote from Wordsworth about writing that action (and I'm paraphrasing here) is best reflected in tranquillity. So is that what Jon is doing here? Letting me know he's safe and warm and writing this from his place of tranquillity? Wordsworth had the Lake District. Jon has his Northumberland fisherman's cottage?

I knew where Bette was. Staying with Jon and Gwen. Obviously. She might have tried to ghost me, make herself dead to me. But I wasn't fooled. I was too clever for that. Jon and Gwen. Simple.

So all I had to do was go round to their house and wait. There was a pub on the corner, some gentrified monstrosity, but I could sit there and watch their street through the window. It wasn't a perfect plan, but it was the only one I could think of. And when I saw Bette, what then? Talk to her. Plead, if need be. Just to get her back.

THE FINAL CHAPTER

The first day she didn't show. None of them did. They were all cooped up safe and sound. Same the second day. By the third day I was getting daggers from the bar staff, even though I was regularly, if slowly, drinking and I'd brought both my notepads and a book to read with me. It looked, to all intents and purposes, like I'd set up my office in the pub and was working from there. Except I wasn't working. Couldn't work, couldn't think until I'd spoken to Bette. Got things sorted with her.

And then it happened. She emerged from the house. I didn't recognise her at first, she looked so different. Gone were the vintage clothes, the make-up. Instead, she just looked like everyone else. Drab, if I'm honest. But I looked beyond that. And she was still Bette. Still my girl.

I got up from my seat and hurriedly packed my things away in my messenger bag, went outside to talk to her.

She hadn't seen me, which was good, as that meant I had the element of surprise. I called her name and she stopped, jumped even, like an arrow had hit her between the shoulder blades. I called again and she turned.

'Bette.'

She looked tired. The lack of make-up just accentuated that. And thinner too. And her roots were growing through her blonde hair. It looked like she hadn't been taking care of herself.

She stared at me, terrified, unspeaking. Unable to move.

'How are you?' I asked.

She kept staring.

'I was worried about you. How you doing?'

'Get away from me.' It was almost whispered. Like she'd seen a ghost and couldn't believe it was right in front of her.

'Come on, Bette, I just want to talk. Can't we work this out?'

She looked round, frantically scanning the street to see if there were any other pedestrians. There were none.

'I miss you, Bette.' I took a step towards her. She flinched, moved backwards.

But she didn't run. I took that as a positive sign.

'Look, we need to talk. Get some of these misunderstands ironed out. I love you, Bette.'

She closed her eyes. As if by not seeing me she couldn't hear me either.

'Please, Bette...' I took another step towards her. 'Look, I can change. If that's what you want. I can change. Become a new person. A different person. A better person. We can start again. Please...'

And then she found her voice. 'No you can't. You can't change. You changed your name, but you stayed the same. You just can't change who you are. What you are.'

'And what's that?'

'Someone who hurt me. Physically hurt me, hit me, hated me...' Her voice rose. There were tears in her eyes.

'No, Bette, no, I love you. I always have, always will...'

I took another step towards her and I was there, beside her, close enough to hold her. Which I tried to do. But she seemed to have come to life, woken as if from a dream or a trance. She dodged around me, jumping into the road to avoid my touch, and made her way, running, back the way she had come.

I ran after her, desperate to talk, but I knew where she was going. If she reached there before me, then she'd be inside, and that would be the end of it. Until next time.

She reached the house before me, even though I'd sped up. Her key was out and she hammered on the doorbell. I stayed by the gate, not wanting to cross over onto Jon and Gwen's property.

THE FINAL CHAPTER

The door opened and she ran inside. And there was Jon.

'She doesn't want to see you,' he said.

Just the sight of him made me angry. 'You've brainwashed her,' I said. 'Turned her against me.'

'You did that yourself. When you raised your fists to Bette.'

'What? No. No I fucking didn't. You just couldn't bear for me to be happy, could you? You're such a cunt, Jon.' I wanted to rush him there and then, pummel his smug face until there was nothing recognizable left.

He gave a small smile. 'Go home. And stay there.'

I was shaking with rage by now. 'Just because you're a failure, you try to take everyone else down with you.'

He slammed the door shut.

I screamed at it for a while until my rage expired. And then, aware of eyes from neighbours' windows staring at me, turned and, did as he had suggested. Went home.

27

I turn but the gun in his hands stops me moving further.

'Hello, Alexander.' I don't actually know what else to say, especially since he's holding a gun on me.

'Hello, Mike.' He says the name as if he's making air quotes around it. 'Sit down. On the bed. Face me.'

I do so. Back straight, ready to move if I need to.

'You got away, then,' I say.

'As did you. And we both came back here. Predictable, really. In your case, certainly.'

'Why didn't you just leave?' I ask.

'Because I don't like loose ends.' He smiles, teeth glinting in the moonlight. It makes the warm room seem colder. 'And you're the loosest of them all.'

I glance over my shoulder at Elizabeth, back to Alexander. 'Your handiwork?'

'Strangulation is a very intimate death,' he says. 'The killer must get up close to the victim. Hate that victim enough to want to end their life with their bare hands.'

'Did you? Hate her enough?'

'She's in your bed, in your room, *Mike*. It seems someone hated her enough to do it.'

'I see. I get what you're doing.'

'Everyone here knows she's with me. But everyone here's seen you both together. Intimately so, at times. A love triangle. The most boring of plot twists, don't you think? But as a crime of passion, or the reason behind one, more than serviceable. Especially in a country like this. Male-dominated, shall we say.'

'You wore gloves when you killed her?' I ask. 'Obviously wouldn't want to leave any prints.'

'Obviously. But thank you for your concern. I'm not an amateur.'

'So how are you going to do this?' I ask. 'You're holding a gun on me. If you use it, then you're charged with my murder. You won't get away with that.'

He smiles again. I see the glint of his teeth and the whites of his eyes in the shadows. As if he's been reduced to base essentials. 'I'm a rich man, *Mike*. In, as I said, a male-dominated country. There will be no trial, even if I chose to stay around for one. Which I don't. I'm walking tonight, so it doesn't matter.'

'Where you going? Isn't the Libya job dead?'

'You really understand nothing, do you? I may not have struck a deal with those two phoney timewasters, but other, shall we say, interested parties have made it clear they want to do business with me with the same objective. So I will be paid irrespectively.'

'And you're leaving me here, tangled up in Elizabeth's death.'

'Precisely.'

I frown. 'But if you shoot me, doesn't that mess things up? You can't have it both ways.' He's about to answer but I continue. 'You want it to seem like I've strangled her. Out of passion, because she wouldn't leave you. Have I got that right?'

He nods.

'And then they find my dead body, shot. Presumably by you, who has now conveniently checked out.'

'As you say.'

I smile. 'That's a mess, Alexander.'

'What d'you mean?'

'You may be the one for destabilising regimes, but setting up scenarios like this is my business. I've made a career out of it. And in all that time I've never made a mistake. Never been able to afford to. But this one? Absolutely stinks.'

I can sense a shift within in, even in the shadows. Not so sure of himself. 'How so?'

'First thing: leaves more questions than it answers. I happen to get angry enough to kill her. Then you get angry enough to kill me. Then you go on the run.'

'As I said, I'm rich enough—'

'I heard you.' As I speak, I feel confidence returning to me. I'm working in my territory now. On the front foot. I don't know where this is going, but it seems to be heading in my direction. 'Rich isn't going to cut it. Not in this situation. Because there's much more to it than that.'

He stays silent, which I take as encouragement. I could almost smile.

'Firstly. Yes, you're rich. But you'll be on the run. I'm sure you have fixers to take care of things but not everyone can be bought or threatened. Your picture might leak out somehow. And that's something I know you've worked hard to avoid. You might say it's even your real life's work. Even Carlos the Jackal was caught eventually. And he had a penchant for staying in places like this.'

'Go on.'

'Next thing, they'll want to know who I am. Obviously my legend is in place and will hold well, but how well? It only takes one loose end from my story for it to start unravelling. As you said, you hate loose ends.'

Feeling expansive, I stand up. He keeps the gun trained on me.

'So they'll look into you, they'll look into me. And also, they'll look into Elizabeth.'

'So? She's no one important.'

'Oh, I know you think that. But here's the thing. She tried to kill me this afternoon.'

He freezes. 'What? That's wrong. She was nowhere near the car.'

'Absolutely right. I didn't say she was. Our little contretemps wasn't the only bit of excitement in the old town today. Someone was shot in the market.'

'Who?'

'Not exactly the right question. Who by, might be the better one. The person who died was my contact. Yes, cards on the table, I was sent here to kill you. As you know by now.'

'Your orders may have changed.'

'If they had, I'm sure I'd have been told. As it happened instead, Elizabeth, or another woman exactly her size and shape wearing those bike leathers piled up down there, rode her bike up to the shop where my contact and I were discussing my extraction, came into the shop and shot him dead. She tried to kill me but I was already armed, remember? I had your driver's gun. She tore off before I could get her.'

'And this was Elizabeth?' Incredulity in his voice. 'Are you sure?'

'Her leathers on the floor, her dead body in the bed.' I sit back down now. 'Bet you're wishing you hadn't killed her now, aren't you? As I said, more questions than answers.'

I hear him sigh. Hesitate before speaking. I wait.

'I didn't kill her.'

I pause. Not the answer I'm expecting. 'Sorry, what?'

'I didn't kill her. I came here to wait for you. She was dead on my arrival.'

I frown again. 'But you told me you killed her. You said you did.'

'I was lying. I assumed you had done it. I was going to use it to my advantage.'

'Kill me and leave a whole mess for you to get tangled up in. Yeah, great idea.' Before he can reply, I continue. 'This makes no sense at all. Of course you killed her. You found out who I am, cover blown, follow me until I meet my contact then try and kill us both. You sent her to kill me. And she messed up. So you killed her and you're now trying to blame it on me. Trying to make the best of a bad situation. Isn't that more likely?'

Prizrak laughs then. Actually laughs.

'What's so funny? Can't you bear it that I've got this right? That I've shown you you're not as clever as you think you are?'

'You are miles away, Mike. Miles away. I know nothing of your contact. I know nothing of Elizabeth's extra-curricular activities. And I know nothing of her death. I'm as surprised as you are. I thought you had done it since you had killed my bodyguards.'

'Self-defence.'

He shrugs. 'Whatever. They are replaceable. You were going to kill me.'

'I think it was fifty fifty for a while, don't you?'

He laughs again, and it sounds more like the old Alexander, the cover story, the mask that Prizrak grew into.

'Oh Mike, we could have been friends, you and I. Good friends. It is a shame. Especially in light of current events.'

'What current events?'

He stands up then, walks towards me. He's smiling but his eyes are unreadable. 'The balance of power has changed since earlier today, shall we say. I don't blame you for not knowing about it.'

He looks at the bed, at Elizabeth lying there. Sighs.

'I was very fond of that girl. In my own way. Very fond. Probably more than she realised.' He looks up, back at me. 'If I can allow myself to indulge in such thoughts. However briefly.'

'So you didn't kill her.'

'No, I didn't. I thought you had.'

'No. She wasn't my target.'

'No.' He nods, to himself. 'You're a professional, Mike. And as such, I acknowledge your own code of honour and ethics. You wouldn't have killed her.'

'I only kill my target.'

He smiles again. 'But not today.'

We stand there, staring at each other.

'Why not today?' I ask. 'We're both here. I could still do it. It wouldn't be pretty, but I would be fulfilling my job.'

'You'd be welcome to try,' he laughs. 'And you may get lucky. Or I may. But it doesn't matter. Our game has been suspended for today.'

'What are you talking about?'

'We're the English and Germans during World War One, playing football in No Man's Land on Christmas Day. That's what we're doing now.'

'I'm missing something, aren't I?'

'You are, Mike.' He looks at the dead figure of Elizabeth once more, then back to me. 'As I said, it's a shame we couldn't be friends. Allies. Perhaps when next we meet – *if* we meet again – we shall be. Whoever you may be then.'

I say nothing, just stare at him. This isn't how I expected this scenario to end.

'I apologise for the misunderstanding over Elizabeth,' he says. 'But now, it looks as if you are the one with the explaining to do.'

He crosses to the double doors, reaches behind with one hand and opens them, still holding the gun on me with the other.

He steps out, disappears into the night.

27 – Notes

All I can say is that by this point, I never wanted to see, hear from or listen to Jon Durward ever again. It was too painful. Being his friend had brought me nothing but pain. He'd hurt me so much. More than I could put down in words.

He had taken away, or killed, everything and everyone I had ever loved.

28

I watch him go. Or rather, I stand and stare after he's departed.

It's a mess. But I've been in messy situations before and got myself out of them. I just need to think. Be methodical. The first thing I need is a shower. It doesn't take me long to pack. Once I've shaved and washed a lighter shade into my hair, dressed in clean clothes, my old ones bundled up in my suitcase along with the rest of my belongings, I'm ready to go. Every inch the anonymous Western tourist. I take my documents from their hiding place, decide who I'm going to be next. Paul Davis. A divorced financial services manager who's counted his money carefully and can afford to treat himself to opportunist holidays abroad in the hope of getting lucky. He'll do perfectly.

All the while I'm doing this, I'm carefully avoiding touching the dead body in my bed. That's how I have to think of her now. The dead body in my bed. She no longer has a name, an identity. That's all gone. Now she's just an impediment to my getaway. The room is filled with my DNA. I don't want any of it getting on her. Hopefully local forensics will notice that, but I can't risk it. I'm still leaving without checking out.

I wheel my suitcase through the double doors into the garden. I'm carrying two bath towels which I throw onto the high wall at the side of my room, the one I came over. I don't want my clothes getting scuffed and dirty. That won't help my cause at all.

I climb up, pull my suitcase after me, balance it on the top, lower it down the other side. Then I follow, pulling the towels with me, bundling them up in a small ball and leaving them at this side of the wall. I'm now where I was before, in the shanty town village, hoping there are no feral dogs or humans around to impede my progress.

There aren't. I begin walking.

Luckily, there are other hotels in the area. It doesn't look like it from the road, which is bleak and arid, even in the dark, but like the one I've just left, they are all walled off, keeping their riches, not to mention their precious, high-paying guests, inside. I walk towards one of them, go up to the gates, knock. I'm greeted by a tired-looking night porter who puts down whatever he was looking at on his phone, comes towards me. Time for some acting. I play the part of the confused tourist, having just been dropped off by a taxi that wanted more money after we had set off. Once I refused to give him any more, he left me here. Am I in the right place? All of that.

I'm taken to reception where I repeat my tale of woe. Am I in the right place? Is this ... I look at my phone, pretend to be checking documents ... and give the name of a place on the other side of Marrakesh. When I'm given the answer I'm expecting, I ask if I could possibly book a car to that hotel compound or do they have a spare room for the night? I make out I'm reluctant to spend money on a room when I already have one booked in another hotel, and if it wasn't for that damned taxi driver ... They sense I'm trouble, or at least obnoxious, so organise a car to take me to the other hotel, payment in advance. I thank them, get in and am driven away.

And that is how it's done.

There are no flights out of Marrakesh but there is a train

leaving for Tangier and I just might be able to get it. I tell the driver that I've changed my mind, I don't want to go to that hotel, I've had enough of Marrakesh, take me to the train station. He does so, dropping me off just in time to get myself a ticket (First Class this time, Paul Davis is like that) and board the train. Since we won't be arriving in Tangier until eight the next morning, I've booked a one bed sleeping compartment; while I should go straight in there, I decide to sit in a carriage first. Get my bearings on the train, see if I'm being followed. Professional stuff. I stow my luggage temporarily in the rack above, get myself comfortable. First class carriages comprise six well upholstered seats, three on either side, with a sliding door connecting to the corridor outside. The kind of First Class compartments I used to see in old black and white films on Sunday afternoons. I have this one to myself. I slide my Panama hat forward until it's over my eyes, and to anyone observing me, settle down to sleep. When next I look up there's someone sitting opposite me.

'Mind if I sit here?' He's tall, blonde, middle-aged, slightly portly and speaks English in heavily accented German. Bearded and smiling. And he's already sitting.

I tell him it's fine with me. I soon find out he's a talker, which I would usually close down as I try not to be memorable, but in this instance I tolerate it, even join in, as, if I'm to be remembered at all on this journey, I want it to be as mousey-haired Paul Davis, irritating financial services manager, not darker-haired Mike Nolan, confident ex-forces bloke with a dead woman in his bed.

I find out his name is Johann and he's from Hamburg. I tell him I'm called Paul.

'Travelling alone?'

I explain the hotel mix up in Marrakesh and say I've had enough, I'm going to go to Tangiers.

'It's nice to have the freedom to do that.'

'That's what being divorced and carefully looking after your money buys you,' I say, laughing. He joins in.

He produces six cans of beer from a plastic bag next to him and offers me one. I decline, saying it'll stop me from sleeping. He laughs. 'Stop you? Help you if anything!'

I laugh politely, still declining, but he's insistent. I decide it'll look suspicious if I keep refusing so I take one, open it and drink from the can. He opens one for himself, joins me. I wish he'd chosen a better brand as this lager doesn't taste good. (1)

As the train moves away from Marrakesh, setting off on its nine-hour journey to Tangier, we settle down to conversation. I tell him about my ex-wife, Erin, who left me for an office intern fifteen years younger than her. And after being upset for about a month or so I realised just how much freedom I now had. And I've never been happier, I insist. Never. As I speak, I see Erin's face, experience the heartache of her leaving me once again, followed by the liberating freedom that a midlife crisis brings. I actually enjoy telling him about my make-believe life, believing in it myself.

He tells me his life story and it's similar to the one I've made up except with some deviations: it was him who left his wife for a younger woman and they're still together. He's on his way to meet her now, having been detained in Marrakesh on business.

'What d'you do?'

He tells me he works in book sales for a German publishing house. He speaks Arabic so his territory, naturally, is North Africa. He shrugs as he says it. What can you do? Got to make a living. (2)

After that the conversation reaches a natural end. We sit in silence, drinking, like two companions. A good thing, as, if the authorities are looking for me at all, they'll be looking for a single traveller.

The next thing I know, I'm opening my eyes and some time has passed. I sit up straight away. Johann looks up from his book, alarmed.

'You OK?'

'I've been asleep.'

'Yeah, you passed out a couple of hours ago. I just left you to it.'

This isn't right. Not right at all. I never fall asleep like that. Never. Years in the field have left me wary of being vulnerable. Something must have happened. 'Where are we?'

'Just left Casablanca.' He laughs. 'Of all the bars in all the world, right?' he says, doing a dreadful Humphrey Bogart impression.

I study Johann intently, trying to see beyond his bonhomie. He just frowns in return. 'You sure you're OK, Paul?'

I tell him I am, that it's time for me to turn in.

'Turn in? Aren't you sleeping here?'

'No, I booked a sleeping compartment. I should have headed off hours ago. But ...'

Is that a look of panic on Johann's face? Why?

'You OK, Johann?'

He composes himself. So well, I could almost believe I never witnessed his unease in the first place.

'I'm fine, fine ...' Another hearty smile.

I stand up, he does the same.

'Let me help you with that,' he says, as I go to take my suitcase down from the rack.

'No need,' I reply. 'I've got it.' I get it down, pull out the extending handle. 'Well, very nice to have met you, Johann. Good night.'

He bids me a cheery good night but I can see there's something else there at the edges of his expression. Fear? No. Panic? Why would there be panic?

I reach my compartment. It's not bad at all. Small, obviously, but quite opulent. And cheap. I could never travel First Class like this for anywhere near the same price at home.

I check the room out, although I don't know what I'm expecting to find. But I do know something isn't right. I sit down on the bed trying to work everything out. I tell myself that falling asleep was a response to the stressful day I've had, my body closing down in order to cope. But that isn't right. I've been in stressful situations before and never done that. Plus, I still feel groggy from my sleep which, stress or not, isn't like me. Isn't right.

And Johann's response when I got up to leave. Off kilter. I'm sure I wasn't imagining things. Both things don't add up. So, think. What do the two things have in common? Nothing. There's—

I stop. Think. Realise. The beer. I thought it tasted off ... Johann managed to put something in it that knocked me out. And, defences down like an amateur, I let him do it.

'You fucking idiot.'

He's done something. I don't know what, but I need to find out. Because if that's the case then it means he knows who I am. And I'm not going to get to Tangiers. Or if I do, I'm not going any further.

Think. What was he so worried about?

My suitcase. He even offered to help me with it. What's he done to my suitcase?

I swing it up on the bed beside me, open it. I don't have to look far. Because there, sitting on the top of my clothes, is a gun. And it looks just like the one that killed Kharis. (3)

28 – Notes

1. And there it is. The final cliché of the espionage novel. The drink that tastes bad. Yes, I know at this point we don't know for sure that he's been poisoned or knocked out or whatever, but isn't it obvious? It's clearly been set up so that the reader will notice it. Why? Because the reader is as fluent in cliché as the writer is. This writer in particular. The reader will reach that section and think, 'Oh ho. I'll bet that drink's poisoned. Or something.' And when that turns out to be the case, the reader will congratulate themselves on being one step ahead of the writer. They're not, of course. The writer – any one, not just Jon Durward – writing a scene like that in a novel like this will know that the reader will expect it. And, consequently, congratulate themselves on working it out. It's a trick. Like so much of this novel, a trick.

2. Working in publishing. How lazy can you get? Jon's not even bothering to find an interesting profession. Is he running out of ideas now? Can he not be bothered thinking up something more imaginative? I mean, yes, it does work. And it would be a textual reason why an Arabic-speaking German would be in North Africa. But, I don't know. I just thought he would try harder. Maybe because he makes something sound plausible, he expects people to believe it. And they do.

3. Would the character know that? Could he remember that detail? Things were moving rather quickly at the

time, and he was fighting for his life. Would he really have been able to take the time to place the make and model of the gun? I don't know. And I'm not sure that, well-trained as he is and often tells us about, the protagonist would be able to do that. But when we see it set down on the page like that it seems plausible. More than plausible, factual. Why? Because it's written with authority. We see it there, we believe it. It helps that it comes as a reveal at the end of a chapter, ending on an emotional highpoint. Put a bit of emotion in with a fact and the reader, while having an emotional response, will be more inclined to believe it and not give it too much thought. No matter how implausible – or just downright wrong – that 'fact' may be.

Case in point: What happened to me next.

I began to notice that I wasn't being invited to as many parties as I used to. I know that in itself it doesn't sound like something to worry about, but when you're in such a small world as publishing, it should send a pulse down a wire somewhere to say that something's not right. I did still find my way to events, though. And when I did, I wasn't blanked exactly or completely ignored. No. I was greeted with a smile (usually a brittle one, hindsight told me), then whoever had spoken to me would then turn away. I was made to feel like an outcast, a pariah. And I didn't know why.

It didn't stay that way for long.

Word reached me, I forget how, as to the reason I was being ghosted. I was revealed as a domestic abuser. I used to beat Bette up. Rape her. Beat her some more. Everyone knew this, it was a fact. Except it wasn't. I didn't beat her up. I barely raised a hand to her. We argued, obviously. Every couple does. But deliberately hurt her? Of course not.

And rape her? I couldn't even countenance such an accusation. If this was what they believed, where was the proof? The proof, apparently, was that Bette had left me and gone to live – or rather 'sought refuge', the phrase being bandied about – with Jon and Gwen. So it didn't take a master detective to work out who the source of those rumours was.

Things had got so bad between us that this was Jon's way of getting back at me. For giving Kari support and encouraging her to leave, for calling him a cunt, for everything else. He just couldn't bear the fact that I'd become successful in my own right and had to bring me down. And pouring poison in Bette's ear, and subsequently, the whole of British publishing, was his way of doing it.

The thing is, when you're accused of something like that, and the person doing the accusing doesn't want to take matters further – for whatever reason – then you have no leg to stand on. And so it was my word against Bette's. And Jon's. And in cases like this, no matter how much I protested my innocence, it's always the woman that's believed. And yes, I'd say exactly the same thing, if I heard it about someone else. And I dare say I'd treat them the way everyone was treating me too. Because it's the last taboo, isn't it? Even more so than murder. Someone controlling, abusing, *raping* another person. Especially a man doing it to a woman. There's no smoke without fire, and all that. Except there was. Smoke. And lots of it. And no fire. But it didn't matter what I said or who I said it to. No one wanted to hear my side of the story. No one wanted to give me a fair hearing. And why should they? Side with me, a rapist, an abuser, and it might rub off on you. You might find you're the next one for a very public shunning, just by talking to me. So, no. Out I went.

And here's the thing that makes me laugh. In a very

bitter, harsh way. It was easy for people in publishing to make me an outcast. Why? Because I'd stopped bringing in the money. My books weren't earning, I was no longer a bestseller. I'd been dropped from agents and publishers. So who cares if the accusations were real or false? There was nothing riding on me, financially, so we may as well let him go.

You don't believe me? Have a look at writers who have been exposed as abusers. Especially the cases that have spilled off the books' pages and on to the news pages of the papers and media. The household names. Have their publishers dropped them? Have they been sacked from showrunning lucrative TV versions of their novels? It might seem as if they have at first glance. But look closer. Check the wording. Their TV shows are 'paused' while allegations are 'being looked into'. Their publishers don't seem to be putting out any new work by these authors 'during this time' but are happy to keep their lucrative (that word again) backlist in print. So what happens to them? Well, unless something definitive and awful is proved about their behaviour, they do their time away from the spotlight, 'learn their lessons' and return with a newfound respect for women, thoroughly chastised, humbled and ready to learn from their experiences. And apologising profusely for the harm and upset they've caused. We see it all the time, especially with male comedians. Are male writers (lucrative ones) so very different?

But hey. No one cared about me. Whether I was telling the truth or not.

I can't tell you how angry that made me.

29

Like Elizabeth's body, I make sure I don't touch it.

It's so obvious. Childishly obvious, when I think about it. He drugs me, and, when I'm out, plants the gun in my suitcase. Then, thinking I'm going to spend the rest of the night in that carriage, its job done for him, and he can keep an eye on me.

Except it didn't work out like that. Thankfully.

So why plant the gun that killed Kharis on me? It doesn't make sense on the face of it. The killer was definitely a woman. She was seen in the act and riding away on her bike. But I was seen too. It's a simple matter to show people in the market my photo and ask if I was there when Kharis was killed. I wonder how silent the lighting shop owners will be about that when leaned on by the police. Plus, the woman – now dead – who was seen in the market, and the leathers and helmet she was wearing, have been left in my hotel room. And I, even under a different name, have her gun. Which, even the thickest police officer could work out, would make me an accomplice who killed his partner for some reason. One which I'm sure they would delight in trying to get me to give up. Simple. Airtight. That'll not just stop me leaving Morocco but, with no back up coming to my rescue, ensure I'm left there to rot indefinitely in some hideous North African jail. Good one. Hats off.

Except for one thing. I know it's there. And I can do something about it. The question is, what?

The rational part of my brain kicks in again. No wild guesses now. Just pragmatic, quotidian even, thoughts. They – whoever 'they' are – have been following me. They knew I was going to leave Marrakesh. Beyond that it's just a question of which exit I would take and which direction I would head in. If they know me, if they've studied me, then the most likely route I'd take would be by train. It's how I always leave a job if I possibly can. I've found it to be the method of transport that attracts the least suspicion. Tried and tested. So they'll have put most of their faith in that. Maybe they had people watching the airport and coach station too. That makes me think that following me, catching me and implicating me is quite a structured operation. Someone's going to a lot of trouble to ensure I don't get out of Morrocco. To make sure I'm blamed for something.

I can think about who it is later. Right now, I've got to find a way out for myself. Literally.

I check the time. About four hours to go. Johann, or whatever his name is, said we'd passed Casablanca. I don't think we've passed Rabat or I would have remembered. After Rabat it's straight on to Tangier. If Johann or one of his associates has tipped off the authorities that I'm on this train and have the gun on me, they might try to board at Rabat, catch me before I can make any possible mistake at the end of the line.

I fight down a quiver of fear at that thought. Try to think of any loopholes within that plan. There's one main one that I can think of: how will they know that Johann's planted the gun on me by then? What if they board the train and he hasn't managed to do so? What then? No. They'll wait until Tangier. I'm sure of it.

Well, pretty sure. As sure as I can be. And I have no choice but to work with that assumption.

Which means keeping my head down until we leave Rabat. And then dealing with Johann. I play over in my mind who he might be working for. Prizrak? I doubt it. Doesn't seem like his style. And considering Prizrak was surprised, although opportunistic, about Elizabeth's death, I feel like his influence on my immediate life stopped when he left my room. So who, then?

Simple: whoever sent Elizabeth to kill Kharis. And me, presumably. And since she botched the job on my life, getting me out of the way by implicating me in two murders seems like the next best thing.

The train starts slowing down. We pull into Rabat. Now I wait.

I leave my room, lock the door behind me. It's dark outside but I can see the platform from the corridor windows. I check whether there is anyone getting on that looks like a threat to me. By now I should be able to get a feeling for danger, or if someone doesn't look right, but thinking that, my senses let me down with Johann. I should have expected something like that, but hindsight's a wonderful thing.

I'm ready to go if I have to. There's nothing in my case that I need or that can't be replaced. My documents, cards and money are strapped to my body, underneath my polo shirt. Or rather Paul Davis's polo shirt. It's the kind of thing he would wear.

We wait in the station for a short while. Hardly anyone gets on or off. And then we're underway again. I release a breath I wasn't aware I'd been holding, then go back to my compartment, again locking the door behind me.

I sit on the bed, trying to decide what the best course of action to take is, when the decision is taken away from me. There's a knock at the door.

My first instinct is to reach for a weapon, but the only one to hand is the gun that's been planted in my case, so that's out of the question. Although, worst comes to the worst and this is who I'm expecting, I may need to use it if I'm to get off this train alive and I'll deal with the consequences later.

I keep the case in my eyeline and open the clasps, ready to move for the gun if I have to and open the door. It's not the authorities. It's Johann. He's smiling.

'I thought I saw you in the corridor,' he says, trying to look beyond me into my room, see whether I've opened my case yet. He flinches as he sees the case is open – just quickly, but I catch it – then the smile is back in place. He holds up a bottle. 'Schnapps? If you're awake it would pass the time.'

My first response is to slam the door in his face. Repeatedly. But I stop myself from doing so. Instead, I match his smile.

'Not for me, thanks,' I say. 'Your last drink was quite potent. But feel free to come in.'

I step aside to allow him to enter. The room is crowded with one person inside, with two it's absolutely rammed. I notice his expression change slightly as he registers my words. He knows, I think. He knows that I know. He's still smiling but there's a wariness behind it.

As there should be.

'Sit down,' I say, pointing first to the bed the case is on, then to the bottle he's carrying. 'Don't let me stop you.'

He makes an apologetic smile. 'Well, you know ... I'm not one for drinking alone ...' He gives a weak laugh.

'Course not,' I say and, while he's still in the process of sitting down, I grab him by the lapels, pulling him up towards me.

He splutters, startled, but before he can speak, I grasp both of his lapels in my left hand and backhand him hard across the face with my right. And again. And again.

Feeling the anger surge within me, and with it my enjoyment of my actions, I let him go, throwing him back onto the bed, where he lands in a painful, crumpled lump.

His hand goes to his face. He looks simultaneously shocked,

in pain and also about to cry. He rubs his face. 'What did you do ...'

'I slapped you,' I say, 'because you're not worth wasting a punch on. And I'll do it again if I don't get some answers.'

He looks at me once more. No fake bonhomie, no laughter. I've let him know I know who he is. Games are over.

'Who you working for?' I ask.

Still rubbing his face, he decides whether to continue with his cover story or to come clean. I try to make up his mind for him, reach forward and slap him again.

'Don't bullshit me, *Johann*.' Using the same tone of voice with his name that Prizrak used when saying *Mike*.

Another slap. 'I found the gun.'

He sighs. 'Fuck ...'

'Oh, you are,' I say. 'Fucked. Clumsy, amateur. Who's paying you? Because I can't believe you're a professional.'

'It was last-minute,' he says. 'We had to come up with something.'

'Who's "we"?'

He looks away from me, as if the answer is in the corner of the room, somewhere else. He's like a cornered wild animal. He hasn't reached the gnawing through walls to make his way out stage but I don't think it's far off.

'Who's "we", Johann?' Ramping up the threat in my voice, pulling my hand back as if to strike him once more.

He winces, twists away, eyes screwed tight shut. 'I ...'

'And don't give me all that, if-I-tell-you-they'll-kill-me bullshit. Please don't insult my intelligence. Does it look like you're going to get out of here alive if you don't tell me?'

Another whimper.

'Again. And I want an answer this time. Who are you working for?'

He looks desperately around the tiny cabin. And yes, if he

could gnaw his way out he would. I can see it in his eyes. 'Please, I'm ... This is not my ... I don't usually get involved like this ...'

'Oh what, you're a desk jockey that they drafted in at the last moment? That it? And you got all excited at the chance to be in the field, is that it?'

'Yes ...'

'Bullshit, Johann. That's the double-glazing salesman's argument. I'm sorry the salesman hasn't turned up but I didn't want to not come and see you, I'm a trustworthy guy from the office, honestly ... Bullshit, Johann. Why are you doing this and who are you doing it for?'

He starts to cry.

'*Johann*, as you know, there's a gun in that case. If you're thinking about going for it, then don't. I'll get to it before you do. And I'll fucking use it.' I lean in closer to him. 'But here's the thing. I don't need it, *Johann*. I don't need it to kill you. I have plenty of other ways to do that. So do I have to ask again?'

The tears are coming full force now. He's a blubbering mess. I'm not letting it throw me off. I stand up, move away, stare down at him.

'You pitiful fucking excuse. I don't need to kill you. I can just hurt you. Makes no difference to me. You picked the wrong person to fuck with.'

He looks for the door and his body language changes. He's contemplating making a run for it, even though he knows he won't make it. Then another look round for something – anything – that can help him.

He realises he's still holding the bottle. Before I can stop him, he puts it to his mouth, upending it as fast as he can so it goes in quickly, gulping it down like the hungriest toddler you ever saw, his eyes closed in pain, whimpering all the while.

'You fucker' I try to grab it off him but he's had over two thirds of it. And he's not giving it up without a fight.

We tussle, but he's insistent on hanging on, his hands like tiny, deadlocked claws. He drains the whole bottle, then looks at me, eyes triumphant.

'You won't get anything out of me now,' he says, laughing, but looking as if he's about to vomit.

'Is that poison?' I ask.

'Won't kill me. But it will put me to sleep. For hours, now . . .' He's slurring his words and I can see the drug is working quickly.

'Bye, bye . . .'

He slides off the bed onto the floor and just lies there, eyes closed, unmoving.

My first reaction is to kick him. So I do, but he still doesn't move. I'm angry now that he's managed to outwit me, even at a cost to himself. I kick him again then decide against doing it a third time. I stare down at him, knowing what I have to do. Tamp down the anger. Think rationally again. Make the situation work for me.

So I do. And then I smile. So easy. Ridiculously easy.

I take my case off the bed, pull the covers back. Then I manage to drag Johann off the floor, taking off his jacket and shoes, trousers and shirt. Then, not without effort, roll him into bed. I grab his shirt, open the case and, my hand wrapped in the shirt, take out the gun. I carry it over to him, force the fingers of his right hand round the stock, trigger finger on the trigger, then take it away, making sure his prints are on it. I then place his left hand on the barrel of the gun, making it seem as if he's handled it a lot. Then I pop it into the right side jacket pocket, hang the jacket in the small wardrobe. I hang his trousers up too, move his shoes neatly to the side of the bed. Leave his shirt on the bed. As a final gesture, I leave my Panama hat at his bedside. If he's alerted the authorities, they'll be looking for a western tourist in a Panama hat carrying a gun. So let them find one.

I fasten my case again, leave the room, locking it from the outside, taking the key with me. Then I return to the carriage I'd been in before. My room is in earshot so if he wakes up and tries to get out, I'll hear him. Also, I'll enjoy putting him back to sleep again.

I find my old seat and get comfortable. Ready to outsit the rest of the night, waiting to be in Tangier in the morning.

29 – Notes

I survived. Of course I did. I wouldn't be here writing these notes now if I didn't. There were a few difficult years where I felt I was in ... what would you call it? Limbo? A liminal space, as Jon used to say, about any place that didn't move quickly enough for him.

How did I survive? I reinvented myself. Found a new identity and worked at it. Someone who didn't have any baggage, somewhere that people wouldn't care about where I'd come from. Or cared enough to be excited by what I represented, not what Jon tried to ensure I dragged with me.

Yes, I went into academia.

I parlayed my writing career – or at least an abbreviated version of it, nothing involving Jon's allegations – into a lecturing position at a university far enough away from London. I retained something of the fairy dust of the published, quite successful author, but without any of the understanding, as they saw it, of the more prosaic aspects of my previous employment. The craft, the parties, the gossip. I was thankful especially about the last one. This was the noughties. Yes, we had the internet but we didn't rely on it like we do today. Most of the accusations against me were word of mouth and none appeared in the media, so I was safe in that respect. Obviously, they were untrue, but more importantly, they were unproven. So, no stigma attached to me.

I taught at both BA and MA level. It wasn't a very prestigious university, not, say the one in Norwich with its famous Creative Writing course. Nothing like that. But I did well. And I was good at it. They say those who can't, teach. I've tried not to let that phrase govern my life. Too much. I didn't fail. I was pushed out. And for a long time I carried a lot of anger. I probably still do if I'm honest, in a very residual sense now. There's no point in dwelling on the past so I just have to look forward to what future I have left and enjoy it.

And now we get to the crux, the heart of the matter (as Graham Greene would say), the bit you've all been waiting for: Jon's disappearance.

So, what happened? What seismic event caused this? You know how people say they can remember what they were doing when, for instance, the World Trade Centre came down on 9/11? Big world events like that? Well, you might think, surely I knew what I was doing when I heard. Surely that moment is imprinted for all time on my memory?

Actually? No.

I didn't hear about it until I overheard other lecturers on the campus discussing it. I had made a conscious decision not to bother myself with the news and gossip of the London literary scene. Like leaving an ex and burning all their photos in order to move on. Another pre-internet reference there, for the kids. We were sitting round a table in a local pub near to the university where a lot of us would congregate. That's when I heard. So OK, maybe I do remember. I do know that despite my self-imposed embargo on London gossip, I was interested.

'He's what? Disappeared?'

'Yeah,' said Grace, another, rather attractive, lecturer. But I hadn't allowed my mind to wander in that direction at all, yet. 'Apparently no one can find him. Just disappeared.'

'Suicide?' said another one of my colleagues. They all seemed to be getting a second-hand contact high off the news. Someone they had read, had kinship with in the world of words. One of their own. Kind of. I hadn't told anyone I used to know him. That he used to be my best friend. And now didn't seem like the right time either.

'What's happened?' I said. 'What's anyone heard?'

'Apparently,' said Grace, 'according to the *Guardian*, he just walked out of the house and never went back. Left no note, nothing. Doesn't seem to have taken anything with him.' She leaned in closer, voice dropping as if about to gossip about some relative just out of earshot. 'They say he was depressed because of the reception of his new novel.'

'How depressed?'

'Very. Apparently he'd been turning up at events really pissed, shouting and screaming, ranting to people. Had to be evicted from award ceremonies. Started fights.'

'It says all that?'

She nodded. 'His wife's reported as saying he hadn't been himself. That he'd been in a real depression.'

'Did they say why?'

'Because of his work, it says. His last few books hadn't been getting good reviews, and he was worried his publisher was going to drop him. Would they do that?'

'They might. They've done it before.' I didn't say they'd done it to me. 'Poor old Jon.' I had to work hard to take the glee out of my voice.

'They think,' Grace continued, 'that he might have just walked into the Thames or something like that. Like Richey Edwards.'

'That was never proved,' said another one.

Referring to the Manic Street Preachers guitarist, of course, who similarly disappeared with no body ever found and rumours of suicide that never went away.

'Suicide?' I thought aloud. 'It says that in the article?'

'In the comments.'

'Ah, well, there you go.'

No. That wasn't like Jon. No matter how bad things would get for him he wouldn't do that. Wouldn't. No. He was more likely to run away. Disappear. Just ...

And I knew where he'd gone. It hit me like an electric shock. Where he'd always talked of going. That old fisherman's hut in Northumberland. His bolthole for when everything went tits up. Where he'd told me he was going to run away to. Become someone else. I thought he'd just been fantasising when he said it. But from the sounds of this, he'd actually done it.

'What are you smiling at?' asked Grace. 'D'you think this is funny?'

'Oh, sorry. I was miles away.' Literally.

Talk of Jon Durward was eventually exhausted, and we turned to other things.

I fucked Grace that night. It felt like my new life could start properly with Jon out of the way. I didn't tell her that I'd known him, though. Although I was very tempted. Either the news or his disappearance or the alcohol. Wouldn't like to say which.

And I thought that would be the end of it. But of course it wasn't. Because a few days later I got a call from Gwen.

'Well this is a surprise,' I said, picking up. I hadn't changed my mobile number. I hadn't thought anyone from my previous life would ever try to contact me.

'Hello,' she said, saying my old name.

'I go by a different name now,' I said. 'Some real arseholes in my previous life tried their best to make sure I could never work again.'

Silence on the line. I should have expected an apology and this juncture in the conversation would have been the perfect time to give it. But none came. I said nothing. Waited.

'Jon's disappeared.' The quiver in her voice as she spoke told me she was struggling to hold herself together. I'm sure that calling me just made everything even more difficult for her.

'I know. I heard.' No apology. If she couldn't offer me one, then I certainly wasn't going to offer her one.

'They say he's ...' Another catch in her voice. I could have helped her out there, shown some compassion, and I wanted to, but then I remembered how she had behaved to me all those years. The poison she directed towards me. And I remained silent once again.

'They say he's commuh – commuh – committed suicide ...'

'But you don't think so?'

'Nuh – no ...' She wasn't disguising her tears now.

I kept my voice as straight and calm as I could. 'So where do you think he's gone?'

'I ... I don't know ...'

'Right.'

'But I bet you do.'

'What makes you say that?'

A massive sniff, like she was recalling whatever had seeped onto her face, then she continued. 'Because you were his best friend. And he told you everything.'

'Everything? Really? You think so?'

'Yes, of course. He told you things he didn't even tell me. I know he did.'

'How d'you know this?'

'Because he told me ...' And the tears started again.

I saw her, then, on the other end of the phone, in that big house she shared with him, that house that I was sure felt really, really massive and haunted now. Haunted by Jon, by his success as much as by his absence. And I felt something for her. This harpy, this witch who had colluded in the ruination of my life. It was fleeting, admittedly, but it was there. And it didn't mean I was going to help her.

'OK,' I said. 'So what d'you want from me?'

'Look, I know I'm the last person you want to talk to. The last person you'd want to hear from. Especially after ... how it all ended.'

'How you made up all those false allegations against me, you mean. Tried to ruin my life.'

She sighed. 'Let's not go into all that. Please. Jon is missing. And I need you to tell me where he is. No. I'm *begging* you to tell me where he is.'

'So you think I know? You think he's told me where his getaway is – if he ever had one – and now you want me to tell you?'

'Yes. Please ...'

I don't know whether she could tell, but I was smiling at that moment. All I had to say was one thing. Give a location, and her unhappiness would be at an end. And what about Jon? If he'd run away, then obviously he intended to do so. He wanted to get away. From his own life. From Gwen. And I couldn't blame him for that bit.

So my way of thinking was that if he was my friend, if he'd ever been my friend and our friendship meant anything to him and, more importantly, me, it was my duty to protect that. And if it was at the expense of Gwen's peace of mind, then so much the better.

'If he has run away, Gwen,' I said, picking words carefully and speaking slowly, relishing the moment, 'then don't you think he wanted to? That it was deliberate? And if he told me about this place – or if such a place actually exists – then surely I owe it to him to guard his secret?'

'No ... no ...'

'I'm not saying that I know where he's gone, Gwen. I'm just saying, that I don't care. You made your decision about me and so did he. Don't call this number again.'

And I hung up. I could hear her voice, small distant and distraught, crying as I did so.

I put the phone down. It felt like a huge weight had been lifted from me.

30

The Strait of Gibraltar is a liminal space. (1) It's there to divide, to keep wilfully separate. And despite the clock ticking away on the journey, the actual time spent in the Strait or on it counts as no time, as nothing. Limbo. This strip of unremarkable water should really be shrouded in fog; the traveller disappearing into it at one end only to emerge at the other, their surroundings totally alien to what has gone before, no idea how long it has taken them in real world time. Not a straight, linear journey, but a one-hundred-and-eighty-degree turnaround.

The Strait itself stands or rather flows between not just two different continents but two different cultures. And the differences couldn't be more marked if they'd been invented by a science fiction or fantasy writer. Everything different: colours, light, noise, language, architecture, people. Everything. And arriving at Gibraltar from North Africa makes for an even bigger culture shock. Perched uncomfortably at the far tip of Spain, being UK owned and administered by British ex-pats, the rock represents the most regressive, dull, colourless aspects of Europe, not to mention the most repressed and boring ones. Imagine Europe as a family Christmas party. Gibraltar is the old drunken uncle who ruins it with his far-right rants. A golf club bore who's mistakenly turned up to an Italian, Spanish or

THE FINAL CHAPTER

French Pride party and refuses to leave until he's told all the guests what's wrong with them and why his views are superior. And after the full-on sensory onslaught of Morocco it's like transitioning from colour back to monochrome.

After the excitement of the previous few hours maybe it's the kind of thing that I need, some dullness, familiarity. But it's not what I want. I want to get out this place as fast as I possibly can, make myself disappear somewhere in Europe.

Leaving the train in Tangiers and getting on the ferry was easy. I was being looked for in the crowd but with my new hair and shop-bought coloured contact lenses as well as another change of clothing, I didn't stand out. As I left the train station, I saw them board the train. Johann, still presumably out cold and wearing my hat, would have some explaining to do.

From there it was a simple matter to board the ferry as a foot passenger for the 36-mile journey across. As I've just said, short in distance, long on culture shock. Now I have to decide whether I want to hang around in Gibraltar or move on somewhere else. Easy decision.

So where do I go now? And what do I do? And, most importantly, who am I?

That might not sound like an important question, certainly not if you're considering what I've endured the last few days to get here. But to someone in my profession it's of paramount importance. Who I am dictates what I do, where I go. And why I do it. I've been Mike Nolan but he's now dead. I'm currently Paul Davis but will he stick around for long? Or do I go home, resume being Garrick Hutton? It sounds, like I say, a luxury but in order to become these other people I have to believe in them, believe in me. Currently I'm Paul Davis so I have to think where he would go. Not Benidorm, that would be too obvious for him. He thinks he's somewhat above that. He wants a posher version of Benidorm. Malaga, perhaps. The north side of Mallorca, even, so he can say there's more to the island than getting drunk in Magaluf. That's if I remain Paul Davis. He seems quite boring to me, but if I have to stay in his identity for a while, until I decide who I want to be for the longer term, then that's what I'll have to do.

On one level, it's fun to change identities. To play at being someone else. To convince yourself you're someone else and see others follow suit. Play may be the wrong word. Because although there's an element of play involved, that part of your brain is accessed in the act of doing it, it's far too dangerous to be considered playing. It's just the terminology; an actor playing a part, an agent playing a role. And it's a wrench as well, emotionally, physically, even. Psychically, if you want to get all woo-woo. As I said, you convince yourself you're someone else and others follow your lead. But what happens when you have to stop being that person and have to become someone else, quickly, like what's just happened to me? Well, usually I have a space to decompress, take myself off somewhere while I shed my previous identity and become used to my usual one, or a new one. But the location for that has gone now, for obvious reasons, and I don't have the time. So I have to cope with all these competing thoughts, impulses and character traits within my psyche, all battling for prominence. It's harder than it might look from the outside, this constant battle to regain identity, and also the reason for the high suicide rate in my profession. Death by gun, alcohol, drugs or behaviour. Not many of us make old bones. At least not with our minds intact.

So. I'm Paul Davis. Boring Paul Davis. And he would go to Malaga. So that's where I'm headed.

Except that's not where I've ended up. I'm in Lisbon now, in Portugal. Which yes, is another kind of place I could imagine Paul Davis turning up in. So in that respect the cover's still intact.

I'm sitting at this bar in the sunshine, drinking a local beer, watching the trams go up and down the heavily inclined, sand-coloured old streets. Very pleasant. Just the kind of place you would come to relax, to get away from it all. To think.

I did go to Malaga. Hired a car in Gibraltar and drove to Malaga. Then ditched the car, went to another rental agency, hired another car and drove the four hundred miles to Lisbon. Just in case anyone was still following me. I decided against public transport this time. You never know who you're going to end up with. I'm booked in at a budget tourist hotel in Bairro Alto in Lisbon, a far cry from where I've been staying in Morocco, but it's very Paul Davis. And, as a recent divorcee, I'm enjoying walks around the city, taking in the local culture, visiting museums and galleries and places of interest, and eating in many of its fine restaurants. If this were Hollywood, I would have become entangled with a single, much younger local woman who is devastatingly attractive and a free-spirited soul, with something lacking in her life that only a middle-aged man can fix. But it isn't, so I haven't. It's just been me. The only person I've spoken to is the hotel receptionist. And he seemed more interested in the two twenty-something Scandinavian women behind me in the queue to check in. No one has approached me, and my tradecraft remains sound. I've never used the same route twice for getting about and I'm pretty sure I haven't been followed. And now that I've established myself these last few days and Mike Nolan is working his way out of my system, it's time to plan what I'm going to do next. And the first thing to do is decide whether I'm going to remain as Paul Davis or become someone else. Even Garrick Hutton.

That depends on whether I'm going to stay here or return to Britain. And if I return to Britain, what kind of welcome will await me? I've failed in my mission. I can't come home without having achieved what I set out to do. Not on the last one. I'll be retired in the most prejudicial manner possible. Perhaps it might be better to just slip away. Take one of my other identities I've got stored for just such an emergency and inhabit it for the rest of my life. As far away from my former life as possible.

But there's also Julia to consider. Would she want to come with me? Do I want her to come with me? Is there still something between us that can be eked out over an enforced retirement in some faraway place? She was a company girl when we met and we've both lived by those rules all our married life. But I do notice that in her absence I haven't missed her. I didn't even feel guilty when I slept with Elizabeth. Although I was someone else then, playing a part. That comes with the territory. If I had allowed myself to have felt guilty then I'd have given myself away. But now, coming down from Morocco, putting the operation in the rearview mirror, do I feel guilty now? When I decompress after a job and exorcise the previous identity, I rebalance myself and thinking of Julia is part of that. That's why the netsuke has taken on such a symbolic meaning. It tells me that I'm Garrick once more and I love my wife. And to demonstrate that I bring her something beautiful. But am I feeling that this time? Honestly? No. Why? Because I don't love her any more? Because to disappear I have to be someone else? Someone without a wife? Or because I don't regard this job as finished?

I drain the last of my beer and look up. It's pretty good here. The city has a good vibe to it. I could stay here. Reinvent myself. Paul Davis, divorcee, having adventures. Perhaps with a Hollywood local girl, although in all likelihood, not. But it would be interesting. Discovering this new person, a total creation from myself and not at the behest of someone else. That's appealing. Starting again, a completely blank slate.

But then there's always the Flitcraft parable to think about.

If you don't know what I mean, read Dashiell Hammett's

1930 novel *The Maltese Falcon*. In it, the lead character, private detective Sam Spade tells Brigid O'Shaughnessy of a case he worked on. A man called Flitcraft lived in a suburb of Tacoma, Washington. He had a wife, kids, a good job, plenty of money an easy lifestyle and regular golf dates. And then one day he walked out of his office and just disappeared. Spade was hired to find him. It took him five years. He found Flitcraft, now calling himself Charles Pierce, living in a suburb of Spokane, Washington, with a new wife, a young son, a good job, plenty of money and an easy lifestyle. Living, in fact, the same life as he had previously left. Spade confronts Flitcraft/Pierce and asks him what happened. He tells him that on his way to lunch one day he was almost hit by a falling beam from a construction site, and it made him realise that life could be over in a flash. Without even knowing it. And, since he had lived such an orderly, responsible life he should go out and have some fun. So he disappeared to do that. So why was he living an identical life to his previous one? Spade explains that Flitcraft adjusted himself to beams falling and when no more fell he adjusted himself to them not falling. He went right back to his previous life. (2)

So where does that leave me? Which life shall I take up? As I sit there, nursing my empty beer glass, wondering what to do next, my phone starts to ring.

30 – Notes

1. And there he is with his liminal bloody spaces. Yeah, we know you've got a degree, Jon, but it's a boat trip. Nothing more, nothing less. Get over yourself, mate.

2. The Flitcraft parable. This was the only part missed out of John Huston's film adaptation of Hammett's novel and it's a shame, because I think its ideas of identity and adaptability are central to the plot. The idea that anything can happen to anyone, even a boring family man walking out on the family he supposedly loves and becoming someone else, is an important one, I think. Both for Hammett's novel and this one. Jon wouldn't have included it if he didn't think so. Passages don't get put in novels by mistake.

   Think of what Jon's lead character has already gone through. He's a professional killer. But not at the start of the novel. He hits on that journey by accident, by expedience. By pragmatism. Interestingly, Charles Pierce, the name that Flitcraft was living under when Hammett's detective found him, was in real life a pragmatist philosopher. Hence the inclusion in Hammett's novel. It helps to explain the subsequent actions of all the characters but mainly Spade. It lets us know that the protagonist could – or will – change depending upon the situation they find themselves in.

   Hammett was asking whether it's possible to become a completely different person, or would we always revert to our base personality. Jon's character goes undercover, assumes different identities, behaves in different ways. Does that make him a different person, or just a person responding to differing scenarios? He's asking here if Garrick Hutton can become Paul Davis and if so, would he really inhabit that character for the rest of his life, or at least until the next beam fell?

Which leads us to the next question: falling beams. Does it really matter who we call ourselves or what identity we assume if we're not going to be left alone to get on with our lives? If we're always looking over our shoulders, checking to see if someone we've wronged in the past – or they think we have – has somehow tracked us down and is trying to get even? How many falling beams does that equate to? And how would we deal with that?

For Jon's character, it seems to be leading towards finishing off the job he started then, obligations discharged, he can take things from there. No, that's not a spoiler. Clearly, he's going to go after the antagonist or there wouldn't be a novel. We haven't shared his story with him until this point to see him just walk away and leave everything undone. This is a thriller, not a literary novel.

Besides, we can't really feel we've moved on until we've discharged our obligations towards the past. Any of us. It's only when we can truly say we've confronted and successfully killed our past, and any ghosts that still lingered there, dragging themselves through to the present, that we can truly move forward.

31

'Well. Long time, no hear.'

I try and disguise my surprise in case anyone is watching. I'm not sure how successfully I manage it. It's my handler. No mistaking her voice.

'How are you?'

I look around, take in my surroundings once again. The day suddenly looks completely different from when I sat down at this bar. Hearing her voice has done that. Even though the sun is still out, the shadows seem longer, deeper. I keep my voice steady as I reply. 'How did you find me? This is a burner phone.'

'Oh,' she says, in mock surprise, 'is there such a thing? In this day and age?'

I know what that means. The tone of her voice tells me. I'm being watched. Followed. And my phone has been hacked or cloned. I don't know how, but whoever has done this, they're very good. I should have expected that, because the organisation I work for are the best in the business. They have someone on the ground and I didn't identify them.

I think of the lecherous hotel receptionist, the only person I've really spoken to since I've been here. Him? Really?

I retain my composure, try not to let anything show in my

voice. 'You've heard what happened in Morocco.' A statement, not a question.

'Quite the fuck up, I gather.'

'Down to Prizrak I'm afraid. Not me.'

'No names on the phone.'

'Oh, who fucking cares? Bit late for that. And it didn't help that your man Kharis decided to show a bit of "initiative".' I put air quotes around that word. 'Got him killed. Almost got me killed. And blew the whole operation. Amateur.'

A pause on the line. 'Well,' she says eventually, 'all for the best.'

'How so?'

'We got what we needed to know. What Prizrak will be attempting next. Regime change in Libya.'

'He told me that was a dead end.'

'Yes, well, that's not the case now. International politics move quickly.'

'Then I'll go to Libya. Finish the job.'

'I don't think that's a good idea.'

'Why not?'

'Because regime change there is rather attractive to us. And if Prizrak is the one who could do that without destabilising the region, then we should let him get on with it. Encourage him, if needs be.'

I pause for a moment, letting what she's said sink in. 'Wait, you're ... you're working with him?'

'The enemy of my enemy, and all that.'

'But you sent me to kill him.'

'And it's a good job you botched it because we need him. He's a man we can do business with. Don't be naive, Garrick. You know how these things work.'

'Did you ever intend me to carry out my assignment? Really?'

Another pause. She sighs. 'I think it's best if you come home.'

'Why?'

'We need to have a discussion about your future.'

'Thought I didn't have one with you? Isn't that what you said?'

'We can discuss it. Once you come home.'

There's something in her words, something behind her words that I can't place. And more importantly, can't trust. Nothing she's said so far feels right. Meaning going home wouldn't be safe. It's not just paranoia building. I rely on my senses for this job and I've done it long enough to know when something feels off. And this does. My handler's response just confirms it.

'I'm fine where I am.'

'Really? You're just going to stay there, are you? Drink beer at your Lisbon bar, eat in your Lisbon restaurants, and what? Buy a house there and retire?'

Again, I don't answer straight away. I can't.

Silence on the line.

'You set me up, didn't you? This whole job was one long set up.'

No reply. I keep going.

'You never wanted me to do my usual hit on Prizrak, if that's who he really is—'

'He really is who you think he is.'

'Oh good, well that's something. So what did you expect? Him to kill me? You think I'm past it, too slow, best days behind me, all that. So you send me up against someone who I'm not going to beat. Or so you think. And you give me Kharis with instructions to stack the deck against me. And when Prizrak eventually kills me it's a plus for you. You've outed him, know where he is, where he's going, so you can send someone else after him. Someone younger, perhaps. Who can get the job done. Maybe not even a Shapeshifter, just an accident man. Or even a wet worker, since no one knows what he looks like. As

THE FINAL CHAPTER

for me, well, you've solved a potential problem. Do you get a bonus for that?'

My voice trails away to silence.

'Are you finished?'

I don't reply.

'There's a team on their way to you now. They'll be with you soon. Stay where you are and wait for them. You are to comply with them and return home. We will discuss your future then.'

The line goes dead. I stare at my phone.

Dead. That's what I'll be if I stay where I am and wait. Instead, I get up from the table, pop the phone in the dregs of my beer.

And run.

31 – Notes

'I bet you never thought you'd hear from me again.'

She's right. Surprise doesn't cover what I'm feeling. It's like some celestial entity has peeled back my life to reveal another one underneath. Like removing a carpet to find floorboards, obviously, but herringbone patterned ones that haven't been touched in years.

'How did you get this number?'

I'd changed it after Gwen contacted me. Breaking my final bond with my old life. If someone wanted to contact me, they wouldn't be able to. Apparently, I was wrong.

This, by the way, happened only a few weeks ago. We're nearly up to date. Jon's been gone for years, and I haven't thought about him in that time. I've just been getting on with things. Living my life, my previous one behind me and all but forgotten. Like a literary witness protection programme.

'Are you supposed to be uncontactable, then? I know the name you're going by now. We all know who C. B. Everett really is. Or was.' Her voice is the same but different. Cadences, tones, all still there. But I can hear the weight of the years pressing down on it, contorting it, changing it. I suppose the same thing's happened to mine but I haven't noticed. It's only when I look in a mirror, I realise I'm not in my twenties any more. Guess we all do. That's ageing for you. It's rough but it's better than the alternative.

It's my old agent. Jon's old agent, I should say, because she never felt truly like she was representing me. Only when I was successful. Only when I was bringing her in money. Jon, she looked after. Me, when the money dried up, I was out.

'How are you? And who should I call you?'

'What d'you want?'

'No pleasantries. Straight down to it. I see.'

'I thought you'd have retired by now.'

She almost laughs. 'I have. Left London. Live in splendid isolation in Cornwall now. Well, not that isolated. It's like all of publishing's retired and moved down here. Barely speak to a local.'

Just hearing her voice works as a time machine, transporting me back to those times. Peeling back the layers I've accreted, revealing who I used to be still underneath. Yes, I know I've just used the carpet analogy, but I'm the one writing this and I can do as I please. It's not pleasant. It really is like another life is being dredged up. One I'd successfully buried.

I'm still in academia. No further beams fell so I stayed here. And, as my waistline expanded and my intellectual curiosity receded, I became comfortable. I used to worry whether I was a popular lecturer. I don't any more. Just do my job. Which, surprising though it may seem, I enjoy. And I'm actually rather good at it. I finally – admittedly accidentally – found my calling. Maybe those who can't do *should* teach. And there's no shame in that.

'The first thing I should ask,' she continued, 'is do you have an agent?'

'What?'

'Do you have representation? I know for all intents and purposes I'm retired, but when you hear what I have to say it'll all make sense.'

'What will? What are you talking about?'

'Firstly, I need to know whether you still have representation and, if so, who it is.'

'No, of course I haven't.'

'There's a market for your backlist, you know. Thrillers do very well as ebooks. Easy money, if you approach the right publisher.'

'Is that why you called me? Because I'm not interested.'

'No, it's not why I called you. Although it is worth thinking about.'

'Then why have you called me?' I could no longer hide the irritation in my voice.

'You've probably heard the news. Even in your far-flung outpost, I'm sure you still keep an ear to the ground.'

'If you mean am I still interested in publishing, then no. I'm not. I go out of my way to avoid publishing news.'

'Oh.' She sounded disappointed. And disbelieving, as if she couldn't understand anyone wanting to do that voluntarily.

'So what's this about, then?'

'Jon Durward.'

'What about him?'

'He's back. And writing again.'

My heart skipped a beat. Several, it felt like. I've always thought that a cliché, but believe me, it's absolutely true. I almost dropped the phone as well. It took a few seconds before I could answer.

'Back? What ...'

'I've received a manuscript from him.'

'Are you sure it's from him?'

'As sure as I can be. As we all can be. Gwen has read it. She's convinced it's by him.'

'How?'

'There are things, she says, that he's put in especially for her to notice. And, more to the point, for you to notice as well.'

THE FINAL CHAPTER

I had no words. I couldn't speak. Surprise, shock, all of that. And more. Much more.

She continued. 'It arrived in hardcopy, a rarity these days. Typed, double spaced, exactly like Jon used to do it. It was accompanied by a letter. A *signed* letter. Gwen insists it's his signature. Poor woman. She's really been through it over the years, and now this. She doesn't know what to think, or what to believe. But she believes the book is genuine. And having read it, so do I.'

'Is it a new book or an old one?'

'New obviously. Although we don't know when it was written exactly. That's something that will have to be verified.'

I found my voice. Or part of it. 'So ... where do I come into it?'

'Well, here's the thing. The letter came with very explicit instructions. I was to act as agent, Gwen was to be involved, and you were to edit it.'

'Edit it? Does it need editing?'

'This is huge. And this is one of the main stipulations to it being published. Oh, I doubt there'll be much to do structurally, in fact he insisted that it be published as is. But he wants you to provide notes in a more general sense. At the end of each chapter. Explaining references, in jokes. Providing a bit of context, of colour. That sort of thing.'

'And he said this himself, did he?'

'It was all in his letter.'

'Has anyone spoken to him?'

'Not yet. But he's promised to make an appearance once the book has been published.'

'So it's a newly written book, then?'

'That's for you to find out. Oh, and when he emerges, he wants you to be there too.'

'I'm not sure about that.'

She sighed. 'Look, I know you two left things on something of a bad note. But surely it's time to put all that behind you? Yes? Let bygones be bygones and all that?'

My turn to sigh. 'I just … don't think I want to. Why should I do it? What's in it for me?'

'This could be the literary find of the decade, century, even. Edited by you … well. You'd be back, for one thing. Publishers would be clamouring for your new novel.'

'I don't have a new novel.'

'I'm sure you could write one. Or dig something out of the bottom drawer, that kind of thing.'

'I'm not interested in that.'

'What about the money, then? I'm sure I could get you half a million for editing this.' And the matter-of-fact way she said it made me believe it too. 'Ah. You've gone quiet. I thought you might. Give it some thought.'

'I am.' Half a million. Even if the book wasn't by Jon, it would be something. And half a million … that's retirement in luxury money.

'There is another thing.'

'Oh, I thought there might be.'

'No, it's an addition, not a condition. Gwen seems to believe that you know where Jon went when he disappeared.'

'What? I told her I didn't at the time.'

'Yes, I know you did, but she didn't believe you. And frankly, neither do I. I think you do know. And I think you didn't tell her out of spite. Oh, not that I'm judging you. Not at all. I remember there were some harsh words said at the time and you didn't part company on good terms. I quite understand why you would do that if that was indeed the case.'

Harsh words. The best of terms. Skating round the truth

of the matter very delicately. She could always do that when she wanted something.

'All I'm saying is, if you know where he is – or where he might be – then give it a go. Try and find him. Talk to him. That'll make a marvellous end to the book, won't it? You tracking him down and getting him to talk on the record? That would be worth much more than just half a million. Don't you think?'

She was right. About all of it. Editing the novel would be easy. Or comparatively so. It would involve me dredging up some very unpleasant memories. But, to be fair, there were also some pleasant ones too. Before it all went wrong. I could cope with that for half a million. At least. But if I could track Jon down, get him to talk ... well, that would be nothing short of miraculous.

'Should I leave it with you, have a think? Only I need an answer soon as. Obviously, we need to get on this straight away.'

'If you can get me half a million without talking to Jon then I'm in.'

I could hear her smiling. 'I'm glad to hear it.'

'But I'll need more if you want me to track him down. And I'll need the money in advance if I'm going to play detective.'

'No question. So you know where he went to do you? Did he tell you?'

'I may have an idea,' I said, grudgingly.

'Wonderful. You know, I thought you would. Don't worry, I won't say a word to Gwen. And I can assume you're on board?'

I paused before answering. Felt my old life coming crashing back towards me.

'I'm on board.'

'Well, isn't this marvellous? All back together again. Have a good day and I'll be in touch soon.'

She hung up. And I just stared at the phone, wondering what I'd just committed myself to. I shouldn't have said yes. I definitely shouldn't have said yes. I should have had nothing to do with it. Just put the phone down on her, got on with my own life again.

But half a million ... *at least* ...

And Jon's new book? Really? *Really?* He'd come back just to write this? And if he didn't write it, who did? Someone who could fool everyone, that's for sure. Even his wife.

Yes. I should have said no.

But I didn't.

32

I step off the plane in Keflavik airport and notice the change in temperature immediately. Even though I've packed and am wearing cold weather gear, I'll need to buy a couple of Icelandic wool sweaters once I get through the airport. It's that cold.

I'm straight through customs and passport control, Paul Davis's identity holding out well, and off into a taxi to my Reykjavik hotel. The photo looks slightly different since I've let my hair and beard grow again. It seems to be the done thing for men of my age in Iceland.

It isn't a beautiful country, in terms of scenery. It doesn't have the lush greenery of somewhere English like Devon or Northumberland, nor can it boast the Atlas Mountains of Morocco. But it does possess a natural drama. If it had a soundtrack it would be by Carl Orff. The car I'm in seems anachronistic, unbelonging, intruding amongst rock cliffs, jagged and unyielding, monolithic, that seem to belong to a much earlier age, thousands of years ago. The occasional bursts of grass or alpine plants don't do much to break it up. The skies are huge and open with scudding, threatening clouds, as if John Martin had painted his Biblical and *Paradise Lost sturm und drang* masterpieces in ice rather than fire. And space. Lots and lots of space. It's a small country with an even smaller population. Less than four hundred thousand people live here.

And the one I'm looking for is only an occasional visitor.

I managed to avoid the extraction team in Lisbon and escape. It wasn't hard. There was no sub-*Mission Impossible* frantic tearing round the streets like Tom Cruise on a stolen motorbike, while being pursued by heavies shooting from the side windows of fast-moving black SUVs. No crashing into the stalls of local independent business owners, no getting stuck in the tram lines. No jumping over two local police cars, forcing them to crash head on. Nothing so dramatic. I'm a trained professional, I just ghosted away and stayed hidden until I was sure they were no longer following me. Until it was time for me to remerge again and get back to work. Finish the job I had started.

I didn't return to London. Given my handler's fervour to apprehend me in Lisbon that was the last place I would make for. Instead, I went to Scotland. It felt like opening my presents before Christmas but it had to be done. As I said previously, I have several other identities stashed away in various places in the world. Some far from London, some much closer. Scotland is one of them. It's a cottage on the outskirts of a remote fishing village on the North-East coast, the kind of place that gets some tourists in certain parts of the year but not many. The kind of place that doesn't take kindly to second homeowners. But since it's far enough away from the village and no one is ever there, they've kind of collectively forgotten about it. I've only been there once before: when I bought the place and had it kitted out to my specifications. It's not a particularly attractive cottage, not the kind that an influencer (1) would want to stand in front of. But it suits me perfectly. It's the kind of place you wouldn't look twice at when you passed it, trying instead to see the prettier cottages along the coast. That way it has its own force field, repelling the interested, too boring to be even thought of.

THE FINAL CHAPTER

I went straight there, opening up, checking the place out. It was exactly as I had left it. Clean and tidy, but with a thin coating of time's dust. I went straight upstairs to the secret safe and checked the contents. Money, in several different currencies, credit and debit cards, passports. All present and correct. The wardrobe holding clothes, the house well-supplied. Everything I needed for as long as I intended to stay.

As I said, like unwrapping a Christmas present before Christmas, as this is supposed to be for me if a cover is blown or if I have to get away quickly. Or to make that ultimate change and have to live somewhere like this under a different identity for the rest of my life. So maybe I'm not premature in coming here. Perhaps I'll have to stay. Perhaps this stone cottage is my future. Perhaps.

It's also the perfect place to plan my next move.

Prizrak thinks he got away. But he doesn't know Elizabeth told me of his retreat in Iceland. It's not much to go on but I can find it. And complete my mission. Things may have changed, allegiances shifted, but I still have a job to do. And then I'm off. I've been thinking on the journey from Portugal that I'm no longer doing this for my handlers, for the company. I'm doing it for myself, for my pride. I'm going to retire on a high, with a full, perfect record. And then I'll disappear.

Yes, it's sad about Julia, at least in the interim. Once I'm established in my new identity, though, I can contact her, give her the choice to join me. That decision will be up to her.

In the meantime, in my Scottish retreat I plotted and planned. I took daily trips into the mountains to be alone, just me and my high-powered rifle. Practicing. I'm not a sniper by trade, but I'll have to learn to be one to see this job out. That's the intention. So every day, working on my aim, on distance, precision, speed. Honing my skill. Turning the rifle into an extension of my arms. Making sure I won't miss.

All for this trip. This soon-to-come moment.

Reykjavik is a gorgeous city. Mainly because it doesn't feel like a city. There are no tower blocks or high rises. The only thing with any height is the cathedral. My hotel looks out on to the lake and it's one of the warmest rooms I've ever been in. They superheat everything here to make up for the crushingly low temperatures outside. And they know how to do restrained elegance.

I open my suitcase. I'm still playing the part of Paul Davis, newly divorced yet solvent single traveller, enjoying what the world has to offer before he gets too old. Tomorrow I'll visit the concierge and act like a tourist, saying I've heard the Westfjords are particularly lovely this time of year and could they recommend any trips or tours in the area? Or is it just better to rent a 4x4 and make my own way? I'm quite enjoying the novelty of travelling on my own after so many years as a couple. I realise it's a long drive from Reykjavik so I intend to take the scenic route and staying away for a couple of nights isn't a problem. Financially, I mean. I want to use the hotel as a base to explore from. All of that. And, given this is one of the friendliest countries in the world, they'll be happy to help.

They might not be so happy if they could see the rifle I'm currently assembling, but hey. You can't have everything.

32 – Notes

1. Did they have influencers in 2009? Is that a way of showing this has been written contemporaneously or just a mistake? Or another piece of clairvoyant prescience? I'm not sure I know any more.

And then I received a letter.

Sent to my address, not the university, a typewritten or printed name and address on the envelope. I could tell there was something different about it as soon as I saw it. Heart pounding, and also wondering whether I should put gloves on to open it like they do in films, to preserve DNA or whatever, I opened it. Without gloves. There was a single sheet of printer paper, folded in half. I unfolded it. And read.

Hey CB, guess who? You got the book, then? I presume you're coming to visit me? Remember where I am? Northumberland. Begins with an A. Fisherman's cottage. I'll be on my own. Still. I'll leave you to work the rest out. After all, you used to write detective stories. See you soon.

The words had been printed. Underneath was a scrawled letter in black pen:

J

My heart was doing summersaults. I read and reread the letter, looking for any further clues. I held it up to the light to see if there was anything imprinted within it. I even thought of putting it near a flame to see if he'd written something in invisible ink – or lemon juice – but decided that would be a bit melodramatic. Northumberland. Letter A. It's from him. Definitely him.

Isn't it? The letter J? Must be him. It's a long shot, I have to admit. He was still there? In his fisherman's cottage in Northumberland, this whole time? After all these years? I tried to calm myself, think rationally. I mean, why not? He'd been sincere in his desire to get away, and if that desire had given him everything he wanted then yes, there was a good chance he'd still be there. Jon wasn't the kind of person to want to travel the world, lose himself and find his mind, that kind of person. He had ambition, but that was always for his books, his art. And it's fair to say he achieved every ambition he set out to accomplish. So what do you do when you've done everything you wanted to? Nothing. That's what.

Because that's what life is, isn't it? Striving for something, reaching for an achievement. And for the majority of us, we never attain that. Not really. Yes, we get to something like it, or our own individually tailored version of it, but never the dream we've set out to achieve. Reach for the stars, you might hit the moon. All that new age bollocks. We're always reaching. Reaching, reaching, reaching. And our grasp is never long enough. So eventually we just settle for what we can reach. We have to. We have no choice. Not everyone is going to be Shakespeare or the all-time top scorer in the Premier League, or Elvis – Presley or Costello – or Jon Durward, we can't be. So we have to find our place and settle for that. Or not. Because as I said, life is for striving. But what about that rarified few who do achieve their dreams? What do they do then?

THE FINAL CHAPTER 365

As I said – nothing. There's nothing they can do. They've done it all. They have to find a way to exist, to live, until they die. They have to find a way to come to terms with the fact that their life no longer has any focus, any meaning. Not in a goal-driven sense, anyway. They have to find contentment.

I suppose I did in academia. I settled, in all senses of the word. And Jon? Well, I'll just have to go and see, won't I? See what he did with the rest of his life.

I take time off work. I explain to the head of department what's come up and why I'm doing it. I try to couch it in ways that will reflect well on the university, and our department in particular.

'Like you're being brought back in to do one last job, eh? Like a heist, or something. From one of those books you used to write.'

I smiled politely and got the time off. He actually thought I was coming back. And I didn't disabuse him of this notion. But I won't be back. One way or another, I'll be somewhere else. Someone else, probably.

I also tell my girlfriend I'll be going away. It's not a serious relationship, none of them have been since Grace, just a mutual coming together and drifting apart when needed. She took the news fine, told me she'll see me when I get back. And when I don't return, I doubt she'll care. Too much.

I then had to try and work out whereabouts in Northumberland Jon might be. It began with an A. Amble? Alnwick? Alnmouth?

Next, I took to the computer, looked on Google Maps. Amble fits the bill the most, seems the likeliest place. It's exactly how I pictured it when he described it to me. A one-time fishing village of stone cottages on the edge of the North Sea. Beaches and dunes. Bleak, but beautiful. Yes, I can imagine Jon living there. Just the place.

So off I go.

33

The car handles well and there's barely any traffic on the road. The concierge tried to talk me into taking a small plane to my destination, but I insisted I wanted to see the country. And the customer is always right. The road is clear of snow although there's plenty of it at either side and on the surrounding rocks. My Nissan X-Trail handles it perfectly.

I have no intention of looking at the scenery, of course. I'm planning, plotting. It didn't take long to find Prizrak's hideaway. Not if you know where to look. I'm quite surprised my handlers haven't found it before now. Perhaps they just didn't know where he would hide out. Or weren't privy to the late Elizabeth's giveaway. It's a cabin in the Westfjords, near the Red Sand, the Raudisandur. All the other beaches in Iceland are black due to volcanic activity, but this one is red. Not that it matters particularly, as everything's covered in snow, but it was part of the concierge's sales talk. Prizrak's house is on a clifftop nearby. Thank you, Google Earth.

It's a nine-hour drive from Reykjavik and after about five hours I find myself speeding. Not because I'm a particular fan of driving fast – I'm not. I don't like attracting attention in that way. But just to counteract the boredom. Judging from the few other vehicles I meet on the road it doesn't seem to be the done thing in this country. For a people descended from Vikings, they seem remarkably passive. Perhaps that's why Prizrak likes it here.

Eventually, after travelling most of the time in darkness, I arrive at my destination. It's a white, block-like building, and should be totally at odds with the grey/red rocks surrounding it, but since everything is covered with snow it blends right in. There's what seems to be a car porch with the majority of the accommodation on top of that. It looks like a Seventies version of brutalist futurism, the kind of place a murder would be committed in a Scandinavian crime drama.

The key is in the box outside where they told me it would be and I let myself in. The interior is as modernist as the exterior. It vaguely reminds me of my apartment in Trellick. I look out of the window. There's a ruggedly beautiful view of the cliffs and down below are the red sands.

I open my laptop, get to work. I have the coordinates for Prizrak's house. Three kilometres from me along the cliff edge. Walkable at any time, but I'm sure he chose it for its vantage point. I would have. I'll wait until tonight, hope the dark hides me.

I don't know if he's expecting me or not. I don't know if he has even thought of me since Morocco, considers me a threat or an irritant. Or whether he's moved on and is leaving his security team to deal with me if I show up again. Or is relying on my handlers to have reeled me in. That's an interesting point: if he's been working with my employers, and recent news reports about how wobbly Gaddafi's regime in Libya is currently looking might point to that, then I can't imagine they've told him I'm still in the wind and still intending to carry out my mission. I'm sure they've told him I've been dealt with, any possible threat has been neutralised, however they've worded it. Anyway. I'll find out later.

I spend the remaining hours until my approach checking the rifle, familiarising myself with its workings. Again. And again. Running through all possible scenarios that I might encounter, constructing narratives for how to avoid or cope with them. I always do this, even though I know that once I'm active on a mission I rely on improvisation should something go wrong. However, like comedians who claim to use improvisation, I know there's no such thing. There's just thinking on one's feet in response to a specific scenario. And it's better to be aware of what they might be. `Besides, I've got something up my sleeve should I need it.`

I do this until it's dark and them I'm ready. I get kitted up, sling my gun over my shoulder and I'm off to complete my mission.

33 – Notes

I took my car because he won't know it. He might not even recognise me. I think I still look the same but I'm sure – in fact, I know – I'm heavier and much greyer. At least I haven't gone bald, so that's something. And will I recognise him after all these years? Will he have changed much? Will he have done a Flitcraft and got involved with someone again? Adjusted his life to no further beams falling? Perhaps. I mean, this might be a wild goose chase. The letter might be a fake and I may never find him. But at least I can say I tried. At least there'll be something to put in the novel.

It's dark by the time I arrive. I've already called ahead, booked into an Airbnb, possibly the only one in Amble, certainly the only one I could find off season. Not many tourists come to Northumberland in December.

The place I'm staying is fine. It'll do me for a few nights. I've signed for a week but I don't think I'll need that long. But you never know. I might need longer. He might be harder to identify. I may have to ingratiate myself with the locals. It's a small, old fisherman's cottage, just like the kind Jon mentioned to me. Or at least how I imagined it to be. Part of me wonders if this is it, the actual one. And he moved somewhere else but still kept it, leased it out and he's going to appear in the morning and surprise me. I admit, the coincidence would be staggering, the kind of thing you'd find in a dreadful, unimaginative novel by a lazy writer, but also the kind of thing that would happen in real life and, if you're a writer, you wouldn't be able to put it into a novel because, well, see above.

But anyway. I spent the first night in my Airbnb. It was fine. No complaints. I thought of going to the local pub but I doubted I would find out anything helpful. Jon wouldn't be the newcomer any more; he'd have been here about fifteen years by now. Unless it was one of those hidden-away places that regarded newcomers as anyone not being born there and not having at least three generations before them born there. Also, I'd seen enough BBC Two early evening shows where cooking celebrities travel round the country extolling local restaurants and produce to know that there would be nothing remote about this place and it was probably on some gastro foodie map because of the locally smoked kippers, or something. So the pub would probably be full of incomers eating kippers and writing reviews for Tripadvisor. So, early night and a new day tomorrow.

I could see the attraction of this place. It has its own kind of beauty. The beach, even off-season, with curling grey and white clouds overhead providing the drama, and a heavy mist rolling in off the North Sea, is evocative. It makes you stand still, embrace it. See the landscape and your place in it the way that cities never do. The way that most people don't wherever they are. Feel like you're both yourself and part of the ecosystem. You can *feel* nature here. You can feel ... something. And it moves you. Or it moves me, at any rate.

I got up early, decided to go for a walk along the sand. It's the opposite of a British seaside resort. There are no arcades, no cheap tourist tat shops selling landfill-destined unnecessary plastic items. Nothing to attract a holidaymaker, a tourist. And that's the place's attraction. Just houses, a pub, a few local shops and cafés, restaurants. A wooden shack on the beach, closed up for the winter, that promises fresh fish, crab, lobster and seafood. It looks simple, rustic, and for all I know it has a couple of Michelin stars.

I've also planned ahead. I couldn't leave this to chance so I got back into my old way of thinking. The crime writer. The detective story writer. Just like Jon – if it was Jon – said. If I wanted to track someone down, how would I go about it? The internet, obviously. Even if Jon wanted to remain anonymous, to stay as off-grid as he could, he would have left an electronic trail. He must have bought the house. There are sites to give me that information. And if he hadn't sold it, those same sites could tell me how long it had been occupied and, possibly, with a bit of persuasion, by whom. And also the current market rate. It was all there if you knew how to look.

I checked for houses in the area bought over fifteen years ago. Narrowed my search to stone cottages, since that was what Jon had said he wanted. I narrowed the search further to seafront properties, as that's what Jon had hinted at. Then, with a list compiled, I checked how many had been sold or changed hands in the intervening years. Some, it was clear to see, were bought and sold by families and, unless Jon really wanted to surprise anyone, I knew I could safely discount them. Some were bought and operated as holiday buy-to-lets by absentee landlords, like the one I was staying in. I could discount those also. I concentrated on the ones – and it wasn't many – that were left. That hadn't changed hands, that seemed to have a sole occupant. There were three. One was in a woman's name, so I discounted that. Again, it didn't feel like Jon's style. Whatever his faults I doubted he would have left Gwen and run away with another woman. His problems were of a much more metaphysical nature.

That left me with two houses. Both within walking

THE FINAL CHAPTER

distance. I had their addresses in my phone and walked towards them using the maps app. I reached the first one and wondered what to do next. I hadn't actually made any plans for this. Was I just going to walk up to the door and ask if he used to be Jon Durward? Or would I recognise him? More to the point, would he recognise me? And even more to the point, would he speak to me? Even after all this time?

I put all that to the back of my mind. I still had to find him first.

The first house was just back from the beach. It looked very run down, as if it was waiting for the owner to die when it could regenerate itself. There were a few dead plants in corroded metal plant pots underneath the windows. In the windows hung filthy net curtains, with sun-faded clutter and debris on the windowsills inside. The window frames looked as if they would fall in with the next gust of wind and the roof seemed to be holding on only by an act of prayer. And the walls were filthy and mildew stained. There were the tell-tale signs of handrails either side of the front door. It was either the house of a very old, very lonely single person, or the local serial killer. Either way, unless something truly terrible had happened to Jon in the intervening years, it was a pretty safe bet that this wasn't his house.

I walked to the other one on my list. If he wasn't here, I didn't know what I would do. I'd have reached a dead end and the denouement for my part of the novel would end not with a bang but with a whimper.

This one was a few streets away, one of the last ones, on the edge of the town (village?) before it became completely rural. It was in altogether better shape than the first one. Well-kept, well looked after. It looked like something from a commercial or a prestige drama, where the hero lives out in splendid and very comfortable isolation. It should have been perched on a clifftop for aesthetic purposes, but it wasn't. And it was hardly a humble fisherman's cottage, either. Yes, it was stone, two storeys, but it had land around it. Mature trees and a garden behind an old stone wall. I felt instinctively that this was the place. It had to be.

So now what do I do? Just go up to the front door and knock? Why not?

So I did. And there was no reply.

I was shaking. Really shaking. I'd built myself up to doing it, and not allowed myself too much time to think beforehand in case I talked myself out of it. And he wasn't there. So what next?

Wait. There was a bench just along the way I'd come, looking out to the sea. I could sit there and wait. And wait, if needs be. So, in lieu of any other, and better, plan, that's what I did.

I sat there for a few hours until I got hungry. I needed the loo as well. They never show you this kind of stuff in TV detective shows. Just another example of how they're totally unrealistic. With nothing happening at the house, I decided to walk back along the beach, make myself some lunch, take care of my needs, and return later.

Which I did.

And the first thing I noticed that was different was the mud-splattered old Land Rover parked outside the house.

My heart flipped. I started shaking again. This was it. He was here. I'd found him.

I could feel my heart pounding in my rib cage and my legs vibrating to a near standstill as I walked towards the house. Short of breath and feeling faint. I'm sure I was seeing blackness at the corners of my vision, stars as well.

Hyperventilating. I stopped, took a few seconds to compose myself, and resumed my walk.

I reached the door.

Knocked.

34

No one will look twice at a man carrying a gun round here, not this far out of the main urban areas. This is a land of hunters, after all. Not that anyone can see me. I've memorised the route from the internet and so far, it's holding. The shadows of the cliffs are keeping me from being seen by anyone, not just Prizrak's putative early warning systems. It's snowing as well, which is fortuitous for me as it covers any tracks I may be making.

I'm bundled up in winter camo, hood pulled round my face, scarf round my mouth. Keeping any vapour down to a minimum. Moving slowly, stealthily. Trying to hear if there's any noise above the shallow crunching of my boots, the white noise of the wind.

In fact, the whole place is white noise, looking and sounding like a static-filled black and white TV. I'm the blurred, phasing image in the middle of the bad reception. Unsure if I've been glimpsed or not, a ghost. Hunting a Ghost.

Up ahead, I manage to make out a change in the light. I blink, unsure whether snow is getting in my eyes and I'm imagining it, an ice mirage. I'm not imagining it. A pale yellow has been added to the black and white mix. I must be approaching Prizrak's house and there's someone home. Or at least there's a light on.

I move closer, wary. Slowly now, in case of cameras, motion sensors. As I walk, I check for wires, cables pinned to the rocks, evidence of hidden lights, traps, find nothing out of the ordinary. I keep looking as I go.

In Morocco, Prizrak didn't strike me as a particularly cautious man. Sure of himself, his world and his place in it. Confident he wouldn't be made or caught, he didn't appear to need the trappings of paranoia. Too valuable an asset to too many people. So part of me – the intuitive part – says he wouldn't go in for an elaborate security system, secure in the knowledge that he's covered his trail too well, can't be followed. He wouldn't have named himself Ghost if he couldn't live up to the name. But I'm still wary.

I near the house. Considering the amount of money he must be worth, it's a surprisingly modest place. Wood and glass, looking over the cliffs out to sea. At the edge of the world. Homely. Elizabeth did say it was a retreat and that's exactly what it looks like. No one would come here because no one knows it's here. I stick to the cliffs for protection as I approach. I can see a 4x4 in front of the house. Big and black, anonymous. Like every other car in Iceland. It tells me nothing, except that someone's home. I look around, assessing the area for the best vantage point to make my shot.

There's a crevasse above me that I can pull myself up through. I should be able to crouch at the top with the rifle, ready to take my shot. Perfect range. I pull myself up. It's pretty easy going. Nothing too difficult. I'm soon at the top, taking my rifle from my shoulder, taking the legs down, positioning it. I look through the scope. A perfect view inside the lounge. Lights on, very chill. Warm compared to the cold outside.

There's movement. Someone walking into view. It's him. Prizrak. Dressed like he was in Morocco, demonstrating just how warm the room is. He's holding a glass of something and talking as he walks. There must be someone with him. Either that or he's using a hands-free mobile. I check the scope again. There's nothing in his ear, there must be someone in the room. I move the scope from side to side, trying to make out who he's talking to. It's a woman, I can see that much. She's sitting on the sofa, legs curled under her, also with a glass in her hand. They both looked very relaxed, old friends, or lovers, even. A married couple. He's replaced Elizabeth quickly. They're comfortable with each other. I can't make out her face, though. She has her head turned away from me. It doesn't really matter. She'll have to go too. Collateral. I can't leave any traces. Cover my tracks. I just need to get them both lined up, do them at the same time so they don't have time to react.

He's walking into shot again, heading for the sofa she's sitting on. He places his glass on a side table, sits down next to her. Strokes her hair while he's talking, smiles.

This is it. The moment. I'm ready. It's a long time since I worked as directly as this. I breathe deeply, focus. Calm my heart rate. Ensure my hands are steady. Two shots, then away. Then I'm the ghost.

My finger tightens on the trigger. I'm calm. Calm.

Tightening . . .

She turns her head, as if she's looking directly at me. I stop. My breath suddenly jagged, my heart jumps. I know who she is.

Julia.

My wife.

I put down the gun, stare ahead, uncomprehending.

Then everything goes black.

34 – Notes

Sometimes chapters don't need notes. Sometimes you just need to take a breath before you continue. Then tell the story your own way.

35

'Ah, there he is, back with us. Come on, Mike. Mike? Should I still be calling you Mike? What name should I call you now?'

'Garrick,' says another, more familiar voice. 'Unless he's being someone else.'

'Are you being someone else, Garrick? Is there a new name for me to learn?' A laugh this time.

I know who this is. I recognise both voices. And judging from the warmth, I'm in his house.

I open my eyes, look around. It's the living room I saw through the rifle's scope. I'm sitting on the sofa recently occupied by Prizrak. And my wife.

They're both looking down on me, smiling. Prizrak's pointing my rifle at me.

'To be honest, I expected better, Garrick,' Prizrak says. 'I even thought that if you were as good as they say you are, you might have actually got me.' He pauses as if waiting for a reply. I don't give him one so he laughs. 'I'm joking, of course. I knew you would come. Expected it. Planned for it. Laid out the little trail of breadcrumbs and along you trotted. Good boy.' Another laugh. 'Cleary you didn't do your prep. You might have spotted the patrols. Although I doubt it. You certainly didn't see my man come up behind you and smack you over the head, did you?' Another laugh. He looks at Julia. 'And this is your reward.'

'Hello, Garrick,' she says. 'I'm not going to ask you if you're surprised because I'm sure you're beyond that. Yes, it's me. Yes, I'm here. Yes, I'm standing next to the person holding your own rifle on you. I'm sure you have questions.'

I stare at her. 'More like a comment, actually.'

She nods. 'I can guess what that would be.'

'Is this the bit where you explain everything?' I ask.

'Do you need an explanation?'

'I'm owed one.'

She thinks for a moment. 'Yes, I can see how you would think that. And I suppose you are.'

I look at her, studying her face. It's like I don't really know her, like I've never been married to her all these years. She seems to sense what I'm thinking.

'You don't know me, is that it? How could I do this to you? After all we've been through? Is that what you're thinking?'

'You look like a stranger,' I say.

She smiles. 'I am, Garrick. You never knew me at all. Know why? Because there was nothing inside you that made you want to know me. You were your job, that's all. You would go to work, take on a new identity, complete your task, shed that identity and come home again. And there was nothing of you there. Beyond your needs that I catered to, you had nothing. Are nothing. A Russian doll, discarding one identity after another until there's nothing left inside. That's you, my husband.'

'So what were you then if you weren't my wife?'

'Your handler, of course, what else?'

'But I've got a handler.'

'You do, for missions. But your line of work is specialised. You need round the clock treatment. That's where I come in. I was there assessing you, reporting on you, attending meetings about you. Deciding whether you were fit for service.'

I just stare at her. 'But I brought you presents home …'

'And they were logged and catalogued with a psychological assessment given to every one. That's what I used to do in the room you never went in. It was my office. And you were never in the slightest bit curious about what I did in there. Never once tried to gain entry. That would have been the first thing a husband would do, a real husband, if he suspected his wife was keeping things from him. But as long as you were regularly fed and fucked everything was fine with you.'

She stops talking, giving me time to reflect, to process. I'll do it later. Right now, I'm working. I look at Alexander.

'And who are you? Who do you work for?'

'Me? I'm who you think I am. I do what you think I do. I just received a very generous offer of work from your employers, so I now work for them. We knew you would come after me, finish the job. That's why we arranged to be here, waiting for you. I was to be your final mission, I take it. You would become me, kill me and disappear, is that it?'

'That's it.'

He smiles. 'Well I'm afraid I'm too valuable to be dispensed with. I've just put a plan in place for destabilising Libya and replacing Gaddafi. It's too late now, it's all going ahead and your employers will benefit hugely.'

'And so will you,' I say.

He shrugs. 'Of course.' He sits down opposite me, my rifle still trained on me. 'So, what do we do now, Mike? Garrick? Who do I call you?'

I say nothing. Turn to Julia. 'It was you, wasn't it? In Marrakesh. On the bike. You who killed Kharis, kidnapped me. Killed Elizabeth and tried to frame me for that. Wasn't it?'

'It was, yes. Guilty as charged to all of the above.'

THE FINAL CHAPTER

'Why? Why did you attempt to ruin my operation?'

'Because by then we'd made a deal with Alexander here. So we needed you to stand down. However, as your handler, I knew that, especially since this was your final assignment you wouldn't. You would see it through no matter what. Because professional pride is about all you've got in your life, isn't it?'

I say nothing. Alexander laughs.

'Take your coat off,' she says. 'You must be roasting.'

I do as she suggests. Slowly peel off my snow camo jacket. I still have my heavy Icelandic sweater underneath, in contrast to their lighter clothes.

'Geothermal heat,' says Alexander. 'Why the heating's always on in Icelandic houses. Winter outside, summer inside. You must still be roasting in that sweater.'

'I'm fine as I am,' I say.

'Suit yourself,' he says.

'So. What are we going to do with young Garrick here?'

'There's a team standing by, waiting for my call. We hand him over and that's that. The end of an illustrious career, Garrick. Sorry it couldn't have gone a different way.'

'What's going to happen to me?'

'Nothing good, I'm afraid to say. The information in your head is too valuable to let you walk around with. You already offered your services to Alexander here. We don't know whether you were being serious or not, and there's no point in asking you as we won't get a straight answer. So I'm afraid it's off to a black site for you to see out the rest of your days.'

'A black site.' A feel a shudder run through me.

'Yes. Don't worry, you might spot some familiar faces there. So it might not be all bad.'

'And if I refuse?'

She smiles. Again, it's the smile of a stranger. 'You're not in a position to, are you?' She picks up her phone, presses a button, places it back down on the coffee table. 'They're on their way.'

I look between the pair of them. Assess my position. 'Any last words?' I say.

'I think I should be asking you that, Garrick,' she says.

'Is that a no? You don't even want a farewell kiss?'

'Not when I'm off the clock.'

'Ok, then,' I say.

I squeeze my left palm, feel something drop into it. An NAA .22 Short handgun loaded with .22 Magnum shells drops into my hand. Effective from short-range only, on a hidden forearm rig. I said I had something up my sleeve.

I turn to Alexander. The most dangerous, since he's armed. He hadn't seen the gun by the way he reacts to it, it's too late for him. I've fired twice into his head. He falls backwards, dropping the rifle. From this range, and from the blood and brain matter spurting from the back of his head, I know he won't be getting up again.

Before she can react, I turn to Julia. She's diving across the floor away from me, trying to get the rifle. I point the gun at her.

'Stop.'

She does so.

'Straighten up.'

She does that too.

'Turn around and walk away from the rifle.'

THE FINAL CHAPTER

She obeys. I watch her all the time. Not trusting her in the slightest.

'There. Stand there.' She's far enough away from me to not be a threat, near enough to be in range of my remaining bullets.

'I'd prefer to sit down.'

'I'm sure you would.'

'I won't go for the gun. Promise.' She smiles. And I recognise her again.

'Yeah, course I believe you. Stay where you are.'

She sighs, but there's something of the theatrical about it. 'Whatever. But I have to say, well done. Couldn't have planned it better if I'd let you in on it beforehand.'

I keep the gun steady on her. I'd expected something like this. 'Really.'

'Really. I . . .' she sighs once more, '. . . this would be much better if I could sit down. We can talk better then. Pick up the rifle yourself if you don't believe me. Cover me with that.'

I keep my tiny handgun trained on her, eye contact all the time, and slowly bend down to retrieve the rifle. She doesn't move. I straighten up, hold the rifle on her.

'I assume you've taken the shells out of this.'

'Check if you like.'

I do so. It's still loaded. I put it under the crook of my arm, hold it on her. In the other hand I hold the gun. I'm not taking any chances.

'So,' I say. 'This is the bit where you tell me that you planned it this way. There's not really a team on the way and we're to go home together as if nothing's happened. I'm given a hero's welcome for getting rid of a target and we all live happily ever after. That right?'

'Sort of. There's definitely a team on the way but it's a clean-up team to straighten this place out. Not an extraction team to bring you in.'

'No, you're going to do that.'

'I am, but not in the way you think.'

'So why go to all this fuss for me to kill him? And do it so badly as this?'

'We had to improvise. You were down to kill him, that was right. But then we found out what Prizrak was intending to do in Libya. And that aligned with our aims. So we contacted him, worked with him. Obviously, the hit was out on him at the time, so we needed to be a bit creative. That's why I stepped in in Morrocco, muddied the water.'

'I might have been killed.'

She shrugs. 'If you want an easy life, go work in a bank.'

'So you knew I would still come after him?'

'We knew. We just had to get what we wanted out of him first. Knowing that you wouldn't let him go was a bonus. We just had to point you in the right direction and boom. Job done.' She smiles. 'And now we get to go home.'

She makes to stand up. I wave the rifle at her, remind her I'm still here. She sits back down again.

'Oh, come on, Garrick. If I'd wanted to kill you, I'd have done it by now.'

THE FINAL CHAPTER

'Really.'

'Yes, really. Come on. Let's go.'

I don't move. Keep the guns on her too. 'You expect me to trust you? After what you've just said?'

She shakes her head. 'That was just for him. I've been working undercover with him. And against you, as I had to make him believe. And now it's done and went even better than expected. You've still got it, Garrick. Maybe you should think about staying on, not retiring just yet.'

'So, I'm not a Russian doll, empty on the inside?'

'That was just for Prizrak's sake. What d'you expect me to do? You'd have done the same thing, if positions had been reversed. You use what tools you have to hand, you know that. And it worked, didn't it? The job got done. And what I said helped.'

'You're a psychologist now, are you?'

'That's exactly what I am. What I have been for years. With only one patient. You.'

I say nothing.

'That's how I knew the exact right thing to say. And I could predict the way you would react. I know you, Garrick. Better than you know yourself.'

I stare at her. Julia, my wife. Looking up at me calmly, a slight smile on her face. Confident that she's said the right thing, done the right thing. Confident I'm going to put my guns down, walk out of here with her.

And then what? Is she telling me the truth? Possibly for the first time in our relationship, such as it is, I'm now discovering.

'I gave you what you wanted, all the way through our time together, Garrick. What you wanted and what you needed.'

Clearly she can read my mind too.

'I've always been there for you. And I am now. Come on, let's go.'

She stands up. And I have a decision to make.

I keep my eyes locked on hers.

And pull the trigger of my handgun. Twice.

The surprise on Julia's face is huge, then the realisation of what I've done hits her almost as hard as the bullets. Blood immediately blossoms on her chest. Her hands going towards the wounds, trying to staunch the flow of blood. Not succeeding. She collapses to the floor, eyes imploring.

'Maybe you didn't know me after all,' I say, as she crumples into a heap, her body assuming the final position it will ever make while she's still alive.

I watch as she dies.

And I feel . . . nothing?

I don't know. It's the end of something, I know that but I'm not sure what. A marriage? A relationship? Was it ever that? And did I care? It was what it needed to be. And now it doesn't need to be that any more.

She's gone now. My work colleague, my whatever. My friend with benefits, even though we were never particularly friendly. We just were.

THE FINAL CHAPTER

I grab my jacket, pocket the handgun, sling the rifle over my shoulder and take one last look around. It's the end of another job. A successful conclusion. That's how I feel.

I can hear the helicopters in the distance as I step out of the door.

I may not know who I am any more, but I know who I'm not.

I step out into the darkness and slip away into my new life.

Publisher's Note

There should now follow a section of notes on Chapter 35, followed by an Afterword, or Epilogue written by C. B. Everett, culminating in a conclusion which contextualises and explains all that you have just read. As you may be aware, there is not. Given the circumstances surrounding C. B. Everett and the part he played in events that led to the creation of this novel, we have decided to intervene. When you read on you will see we have reinstated the final chapters as they were originally written before Everett rewrote them himself. You may have noticed a change in the typeface towards the end. This was Everett rejecting the novel as written and creating a conclusion that we can only presume he regards shows him in a better light, no matter how slight that may be.

You will also see that following the reinstated chapters there is Everett's original notes on the ending. We debated whether to include this and eventually decided we would. To explain this decision, we have followed it with a new notes section, not written by Everett. It will become clear who this is written by. This creates not only balance but also a refutation of Everett's notes and has been included at the behest of the original author of the novel. It not only contextualises and explains events in the chronology of the notes as they stand but also the creation of the novel itself. And, of course, the part C. B. Everett played in this.

We understand that this may be regarded as unusual practice and we, as a publisher, thought long and hard as to whether we should actually release this novel in the first place. However, given the extraordinary facts surrounding the creation of it, the need for it to be written in the first instance and, of course. the purpose to which it ultimately served, we felt we had no choice but to honour the author's wishes.

We also felt it germane, in the circumstances, to retain Everett's original notes at the end of each chapter.

We hope upon finishing, that you, the reader, agree that this is not only the best but indeed the only option we could take. We hope you find the remainder of this book an enlightening and worthwhile reading experience. And, ultimately, a prevailing corrective to any misinformation regarding the life of Jonathan Durward himself.

35

'Ah, there he is, back with us. Come on, Mike. Mike? Should I still be calling you Mike? What name should I call you now?'

'Garrick,' says another, more familiar voice. 'Unless he's being someone else.'

'Are you being someone else, Garrick? Is there a new name for me to learn?' A laugh this time.

I know who this is. I recognise both voices. And judging from the warmth, I'm in his house.

I open my eyes, look around. It's the living room I saw through the rifle's scope. I'm sitting on the sofa recently occupied by Prizrak. And my wife.

They're both looking down on me, smiling. Prizrak's pointing my rifle at me.

'To be honest, I expected better, Garrick,' Prizrak says. 'I even thought that if you were as good as they say you are, you might have actually got me.' He pauses as if waiting for a reply. I don't give him one, so he laughs. 'I'm joking, of course. I knew you would come. Expected it. Planned for it. Laid out the little trail of breadcrumbs and along you trotted. Good boy.' Another laugh. 'Cleary you didn't do your prep. You might have spotted the patrols. Although I doubt it. You certainly didn't see my man come up behind you and smack you over the head, did you?' Another laugh. He looks at Julia. 'And this is your reward.'

'Hello, Garrick,' she says. 'I'm not going to ask you if you're surprised because I'm sure you're beyond that. Yes, it's me. Yes, I'm here. Yes, I'm standing next to the person holding your own rifle on you. I'm sure you have questions.'

I stare at her. 'More like a comment, actually.'

She nods. 'I can guess what that would be.'

'Is this the bit where you explain everything?' I ask.

'Do you need an explanation?'

'I'm owed one.'

She thinks for a moment. 'Yes, I can see how you would think that. And I suppose you are.'

I look at her, studying her face. It's like I don't really know her, like I've never been married to her all these years. She seems to sense what I'm thinking.

'You don't know me, is that it? How could I do this to you? After all we've been through? Is that what you're thinking?'

'You look like a stranger,' I say.

She smiles. 'I am, Garrick. You never knew me at all. Know why? Because there was nothing inside you that made you want to know me. You were your job, that's all. You would go to work, take on a new identity, complete your task, shed that identity and come home again. And there was nothing of you there. Beyond your needs that I catered to, you had nothing. Are nothing. A Russian doll, discarding one identity after another until there's nothing left inside. That's you, my husband.'

'So what were you then if you weren't my wife?'

'Your handler, of course, what else?'

'But I've got a handler.'

'You do, for missions. But your line of work is specialised. You need round the clock treatment. That's where I come in. I was there assessing you, reporting on you, attending meetings about you. Deciding whether you were fit for service.'

I just stare at her. 'But I brought you presents home . . .'

'And they were logged and catalogued with a psychological assessment given to every one. That's what I used to do in the room you never went in. It was my office. And you were never in the slightest bit curious about what I did in there. Never once tried to gain entry. That would have been the first thing a husband would do, a real husband, if he suspected his wife was keeping things from him. But as long as you were regularly fed and fucked everything was fine with you.'

She stops talking, giving me time to reflect, to process. I'll do it later. Right now, I'm working. I look at Alexander.

'And who are you? Who do you work for?'

'Me? I'm who you think I am. I do what you think I do. I just received a very generous offer of work from your employers so I now work for them. We knew you would come after me, finish the job. That's why we arranged to be here, waiting for you. I was to be your final mission, I take it. You would become me, kill me and disappear, is that it?'

'That's it.'

He smiles. 'Well I'm afraid I'm too valuable to be dispensed with. I've just put a plan in place for destabilising Libya and replacing Gaddafi. It's too late now, it's all going ahead and your employers will benefit hugely.'

'And so will you,' I say.

He shrugs. 'Of course.' He sits down opposite me, my rifle still trained on me. 'So, what do we do now, Mike? Garrick? Who do I call you?'

I say nothing. Turn to Julia. 'It was you, wasn't it? In Marrakesh. On the bike. You who killed Kharis, kidnapped me. Killed Elizabeth and tried to frame me for that. Wasn't it?'

'It was, yes. Guilty as charged to all of the above.'

'Why? Why did you attempt to ruin my operation?'

'Because by then we'd made a deal with Alexander here. So we needed you to stand down. However, as your handler, I knew that, especially since this was your final assignment, you wouldn't. There was no point even asking you. You would see it through no matter what. Because professional pride is about all you've got in your life, isn't it?'

I say nothing. Alexander laughs.

'So. What are we going to do with young Garrick here?'

'There's a team standing by, waiting for my call,' says Julia. 'We hand him over and that's that. The end of an illustrious career, Garrick. Sorry it couldn't have gone a different way.'

'What's going to happen to me?'

'Nothing good, I'm afraid to say. The information in your head is too valuable to let you walk around with. You already offered your services to Alexander here. We don't know whether you were being serious or not, and there's no point in asking you as we won't get a straight answer. So I'm afraid it's off to a black site for you to see out the rest of your days.'

'A black site.' A feel a shudder run through me.

'Yes. Don't worry, you might spot some familiar faces there. So it might not be all bad.'

'And if I refuse?'

She smiles. Again, it's the smile of a stranger. 'You're not in a position to, are you?' She picks up her phone, presses a button, places it back down on the coffee table. 'They're on their way.'

'So what do we do now?' I say. 'Just wait? Chat? Drink coffee? Make small talk?'

We stay that way in silence until I hear in the distance the helicopters approaching.

'So I guess this is goodbye,' I say to Julia. 'D'you want a farewell kiss?'

'Not when I'm off the clock.'

'But you're right. It is goodbye. Just not to you.'

She pivots quickly and from somewhere a handgun appears. She fires two shots into Alexander, one heart, one head, and he drops to the floor in a shower of blood and brain, what remains of his face frozen in surprise as he drops the rifle. I stare at her.

'What . . .'

'Shut up,' she says, swinging the gun onto me.

'My turn next, is it? Tidying up all your loose ends?'

'It would be quicker that way, yes. And easier. But it's not to be.'

'What d'you mean?' The helicopter blades get louder. 'Is this the bit where you tell me you planned it this way? There's not really a team on the way and we're going home together as if nothing's happened. I'm given a hero's welcome for getting rid of a target and we all live happily ever after. That right?'

'Sort of. There's definitely a team on the way but it's a clean-up team to straighten this place out. Not an extraction team to bring you in.'

'No, you'll be the one to do that.'

'I am, but not the way you think it.'

'So why go to all this fuss for me to kill him? And do it so badly as this?'

'We had to improvise. You were down to kill him, that was right. But then we found out what Prizrak was intending to do in Libya. And that aligned with our aims. So we contacted him, worked with him. Obviously the hit was out on him at the time, so we needed to be a bit creative. That's why I stepped in in Morrocco, muddied the water.'

'I might have been killed.'

She shrugs. 'If you want an easy life, go work in a bank.'

'So you knew I would still come after him?'

'We knew. We just had to get what we wanted out of him first. Once we'd got that, he was expendable. And we've got it.

Knowing that you wouldn't let him go was a bonus. We just had to point you in the right direction and boom. Job done.' She smiles. 'And now we go home.'

She makes to stand up. As she does so I reach for the rifle Prizrak dropped when he died. I bring it up quickly, aim it at her before she has a chance to reach for her gun again. She sits back down again.

'Oh, come on, Garrick. If I'd wanted to kill you, I'd have done it by now.'

'Really.'

'Yes, really. Come on. Let's go.'

I don't move. Keep the gun on her too. 'You expect me to trust you? After what you've just said?'

She shakes her head. 'For God's sake, Garrick, don't develop a conscience now. That was just for him. I've been working undercover with him. And against you, as I had to make him believe. And now it's done and went even better than expected. You've still got it, Garrick. Maybe you shouldn't retire just yet.'

'So I'm not a Russian doll, empty on the inside?'

'I said and did what I had to. You'd have done the same thing if positions had been reversed. You use what tools you have to hand, you know that. Whatever works, whatever gets the job done.'

'You're a psychologist now, are you?'

'That's exactly what I am. What I have been for years. With only one patient. You.'

I say nothing.

'That's how I knew the exact right thing to say. I know you, Garrick. Better than you know yourself.'

I stare at her. Julia, my wife. Looking up at me calmly, a slight smile on her face. Confident that she's said the right thing, done the right thing. Confident I'm going to put the rifle down, walk out of here with her.

And then what? Is she telling me the truth? Possibly for the first time in our relationship, such as it is, I'm now discovering.

'I gave you what you wanted, all the way through our time together, Garrick. What you wanted and what you needed.'

Outside, I hear the helicopters land.

Clearly she can read my mind too.

'I've always been there for you. And I still am. Come on, let's go.'

She stands up. And I have a decision to make.

'No,' I say. 'I'm not coming.'

'What? What are you talking about? We're going now, come on.'

'No. You go. I'll just disappear. Like I was never here. Don't worry, everything in my head will be safe. I just want a quiet life from now on. You'll never see me or hear from me again.'

Outside, the blades power down. I hear boots crunching through the ice and snow to the front door, catch glimpses of the team through the window.

'We can't have that, Garrick. You can't just disappear. You know that. You have to come back.'

'Well, I guess we'll just have to differ. Maybe you never knew me at all. Because I'm going now.'

I see her eyes slide over to someone behind me and as I turn to see what's happening and who's there I feel a bolt of electricity coruscating through my body. I scream, or think I do and drop to the floor writhing in agony.

I look up. She's standing over me. As my world darkens, she smiles.

'You're wrong,' she says. 'I do know you better than you know yourself.'

And my world goes black.

36

I open my eyes. Honestly? I didn't think I'd ever be doing that again. I blink, again and again, trying to make sense of my surroundings.

I'm in a room, a concrete chamber. There's a mirror at one end which I think I can safely assume is two way. I'm in a huge, heavy metal and leather chair, like an old barber's chair, but modern in design. It has ports and inputs. That doesn't bode well. Neither does the fact that I'm strapped into it. I look down at my body. I'm wearing a plain pair of joggers and a T-shirt. Feet and arms bare. It's cold in the room but I'm in no position to do anything about it. I'm sure it's meant to be this way. Above the mirror are lights. A red one goes on, flashes. The heavy metal studded door opens. As it closes, the light goes off again.

'Ah,' says a voice, 'I heard you were back with us.'

It's my handler. Not Julia. She looks just as she always does, her bohemian apparel in even starker contrast to the current surroundings, like a peacock in particularly drab captivity.

'Where am I?' I ask. 'Is this the black site you've taken me to?'

'All in good time,' she says. She crosses the room, gets closer to me. 'How are you bearing up? They treating you all right?'

'I've only just opened my eyes. How did I get here?'

'Brought from Iceland. You were given something to make

you less garrulous and cantankerous than usual. You probably feel as if you have a particularly vicious hangover about now, I should think.'

My head was pounding. 'Just about. You going to let me go?'

A look of what could have been genuine sorrow crosses her features. 'I'm so sorry, Garrick, but I can't do that.'

'Why not?'

'Because you were a naughty boy,' she said, in that tone she must have also used on recalcitrant three-year-olds. 'You see, if you'd just come along without any fuss as Julia asked you to, you wouldn't be in this situation. But you tried to walk away. And we can't have that, can we? Can't have you walking around with all that knowledge in your head. Too dangerous.'

'I won't give it up.'

'Oh, I'm sure you won't. But you might not get a say in the matter, might you? I mean, who's to say you might give it up against your will? Who's to say you won't be kidnapped, tied to a chair in a room and be forced to give it up?'

I pull my wrists against the heavy leather straps. 'That's what's happening here, is it? You're going to torture me? Get me to give up everything I've got in my head?'

'Torture?' She both looks and sounds appalled. 'We don't torture, Garrick, we're the good guys. We leave torture to our enemies. No. We don't torture. We *coerce*.'

A shiver runs through me. 'Why does that sound worse?'

'Because you've got a good imagination, I suppose. And also the years of experience you've had in the field. Selectively sharp instruments work so much better than blunt ones.'

I try to control my breathing. I hate being confined. Hate subjugating my will, my body, to someone else. Years ago, when I was training, they used to run psychological tests like this on us. I managed to find ways to cope but if I was honest, my first instincts would be to scream until they stopped. Not the pain.

I managed that. Just the subjugation, as I said. I've never successfully coped with it. I have coping mechanisms, strategies. But I've never really been called upon to use them. Until now, that is. And when whatever is going to happen is administered by someone you know, that makes it all the worse.

'Get on with it, then,' I say. Steeling myself, trying not to give my discomfort away. 'Do what you're going to do.'

'Very abrupt. Don't you want to try and negotiate?'

'What's the point? You're going to do this whatever I say, do or promise. Just get on with it.'

'Negotiations set parameters, Garrick.'

'I'm sure you know me well enough by now to know what my parameters are.' I hope I sound as confident as I'm trying to.

She shrugs. 'Very well, then.' She turns to the mirror, nods.

The red light goes on once more and the door opens. In come a couple of lab-coated drones carrying a plastic box each. One kneels in front of me, opens the box and begins attaching electrode pads to the soles of my feet. The other one does the same with the palms of my hands. They then attach the other ends of the wires into sockets in the chair. When they've finished that, they attach pads to my forehead and chest, the wires again connecting with sockets in the chair. Tasks completed, they snap their boxes shut and leave the room.

'The electricity comes through here? You haven't done my bollocks. You're missing a trick.'

'As I said, Garrick, we don't used torture. Crocodile clips and a wind-up battery is far too crude. That went out with the Krays and the Cold War. Plus, you'll say anything we want you to just to make it stop. We just want to persuade you. That's all.' She steps back from me. 'I'm going to leave you now. Hopefully when I next see you, we'll all be in a much happier place.'

I try not to speak to her as she leaves the room, but I can't help myself. In fact I don't speak, I shout.

'Is this how you repay me? Is it? All those years, all those jobs I did, and it leads to this?'

She stops at the door, turns. 'You were paid. Well.'

'Yeah, I was paid. But I gave you everything. Everything. It wasn't just money. I gave you loyalty. You don't think I could have gone somewhere else in all that time? You think no one tried to tempt me across?'

'I'm sure they did.'

'And I always stayed with you. I always stayed loyal.'

Her expression changes. Something less than her usual exaggerated bonhomie. Something more real. 'And it hurts to have to do this, Garrick, it really does. But this is business. It's what happens at the end of a career of usefulness. And I'm sorry. But it has to be done.'

She turns and leaves the room.

I don't say anything more. She's gone, even if she's listening behind the glass. But there's no point. I know that. She knows that. Whatever is to happen to me is beyond words now.

As soon as she leaves the lights go out.

And it starts.

37

I feel it in my feet first. A tingling sensation, like an itch I can't scratch but want to. Niggling away, irritating. My handler was right. This wasn't the flashing lightning bolts of crude torture. This is something much subtler. The current is almost gentle but insistent. I can imagine how this is going to work.

It continues. Roving all over the soles of my feet, that irritating, itching feeling building, making me want to scratch, but knowing it still wouldn't be enough because this isn't going to stop. The same with the palms of my hands. Tingling, nerve deep. Playing all the thousands of nerve endings in my feet and hands like a symphony, building up to crescendo after crescendo. I want to rive the skin off my hands and feet, scratch and scratch, dig my nails in and pull, pull, pull until there's nothing left but bleeding, nerveless stumps. It's unbearable.

The darkness only intensifies this.

Then, slowly, in unison with the pulsing in my hands and feet, lights throb around the chamber. Red. Red. Blue. Red. Red. Blue. Red. Red. Green. Blue. Just when I think I've worked out a pattern it changes. Gives me nothing to hang on to.

The feeling in my hands and feet is now excruciating. I strain hard against the leather straps but I'm never going to get them loose. I don't know how long I've been sitting here. I have no sense of time. I try counting the seconds of the light bursts but it's never the same twice and I quickly lose count.

The pain throbs, builds, builds... falls. Then throbs harder. Shocks up my legs too. Round my heart.

The lights, throbbing.

Red. Red. Blue. Red. Green. Blue. Blue. Blue. Blue. Red.

Building... building... building...

Screaming inside. Near unbearable.

I've been trained to withstand torture. But not this. They never taught us how to live through this. Our own side... *my* own side... and they never taught us.

Harder. Harder. My feet, my hands...

Pulsing. Throbbing.

More than pain. The nerves, *my* nerves all singing together, against my body's will.

Then the voice starts.

'Who was your first assignment?'

I don't recognise the voice. Or maybe I do, I'm just in a position to recognise it.

'Who was you first assignment?'

Calm, measured.

'Who was your first assignment?'

Do I talk? I've been trained not to. But this is my own side. I don't know. What do they want?

'Who was your first assignment?'

I say the name. Nothing changes.

The voice again.

'Who was your second assignment?'

I say the name, not wanting to be told twice. Again nothing changes.

I've got the measure of this now. Say the name when prompted. Get it over with quickly. Get out of here. I can do this. I can *contain* this.

'Who was your third assignment?'
I say the name.
Nothing changes.
'Who was your fifteenth assignment?'
'What?' I have to think. I wasn't expecting that.
'Who was your fifteenth assignment?'
'I ... I ...'
The voltage increases on my feet. I scream aloud this time.
The colours flash. Fast. Faster. Faster.
'Who was your fifteenth assignment?'
I screw my eyes tight shut, try to block out the light at least. I can still feel miniature sunbursts on the inside of my eyelids. I can't block out the voice. Repeated over again, over and over, that same, calm measured voice but coming faster now, much faster. And my hands ... my feet ...
I black out.

'Who was your ninth assignment?'
I come round again. I've had no rest, no respite. I don't know how long I've been out, minutes or seconds. Or hours.
The voltage.
The colours.
The voice.
It's all I know now. It's become my world. My whole world.
'Who was your twelfth assignment?' And again. And again.
I'm tired. So tired. I want to sleep. I want oblivion.
I black out again.

That voice again. I can't tell what number assignment it's now asking for. I can't remember the answer to its question. I don't understand the question.
Blue. Red. Red. Blue. Blue. Green. Red. Red. Red. Red. Red. Blue. Blue. Green.

Faster. Faster. *Faster.*
My feet ... my hands ...
My assignment ... my assignment ...
I don't know ... I don't know ...
Colours.
Hands.
Feet.
I don't know ... I don't know ...
Black.

I come round and I'm talking. Talking. I don't know what I'm saying, how long I've been saying it. Part of my mind speaking while the other is resting. Saying names. Names. Lots of names.

No order. Just names.

Any names. Any order. All the names. Tell them everything. Tell them anything.

Just make it stop.

Make it stop.

'Who was your ...'

I don't know. I don't know. I don't ...

'Who ...'

I don't know. Have a name. Any name. All the names. Have them. Have them. *Have them ...*

The lights. The colours.

The blackness.

Deep this time.

Black. Final.

Black.

38

I open my eyes. I'm still in the same room, the same chair. I'm beyond tired.

I try to take stock. The lights have stopped. There's just a dead, overhead light on.

I look at my hands. The wires and pads are gone. My palms look red raw, bleeding in places. My fingernails have skin and blood in them. Same with the soles of my feet. They're crusted over but have been bleeding. I tried to scratch at my hands and feet. I must have done it while I was blacked out. And some time ago, judging by the fact that the blood has dried.

I listen. My ears are ringing with grade-A tinnitus. And silence. The silence is deafening.

I look round. There's no one else there. The room is empty.

I study the glass in front of me. Look at the red light above. It's off. They must be watching me. I'm sure of it. They wouldn't leave me alone like this.

And something else. I can move my arms. I'm no longer strapped to the chair.

I lift my arms. They ache as if I've spent three days on free weights in the gym. I try to move my legs. The muscles are near rigid. But I manage it. Place one bare foot gently on the floor, then the other. The pain. My feet are red raw.

I need to stand. Do so, but very, very slowly. I feel dizzy when I'm upright. I glance up at the light. It hasn't come on. I'm sure they'd come running when they saw me get up.

Perhaps this is another part of the test. They're waiting to see what I do, how I behave. If I move around, they might have electrified the floor or something. Shock me to my knees. I have to try, though. I have no choice. I can't sit in that chair for ever.

I walk. Slowly. One foot painfully in front of the other. Nothing. No voltage. Just bare, cold concrete.

I make my way to the door. It's open.

I'm even more wary now. This is a test. It must be. There's something, or someone waiting for me on the other side of that door. I just swing it open and ... nothing happens.

I pull the door towards me, bracing myself for whatever may be there.

Nothing.

Just a poorly lit concrete corridor.

I step into it. Listening all the time, alert for anything. There's no other noise. Only my breathing. My shuffling feet.

There's a door to the right. Closed. That must be where they control everything, watch me through the mirror. I try the handle. Locked. I try it again, pushing this time. Nothing. Definitely locked. All I succeed in doing is leaving a bloodied smear on the handle. I keep walking.

The corridor is quite long. There are several other doors to either side, all locked. The overhead lighting is grim, oppressive. I'm sure it's designed that way. Designed to take away hope. There'll be no Disney murals anywhere in this building.

I keep walking until the corridor ends with a door. It has a bar across, looks like it leads to the outside. Unless it's another trap. Perhaps I've walked in a circle and I'm back in the room again, ready to go for the next session. They just wanted to give me a taste of freedom then snatch it away at the last minute. Make my fate even more unpleasant.

I have to try. I have no alternative. I reach for the bar, depress it. It gives, opens.

I stand back, fearing another trap. If not the room, then someone on the other side waiting to attack me. Or, I don't know, gas or something? A spring-loaded spear?

I pull the door towards me, body tensed and ready.

Nothing.

I step through it. And find myself in a street.

As I look round, the door swings shut behind me. I turn, try to open it again, but can't. There's no handle, nothing to grip. I push but it won't give. Almost like it was never there to begin with.

I look at what's in front of me. A city. Rain. Cold. I see a bus go past, a taxi.

I'm in London. Definitely.

I step into the street, away from the door, look around again. The bus is headed towards Hackney. Up the street to my left is an Underground station. Barbican. I turn again to where I've just exited. I can't see the door. It just looks like an expanse of grubby wall down an alleyway. At the front of the building is a kebab shop.

I need to go . . .

Where? Where do I need to go? I can't think. I don't know.

I try again. What's my name? That's easy it's . . .

I can't think of my name. I know I had one. No. More than one. I had several. Names. I used to change them. I used to be different people. With different names. And now . . . no. I don't know. I can't think of one.

If I can't think of my name, do I know where I live? Yes. I live in . . .

I live in . . .

No. I can't remember.

I look again at the door I've just stepped through. What was I doing in there? In that building behind the kebab shop? I can vaguely remember something, something unpleasant. But it's fading, detaching itself from my mind and floating away, as if unmoored. A dream I've tried to drag with me through to waking.

I need to ... I have to ...

I don't know. I don't know who I am. I don't know where I'm supposed to go, what I'm supposed to be doing.

I check my pockets. Nothing. I'm wearing joggers and a T-shirt and I'm freezing cold and soaking wet. I have nothing on my feet and my feet are cut and sore and bleeding. They hurt. Really hurt. So do my hands. What happened to my hands? How did they get like this? And my feet? What happened in there? Behind that, that, that door?

What door?

I don't know who I am.

I don't know where I belong. Where I should have a memory there's just a ... nothing. Just grey. Just nothing.

I can remember some things. I know I'm in London. I know how to talk. I probably know how to write. I understand things. I know where Hackney is because there's a bus going there. But I don't know how I got here.

'I don't know who I am ...'

I said that out loud. People look away, move round me on the pavement. Try not to see me. Pretend I'm not there.

Maybe I'm not. Maybe I don't exist. Maybe I'm invisible.

Maybe I'm nothing.

Maybe I'm nobody.

I look round again. I have nowhere to go, nowhere to be. No one I know. Least of all myself.

I know one thing, though. I can't stay here.

So I start walking. And walking. And walking. Hoping to find, if not myself, then something. Anything.

THE END

35 – Notes

I recognised him straight away. Yes, he was older but then so was I. It took him a few seconds but then he recognised me too.

'Hello, Jon. The beard suits you.'

Not just a beard, but grey hair too. In his plaid shirt, jeans and boots, he looked like an aging bookish lumberjack. Designer glasses frames did the heavy lifting for the bookish part. I looked through to the house behind him. Reusable bags were piled in silhouette against a further doorway. I seemed to have caught him doing his supermarket shop.

'I've got to admit, I'm surprised you're still here. But then I got your message. You made it quite easy.'

His frame relaxed and whatever tension he'd been holding slowly dissipated. 'Right. I just … right.' He stood aside, opened the door wider. 'Come in, then.' He didn't sound happy about it. More like a criminal who had spent a lifetime on the run and who finally had been brought to ground.

I stepped in. The cottage was as I would have expected. Tasteful. Discrete. Lots of bookshelves, TV and blu-rays, CDs and vinyl. I smiled. Bare wooden floors with an old wooden chest acting as a coffee table. Some things never change.

'Erm, d'you want a coffee? Tea?'

'Whatever you're having.'

He busied himself in the kitchen. I sat on the sofa. He brought out two mugs of tea. Placed them down on the wooden chest in front of me, say down in the armchair.

'I can't remember whether you have sugar or not. So I haven't put any in. It's in the kitchen somewhere if you want some.'

'Thanks. I'm good like this.'

I looked round the room again. The kitchen that I could see glimpses of seemed slightly messy, as if he didn't have anyone to impress. The living room was tidy enough but definitely looked lived in. As did Jon. When he sat down, I noticed his spreading paunch, his thinning hair on top. The curse of middle age.

'So you found me, then?'

'I got your letter. Worked it out from that.'

He nodded.

'So why all this? After all these years? You've got my address, so if you knew where I was, why didn't you just call me?'

'Why didn't you come and see me, all these years?'

'Because I didn't know where you were. You disappeared, no one knew where you were.'

He frowned. 'Really? Everyone knew.'

'No they didn't. I felt myself becoming defensive. 'Gwen phoned me, begging me to tell her where you were. I said that if you wanted your privacy so badly, I had to honour your wishes.' That wasn't the reason why, obviously, but I wasn't about to go into that.

Jon looked puzzled, shrugged. Then nodded, understanding something. 'Right. Ah. She was testing you. Seeing whether you'd give my location up. Tell anyone. If you didn't tell her then I was safe.'

It was my turn to frown. 'What d'you mean?'

'Just what I said. She knew. They all knew. Well, my agent and Gwen. And I knew they'd never tell. I didn't tell the publisher. That way their reaction would be more genuine.'

'Sorry, Jon, I'm a bit lost. They told me I had to track you down, get an exclusive interview for the end of this new book. If I could find you, that is. Made it sound like Salinger, or something. Pynchon.'

He laughed. 'Sorry. I thought they'd have told you.'

This wasn't the confrontation I'd been expecting. I had thought it would be dramatic, me turning up here, Jon staring at me in shock, horrified, surprised. Slamming the door on me, saying he'd never sent me a letter. Me having to talk him into just seeing me, never mind saying anything. Me forcing an interview with him, using whatever skills I could to get him to talk. And then taking that conversation home, writing it up, making it the final, brilliant chapter of the book. But not this. Not sitting down, drinking tea. Chatting. Not this at all.

'You look disappointed,' he said.

'Well, yeah,' I said. 'I didn't think you'd want to talk to me.'

He laughed. 'What makes you think I want to?'

'You sent the letter.'

'So?'

I took a mouthful of tea. Too hot. Replaced the mug on the chest. 'So we're still like we were when we last saw each other, then? Nothing's changed for you?'

Another frown. 'What d'you mean? Oh yeah. We weren't speaking. We left on bad terms, that's right.'

'Yeah, we did. Just about the worse terms we could have left things on.'

'Well...' He shrugged. 'That was then, wasn't it? Doesn't bother me now. Sixteen years have passed. I wouldn't have asked you to work on the book if it bothered me now.' He laughed. 'I wondered why you didn't get in touch.'

'You mean I was meant to?'

'Well, I thought Gwen would have told you where I was eventually. But then you up and left. Went somewhere else. So I guess we felt that you just didn't ... that that part was all done with. You'd moved on, that was that.'

'Right.'

'Don't worry. You can still have your interview with me. But it might not be the one you were expecting.'

'What d'you mean?'

'When I came up with the idea of this book, especially with what it was about, I thought that enough time had gone by to tell the truth at last. Not just make a comeback but explain everything that had gone on in the first place. Tell the whole story, as it were.'

'What whole story? I know the whole story.'

'No you don't. You wouldn't be sitting here now if you did.'

'OK, then. Tell me the whole story.'

Jon smiled again. 'Like a confession, isn't it? Like you're a priest and I'm the sinner. Well, a defrocked priest.' He laughed. 'Anyway. Ask me something. And I'll tell you the truth.'

It felt like things were moving too quickly and in a way I had no control over them. It felt unreal, like I was in some kind of waking dream, talking to my best friend of twenty years ago, thinking of the distance, the time that had elapsed between us. But also in a way it felt like no time at all had passed. I just hoped I could keep it together to get what he called the whole story.

'OK, then. Why did you disappear?'

'Right. To answer that I've got to go back to the beginning. To first meeting Gwen in the pub that night. You know the story.'

'I've heard it enough times.'

'Course you have. Everyone has. One of my best bits of storytelling. You see, Gwen found me in the pub that night, with me talking about stories, telling her I was going to be a writer, all of that. And yes, we did spend the rest of the night and into the morning talking. But we were young. It was the kind of thing you did then. No big deal, really. In fact, when I'd finished my shift in the pub, I used to go out clubbing, and then out somewhere after that. Staying up all night wasn't rare. It happened all the time.

'I took Gwen back to mine and, amongst other things, showed her what I'd been working on. And she knew straight away that it was shit. Really derivative, awful shit. Embarrassingly bad. Never get published in a million years.'

'But you got better. We're all like that at the beginning.'

'Maybe. Or maybe not. But Gwen could see that I was marketable. As me. As this tall, good-looking bloke. This working-class prodigy. I could tear the publishing world apart. All I needed to do was know how to write.'

'So she showed you.'

'Well, kind of. You see, she could write. Really write. But she couldn't write the kind of stories that I could write. Or I could be seen to be writing. Because it wouldn't look genuine. She'd just be accused of being another dilettante. What she needed was someone to front the writing. Someone believable. And that was me. She chose me. I was what she'd been looking for all along.'

'What?' I don't know what I'd been expecting to hear, but this wasn't it.

'Yeah, that's right.' He grinned. 'I'm a massive fraud. Always have been.'

I didn't know what to say. I just stared at him.

'Don't let your tea go cold.'

I took a swig. More to have something to do than any other reason.

'James Dean if he could write. That's how she pitched it to me. I was as manufactured as a boy band. Another question?'

'Just ... I can't think of anything. Just keep talking.'

'OK. I mean, I did try to write at first. And she tried to edit me. Rewrite what I was writing. Improve it. But she soon realised – *we* soon realised – that it just wasn't happening. And it never would. She tried telling me that the first novel I wrote was my novel, or still my novel after all the rewrites but we both knew it wasn't. She even tried telling me that her rewrites were just tweaks because she knew which market to aim for. She knew the kind of thing that would sell. Knew it all better than me. And all that was true. She did. But we both knew that I just couldn't write. That was the truth of it. So that's when she came up with the ghosting idea.'

'And you went along with it? Didn't that hurt? Wasn't it your dream to be a writer? The kind of writer you became?'

'Yeah.' He nodded, mind back somewhere else. A cloud passed over his face. Momentarily. Then it was gone. 'But you know, I told myself, did I really want to write? Did I really want to put all that work in? All those hours, all that self-doubt, all that conflicted inward-looking flagellation? Or did I just want to be known as a writer?'

'OK. Put like that, I can see the attraction of it.'

'I could be the kind of writer that people who don't read think of as a writer. Just by living the lifestyle. So I became the public face of the books. Gwen's books, really. The very handsome public face, she used to say. James Dean who could write.'

'And it was a massive success.'

'Yeah. It was.' Wonderment in his voice. Still. After all these years. The voice of a man who had got away with it.

'And the rest is history.'

'Well, not quite. I mean, we worked on that book to be successful. But neither of us thought it would be that successful. That big. The film, and everything. That took us by surprise. That was just luck.'

I felt that old, coiled anger inside me that I thought I'd long since repressed. Luck. It all came down to luck. Always. And Jon was like that, even if he hadn't written anything, he still had luck. And that was the difference between him and me. Between him and all the rest.

'So you write another one?'

'I tried. I thought I'd really give it a go, especially after the first one had been so well-received. But . . .' He shrugged. 'It wasn't there. The rough outline of the first one had been mine and I really didn't have anything left after that.'

'So Gwen took over again.'

'Yeah. I mean, she encouraged me to have a go. And then stepped in to steady my hand, as she said. But she just took over again. Wrote the whole thing this time. I mean, I *may* have given her an idea. Just the small spark of one. But it was all her work. With my name and picture on the cover again.'

'And another massive success.'

'This one was even bigger. But you probably remember that. I think you were there by this time.'

'I was. And I have to say, I had no idea.'

He laughed. 'You weren't meant to. That was the point. I was enjoying myself by now. And having a great time on our nights out. That's what it was all about, really, wasn't it? Living the writer's life.'

The *successful* writer's life, I thought. But said nothing

more about it. 'Didn't Gwen mind you out all the time? Taking credit for her work?'

'No, that was the point. She genuinely didn't want any of that. All she wanted was to stay home and do the work. She knew that I had to play my part too. Get out there, show my face, ramp up the publicity. And this was all going great until the third novel.'

'Oh. Right,' I said. 'The third novel.'

Jon looked slightly shamefaced. 'Another tea?'

'I'm good, thanks.'

'I haven't asked about you yet. You're a university lecturer now, yeah?'

'Yeah. But never mind me. You were going to talk about your third novel.'

'Right.' He nodded, not able to put it off any longer. 'Firstly, I'm sorry. I know I should have said that years ago and it was wrong of me.'

'Or wrong of you and Gwen.'

'Right. Yeah. Sorry. I had no right to do that.'

'So why did you?'

'Because ...' He sighed. 'Because I was a cunt. I was full of myself. I could do no wrong. And I was stuck for an idea. We both were. And when you told me about your marriage and how it was falling apart, I told Gwen one night, at home, just in conversation. And she said, that's it. That's the next book. I told her I thought it was your story, you had the right to write about it. And you did, you know. And really well. It was a great book. But she said she wanted the idea as well.'

'But it wasn't just the idea, was it? It was the whole thing. There were things that I'd told you, things I'd said to her and she'd said to me, that popped up in yours, word for word.'

He looked down at the Persian rug. 'I'm sorry. Really, I am.'

An idea occurred to me. 'Was it Gwen who told you to become friends with me? Real friends with me? Close friends?'

He didn't lift his face. 'I mean ... she didn't not ...'

I let the words hang in the air. Said nothing. Waited for him to continue.

'I mean, what could I do? It's what Gwen wanted to write about. We had nothing else. I had to have something to show the publisher. To keep the ball rolling. You have to see the position I was in.' He paused. I said nothing. 'For what it's worth, I thought your novel was the better of the two. By a long way.'

'Thank you,' I said eventually. What else could I say? This was years ago. There was nothing I could do about it now.

'Anyway. After that, Gwen found herself drying up. Couldn't think of any more stories to tell. Taking yours had been the last thing she could do and I think she knew it.'

'So why didn't you just stop then?'

'Because we were on a roll. I had the world at my feet, to use a cliché. And I was having the time of my fucking life. I didn't want to stop. I couldn't stop. So we got another ghostwriter.'

And then I understood. 'Right. Kari.'

'Yeah. Kari.'

'That's what she was doing. You weren't fucking her, you were ... what?'

'Paying her. And who says we weren't fucking?'

'Were you?'

'Maybe it was me, maybe it was Gwen. Maybe both, maybe neither. Does it matter? Really? Now?'

'I suppose not.'

'Right. I took her on as my protégé. Got my lawyer to write up a binding contract for her. And off we went again.'

'Where did you find her?'

'She was a student. That bit was true. A hugely talented one. And I promised her she could write under her own name too. That I'd introduce her to my agent, my publisher and make her as big as me.'

'Or Gwen, rather.'

'Whatever. But it didn't happen. For whatever reason. And she got pissed off and left.' He looked up from his cold mug, directly at me. 'And you had something to do with that, didn't you?'

I thought back. Remembered the conversation I'd had with her. 'She asked my advice for what to do at the time. I gave her it. I didn't know she was ghosting for you. Didn't know any of that. She just seemed like she'd have been happier out of it. Whatever "it" was. And I told her so.'

'And then she took off. And I was back to square one.'

'Sorry. I didn't know.' I'm sure that apology didn't sound sincere. But then considering what he'd just admitted to doing to me, I didn't really care.

'I was pissed off, then. Really pissed off. And desperate. Because there was nothing more I could do. Gwen was burnt out, I couldn't write and Kari had gone.'

'You could have found another one.'

'I suppose so, and I tried. But writers as good as her are hard to come by.' He gave a small, mirthless laugh. 'Here's the thing. I nearly approached you.'

I was genuinely astounded. 'What?'

'To write for me. I was toying with the idea of asking you to do it. I knew you were good enough. And you were writing under a pseudonym, what would another name be to write under?'

I can't believe he actually said that. I honestly don't know how to respond. So I don't.

'Would you have done it? If I'd asked?'

'Probably not.'

'There you go, then. That's what Gwen said you'd say. That's why I didn't.' He leaned forward, fingers steepled together. 'You see, I've always rated you. Really rated you. If I'm honest, you should have had the career I had.'

'After everything you've said, I'm not going to argue with you.'

'No. Don't. I mean it. And the fact you had to write those thrillers when you should have been writing ... well, my books, really. But under your name. No wonder it fucked you up in the end.'

'I'm sorry?'

'Well it did, didn't it? That's why you got dropped. It's what I was trying to avoid in my career. Or Gwen's career, whatever. But the fact that you were doing something you hated told in the end.'

I'm angry at what he's said but I know he's right. I was complicit in my own downfall as a writer. I let my own ego get to me. But it wasn't just me. 'You played a part in me being dropped by everyone, though.'

'Me?'

'You know you did. What was it, you were so pissed off because I'd told Kari to leave that you decided to ruin things with me and Bette?'

He sat back, hands out in front of him. 'Oh, now look, I wasn't ... I didn't do that. That wasn't me.'

'Really? Didn't you tell everyone I was beating her up? Hurting her? You had everyone convinced. Even Bette in the end.'

Jon paused. Thought. Continued. 'Yeah. I was pissed off. I was. Really pissed off with everything. And I was lashing out. My career was ending. My life was ending. Everything

I had was going. And I had to do something. Kari had gone and you helped in that. You helped to end my career. I was so fucking angry. Can you imagine that? Do you know what that's like?'

'Oh yes. I can imagine it. I know exactly what that's like.'

'It was all ... it was a bad time. That's why I had to get away. Gwen was writing the books again but the magic, whatever, the spark was gone. She was just repeating herself. We even tried taking gaps in between, and the gaps got longer and longer. And in the end, I said to her, this is no good. We have to do something. Something drastic. Something that'll give the books a new lease of life, even if there won't be any more.'

'So you came up with this?'

'Yeah. I'd already bought this place. It was going to be our little country hideaway that absolutely no one would ever know about. Not even my agent. But I got drunk and told you. That's why Gwen called you, like I said. Testing you.' Another bitter laugh. 'You were so pissed off with me that you played it perfectly.'

'Didn't Gwen mind you doing this?'

'It was her idea as well. Like faking my own death, except if I just disappeared, I could come back at any time. And say I'd been living off the grid, like a hermit. All of that.'

I looked at the supermarket carrier bags in the kitchen doorway. 'Yeah. A real hermit.'

He laughed, and in that laugh I heard the old Jon. The man who – I thought – had been my best friend.

'Anyway, Gwen and, our relationship by this time was nothing more than a business partnership really. So she didn't mind me coming here. And I wanted to. I've always had this fantasy of living somewhere like this. Somewhere *exactly* like this. And spending my days just how I want to. I like my own company. Enjoy it.'

'Thought you'd have a dog.'

'Me too. Just never got round to it.'

'So what do you do here all day?'

'I keep busy. Plenty to read. Films to watch. Music to listen to. I go for walks. Newcastle's just down the road if I want company. Any kind of company.'

'D'you have friends? Do they know who you are?'

'Who I was, you mean. Yeah, I've got friends round here. I just tell them I used to work in tech and made enough to take early retirement. And now I hate tech so much I try to live without it. They accept it. I think they're kind of envious of that, really. I don't even have a laptop.'

'And what about Gwen?'

'We talk on the phone. Now that it's safe to, she comes up and stays sometimes. Usually when there's something about the business she needs to talk to me about. She's happiest in London, though. She's here a few days and starts getting antsy. Wanting to go home. She'd never leave there. And she's seeing someone else. They don't know about me being here, by the way.'

'And you're happy?'

'Yeah. As happy as we get in this life. I mean, things could be worse. A lot worse.'

I looked round the room again. It looks like a home, like the kind of place someone who's happy, or at least content, with their life would live in. And I suppose he is. The things he's done in the past, the heights he's reached. Why wouldn't he be content with this now?

'So why the new book? Why now?'

'Well ... I just got to feeling that there were things I should say. Amends to make, that kind of thing. Or set a few things straight. I think that's the best way of saying it. Plus, and this is a biggie, the money was starting to dry up. Jonathan Durward was starting to slip out of people's memories. The sales of the old books were slipping. I thought it was time to remind people of who I was. Or who I'd been, at any rate. So Gwen and I had a chat, decided that a newly discovered, newly found novel would be just the thing to revive interest. And so we came up with *Russian Doll*. A novel of identity, we described it as. Which was our idea of a joke. And we wanted you to edit it. Get the old gang back together again. And when you edited it, you'd follow all the clues and find me. And that would be the real ending of the book. And this conversation would be my way of telling the world, through you, that Jonathan Durward was a fraud.' He laughed.

'So that's it, then.'

'Yeah. You found me. I knew you would. I didn't know when it was going to happen. Like I said, I thought Gwen might have said and we could have done this with a phone call. Still, I suppose it's better this way. More colour and all that. Seeing me in my new life. Well, it's not new any more, not after all this time, but you know what I mean.'

'So is that my signal to leave?'

Jon shrugged. 'I suppose so. I mean, we have very little in common now. You have to admit that. And I don't think we're going to be friends for the rest of our lives again, are we?'

'I don't know,' I said, honestly. 'I hadn't really thought that far ahead.'

'No. I think it's better like this.'

He stood up, which I guessed was my cue to do the same. So I followed suit.

He looked at me then. Really looked at me. As if scraping

all the years away to see the person he used to know. To look through the layers. To reach the old me.

'I like you. Honestly. I always liked you. I think that's why it hurt the way it ended like it did. Because we were friends. Real friends.'

'Well, I thought so.'

'We were. You were a good friend to me. Better than I often was to you.'

'D'you want me to argue?'

'No. Because having said that, you used me. And you don't need to argue about that either. Because it's true. You used me. My access to things, my name. My coattails. But that's OK. Because I suppose we used each other. Just for different things. Best you could say, it was symbiotic. Because you see, you always thought you were better than me.'

'I—'

'No don't argue with that either. You did. And you were right. You were better than me. A much better writer. More than you ever knew.'

We stood there in silence, looking at each other, seeing the people we used to be. Or thought we used to be.

'So let's just walk away now, as friends. My agent'll sort everything out. And when the book comes out, maybe we'll see each other again. But I doubt it. Maybe I'll have gone again. Found somewhere else to go, someone else to be. I don't know.'

'It was good seeing you again.'

Jon smiles again. He looks weary. Old. I suppose I do too. 'And you.'

He offers his hand. I take it.

'We won't see each other again. So goodbye. I hope you can be happy in your life.'

'And you, Jon.'

And I left him there.

He could still be standing in the front room of his little cottage now for all I know.

The Final Chapter

I recognise him straight away. Yes, he's older but then so am I. It takes him a few seconds but then he recognises me too.

'Hello.' I call him by his old name. 'The beard suits you.'

If I'm looking for signs that his actions have been eating away at him over the years, I don't find them. He looks comfortable in his own skin. Replete. Like he's grown into who he was always supposed to be. A wave of anger passes through me. He shouldn't look like that. It's wrong. Not after what he did. Not after what he put me through. *All of us through.*

'Didn't think you'd come,' I say.

'I received a letter telling me to come.'

I consider smiling. 'Just in case you forgot where to come to. Although I doubted you would. Not really. Not after what happened here. What you did.' I force my voice to not break on the final word.

He sighs. Like I'm telling a story he's heard over and over again and am getting all the details wrong. 'I don't know what you're—'

'Oh, don't even bother. Please. Give me that much respect, at least.'

His mouth closes. Whatever he'd been about to say goes unsaid.

We stare at each other across the floor of the living room.

'Is it like you remember it? This place? I haven't done much to it. Had someone come in to clean it, that's about all. Rent it out as an Airbnb mostly. Surprised you didn't stay here. Oh, but listen to me, prattling on when we have such a lot to discuss. Why don't you sit down? I'm afraid I can't offer you tea or coffee, I'm out of milk.'

I sit down on the armchair. He sits on the sofa.

'Why did you ask me here?'

'Don't,' I say. 'Respect, remember? It's time for honesty. After all these years. We're going to be honest with each other. At least you are. You're here to tell me the truth. And you must want to, even if you don't think so, because look at you, you've turned up. So who goes first?'

He opens his hands as if about to explain something to a class. 'I came because I received a letter inviting me to. From my old friend, Jon. Who's book I've been editing. I came because I assumed it was part of the process of what I was doing. He wanted to talk it through with me. Is he not here?'

I do smile this time, but there's no warmth or humour in it. None at all. 'You know he's not here. He hasn't been here for years.'

'So where is he, then?'

'Don't. Just don't.'

'I came to see him. He contacted me, and I came. He—'

I stand up, unable to take any more of this. 'Stop it,' I shout, 'just stop it. All this ... this fucking bullshit. Stop. I know. I know what happened. I know what you did. I've read your edits and commentary and I can't believe the self-serving bullshit you've put in. And the lies, all those fucking lies ...'

'I haven't lied. I told the truth as I remember it. About what happened. Everything that happened. If you don't like it that's not my problem. And if you disagree with it, then you shouldn't have asked me to do it in the first place. Or Jon shouldn't.'

My turn to sigh. I sit down again. 'OK. It's going to be like that. OK. Want me to go through it? Want me to tell the story again? From the start? Because if that's the only way to get you, I will.'

He shrugs. 'Whatever. And if you could provide some answers for me being here, I'd appreciate that too.'

'I'm sure you would. Let's go back to this conversation you said you had with Jon, in this very cottage. You wrote it before you came here and went back and added the letter in. Nice touch. Muddy the waters. But let's go through that conversation, shall we? Let's look at what was actually said between the pair of you.'

'How do you know what was said? You weren't here.'

'Oh, I know. Let's start from the beginning. Yes, Jon and I met in the Prince of Wales pub in Clapham. That's now a matter of record. And we fell in love straight away. And then we started to write together. It was partnership. But his name would be on the cover. Expediency. Marketing – I already had a career on the other side of publishing. We knew what we were doing. And yes, maybe my input was greater than his as we went along. That's OK, that's fine.

'The plan was to reveal that we'd been writing together after the first one. We never thought that the first one would be so successful and we had no choice but to continue with Jon's face on the front. We talked about it and decided that was the way forward. Then the film money came in, and they wanted another book, all of that. So we gave it to them. And yes, Jon's contributions were becoming smaller than mine, but his face was on the cover and he was involved and the money rolled in. No problem. Then he met you.'

'And stole the story of my marriage,' he says. 'Both of you.'

'Yes, I admit we did that. And I'm sorry.'

'Which fucked me off no end.'

'I'm sure it did. And I'm sorry. If I could have made it up to you then, I would have. And it's too late to do that now, obviously, with everything that's happened. But I've had years to think about this and that's where it started. Your hatred of Jon. And me. And maybe you didn't want to get even or do something then, but that's when it started isn't it? That's when you first had the idea of doing something against us? Getting your own back?'

'What am I supposed to say?'

'The truth. For once. How much you hated him for what he did.'

'OK. Right. I did hate him for what he did. Both of you. And the smug way you both had, the way you looked at the rest of us like we didn't matter. You, especially. Like all my work was nothing, especially compared to Jon. Sainted fucking Jon.'

'And you wanted to get your own back on him so you became a parasite, hanging around him, hanging onto our lives.'

'Oh, fuck off. This is bullshit.'

'Is it? Because next we come to Kari. We needed help with the books, keeping them going, keeping the quality up. So we brought in Kari to help. And all that bullshit you wrote in the notes about Jon having an affair, or maybe me having an affair with her, all because you knew what was happening and you hated it. And yes, Jon had even thought of asking you, but he knew you'd say no. But all that stuff you wrote about what a great novelist Jon thought you were? Don't fucking flatter yourself. You made all that up.'

'Did I? Really?'

I smile. I've just got him to admit he was here in this house with Jon. Something drains from his face as he realises it too. I continue.

'So you wanted to get back at us. So you started seeing Kari.'

'Bullshit.'

'No it's not. You started seeing her and you got her pregnant. You knew she was young, impressionable, so you tried to destroy her to get back at us.'

'I can't believe this.'

'She was terrified, poor kid. Pregnant by you, hurt by you and you didn't want to know. You told her it was nothing to do with you and you'd always taken precautions even if she hadn't. It must have been someone else. She was heartbroken after what you did to her. And then you started to put the word around that Jon had got her pregnant. And he'd sent her away with money for an abortion and she'd never come back. Oh, we knew it was you saying that. We knew it. Your way at hitting back.'

'And why would I do that?'

'Revenge. But it didn't work. Because she did go away and I was the one who sorted out her abortion. After that she didn't want to stay around in case she saw you. You do try to paint her as irrelevant and unattractive in your notes. But I'm not fooled. And all that hysterical wailing from Jon when she went? Never happened. But it did cause problems for us and our novels, so well done you. You tried to destroy both of our careers and a life. But we bounced back. And you hated that.

'Then came Bette.'

'Get her name out of your mouth . . .'

'Getting angry, are you? You did a lot of that with her. Get angry. Show her who was boss. Throw her around, hit her. Poor, poor kid.'

'Lies. Fucking lies. You did that, you put the story around I'd been abusing her.'

'Yeah, you say in the book that it was Jon doing it, but it wasn't. Everyone knew what you'd been doing to her. And no one wanted to be near you. Certainly not Bette. That's why she came to us. We looked after her until she was well again and you'd gone. I didn't destroy your career. Jon didn't destroy your career. You did. Just you. It's always been you.'

He stands up, takes a step towards me, and this time I'm scared. He looks capable of doing the things I've been accusing him of, things that I know he did. He's looking round, seeing if there's anything to hand to hit me with.

'You can't get away with saying that. You can't.' His voice quiet, like the earth before an earthquake.

I try to find strength, not to show weakness. 'I can because it's the truth. And you know it's the truth. And we haven't even got to the best bit yet, how you killed—'

And he's on me before I can finish my sentence. Hands round my throat, squeezing, choking. I don't have time to . . . to . . .

Publisher's Note on the Final Chapter

My name is Gwen Durward-Hartmann. And this is my confession.

I'm on the other side of the two-way glass so he can't see me or hear me. But I can see and hear him. The interrogator is very good at his job. He's got him talking which is more than I managed to do. I got him to attack me, yes, but not confess. And it won't be long now.

I was at the cottage waiting for him. I sent him the letter to entice him to come. And I wrote the novel, *Russian Doll*, and claimed it was my husband, Jon, who had written it. I confess.

Why? Short version: To get a confession from the murderer of my husband.

I knew it was him. I've always known it was him. I just haven't been able to prove it. Jon disappeared in 2009. C. B. Everett, as he's calling himself now, went and found himself a new life then, a new identity. And I was bereft. Jon hadn't just disappeared. He would never have done that. Never. Admittedly I didn't know about the cottage in Northumberland at first. But that wasn't because Jon was hiding it from me, it was because he'd bought it as a surprise birthday present for me. That's what no one knew at the time. The property was searched thoroughly, including digging up the back garden. Neighbours claimed they heard two men arguing but they couldn't give a description of either man. Then the house went silent.

It took months to put the two things together, Jon's disappearance and the two men arguing. Months. And there was no indication that there had been a physical fight. And no DNA left at the scene either. He had been very careful. But I know what happened now. He's told his story. The truth. Or his version of it. It might be true, this time as he doesn't come out of it very well.

This is it: he killed Jon because he blamed him for every failure in his own life. He went to the cottage knowing Jon would be there, renovating it, and with the express purpose of doing so. Pre-meditated.

Yes, he ruined Kari's life.

Yes, he attempted to ruin Bette's.

Yes, he ruined mine.

And he's sitting there, on the other side of the glass, admitting everything. Because when you're discovered with your hands round the throat of someone else, there's generally only one way things can go.

They found a body. This would have been about three years ago now. Just when I'd managed – as best I could – to get back on with my life. To accept things as they were. When I say 'they', I mean a member of the public who alerted the police. And when I say 'a body', I mean the remains of one. Buried in a field in Northumberland. A field that had lain derelict for years but had been sold to a developer to build new executive houses. It wasn't until DNA tests were done on the remains and compared with historic missing persons cases that they confirmed it was Jon. And then I was informed. I managed to keep it out of the media. Spoke to a lawyer straight away. Because I knew, as I said earlier. I knew who had done this. And if details were released, made public, he might hear about the find and disappear again. And I couldn't have that. So, again with my lawyer, I approached the police. Suggested a deal. If I can get the murderer to come forward and confess, would they support me? It was an unorthodox request, but it was made in good faith. And I knew how to go about it. Once I'd explained to them what I intended to do, they agreed. Possibly more for their own curiosity than anything else. A murder case had never been conducted this way. Not out of the pages of a novel, of course.

So I wrote a novel, *Russian Doll*, claiming it be the handiwork of Jon, who had come out of hiding. I contacted Jon's old agent, who thought the whole idea extraordinary but believed it would work. Together we went about contacting the only person we knew to edit it. And we found him. C. B. Everett.

We knew he would agree. He would be too intrigued not to and his ego wouldn't say no. Plus, as Jon's murderer, he would want to know what was going on. He would be wary, so we knew we had to play it as straight as possible. Which we did. Even alerting the media to say that it was all the work of Jon and had been authenticated as such. I wrote the story with him in mind, made the narrative something in which I knew he would find comparable triggers for in his past relationship with Jon. And sat back and waited.

He didn't disappoint. The notes told a story as he claimed to remember it. Showing himself in a good light, and Jon – and especially me – in a bad one. He muddied the waters too, put things in, conversations that didn't happen when he claimed they did. Such as his climactic argument with Jon. It happened much later. When he confronted Jon at the cottage. And we know how that conversation concluded.

The final touch was the letter, just in case he wasn't going to show up. The police had been observing him for quite some time and notified me when he left for Northumberland. I was waiting for him, the police hidden out of sight and ready to intervene. Which, thankfully, they did.

And there he sits. Confessing.

So was it all worth it?

Yes and no. I should feel some elation, especially after all these years, but I don't. I just feel numb. Perhaps it hasn't sunk in yet. Perhaps confirming what I've always known wasn't what I've needed all these years. Perhaps the idea of closure is just bullshit. Because it's never closed, no matter what happens. He's gone, Jon's gone, and that's that. And because I've always known that it was him. Always. Even without any evidence, I knew. It's like being right about something. You just know you're right. You don't need anyone else to confirm it for you, you already know it.

But this confession isn't just for me. It's for everyone else. The people he knew and who knew him. The readers. His friends. That's why I wrote the novel. Why I went on this ridiculous roundabout way to get a confession, the one he's now giving. It's all been for this moment.

This empty moment.

He looks up. The interrogator leaves the room. He's done. That's it.

He looks at the glass. At me?

And smiles. Mouths something.

Well played.

He begins to applaud.

I turn away.

Notes on the Final Chapter

The detective stands up, stretches, leaves the room. I've given him what he wanted, there's no reason for him to stay here. There is, unfortunately, every reason for me to stay here.

They say confession's good for the soul. Or Catholics say that, but then they would. Not me. I've always believed in keeping things close, bottled up. Not sharing. Like the Hell's Angels say, two people can keep a secret if one is dead. And Jon is dead. I know, because I killed him.

It went down just like they said. In the cottage, arguing, and my hatred of him got too much.

Afterwards, I didn't feel bad. In fact, I didn't feel anything. It just became a question of logistics, what would I do with the body? How would I get rid of it? How would I get away with this?

I kept calm, worked it out. Drove around, found a field that looked abandoned, waited until night, pulled my car off the road where it couldn't be seen, dug a deep, deep hole. Walked away. Simple.

Walked away from everything. My life, my name.

Maybe I am the title character of *Russian Doll*. Maybe I am Garrick. Or was. Maybe I'm not so vain. Maybe it was all about me. Oh, you know what I mean.

And say hello to C. B. Everett. University lecturer. Academic. Tweedy, cardigans. Another disguise. Another identity.

And a long-lasting one until this book appeared.

I should have known something was amiss. I mean, I

suspected something, but I had to be involved to find out more. There's no way I could not be. Unfortunately, I didn't foresee it ending like this. If I had, I wouldn't have become involved. Silly me and my ego.

I look at the glass. I know she's behind there, watching. Waiting to see what I do.

I smile at her.

'Well played,' I say, and start to clap.

Because I have to admit, she's won. Or she's won this round. That's the way I have to look at it. I have to think what's ahead for me. A courtroom trial. Prison. Life? Possibly. Infamy? Certainly. Celebrity? Definitely.

Because everyone will want to know me. Want to tell my story. But no one will be able to tell it as well as me. So, a new publishing deal. My backlist in print again, eagerly read by true crime fanatics hoping to see into my soul. Everyone I've ever known stepping forward to tell their story. And none of them doing it as well as me. Who knows, I might even win awards.

So, I haven't got to look on this as the end. It's just the end of C. B. Everett. And the start of . . . who? I don't know yet. I haven't chosen my new identity. But I will.

I'm still looking at the glass. And I'm still smiling.

And I'll stay that way for a long time.

The Other People

C. B. EVERETT

'Hellishly good fun'
THE TIMES

Ten strangers wake up inside an old, locked house.
They have no recollection of how they got there.

In order to escape, they have to solve the
disappearance of a young woman.

But a killer also stalks the halls of the house,
and soon the body count starts to rise.

Who are these strangers? Why were they chosen?
Why would someone want to kill them?

And who – or what – is the Beast in the Cellar?

Forget what you think you know.

Because while you can trust yourself, can you
really trust THE OTHER PEOPLE?

'A blackly funny twist on the Country House
mystery, with bodies and wit galore'
JOHN CONNOLLY

AVAILABLE IN PAPERBACK, EBOOK AND AUDIO

SIMON &
SCHUSTER